Also by Kait Ballenger

Cowboy Wolf Trouble

THE LAND OF THE

SEVEN RANGE SHIFTERS

MONTANA

BILLINGS

Wolf Pack Run

BOZEMAN

HELENA

Missoula Ranch

MISSOULA

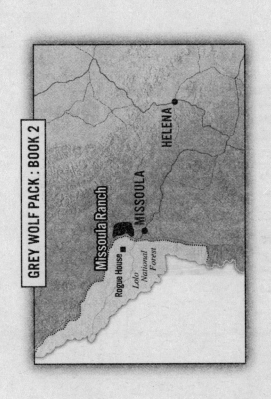

GREY WOLF PACK : BOOK 2

HELENA

MISSOULA

Missoula Ranch

Rogue House

Lolo
National
Forest

COWBOY IN
WOLF'S CLOTHING

KAIT BALLENGER

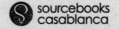

sourcebooks
casablanca

Copyright © 2019 by Kait Ballenger
Cover and internal design © 2019 by Sourcebooks
Cover art by Kris Keller

Sourcebooks and the colophon are registered trademarks of Sourcebooks, Inc.

All rights reserved. No part of this book may be reproduced in any form or by any electronic or mechanical means including information storage and retrieval systems—except in the case of brief quotations embodied in critical articles or reviews—without permission in writing from its publisher, Sourcebooks.

The characters and events portrayed in this book are fictitious or are used fictitiously. Any similarity to real persons, living or dead, is purely coincidental and not intended by the author.

All brand names and product names used in this book are trademarks, registered trademarks, or trade names of their respective holders. Sourcebooks is not associated with any product or vendor in this book.

Published by Sourcebooks Casablanca, an imprint of Sourcebooks
P.O. Box 4410, Naperville, Illinois 60567-4410
(630) 961-3900
sourcebooks.com

Printed and bound in the United States of America.
OPM 10 9 8 7 6 5 4 3 2 1

Chapter 1

COLT CAVANAUGH STRODE ACROSS THE PASTURE, HOLDING the rim of his Stetson against the wind. The heels of his brown leather cowboy boots dug into the frozen ground, each step punctuated with murderous intent. He'd read the note scrawled in his packmaster's hand an hour ago, yet he still seethed with anger. He'd never contemplated disobeying a direct order before, but there was a first time for everything.

Not unless provoked, Maverick's orders had read. During active wartime, no less. What a load of horseshit.

When Colt reached the stables, he tore open the doors. The cold mountain air seared through his lungs, mixing with the familiar scent of manure and fresh hay. The soft purrs of several sleeping horses filled the small space. Colt spied Silver in the third stall down. In the glowing orange of the heat lamps, the silvery threads of the white Arabian's coat shimmered. At the sight of Colt, the horse's tail lifted high and proud. Silver was a horse fit more for a purebred high commander than the cowboy Colt was at heart, and the animal damn well knew it.

Even his own horse suspected the dark truth of his past.

Colt was anything but purebred.

He grabbed an available saddle, and the *attention whorse* wrinkled his nose in distaste at the old, worn leather. Colt ignored him. He needed to reach the location, scope out the perimeter, and strategize his men's placement before their enemies arrived. Thanks to Maverick and the Seven Range Pact's orders, Colt and his men wouldn't be running headfirst into battle tonight, but they would be armed to the teeth all the same.

Colt led Silver from the stable, mounted, and gave the beast a commanding kick. Silver shot through the camp and into the nearby forest at breakneck speed, rushing past the darkened pines and navigating the underbrush with ease. Colt would give Silver that much. He wasn't the most obedient working horse for rounding up cattle on the main Grey Wolf ranch back home at Wolf Pack Run, but his speed was rivaled by none.

As they rode, the setting sun painted the Montana mountain skyline in pink and orange. Shadows elongated, chasing Colt like dark, snarling demons as evening descended onto the forest. When they reached their destination, Colt tugged Silver to a halt, dismounted, and scanned his surroundings. The forest was deadly quiet. The remaining late-spring snow blanketed even the most dangerous of sounds. He led Silver to a nearby bush, allowing him to graze on the frozen grass beneath.

With his horse content, Colt searched for the moon. The white crescent cast a dim glow over the pines. His wolf stirred, and his eyes flashed gold before he threw back his head and released a long howl.

The sound reverberated off the trees, and his men answered, providing him with a keen sense of his soldiers' positions and acting as a warning to their enemies. Though Colt was the only wolf in the clearing, he was far from alone.

Maverick hadn't specified anything against intimidation.

As his howl ended, Colt inhaled a sharp breath. Three vampires several meters upwind. A low growl grumbled in his chest as the scent drew nearer.

"You failed to follow protocol," he called out.

One of the vampires emerged from the trees. At first glance, he appeared human, but he was far from it. The bloodsucker smiled, the moonlight revealing a sinister, sharp-toothed grin.

Colt recognized the vampire instantly. As Grey Wolf high commander, he made it a point to know his enemies. Lucas was a crony of Cillian, the ancient bloodsucking leader of the Billings vampire coven. Lucas, neither the most powerful nor eldest of bloodsuckers, was hungry for power and a force to be reckoned with. But what the hell he was doing all the way out here near Missoula in one of the Grey Wolves' subpack territories, requesting a negotiating meeting during wartime, Colt hadn't the slightest clue.

"You said one representative."

"You have exactly that, Commander. One representative...and my two guards. We also requested the packmaster, so promises were broken on both sides." That sinister smile flashed again.

A vein pulsed at Colt's temple, but he held his features steady. He had learned long ago never to betray his emotions.

"Maverick made no such promise. State your purpose or leave," he said.

Lucas broke a piece of peeling bark off a nearby tree, grinding the wood to dust in his palm. "My coven thought we might offer a deal." He broke eye contact, turning toward the trees in a way that raised the fine hairs at the nape of Colt's neck.

The bloodsucker was anticipating something. Colt sensed it.

"We'll cease all war efforts immediately for the span of one year," Lucas continued. "It will give you time to prepare, rally and train your subpack troops, and get the other *animals* in that Pact of yours on board."

Throughout Montana, the seven shifter clans that called Big Sky Country home formed the Seven Range Shifter Pact. They agreed to band together as allies in the face of their common enemies and for the greater interest of all shifters. If one pack went to war, all went to war.

But Lucas's proposition lacked long-term logistical thinking. This early in the battle, they weren't going to strike any deals with the enemy. Colt wasn't eager to hear what came next. He'd rather call bullshit now and rip this bloodsucker's heart out. But there must have been a reason the vamps wanted a delay...

"Name your price."

Lucas's face turned businesslike. "Ten of your strongest warriors."

"No deal." Colt betrayed none of the hatred he felt.

A smile curved Lucas's lips. "Be logical, Commander. It's only ten men. I'm offering you the lesser of two evils. Think of the lives lost in a year of war. Far more than ten."

"No deal," Colt repeated.

"You can't walk away from this." Lucas's eyes flashed a deep crimson red.

Colt allowed his wolf eyes to glow through the darkness. "That's where you're wrong." Colt might not have been born a true Grey Wolf, but he was loyal to the pack, to Maverick. He'd never consider an offer that would endanger their packmates, his men. Colt advanced, forcing Lucas to ease back. "These are *my* soldiers. No deal," Colt growled, low and foreboding.

He and the vampire stood nearly nose to nose now. The heat of their breath swirled together in a smoky dance.

"I was afraid you'd say that. You see, Commander, I really was giving you my best offer, because if you failed to accept, our intent was to take what we need by force. You didn't think I'd play by the rules, did you?" Lucas snapped his fingers, and his two bloodsucking cronies emerged from the trees.

Provocation enough. Colt lifted a hand and tipped the edge of his Stetson lower, signaling to his men watching through the underbrush.

"On the contrary," he said. From beneath the rim of his Stetson, he glared at his enemy. "I counted on it."

The Grey Wolf soldiers burst through the tree line just as Colt tore his blade from his ankle holster. The hilt disconnected to double as a stake, and he intended to use it.

Four of his men took on Lucas's cronies, which left Lucas to Colt. Despite his bravado, the bloodsucker fled. Colt bolted after him. With a quick whistle, he signaled Silver. Gripping the reins, he hooked his foot in the stirrup and swung into the saddle, leaning forward to urge the horse into a gallop.

As Colt rode after Lucas, a howl from one of his men echoed through the forest, cut short by a sharp, piercing yelp of pain and confirming his worst suspicions. He should have ignored Maverick and the Seven Range Pact's orders, gone with his instincts come hell or high water, and attacked first.

He'd make their enemy pay for the mistake.

Colt steered Silver into the trees, maneuvering the beast into a quick turn until they rounded off Lucas at the pass. Colt dismounted into a drop-crouch with his blade in hand. But as he rose, another bloodsucker lunged from the nearby bushes, colliding with him in a tangle of snarls.

One of those damned half-turned vampires. He'd thought the pack had all but eliminated them at the start of the war.

The half-turned vampire screeched as it lunged for Colt's throat. Colt dislodged his blade, revealing a small stake on the other end. Clutching the vampire by the throat, Colt drove his stake into the vampire's undead heart. The vampire lurched. Colt shoved the dead bloodsucker off him, stake in hand, but Lucas had escaped.

And whatever Lucas wanted Colt's men for, he wouldn't succeed, because Colt wouldn't rest this night until he found him and bled his enemy dry…

―――

Dr. Elizabeth "Belle" Beaumont had been waiting for this moment, and she'd be damned if she missed this chance. Belle leaned against the wall of her cell, feigning sleep, the tattered blanket they'd given her draped over her legs.

Tonight, she would set herself free.

The sounds of shouting above the dungeons rang overhead. Whatever had caused the emergency throughout the Missoula Grey Wolf subpack had drawn the attention of every guard.

Her breath swirled as she released a slow sigh. The air in the dungeons bordered on freezing. She'd never been more thankful that she was a werewolf than at this moment. Had she been one of the many humans she'd treated over the years, without the benefit of her wolf heating her from the inside out, she would have died from hypothermia days ago.

The hurried voices of the last two guards trailed off as they pounded out of the dungeons.

Now was her chance.

Belle pulled the bobby pin from the nape of her neck, digging it free from the mess of snarled curls and frizz. She crept over to the entrance of her cell and wiggled the hairpin into the housing of the lock, pressing up until she felt the slight pop of the springs releasing. With shaking hands, she eased the cell door open. The hinges released a whining creak.

Another round of shouts overhead spurred her forward. She needed to get the hell out of Dodge and fast. Slipping through the darkness, she found her way to the stairs leading out of the dungeons and climbed.

When Belle emerged into the night, the fresh scent of the surrounding pine forest filled her nose. She hadn't realized how dank the dungeons had been until she was here now, in the fresh mountain air. She scanned her surroundings. To the left, the open pastures and ranchland of the Missoula subpack. To the right, lit by firelight, was an army encampment temporarily housing the Grey Wolf soldiers. With the start of the war only weeks earlier, the Grey Wolf soldiers from Wolf Pack Run, the main ranch and compound, were here in Missoula to train the cowboys of the Missoula Grey Wolf subpack into soldiers. Considering her ties to the Wild Eight, they'd see Belle as an enemy—even without knowing the dark truth of her circumstances.

Shouts and yelling sounded from that direction.

It was now or never.

Belle bolted toward the safety of the forest.

Toward freedom.

As she ran, her foot landed in a bramble bush, the icy thorns slicing at her leg. She bit her lip to keep from crying out but didn't stop to assess the wounds. She needed to keep moving.

Belle wasn't sure how long she ran, but she didn't stop until her legs refused to carry her any longer and she collapsed on all fours into the snow. The cold tingled into her limbs, but she ignored it, staring up at the gorgeous crescent moon shining through the tree-tops overhead. She fought the urge to let out a victorious howl as she prepared to shift into her wolf for the first time in days. The feeling would be exquisite. She felt the rapid thrum of her pulse as she struggled to calm herself enough to find her focus.

And then she heard it.

A rustling nearby in the trees.

She rose onto her knees. The blanket of snow covering the ground had soaked through her worn jeans, chilling her to the bone. From the close proximity of the noise, her options were limited.

Find or be found.

Lowering herself onto all fours, she calmed her breathing and steadied herself, finding the place deep inside her where her wolf struggled to break free. In the pale moonlight, her beast came forth with ease. A quick twinge of pain followed by a sweet release, and her fur instantly warmed her. Her clothes fell to the ground beneath her. Shaking the snow from her furred coat, she dragged her clothing beneath a nearby bush to cover her tracks and slipped into the cover of the underbrush.

Slowly, she prowled toward the source of the noise. Keeping downwind, she zeroed in on the rustling coming from the edge of a nearby clearing. As she peered through the undergrowth, her heart stopped.

The first thing she saw was a horse. From the thin shape of its face, she recognized it as a purebred Arabian. They may not have bred yearlings on her mother's ranch growing up, but they'd owned enough horses for her to know what she was seeing. But it wasn't the horse that caused her pulse to race into overdrive.

It was the sight of the cowboy beside the steed.

In this neck of the woods, if his Stetson wasn't enough to give him away as one of the Grey Wolf cowboys, the earthy scent that drifted on the winter breeze was. She recognized him instantly as one of her kind. He smelled of pine, dark spices, and clove, a warm and welcome scent that was far too pleasant for her liking. But if he was a guard, he hadn't served on her cellblock. She would have remembered, because whoever he was, he smelled divine.

The Arabian sniffed through the undergrowth again, causing the rustling noise she'd heard.

Inhaling a steady breath, Belle inched backward. She needed to get the hell outta here before he discovered her, but the sound of his deep voice froze her in place.

"Find anything?" he asked.

A small band of wolves stepped into the clearing, all in human form. One of them stepped forward. "No, Commander," he answered.

Commander. The haunches of Belle's fur bristled. These weren't just any wolves. They weren't even guards. These cowboys were Grey Wolf *warriors*.

If they found her, she'd have no choice but to run for her life. She'd never been much of a fighter, and she-wolf or not, her skills would be no match for a well-trained alpha male. Did they know she'd escaped?

The fur of her tail prickled. No. She couldn't go back to a cell. She was innocent, though she knew they'd never believe her. She was a Rogue, an outcast. According to pack wolves like them, not to be trusted. It was the unfortunate way of their world.

The commander's voice chilled her. "Spread out and cover more ground. We can't let this one go."

The other wolves obeyed, leaving the commander in the middle of the clearing. Her heart sank further as each wolf prowled in a different direction, lessening her chances for an easy escape.

With his back still turned to her, she watched the commander's wide shoulders rise and fall. For a moment, he leaned his weight against his horse before he removed his Stetson. Setting it on the horse's saddle, he ran a hand through his short hair, leaving it slightly ruffled. It was pale brown in color, almost dirty blond.

He must have decided to shift and search like the men he'd given orders to, because he chose that moment to reach down and tug the hem of his shirt over his head.

Had Belle been in human form, she would have had

to stifle a gasp. The spine and musculature he revealed were rippled with sinew, but the scars were what stole her breath. Even in the dim glow of the moonlight, her wolf eyes allowed her to see. The commander's body was a history of battles won and lost, wars waged on behalf of a supernatural empire.

And then he turned around and Belle's breath caught.

He wasn't any commander. He was *the* commander. In an instant, she recognized *exactly* who he was. This cowboy wolf was none other than Colt Cavanaugh, high commander of the Grey Wolf armies, infamous Grey Wolf warrior, and one of the fiercest wolves ever to live.

Anytime one of the Wild Eight had returned to their compound near death's door and clinging to a thread of life, this man had almost always been the one singularly responsible—and that didn't begin to cover the damage he'd done to the Wild Eight through the information-gathering and patrolling schedules demanded of his men.

If she'd thought his battle scars made him intimidating, the pair of eyes locking onto the bush she hid in, as if he saw straight through the shrubbery, chilled her more than the snow beneath her paws. Irises the color of steel bore into her, distant and cold.

Those steely eyes framed a harsh, handsome face. The brown hair of his close-trimmed beard framed his strong jaw, and she realized the chill of his gaze made him more rugged than his features should have allowed. With high cheekbones and a perfectly straight blade of a nose, he should have been a charming, handsome cowboy. Yet years of a hard life had roughened him around the edges with a rugged, raw masculinity.

As he stepped toward her, Belle hunkered lower into

the leaves, hoping it wasn't *this* wolf, *this* cowboy to discover her, because what she saw in those steel-gray eyes told her this wolf showed his enemies no mercy. He drew so close that only the toes of his brown leather boots remained visible. Just as she was certain he had detected her, his horse let out a frustrated whinny, drawing the commander's attention.

Belle breathed a sigh of relief.

Stepping away, the commander placed his shirt in his horse's saddlebag before starting on the buckle of his worn, ranch-worked jeans. She averted her eyes, trying not to ogle him, but it wasn't as if she could move from her position. She watched as he shifted into his wolf—a massive, gorgeous grey, larger than most others she'd seen of their kind—and bounded away into the woods. It was only once he was gone that the tension in her limbs eased. Slowly, she started to ease backward from her hiding spot, causing the leaves to rustle.

As if his horse had known she was there all along, the beast trotted toward her, sniffing across the ground until the soft warmth of its mouth tickled her paw. The beast examined her with dark eyes, sniffing in her scent. It must have decided it liked what it smelled, because it nudged her with its wet nose.

The horse nudged her again, this time harder, forcing her to adjust her balance. When the horse persisted, she finally shifted into human form and stood, taking in the full sight of the beast and the old, worn leather saddle on its back.

Its saddle. Her eyes widened.

Having grown up on a ranch in central Florida and after spending several years working the rodeo, she was an accomplished horseback rider. She knew her way around a stable well enough that she could tell this animal was not only well cared for, but also powerful, fierce in strength and, more importantly, speed. She would move faster on horseback. Deep into the safety of the mountains, far past the Missoula Grey Wolf territory, if she could help it.

What was petty thievery compared to the horrible crimes she'd been charged with? Little consequence, if you asked her. The false accusations failed to take into account the truth of her circumstances.

Treason. Murder.

And now...

"Horse thief."

Belle froze. She felt the blood drain from her face as she turned toward the sound of the commander's voice.

Chapter 2

COLT CROSSED HIS ARMS OVER HIS CHEST AS HE STARED AT the naked she-wolf holding Silver's reins. "We can add horse thief to your growing list of violations."

He'd sensed a pair of eyes on him from the bushes moments ago. He had caught an unfamiliar scent, but then he'd passed it off as his own sense of paranoia. It was only when he'd paused while leaving the clearing and heard Silver huff that he trusted his initial impression. He should have known better by now. His time as high commander had honed his instincts into a lethal weapon. Not to mention that working a ranch the size of the Grey Wolves' lands tended to teach a cowboy to trust his gut. Colt's intuition rarely proved wrong.

And neither did Silver's noises. The horse always made that same huffing sound when he'd found a new loyal subject from whom to demand attention. Silver was the worst kind of bleeding heart. Friend to all and foe to none, as long as they gave him the ample attention he thought he deserved. Apparently, even from a lost she-wolf.

Whoever this she-wolf was, Colt didn't recognize her. Though he knew every wolf at Wolf Pack Run, he'd only been at the Missoula ranch a handful of days and had yet to meet everyone. Between the dozens of Grey Wolf territories with hundreds of wolves at each ranch, it was nearly impossible to know them all.

Colt stepped toward the pair, shaking his head in disbelief. "Breaking pack curfew and prowling through the woods during a hunting ban, while there's an active vampire threat, and now stealing my horse." He ticked off the list of offenses. "Not to mention hiding in the bushes while watching me strip naked like some sort of delinquent. Are you *trying* to get yourself killed?"

She bristled.

Silver mimicked her outrage, huffing and flicking his tail as he drew closer to the she-wolf, his loyalty instantly gone.

Colt shot him an annoyed look. *Et tu, Brute?*

"I...I wasn't watching you strip naked," she stammered.

"No?" He raised an amused brow. "By my calculations, you've been hiding in that bush since well *before* I shifted." He stepped closer. "Typically, when a woman wants to see me nude, she doesn't risk bodily harm from vampires to do so."

"I wasn't risking bodily harm," she shot back.

"Really?" He gestured to the surrounding forest. "What else were you doing standing out here in the middle of a vampire raid?"

She gaped at him as a flush of pink colored her cheeks, reaching all the way to her beautiful hazel eyes fringed by heavy black lashes. Standing where she was, her lower half was shielded by the darkness, but her breasts were barely covered by the shadows and her shoulder-length brown hair. The dark curls glittered with bits of fallen snow in the moonlight. She looked every bit like Eve, standing in a wintery Garden of Eden.

She was breathtakingly beautiful with thick,

mouthwatering feminine curves that stirred something low in his belly—and that didn't even begin to cover her scent. A delicate mix of baby powder, lemon verbena, and wildflowers, like spring in full bloom.

Shaking his head, Colt tried to clear his mind. He needed to remain focused. Not only did he make it a point to keep his fair distance from the females of the pack while working, but this woman—whoever she was—was in jeopardy, standing out here in the middle of the woods during an active vampire raid. He needed to protect her.

You're meant for violence, not love. The words of his birth father echoed in his head.

He'd already failed to protect one she-wolf in his lifetime. He had no intention of doing so again. Colt cleared his throat, falling into the role of stern commander with practiced ease. "So, delinquent horse thief, what do you have to say for yourself?"

"I…" She stared at him like a doe caught in a hunter's sights.

Suddenly, she shifted into wolf form and bolted into the trees.

Colt swore. He stepped forward, prepared to chase after her, but he hesitated. He had more pressing matters to attend to than some she-wolf's disobedience. He turned to mount Silver and continue his search for Lucas, but he caught the scent of a vampire on the breeze.

The vampire was headed in the same direction as the she-wolf, but downwind from her. She wouldn't detect it. She was in real danger now. Instantly, Colt's protective instincts took over.

"Shit." Colt shifted and sprinted after her, running as

fast as his four legs could carry him. She was fast, but he gained on her quickly. She dodged left, then right, trying to throw him off her trail. Had he been any other wolf, she might have outmaneuvered him. But he wasn't just any wolf. He was Colt Cavanaugh, high commander of the Grey Wolf armies, and he'd made it his life's work to be outplayed by no one.

Anticipating her next move, he leaped from the bushes, tackling her. They rolled in a tangle of legs, teeth, and limbs until Colt came out on top, pinning her underneath him by biting onto the scruff of her neck as if she were no more than a pup. In wolf form, he outweighed her by at least fifty pounds and was nearly twice her size. Dragging her by the scruff, he pulled her back into the bushes with him and into hiding.

The vampire likely drew closer by the second.

Under the cover of the brush, Colt pinned her on her back, using his weight to keep her down and still before he shifted into human form. She followed suit.

As his fur receded, he clapped a single hand over her mouth, silencing her. She struggled against him and let out a strangled cry against his hand.

Lowering his mouth next to her ear, he whispered, "Vampire. To the left." The bloodsucker was still a considerable distance off. But that didn't mean it couldn't turn in their direction.

Immediately, she stilled.

As if in confirmation, a hiss sounded in the distance. Her head turned toward the noise, and Colt felt her breathing quicken.

Slowly, he removed his hand from her mouth. She didn't make any further sound. There was fear in her

eyes, but there was also resolve—a will to survive he'd
seen before—which meant whoever this she-wolf was,
she was more than beautiful. She was brave. As they lay
there together, naked bodies tangled in hiding, he watched
her face. Adrenaline heightened every sensation, and the
strength and force of will in her hazel eyes entranced him.

She clutched his bicep and braced her other hand
against his chest.

Another flicker of sound rustled off to the west,
moving away from them. The vampire could still circle
back, but for a moment, they had a reprieve.

Colt leaned down until his lips brushed her ear. "I'll
protect you," he whispered. "You have my word."

At his promise, she relaxed against him.

It was a gloriously awful mistake. Her acceptance
of his touch changed the situation entirely, bringing a
whole new awareness of the smooth, creamy softness of
her skin, the hint of wildflower that lingered in her hair.
Her naked breasts pressed against his chest, deliciously
warm and soft. He could feel every inch of her—the
hourglass shape of her waist, the wide curve of her hips.
He tried to fight his arousal, but he couldn't. Not with
her naked against him like this. His cock stiffened and
brushed against the warm crease of her thighs.

In response, her breath caught, and what Colt saw
reflected back in her golden wolf eyes gave her away. It
was unmistakable.

Desire. Intrigue.

His own eyes flickered to the gold of his wolf. She
inhaled a sharp breath. Slowly he shook his head, urging
her to remain quiet. In response, she bit her lower lip,
drawing his attention there. Their mouths were only a

hairbreadth apart, so close to touching, he could practically taste her on his tongue.

If only she granted him permission…

Minutes seemed to stretch into hours as they slowly drew nearer to each other. Just when Colt felt certain he couldn't take the torture a second longer, that he would close the gap between their lips and kiss her, the rustling of the vampire drawing closer to them once again broke the silence. They both froze, the spell between them instantly broken. He felt the terrified thrum of her heartbeat against his chest. So many creatures had prowled through the forest tonight, Colt hoped it was enough to mask their scents.

The bloodsucker lingered for a moment, then pivoted north. It must have decided to follow a different scent. After several minutes, when Colt felt certain the immediate threat had disappeared, he whispered, "It's gone."

He pushed into a plank position and lifted himself off her. Like a bat out of hell, she tore from the bushes, brushing the mixture of dirt and snow from her behind. He tried not to notice how her round, ample ass and hips swayed as she did so, but it was a lost cause.

Colt mimicked an owl's hoot, ordering Silver to return. A minute later, the steed trotted through the trees toward them, having been trained to follow close by whenever Colt made chase. When the horse came to a halt, Colt opened his saddlebag, digging inside. He retrieved an extra pair of pants from his bag and slipped them on, eager to cover his massive cock-stand.

Locating an old T-shirt balled at the bottom of his saddlebag, he extended it toward her. He half expected her to refuse it, to shift again and run, but she didn't.

Instead, she accepted the shirt. Once his jeans were on and fully fastened and he'd given her sufficient time to cover herself, he turned around to find her standing, arms crossed. The shirt proved just long enough to cover her most intimate parts. Not that he wasn't well acquainted with the feel of them by now.

"Did you just…?" She gestured to his lower half, struggling to find the words until finally she settled on glaring at him.

If Colt hadn't been so apt at reading facial cues, he might have actually believed her outrage. She was obviously trying to save face and cover up her embarrassment. He'd smelled her desire clear as day, but his closeness had been a necessity to keep her safe, plain and simple. She had to know that. Engaging in a battle with the bloodsucker would have made her a target as well—and he couldn't have that. It was his duty, his *honor*, to protect her and their packmates.

He would have said as much, but something about those narrowed eyes pleased him, and he found he didn't need or *want* to explain himself. He knew exactly what she meant, but he wasn't going to make this easy on her. Not by a long shot.

"I'm not certain what you mean," he said, feigning innocence.

A defiant spark lit in her eyes. When she looked at him like that, he wanted to bend her over his knee and make that gorgeous behind of hers as pink as the blush on her cheeks. She indicated the lower half of his body again, making some bizarre, ridiculous signals with her hand as she pantomimed. From the growing fire in her eyes, she had to know how amusing he found this.

"A banana? An eggplant?" he teased. "I'm not very good with charades."

Her hands clenched into fists. "You know *exactly* what I mean."

A wicked grin crossed his lips. "My cock…" he finally offered, putting her out of her misery.

The blush that burned on her cheeks and spread down her neck caused the appendage in question to stiffen. She had looked downright delectable flushed pink and bare in his arms. At least this time, the evidence of his thoughts was safely tucked beneath the fly of his jeans.

"Yes… Yes, *that*," she finally managed. "First, you accuse me of stealing your horse and watching you strip nude, and then you mount me with something that may as well have been attached to Biscuit over there." She cast a quick wave toward Silver.

Colt didn't know where to begin. He wasn't certain which part of that sentence he was hung up on more. The fact that she *had* been trying to steal his horse and watching him nude, that she thought Silver's name was something as ridiculous as Biscuit, or the fact that she'd announced *he* may as well have been part horse between the legs.

At least the last point was a fair assessment.

"You *were* trying to steal my horse," he said, deciding to start there.

The horse in question gave a small, enthusiastic shake as he lifted his tail and batted his large, dark eyes. He puffed up like a damn peacock, eating up all the attention as if it were sugar cubes.

She released an impatient huff. "That's beside the point."

As far as Colt was concerned, that was *entirely* the point.

But as amusing as this frustrated little she-wolf was, he didn't have time for this. "Look. I don't know why you're running around the woods during a vampire raid and stealing horses, but I won't allow it. Not in my woods."

"Your woods?" She looked at him as if *he* were the insane one. "Last I checked, I had every right to be standing on this mountainside, no less than you do, and I didn't steal your—"

"That's beside the point." He turned her own words against her. Releasing a steady sigh, he raked his fingers through his hair. "Let's start with something simple, then. What's your name, sweetheart?"

"I'd prefer not to start there, Commander." She uttered his title as if it were little more than a participation trophy. From the way she said it, she knew who he was. She just didn't care.

Colt fought down a growl. Few would dare to defy him, but from her, there was something he almost *liked* about it. The woman was as frustrating as she was beautiful, and she had a saucy little tongue to match. In any case, he needed to get her to safety and fast. It was his duty to protect the pack, even viper-tongued she-wolves.

"Fine," he said coolly. "But you're still going to march that sweet little ass of yours over to *Biscuit*," he said, highlighting the absurdity of the name, "and get on the godforsaken horse so I can take you to safety."

At the very least, Silver had the presence of mind to look confused at the unfamiliar name. He stared at them while chewing on a blade of grass.

The she-wolf looked at Colt as if he'd grown two heads. "No one has ever called my ass little."

That was what she gathered from this? He couldn't

help raking his gaze over her. She was fuller-figured than many women of their kind, but to him, she was perfect. All luscious feminine curves to his hard muscles.

"No, I'm certain they haven't," he said.

Judging from her frown, she hadn't caught the appreciation in that statement.

She nodded toward Silver. "What if I don't get on the horse?"

His cock gave another eager pulse. Maybe he *did* like the defiance—at least from her. Judging by the growing ache in his jeans, his lower head had different opinions than his ego.

Colt was about to tell her that if she didn't get on the horse, he would take one of each of her ample ass cheeks in his hands, bend her over, and give her a proper spanking for disobedience as any good cowboy would—a spanking that would leave her thinking of him with every bounce of the ride back to the camp—but as he opened his mouth, a familiar scent on the edge of the breeze alerted him, and Silver let out a warning whinny.

Instead, he only managed to breathe out one word to her before the vampire came crashing into the clearing.

"Run."

Three things occurred to Belle as she watched the vampire charge the alpha wolf as if in slow motion. The first was that, based on those bloodstained fangs diving toward them, vampires were far more lethal than stories had led her to believe. As a Rogue who'd grown up in the countryside of the Sunshine State, she hadn't had occasion to encounter many. Aside from being in New

Orleans, they were more common in the northern parts of the country, and they tended to keep to big cities with high human population density—the sort of places where she'd never spent a day in her life.

The second revelation she had was that not only was she without an ounce of fighting ability to fend off this creature, but she wasn't athletic. She was soft and feminine, and running without a proper sports bra was unworkable. That was certainly an annoyance, but it had never occurred to her as a survival problem. Until now that she stood frozen in place.

The third and final conclusion she came to was that this arrogant commander was likely her only chance at survival. Though he *had* told her that her ass was large, and she felt certain that was enough for any man to deserve death. But at the moment, she needed him in full fighting capability, so he'd have to live for now.

He was yelling at her. She saw his mouth moving, but someone seemed to have turned off the sound. Instead, there was a harsh ringing in her ears.

Run, she finally deciphered.

Unfortunately, it was too late for that.

The slow motion stopped as the commander shoved her square in the shoulders, sending her stumbling backward several feet and out of the way as the vampire collided with him. Sharp pain shot up her spine.

At least her ass cushioned her fall.

Scrambling to her feet, she bolted away from the melee. Belle only made it several yards before a second terrifying hiss stopped her in her tracks. Another vampire.

Glowing red eyes glared at her from the darkness. Adrenaline quickened her pulse. She didn't think about the fact that she had no idea how to battle a vampire. Instinct took over. It was her or this red-eyed bloodsucker, and hell would freeze over before she went down without trying.

She shifted into her wolf as the vampire lunged. Fangs and canines clashed. Belle snarled and bit indiscriminately, her canines locking down and sinking in. The taste was awful. Like putting something dead in your mouth, which she supposed she was, but still she held her grip, shaking her head back and forth to cause further damage.

But the vampire wasn't having it.

It leveraged her hold, throwing her onto her back. She yelped and released it. Poised above her, the vampire reared to strike. No. She couldn't let it damage an artery. She blocked her neck with her front paw. The vampire's fangs sank into the furred flesh of her foreleg and a high-pitched keen tore from her throat. Pain, the likes of which she'd never known, seared throughout the limb.

Suddenly, the vampire's weight lifted. The commander stood over her, having thrown the vampire off her. His eyes blazed the golden of his wolf's, and even in human form, his teeth were bared in a feral snarl. He clutched a bloodied stake in his hand.

He was lethal and glorious, and she couldn't bring herself to look away.

The commander charged the bloodsucker head-on, meeting its attacks blow for blow in a calculated battle that was every bit as mesmerizing as it was terrifying. Belle shifted back into human form. He had a knife at his belt, but the fury of his fists and the stake in his hand seemed enough. She'd never seen someone so skilled at combat.

A thread of hope for their safety grew in her. Until she spotted movement in the trees. The glowing red eyes of another vampire watched the commander with malicious intent, but this one was less animal-like than the other, almost human in appearance.

"No!" Belle shouted a warning.

The commander's attention snapped toward her as the vampire looming in the trees retreated with a terrible, sadistic grin. The other bloodsucking beast he'd been fighting seized the moment of distraction and dove in for the kill. Belle screamed, covering her eyes. She couldn't look. She couldn't.

And then everything went quiet.

Keeping pressure on her bleeding arm, she slowly lifted her gaze. Relief flooded her as she stared up at the face of the commander. He stood over the vampire, who was now truly dead, the stake sticking from its chest. Colt looked lethal, panting with exertion.

"You saved me." Her words came on an exhale. "Thank you," she whispered.

He didn't acknowledge her gratitude, as if he often saved people's lives with random acts of bravery. He glanced toward her without fully facing her. Something dark flashed in his eyes as he noticed her wound. "You're hurt."

As he watched her, the hard planes of his face softened, and the open concern in his steely eyes caught her off guard. It was as if the mask he wore had fallen away. This was a man who shielded his true self under layers of jagged battle scars, hiding away behind lock and key.

He faced the world as a hardened warrior, but he was far more complex than that. She realized that now with total certainty, because for a brief second, she had seen him as he truly was.

This was a man who carried the weight of the world on his shoulders, who saved others pain by making it his own. The hurt in his gaze at the sight of her injury tore her to shreds. She was a stranger to him, but that failed to matter. It was as if he held himself personally responsible for her injuries, her protection, and her safety. In that moment, her pain was his pain.

The intensity of that stopped her breath short.

In an instant, he broke the contact between them, his face hardening again as he glanced away. But her heart had been warmed by that intense gaze, brief as it had been. There'd been so few times in her life when someone had looked at her that way—as if they cared for her, as if she mattered, as if she meant something to them.

As if she were someone worth fighting for...

But for a moment, this man who was supposed to be her enemy had given her just that, and now that she'd seen it, she'd give anything to see just a glimpse of his tenderness again.

"Are you all right?" he asked, further breaking the tension between them.

With careful movements, she probed the tender flesh to test the depth of the lacerations. An inch or so deep, but it would heal within a night. She cradled her arm against her chest, applying pressure to slow the bleeding. The pain was sharp, but it was far from the worst that could have happened.

"It will heal. Trust me. I'm a doctor. A few stitches will take care of it."

She may have been a miserable fighter, but she knew medicine. She'd been tending animal wounds on the ranch since she was a small child, long before she'd gone to medical school. Animal, human, a werewolf cross between the two: it didn't matter. As an orthopedic surgeon for the rodeo, she'd had a fair amount of experience handling organs and protruding bones.

She could handle the aftermath of fighting. It was the violence she couldn't handle. Not after Wyatt. She'd experienced violence every day for the past several years at the hands of the Wild Eight.

The commander sounded breathless from the fight, though she didn't blame him. What he'd done had taken amazing strength. "There's antiseptic and medical thread back at the ranch," he said.

On the Missoula Grey Wolf ranch. The very prison from which she'd escaped.

She shook her head. "I can't go back there."

His brow crinkled. It made him look far older than she guessed he was. Those golden wolf eyes blazed with unchecked frustration. "You're going back there whether you like it or not. For your own s-s-safety." He slurred his *s*.

Belle raised a brow. She was about to tell him that saved life or not, he was no boss of hers. But that was when he turned fully toward her, and she noticed the blood, pooling beneath him in the snow. Her gaze followed to the bloodied blade in his hand, which he'd clearly removed from his own abdomen. She blanched.

With slow, unsteady movements, he followed her

gaze, weaving slightly as he did so. "Shit," he muttered as his eyes rolled back into his head. He collapsed, dropping like a stone.

Belle scrambled toward him, allowing her medical training to take over. She checked his pulse, measuring the beats and feeling them quickly dropping. The rise and fall of his chest seemed weak. His lips were slightly bluish around the edges. Placing her ear to his chest cavity, she listened to the sound of his labored breathing.

From the looks of it, the knife had pierced the pleural space of his chest cavity, causing a steady stream of air and blood to flood in. The gravity and pressure had created a tension pneumothorax—a collapsed lung. With only one functioning lung, the air supply in his blood was dropping, causing his pulse to slow, and he was going into shock.

If the blood continued to pool in his lungs, his prognosis was grave. He could die within minutes if the condition continued to deteriorate. Faster than even the most powerful of wolves could heal. She used both hands to hoist him onto his left side.

Blood drenched the snow beneath them. She held him like this, checking his pulse and noting a slight increase. The drained blood would relieve enough of the pressure for now. Not enough for a human, but for a werewolf, it would suffice. He'd need to be transported back to the Missoula ranch to receive further care. He needed a tube inserted to fully relieve the pressure and prevent further collapse.

Leaving him on his side, she tried her best to mimic an owl's hoot like she'd heard him do before. A moment later, his horse bounded back into the clearing, having

retreated during the melee. The horse must have seen
its fair share of war and injured riders, because it knew
exactly what to do. Coming to stand beside them, it
nudged Colt a few times with its nose, then lay down
next to him with a sad look in its eyes so Belle could
hoist the commander into the saddle. The commander
was all muscle and far outweighed her, but after several
attempts, she managed to lay him across the old leather.

As she released him, the horse's ears perked up in
alert and Belle froze. It was distant, but she heard it, too.
Hushed voices. The hairs on the back of her neck rose
on end. Maybe the commander's fellow soldiers. If she
could draw them to where he lay, they would take him
back to the Missoula ranch and he would get the urgent
medical care he needed. If she was careful, she could
do so without alerting them to her presence, then make
her escape.

She shifted into wolf form and eased into the underbrush. With steady, silent movements, she followed the
source of the noise until she came to a clearing. Instead
of the woodsy scent of werewolf, the sickly dead scent
of vampire filled her nose. Belle didn't dare approach
further, but she heard the conversation of the two bloodsuckers loud and clear.

"Did you find him?" one asked.

"No yet, sire. But we've followed Lucas's directions,
so we must be close," a second answered.

"Well, keep looking. You heard Lucas. One of
the half-turned may have injured him, and it will
be our heads if we don't return to the coven with the
commander—alive—by night's end."

Belle stiffened. Her thoughts turned to the vampire

who'd retreated during the battle. That must have been Lucas.

"I don't see why we need the commander anyway. Why can't we take one of their other warriors and be done with it?"

"Lucas said it *has* to be him. You heard what happened with the other shifters, the bobcat and the cougar. Too weak. The wolves have been the best result, and the purer the blood, the better. If we capture the commander, then Lucas can synthesize his blood and we'll be able to control those mongrels once and for all."

The second voice grumbled. "They smell awful. Do you think it will taste okay? Werewolf blood instead of human?"

Belle stiffened. Vampires normally fed only on humans, but if they were capable of feeding off werewolves and other shifters...

Forget the war; it would change the fate of her entire species *forever*.

"It doesn't matter how they taste. Once we rule, we won't need to feed off them. We'll have all the humans we need without them or those pesky Execution Underground hunters patrolling our every move." The first vamp cleared his throat. "Position our men outside the wolves' ranch. We have to strike when he's weak, and if we don't find him in the woods, then he'll be ours when he returns tonight."

Belle had heard enough. Taking care that she wasn't followed, she retreated. When she found the injured high commander where she'd left him, she hesitated. She couldn't take him back to the Missoula ranch, not if the vampires were lying in wait for him there.

And she couldn't abandon him either. He desperately needed medical care, and she'd sworn an oath.

No, she'd take him with her. They were about equidistant between the Missoula ranch and the Rogue house. With her tail, Belle beckoned his horse to follow her. The beast stood, balancing the commander's weight.

As she and the horse carried their patient through the woods, Belle didn't think even once about her own safety or what the repercussion of saving an arrogant Grey Wolf commander might bring her. As she and the horse transported the man who'd saved her life to the Rogue house, the only thought that echoed through her head was a purely selfless plea.

Please, don't let him die.

Chapter 3

AT FIVE YEARS OLD, COLT LEARNED THAT LIES SHAPED reality. It was the first night his father, or the man he would one day call his father, had brought him to Wolf Pack Run, the main Grey Wolf ranch, days after his mother's death. That evening, around a campfire with the whole of the pack in attendance, James Cavanaugh, then high commander of the Grey Wolf armies, had stood in the flickering orange glow of the flames and announced he had a son that he hadn't known existed.

That son was Colt.

As Colt had stood with James by his side, the massive man's hand wrapped around his tiny shoulders as if James were his father, as if he were proud of him, Colt had looked out at the faces of the Grey Wolf pack. Their expressions had been filled with affection, as if they'd found a long-lost family member in him. Every one of the pack members believed in him, wanted him, loved him. And in that moment, Colt had wanted James's words to be true so badly, even *he* almost believed it.

Despite every word being a complete and total lie.

No one searched for the body of his supposedly Grey Wolf dead mother. No one verified she'd been killed at the hands of vampires, rather than the monster who'd really caused her death, and no one double-checked that he really was James Cavanaugh's son. Everyone had simply accepted the lie as reality. And from that point forward, it became so.

That same night, Colt had sworn to James that he would never speak the truth to any packmember. Colt had repeated the oath with eager gratitude. For saving him. For making him his son. For giving him a life he never could have had otherwise.

And it was the lie Colt had lived every day since.

Because Colt Cavanaugh, now high commander of the Grey Wolf armies, was not and never had been a Grey Wolf. In many ways, he'd *become* the lie. But as Colt floated through his unconscious mind, he felt this hidden truth inside him, and a pair of bright, glowing red eyes, terrifying eyes, screamed at him.

Liar.

Colt lurched forward, but a small firm hand pushed him back down.

"Don't move. You'll dislodge the tube," a feminine voice reprimanded.

Colt wasn't used to following orders, yet the urgency in those words held him in place. Slowly, his vision came into focus. He was lying in a bed inside what appeared to be a rustic one-room log cabin. A fire burned at an old wood-burning stove, and another blazed in the hearth. Sun streamed through a nearby window. Silver was outside near the snow-dusted pines, and his Stetson hung on a hook beside the door.

Yet he didn't know where he was.

He didn't know the name of the woman beside him either, but he recognized her. Dark curls, wild and untamed, framed her face. Her hair was damp, as if she'd recently bathed. Her skin was so pale, she looked like she'd been carved of alabaster, and her lips were rosy pink. And those eyes. Emerald with hazel starbursts around the iris.

He hadn't spent the night with her. He knew that much. When he did bed a woman, he never stayed the night. No exceptions. Too often that led to expectations of a relationship, and that was something he couldn't offer. He always made that clear.

Whoever she was, he couldn't recall her name, and even *he* wasn't *that* much of an asshole.

"Where am I?" he rasped.

"Not far from Missoula Grey Wolf territory."

The Missoula territory. It all came flooding back now. The vampires. The attack. The search and then her standing naked about to steal his horse—after watching him strip.

He tried to sit up, but she guided him down again.

"It took a lot of work to get that tube into place with the few makeshift tools I could find," she warned.

He glanced toward his chest. The tube stuck out from his sternum, leaving a small opening to his chest cavity. Beneath it, a pink wound from where the vampire stabbed him had started to mend. With his true nature, it'd be gone by tomorrow.

His thoughts turned to his men. They'd eliminated a large number of the vamps before he'd found her, but a few had remained. He needed to assess the damage, and then there was the matter of Lucas's offer. He needed to warn Maverick.

"I need to get back to my men." He moved to sit up again, but a blade pushed against his throat. *His* blade. Though it'd been cleaned since he last saw it sticking

out of his chest. And it was none other than the delinquent, horse-thieving she-wolf who held it. He raised a
brow. "You realize there's some irony to threatening my
life so you can keep doctoring me?"

She shrugged. "I know, but I needed to get your
attention in a way you'd understand. You're a commander and a cowboy to boot, so I get that you're not
used to taking orders, but *this* is an order you can't
ignore. As long as you're *my* patient, you will listen
to my care directives. If there's one thing you'll learn
about me, Commander, it's that I have little patience
with noncompliance."

This woman had no idea what kind of fire she was
playing with. Colt turned his gaze toward her, carefully
planning his next move as he spoke. "And if there's
one thing you'll learn about me, *doctor*, it's that I don't
respond kindly to threats."

He knocked the blade from his throat, pushing past
the pain and seizing the weapon with ease. He slammed
the knife down on the bedside table with an audible thud
as he pegged her with a hard stare. Even in a recovering
state, Colt had more than a few tricks up his sleeve.

He smirked. "Don't pick battles you can't win."

From the look of alarm in her eyes, he'd made his
point clear.

He lowered himself back into the bed, propping an
arm behind his head. He relaxed into the sheets again.

In response, she growled, actually *growled* at him.
He wasn't sure any lower-ranked wolf, particularly a
female, had dared to growl at him in years, other than
maybe his sister, Sierra. Sierra had been born to James
and his stepmother, Sonya, a handful of years after they

had taken Colt in, but she was hardly typical and he'd had years of practice ignoring her troublemaking.

But *this* woman he couldn't ignore. She riled his control. It was both infuriating and arousing.

"Your lung collapsed," she said. "Until a few hours have passed and the pressure has released, you'll listen to my orders. If not because I saved your life, then as a physician. Do I make myself clear, Commander?"

Crystal. She made herself crystal clear. And from the feel of it, he was convinced his cock was currently made of crystal as well. Thankfully, this time, he was covered by the sheets and still wearing his jeans. He cleared his throat. "How's that work, considering I saved your life first?"

She waved a hand in dismissal. "It was your duty to save me."

It was his duty, but it was also his privilege, though he wasn't about to tell her that. "And as a doctor, isn't it *your* duty to save *me*?" he shot back.

Her lips drew into a tight line. He had her on that point, and she knew it. "The Hippocratic oath only requires I do no harm. It doesn't require me to save you," she countered.

"Says the woman who held my own knife to my throat."

She shrugged a single shoulder. "It was a bargaining tactic."

He huffed. "Well, that's reassuring."

She smiled, clearly toying with him. "It wasn't meant to be, Commander."

The witty retort caught him off guard, and Colt fought a grin as he took in the sight of her. If they were so close to the Missoula packlands, why hadn't she taken him back to the ranch? Though few pack wolves would recognize it, he knew where they were. This cabin looked like every other Rogue house he and his mother had stayed in during his early childhood. Before her death, before the Grey Wolves had taken him in.

Yet this she-wolf had been on Missoula pack territory. Rogues weren't allowed to roam packlands, not without an escort, which must have meant she was a Grey Wolf, not a Rogue.

As he stared at her, trying to determine her affiliation, she looked away, but before she did, he recognized she was trying to hide something. He'd seen that same look on his soldiers when they were trying to get away with murder—figuratively, not literally. Whoever this woman was, she had secrets. He saw it in her eyes, and before he returned to the Missoula ranch, he intended to find out what those secrets were.

"It's Colt." He offered his name. "You can call me Colt."

"Like the horse or the gun?" she asked.

"You may as well ask if I'm more cowboy or wolf."

She looked away, but he saw a hint of amusement on her lips. "Well, Colt like the gun and horse, do we have an agreement that you'll stay in this bed for at least five more hours? The knife wound won't be healed, but you'll be stable enough to ride."

He glanced out the window. A thick layer of snow blanketed the mountainside, the sun overhead blinding in its brightness. He didn't know this woman, but her medical expertise and intelligence were clear, since he was still breathing. And she had to be resourceful to boot, managing to keep him well in such rough conditions. From the position of the sun, in five hours, it would be just before nightfall. It'd give him enough time to get back to the Missoula ranch within several hours if Silver ran fast. Enough time to find out who this woman was, and why the hell she'd been out in the middle of the woods during a vampire raid.

His eyes flicked to the bedside where he'd put his knife. His instincts told him she was no true opponent of his. No, this woman was a different kind of threat. One he was far less equipped to handle.

"Unless you want to die a painful *death*." She emphasized the word as if he hadn't stared down death countless times before.

"By my own blade or the collapsed lung?" he quipped.

"Does it matter?" She smiled.

As she did so, she tilted her head to the side, a funny little quirk he'd noticed. Each time she did, a single stray curl fell over the edge of her eye. He wanted to wrap his finger around that curl and use it to pull her gently closer.

He shook his head. No. He couldn't begin to go there. Colt knew firsthand the danger of temptation, and to a warrior like him, it could be deadly.

You're made for violence, not love. His birth father's words echoed in his head. The only words the man had ever spoken to him. His birth father had been a monster, but there was truth in those words all the same. The Grey Wolves might have taken him in, but the violence of his birthright thrived in him. It was how he'd conquered so many on the battlefield, how he was known as more cunning than any warrior before him, including the Grey Wolf commander who'd raised him.

He glanced out the window again. The branches of the pine trees hung heavy with snow. He'd be no use to his men or Maverick dead on the Montana mountainside.

"I don't see I have much of a choice," he answered.

"In that case, we need to go ahead and remove the tube."

"I thought you didn't want me to remove it."

"I didn't want you to dislodge it and cause further injury. The tissue is open and sensitive. Once I remove and clean it, I'll monitor your vitals while the hole closes. By evening, if your breathing remains steady, you'll be almost as good as new. The stab wound will be tender for a few days and may bleed some, but considering the scars on your body, I bet you already know that."

He did. On the battlefield, he'd endured worse than knife wounds. He laid his head back into the downy pillow, staring up at the wooden timbers of the ceiling. "Go ahead then."

"You don't want some alcohol to numb the pain?" She pointed to a corner table, where a half-empty bottle of Jack Daniels sat.

"No, I make it a point not to drink." If anything was his vice, it was women, not liquor.

"Suit yourself." She leaned over him, examining the clear tube and surrounding skin. "Are you an alcoholic?"

He frowned. "I said I don't drink."

"Like many recovering alcoholics." As she depressed the tender flesh of his wound, he grumbled. It wasn't the worst pain, but it still *hurt*.

"I'm not an alcoholic," he repeated. "Not that it's any of your business."

She gripped the tube, rotating it ever so slightly so it loosened. He grimaced. Slowly, she started to inch the tube out.

"In the past twenty-four hours, I've seen and *felt* you naked, been drenched in your blood, lifted you onto a horse, and saved your life, and now I'm removing a tube from your chest." She shot him a pointed stare. "I think it's my business."

"You only saw me naked because you appear to have a thing for voyeurism."

She laughed. "You don't know the first thing about my fantasies."

"After your reaction in the clearing, I beg to differ." He cast her a wolfish grin.

She tugged on the tube, though an amused grin curled over her lips. The quick shot of pain caused sweat to break on his brow. Message received loud and clear.

He gritted his teeth. "In any case..." She'd returned to being gentle. "I don't drink because I make it a point never to lose myself. I need to have my full judgment at all times."

"In other words, you're a control freak." She wiggled the tube more. "A commander for the Grey Wolves would be."

Grey Wolves, he noted, not *our pack*, catching the word choice instantly. Colt had interrogated enough enemies over the years to notice subtle cues in language, facial expression. She may as well have been an open book. And without a doubt, whoever this woman was, she was no Grey Wolf.

He supposed that made two of them.

With one last gentle pull, the tube was out. She busied herself gathering a bowl of steaming water and a washcloth sitting on the basin. When she returned, she dipped the washcloth in the bowl, then wrung it out. A few stray drops spilled onto her jeans.

She leaned over him, placing the warm washcloth to

his chest. As she did so, his attention on her pack affiliation faltered.

"What are you doing?" he growled.

As if the incident they'd had in the clearing hadn't
been enough.

She glanced at him through a thick layer of lashes.
"Cleaning your wound."

With each stroke, he imagined that warm washcloth
drifting lower. Fuck.

Clearly, she had no idea what she was doing to him.
She was like some sexy Florence Nightingale, caring for
him with gentle yet strong feminine hands. Except she
wasn't, because Nightingale had only been a nurse, and
this woman was a doctor, which meant not only was she
beautiful and caring, despite having the demeanor of a
docile viper, but she was smart. Damn smart, and from
that fire in her eyes likely passionate, too.

He growled again.

"Hold still, Commander." She must have thought he
was warning her away instead of fighting not to haul her
into bed with him, because her eyes narrowed and that
pink mouth pulled into a disapproving pucker again as
she rubbed the washcloth in tender, sensual circles.

She was testing Colt's self-control. He was certain.

"No one's ever dared call me a control freak," he com-
mented. At this point, he was trying to distract himself.
Maybe if he could focus on conversing, he could ignore
the caressing of that warm washcloth and tender touch.

So far, it wasn't working.

"I imagine they'd be too scared, *High Commander*,"
she said guardedly. She swiped the warm cloth over
him again.

"But you're not," he challenged. Which meant she was not only intelligent and resourceful, but she'd proven again she was brave to boot. He'd seen as much when they'd hidden from the vampire in the clearing.

"I'm not most people." She shrugged before a small smile twisted her lips. "And at the moment, you're at my mercy."

Colt couldn't help his amused grin. He cleared his throat, trying to hide his appreciation. "In any case, I may be a control freak, but that's because I know the truth. People think they're in control of their lives, but fate and circumstance have a way of messing with plans. I'm only so bent on control because I know I have so little of it."

His choices were the only thing he had true control over. He'd learned that the hard way, and the consequences had been deadly.

She paused, the heat of the warm washcloth poised over his heart. His pulse thumped against her hand. In an instant, the walls that kept her sharp-tongued and saucy fell. He saw it, and as those large hazel eyes found him, he suddenly felt as if she saw through all his shields, straight to everything he'd ever tried to hide.

"And that terrifies you," she whispered. "Doesn't it, Commander?"

Colt stilled. Her words cut through him. For a moment, he could have sworn she saw him—truly *saw* him, raw, open, and vulnerable—for what he truly was. But his mind had to be playing tricks on him. No one ever saw the real him. No one ever dared to challenge him that way. He was one of the most fearless wolves ever to live. Ask any one of his packmates, and they'd say he didn't have fears, vulnerabilities, weaknesses, and secrets that could be exploited.

And yet...

A pang of longing shot through his chest.

No. He shook his head. She couldn't see the real him. No one could. Not without risking his secrets. That was dangerous. Far too dangerous.

Colt cleared his throat again. The sudden warning in his eyes instantly cut the tension between them. "Fear is a weakness I can't afford."

The fire returned to her hazel irises. "Everyone has fears, Commander. Even alpha wolves like you." She gave him a knowing look. "Some of us are just more willing to admit it than others."

"And what gives you the know-how to make that call?" he asked. His tone was more defensive than he'd intended, but he couldn't allow her to get too close.

"Chalk it up to good judgment," she said.

Good judgment indeed. Colt refused to look away from her. Perhaps she was right; perhaps she was good at reading people. But as he stared into her eyes, he had a sneaking suspicion it was something more than that. Something so out of his control, he couldn't begin to acknowledge it.

To his satisfaction, she was the first to look away.

"Don't worry. Your secret is safe with me." She was baiting him again.

Tracking her every movement with his eyes, he inhaled, and the tantalizing scent of her hair flooded his nose. Those gorgeous still-damp locks were so close, he could have reached out and buried his hand in them.

"There." She'd finally finished. She stood and deposited the washcloth in the ceramic basin.

After wiping her wet palms on an apron hanging nearby, she placed her hands on her hips. Her eyes darted to his Stetson hanging from the door hook. "I know commanders—and cowboys, for that matter—aren't very good at taking orders, but you should rest now."

A sudden wave of exhaustion overcame him. The idea wasn't half-bad. A few hours would make little difference in getting news to Maverick, and he wasn't ready to be done being cared for by this minx of a doctor.

He relaxed into the bed. After several quiet minutes, as his eyes grew heavy, he muttered the request dancing on the edge of his tongue since he'd first seen her. "Tell me your name."

She hesitated, but finally she answered, "My friends call me Belle."

Belle. Why did that sound so familiar? As he attempted to repeat it aloud, his lips formed the shape, but the name came out as little more than a whisper as he fell into a deep sleep.

As Belle monitored Colt's pulse, she spent the next several hours alternating between watching the snow-capped mountains and memorizing the relaxed lines of his handsome face. There wasn't much else to do inside the cabin, and she tried to reassure herself that was the sole source of her intrigue with him—but she was failing *miserably*.

Every time she looked at him, especially in this relaxed state of sleep, the vulnerability and emotion she'd seen from him in the woods haunted her, softening her opinion of him. He'd been so stoic throughout her wound care, the perfect image of the hardened soldier, yet when she'd turned away, she'd heard him wince in pain.

He was strong, fierce, brave, hardened by war. All the things he showed the world, yet...

There was softness underneath it all. She'd seen it. And now that she had, she couldn't bring herself to forget it.

She shook her head. She should know better than to get too involved with another alpha wolf. Wyatt had never been charming like Colt, and look where that had gotten her.

She glanced out the window. The snow-covered pines glittered white in the distance. While the Rogue houses scattered throughout the state were a godsend for packless Rogue wolves like her who needed a safe refuge or a place to hide, they were anything but high-tech. Most Rogues lived off the grid and liked it that way, favoring intense privacy over modern amenities.

The houses were funded by a collective run by an anonymous benefactor, a wolf as infamous among Rogues as Maverick Grey was among the Grey Wolves. They called him the Rogue. Not *a* Rogue, but *the* Rogue. If there was a leader among the packless, the unwanted, the underdogs and scoundrels of shifter society, it was him. Though few had met him and lived to tell the tale, rumors painted him as a dark Robin Hood, fighting for the better treatment of her kind. He was as much myth and legend as he was a hero.

In any case, whoever he was, Belle appreciated the Rogue houses. For a wolf like her who'd been born without a pack—a Rogue by birth, not choice—they provided a safe space. Even when she needed to escape the law, like now. No reservations, no booking, simply show up at the property and hope no one else was there. Packless wolves only.

She was bending that rule now with the high commander of the Grey Wolf armies lying asleep on the cabin bed. She wasn't doing the greatest job of hiding from the law either, considering he *was* the law, at least for their kind.

She looked toward Colt again. He was still asleep but he stirred, his eyelids fluttering. He looked years younger when he slept. All the harsh angles of his face softened.

How had she ended up here? Alone in a cabin with a Grey Wolf cowboy—and not just any cowboy but the highest-ranking Grey Wolf soldier in existence. Subordinate only to Maverick Grey and whoever the Grey Wolf second-in-command was. Though the last she'd heard several months ago, the Grey Wolves still hadn't appointed someone after the death of their last second.

One word from this man, and she'd be in a cell again before she could blink.

At the very least, he didn't recognize who she was. Even her name hadn't triggered any recollection, which meant when he left, she would return to her original plan. She knew exactly where she was headed. Back to the rodeo. To her old life. To healing cowboys' wounds and broken bones. The life she had loved before the Wild Eight. It hadn't been perfect, but it had treated her well.

She perched on the edge of the bed to check his pulse again. But as she did so, a sudden blur of movement caught her off guard. She was suddenly on the bed and he was on top of her, the knife, which had been sitting on the bedside, clutched in his hand. The blade pushed against her throat as she lay caged on the mattress beneath him.

Fear froze her in place. Maybe he *did* know her identity after all.

He stared down at her with alert eyes, far more alert than someone newly awake should be. His breathing was rough, labored as if he'd run a marathon. As his eyes scanned over her, he swore under his breath, immediately casting the blade aside, much to her relief. She was suddenly breathless herself as she marveled at the intense gray of his eyes. Cold, calculating, yet they burned into her.

What she wouldn't give to see that tenderness reflected there again...

They lingered like this, their bodies pressed together for a long beat. That same blazing heat returned to her center, the one she'd first felt when she'd been in his arms. She knew she should have been terrified, but there was something about this man, despite the evidence of the violent life he lived, that made her fearless, brave—terms she never would have used to describe herself.

Or maybe reckless and stupid. She couldn't be certain.

"Oh, it's you," he mumbled.

Any thought of romance flew out the window. "I see you're feeling better."

He cleared his throat and pushed off her, scratching a large, masculine hand through the scruff on his face before he ran his fingers through his hair. It gave him the sexiest kind of bed head. Belle bit her lower lip and averted her eyes. The Grey Wolf high commander held the power to destroy her with a single word, and here she was, panting after him like a she-wolf in heat.

Colt grumbled some unintelligible just-woken-male response.

"Don't tell me you've forgotten my name already. 'Oh, it's you' isn't exactly what a woman wants to hear after she saves your life."

"I didn't forget your name, Belle." His voice was still graveled from sleep, and there was a glint of teasing in his eyes. "Would you have preferred 'Oh, it's the horse thief'? or 'Good afternoon, she-wolf voyeur'?"

Yes, she *much* preferred him when he was sleeping. Already he was trying to get a rise out of her. Though in some ways it frustrated her, she liked their banter more than she cared to admit.

With the early afternoon light streaming through the window, the sun highlighted the blondish undertones of his messy brown hair. God, he was equal parts gorgeous and terrifying. He was still shirtless from where she'd tended his wounds, exposing the rippled muscles of his abs and pecs as well as the scars and ink that made him appear rough. The snug blue jeans he wore accentuated the trim of his legs and that behind she knew was so muscled, she wanted to take a bite out of it. His body had been hardened by a combination of ranch work and battle, and her eyes fell to a black tribal tattoo of the sun that sat on his left pectoral overtop his heart.

It was entirely unfair. This man had everything going for him. Looks, power, privilege.

"We need to head back to the Missoula ranch," he announced, instantly cutting the tension between them. "I'd like to arrive by morning, and it will slow Silver down to carry us both."

He said it as if it were an order. He was likely used

to making decisions for others without consulting them. But *not* for her. She was done with a life of alpha males bossing her around.

She straightened the bedsheets, refusing to look at him. "We?"

Those intense eyes followed her. "You're not returning to your pack?"

She made a show of fluffing the pillows. Really, she was beating out her frustration on them, but she didn't think he'd notice. "No, I'm not."

"Are you running from something?"

She pretended not to hear him. The question cut straight to the heart of the matter. She couldn't tell him the Grey Wolves weren't her pack. Some would have called the Wild Eight her pack for a time when she'd served as their physician, but she hadn't been able to leave. Not then. Not without abandoning Dalia to Wyatt's mistreatment. Her thoughts turned to the old woman, and a tinge of sadness hit her heart. If only she'd known what the outcome would be. As far as she was concerned, she'd never had a pack. And she *was* running. From the Grey Wolves, the Wild Eight. All of it. She was running back to her old life, to freedom, to the rodeo.

When she finished beating the ever-loving piss out of the pillows until they were puffed, fluffy clouds, she started tucking in the bedsheets.

"If this is about you being out in the woods after curfew, forget it. I'm a man who pays my debts. I'll overlook it," he said.

She stilled at his words. So that was what she'd be to him? A debt to be paid. She shouldn't have cared how he would remember her. They were strangers, and after he left this cabin, she was certain she'd never see him again.

Years ago, before she'd gotten tangled up with the Wild Eight, she'd tended countless riders in the rodeo she never saw again. There was likely to be a rodeo within fifty miles anywhere in the States, so she'd worked wherever she wanted and kept only a handful of connections. She'd never needed anyone, never cared what they thought, so long as she did her job and healed them. So why did this cowboy's opinion matter so much?

Because he risked his life for you, and you know he would do it again in a heartbeat...

Pushing the thoughts aside, she finished making the bed. "I'm not going back to the Missoula ranch."

He towered over her, dwarfing both her and the cottage, examining her with weary, suspicious eyes that seemed to know too much. "You want to be alone? Out here in the woods?"

"I do." She gathered the dirty rags and threw them into the sink before she turned on the cold-water faucet. There was no washer or dryer at a Rogue house, but the cold water and some dish soap would work the blood out all the same.

"Where are you going?" he asked.

"West."

"And what's your plan?"

She remained silent.

"You could just tell me the truth, you know." He pegged her with a scrutinizing stare. "You're not a Grey Wolf."

Belle stiffened.

"I'm the Grey Wolf high commander, Belle. You

thought I wouldn't recognize a Rogue house when I saw one?" he asked.

Glaring at Colt, she snatched the bowl of bloody water off the table. She didn't address him. If she spoke, she'd give too much away, though her silence was likely doing so already. His questions were a double-edged sword, and there was no way she'd win this battle. Better not to engage.

"The Rogue is one of our top enemies. He's a troublemaker for all packleaders. The houses may be convenient, but it's not worth the chance of getting mixed up with the likes of that bastard vigilante," he added.

Belle disagreed. From her knowledge, the Rogue in all his mysteriousness didn't condone violence against the packs. He might have been a troublemaker, and she wouldn't want to cross paths with him in a dark alley, but he worked for the betterment of her kind. Carrying the bowl carefully, she exited the cabin. She'd dump it in the utility sink around back.

"There're a few men's shirts in the closet. Go ahead and take your pick," she said over her shoulder as she went. Another fortunate feature of the Rogue houses was that they remained packed with plentiful survival supplies and essentials.

As she stepped outside, the cold wind hit her hard, chilling her to the bone. But that was the lingering Montana winter. She couldn't wait till spring gave way fully. She descended the porch steps and headed around back, her cowgirl boots shielding her from the inches of snow she trudged through as she dumped the bloody water into the utility sink, trying not to think of Colt's realization about her pack affiliation.

She was ready for him to leave. When he'd been passed out, he'd appeared harmless. Not to mention she'd felt grateful to him since he'd risked his life to save her. It had all worked as a horrible cocktail that softened her to him.

But now, she was growing more anxious by the second. There was nothing harmless about this man. And that had little to do with her unwanted attraction to him or the way his nearness made her melt like chocolate in the hot sun, thank you very much.

When she returned to the cabin's small wooden porch, he stood there, watching her. She wasn't sure what alerted her, but something about his gaze had changed. He stared at her as if she were a piece to a puzzle he was trying to solve.

"You said your friends call you Belle, which means your true name is something different. Perhaps…" He examined her with careful eyes. "Elizabeth?" he questioned. As he tested her name on his tongue, his eyes narrowed and his brow scrunched low.

Belle froze. She watched in fear as the creases in his brow disappeared. Those liquid gray eyes grew wide, and that was when she knew he'd recognized her.

Which meant she had no other choice but to run.

Chapter 4

COLT HAD BEEN ABOUT TO ASK WHERE HE'D HEARD HER NAME before, but as he'd watched her pretty features become stricken with terror, he'd recognized her in an instant. He'd seen her once before in a photograph. A photograph inside a file at Grey Wolf command control back at Wolf Pack Run.

A file labeled *Wanted Wild Eight*.

"Belle Beaumont," he said, recognition flooding over him.

The Wild Eight's only physician.

Which meant this woman who'd saved his life, who he'd held naked beneath him until he was aching with anticipation and pleasure…was his enemy.

She dropped the empty basin in her hands as the fear in her eyes deepened. And then she ran.

Shit.

Colt raced after her. He couldn't let this woman go. She bolted into the trees as he chased her, rounding pine trunks and leaping over mounds of snow. She was fast, but even with her head start, he gained on her quickly.

She darted off course to where the trees thickened. Colt followed, but by the time he reached the trees, she was gone, hidden behind one of the thick layers of pine needles.

"You can run, Belle, but you can't hide," he called after her. "Not from me."

Silence answered him, but he knew she was close. He sensed it. Slowly, he prowled through the trees, searching for her. A rustling of branches sounded behind him. She was trying to keep moving to throw him off her trail. But he was only a few feet away from her.

It was now or never.

Colt pounced, tackling her from the side. She shrieked as they both toppled to the ground in a tangle of limbs. They landed in the snow, Belle on top of him, writhing and struggling. The ordeal sent a sharp burst of pain through his still-healing wound, but Colt locked his arms around her. With one quick twist of his hips, he had her pinned beneath him.

"Let me go!" she growled. Her dark curls sprawled out over the melting snow beneath her. Anger blazed in her eyes.

"I can't do that." Not now that he knew who she was.

She tried to wiggle away, but that did nothing except draw his attention to the soft mounds of her breasts pushed against him.

With her beneath him like this, his body was instantly back in the Missoula territory, where the feel of the heat between her legs had pressed over his throbbing cock. The darker part of him was enjoying this. Yet she was his enemy and his own darkest secret rolled into one. Even if she'd saved him. *Damn it all to hell.*

He moved to stand, drawing her up by the arm. As soon as she was on her feet, he had ahold of her. There was no way she'd dare try to overpower him. It would be a losing battle, and she had to recognize that.

"Walk," he ordered, nodding in the direction of the cabin and, more importantly, Silver. He needed to get this woman subdued and back to the Missoula ranch. Savior or not, she was one of only five active Wild Eight remaining. The nefarious pack had been disbanded following the start of the war, and the Grey Wolves had been searching for the remaining few survivors ever since. Maverick wasn't a fan of loose ends, and neither was Colt.

Especially not when it came to the legacy of the Wild Eight.

"You're making a mistake," she pleaded.

As far as he was concerned, this was the first action he'd been certain of since he'd found her naked and stealing his horse in that clearing. He should never have gone after her.

"Please," she continued. "Don't put me back in that cell again."

The pieces of the puzzle fell into place. That was why she'd been in the forest. She hadn't been violating the ban; she had been making a run for it. Her capture must have been recent, because her paperwork had yet to be forwarded from the Missoula ranch to the main ranchlands at Wolf Pack Run. With all the pack's guards and soldiers addressing the vampire threat last night, she must have found a way to escape from the cellblock, right out from under his and his men's noses.

She'd made complete fools of them all.

Colt growled. "How did you escape?"

"I used a bobby pin to pick the lock," she confessed. "It was stuck in my hair from when they took me captive."

He scowled. Not shy and meek or innocent as he'd first thought in that clearing. Not at all. If anything, she was smart, clever, brave, and defiant as all get-out, with a past as complicated as his own. He'd been misjudging her from the start. To think she'd escaped a Grey Wolf prison. While the subpacks weren't as tight on security as Wolf Pack Run, a fact he'd come to their territory to help correct, courtesy of the war, her escape was impressive nevertheless.

And she'd done it with a bobby pin.

It was an oversight he couldn't afford to risk. Not again.

When they reached the cabin, Colt beckoned Silver. The horse trotted obediently to his side, allowing Colt to reach into the saddlebag and retrieve a pair of silver handcuffs. At the sight of the cuffs, Silver's eyes darted to Belle. He clearly had an impression of what was about to happen, because he chose that moment to snap at Colt's hand.

Colt swatted the horse away. "Disloyal bastard." He wasn't sure what made Silver so taken with Belle, but he supposed that made two of them.

"You keep spare handcuffs in your saddlebag? You really are a control freak," Belle said.

"You have no idea," Colt grumbled.

Silver huffed as if in agreement, and Colt scowled.

Enemy or not, Colt could think of a few things he'd like to do with this she-wolf and a pair of handcuffs, things that involved him burying himself between her thighs and pleasuring her so thoroughly, she wouldn't walk straight for a week.

Pushing the fantasy aside, Colt slapped the cuffs on her wrists. The cuffs would suffice to hold her for now.

"You don't have to do this. I saved your life."

Colt almost laughed. "After dragging me miles away from the Missoula ranch. You can't expect me to believe you had no ulterior motive, sweetheart. I wouldn't be surprised if your Wild Eight buddies showed up any minute."

"If by 'ulterior motive' you mean saving your life from the vampires trying to abduct you, then yes, I did have an ulterior motive," she said.

Colt froze. *Abduct. Not kill or maim.* His thoughts turned to Lucas's offer. Gripping her shoulders, he guided her until she faced him. "Abduct? You mean take me alive?"

"That's typically what abduction means," she quipped.

He knew *exactly* what it meant. It meant this situation was growing more complicated by the second.

"How do you know this?"

"After the vampire attacked you and *I saved your life*," she emphasized, "I overheard something nearby. I might not have noticed if it weren't for Biscuit over there." Her gaze darted toward Silver, who flicked his tail appreciatively at the attention. He might as well have been blushing like a bride.

Colt scowled in response.

From the annoyed look the horse cast him, he was clearly pleased by only one wolf's attention over the past twenty-four hours—and it wasn't Colt's. Needy beast of a horse.

"What did you overhear?" Colt urged.

"Just voices. I followed them," Belle continued. "I thought it might have been some of your soldiers. I figured I could draw their attention to you, then hightail it out of there, but I found vampires, not wolves. They were talking about finding you. A vampire named Lucas saw you get injured, and his men were looking for you.

They said if they didn't find you in the woods, they'd take you when you returned to the ranch. That's why I brought you here instead. And…" Her voice trailed off.

"Go on," he urged.

She was shaking her head in disbelief. "And I know this sounds crazy, but I overheard them say…" She struggled to find the words. "I…I heard them say they planned to use your blood for a…a serum. They were talking about vampires being able to feed off were-wolves. They said the purer the blood, the better. They made it sound like it made them stronger by drinking it. They mentioned a bobcat and a cougar not being as effective. I'm not sure what it all means but…"

Colt's anger flared, but he kept his breath steady, even as he felt his pulse beat inside his temple. He would destroy Lucas…

He searched Belle's face. If she was lying, she was excellent at it, but his instincts told him she was telling the truth. This woman wore her heart on her sleeve. If she was lying, he would know, and from what he remembered of her file, she'd only served as the Wild Eight's physician. She'd never directly hurt anyone, only served their misguided cause. As far as enemies went, she was on the lowest rung of the list. Hardly dangerous or full of evil intent.

It wouldn't be the first time one of their enemies had targeted him personally, but he'd make certain it was their last. And if what she said was true, this would change not only the war, but the future of their species. This had deep implications for the entire Seven Range Pact.

But why him? What made his blood different from any other Grey Wolf?

Colt froze.

There was only one thing that made his blood different from any other Grey Wolf's—that he wasn't truly a Grey Wolf at all. Colt's thoughts raced. No, it wasn't possible. How could Lucas know? His father, James, the only person who knew, had passed years ago. Not even Maverick or his own sister, Sierra, knew the truth. Lucas couldn't know, unless...

They needed to get back to the Missoula ranch—and fast.

"We're leaving." He reached for Belle, but she pulled away.

"I'm not going back. I was trying to escape when you found me," she said.

"I'm aware. It's not often I encounter jail-breaking horse thieves streaking naked through the woods."

"I saved your life," she challenged. "You said so yourself."

"After I saved yours." He gestured toward the horse. "Ladies first."

She rolled her eyes. "What a gentleman."

He rattled the handcuffs on her wrists. "I'm not a gentleman, Belle. Don't forget that."

"Believe me, I won't." Her cheeks were flushed red now, and that saucy little tongue he enjoyed peeked out to wet her lips.

"I wouldn't have run into that vampire if you weren't chasing me," she added.

"And I wouldn't have been chasing you, had you not been stealing my horse," he shot back.

Gripping her by the handcuffs, he marched her toward Silver.

She must have known it was a lost cause, because she didn't try to resist. "I knew you were a Grey Wolf soldier."

"Yet knowing who I was, you still saved me?" She'd risked not only her life, but also her freedom and safety. For him. Her enemy. The thought turned sour in his stomach.

"Yes." She straightened her shoulders, standing tall and confident. "Yes, I did."

"Why?" he breathed.

"Because it was the right thing to do."

The raw honesty stopped his breath short.

She glared at him. "The Wild Eight may be murderous traitors, but in my experience, the Grey Wolf cowboys are just as violent and at least twice as arrogant." She eyed him up and down.

The insult hit home. She wasn't the first and likely wouldn't be the last to call him arrogant. But if she knew his true origins, she'd think twice.

"Spoken like a true Wild Eight," he countered.

She stepped toward him. "I'm not going with you."

He gripped the handcuffs at her wrist again. "I don't think you have much of a choice."

When she didn't move, he stepped closer, bringing them nearly nose to nose, their gazes locked in a battle of wills. "Get on the damn horse, Belle."

Returning to the Missoula ranch and then Wolf Pack Run was the best decision. For both of them. Enemy or not, after she'd saved his life. He wouldn't be able to live with himself if he abandoned her in the woods, though he'd never dare to admit it, especially not to her. If the vampires had caught his scent, they could find her in his place, and the consequences would be deadly…

When she still refused to move, he shook his head. He couldn't fully release her from custody. If he spared her and anyone found out, it could raise questions about his loyalties, and those questions could reveal the secrets of his past. Secrets he had no intention of revealing.

"You really want me to let you go?"

"Obviously." She rattled the cuffs on her wrists.

"Fine," he grumbled. "As long as you don't try to steal my horse again." Stepping behind her, he unlocked the cuffs.

When her wrists were free, she stepped away from him—tentatively at first—before she quickly placed several paces between them. She eyed him with weary suspicion. "I'm really free to go?"

Colt pocketed the handcuffs, heading down the mountainside to where his Stetson had fallen off in their scuffle. "Sure, you're free to go."

He retrieved the hat, brushing the snow from its rim before he tipped it onto his head. "Just don't expect any mercy when someone turns you in for the reward money."

Belle was certain no other person—wolf, human, or otherwise—had ever infuriated her more than Colt Cavanaugh. She'd always considered herself a mild-mannered person. Having grown up on a ranch in the Deep South, she'd been taught to be polite, accommodating, and generally pleasant. *Sugar wouldn't melt in her mouth*, her mother used to say of her. Some would have called her bookish, shy even—when she wasn't donning her lab coat overtop her cowgirl boots, that is.

Yet, at the moment, as she looked into this cowboy's

ruggedly handsome face, all Southern hospitality flew out the window. Everything about him turned her to salt instead of sugar. Who did he think he was, bossing her around and acting as if he gave a crap about her safety?

The high commander of the Grey Wolves, that's who.

And now he was baiting her. Playing on her sense of curiosity with that dark, playful grin on his face. And she was falling for it, hook, line, and sinker. *Damn him.*

"What you do mean, reward money?" she asked.

He strode toward his horse, untying the animal's reins from the cabin's fence post. "It means it's in your best interest to come with me."

The horse flicked his tail excitedly.

"We're outside Grey Wolf territory, Commander, so unless you're as much of a monster as the Wild Eight, I'm not going anywhere."

His features hardened, darkening in a way that stirred something low and forbidden in her. "I'm more like them than you'd ever believe." The words were nearly a growl.

She wanted to ask him what he meant by that, but the question was lost as he stalked toward her, each movement the calculated prowl of a predator. She retreated until she was flush against the porch railing.

His hands locked on the posts beside her, caging her in. The liquid steel of his eyes blazed. "A week before the Wild Eight staged their attack on the Grey Wolves and started the war, Wyatt Maxwell was found dead in his apartment in downtown Billings. He was one abusive, sick fuck."

Boy, didn't she know it.

"We wanted that bastard dead, but we don't know

who the perpetrator was. There're only five remaining Wild Eight members. You; Wyatt's brother, Eli; Brent Remington; Clint Mack; and Silas Buck. We believe one of those five killed Wyatt, so the Grey Wolves put out a ban on any interaction with Wild Eight members and offered compensation to any wolf who turns any of you in. Do you know what that means, Belle?"

She was too breathless at his proximity to answer. He couldn't possibly know. He couldn't see the guilt in her eyes, could he? He was so close. She could practically feel the weight of his muscled body pressed against hers. She inhaled a sharp breath. This was the first she'd heard about the price on her head, but she knew exactly what it meant.

Her only option would be to take an alias, change her identity, which meant she wouldn't be able to practice medicine any longer, not even for the rodeo. And that was if no one discovered her identity and sold her out.

"What had you planned to do with your freedom, Belle?"

Immediately, her thoughts turned to the rodeo. It hadn't provided her much in the way of a community like a pack would, but she'd had a few companionable acquaintances there, other Rogues who'd worked the circuit. She wouldn't call them close, but it was more than the isolation she'd been accustomed to in her younger years. She'd enjoyed the challenge of her work, as well as the travel, and she'd gotten to see parts of the country she never would have visited otherwise, had she been practicing medicine in a more traditional setting.

To think she'd come to Montana wanting more than the rodeo had offered her! A family, friends, a pack to call her own. They'd been the dreams of her childhood—young and overly optimistic—and she'd been fool enough to chase them.

She'd given up something good, and now that she knew better, she'd give anything to go back. But if Colt was telling the truth, she would never have any of that again.

"I can give you your freedom." His gaze seared into her. He was so close that the scent of his skin wrapped around her. His wolf scent smelled of sandalwood and soap and all things deliciously male.

"I thought you already did," she said.

Colt smiled again as if she'd amused him. In an instant, his face changed from hardened soldier to dark, sexy cowboy. That grin alone was enough to make a woman weak in the knees.

"I mean true freedom, Belle, from living your life on the run and having a price on your head."

She didn't like where this was going. Favors like that didn't come without payment. "I'm not going anywhere with you."

That sexy grin widened. "Do you often lash out at people who try to help you?"

She laughed. "You? Want to help me? A she-wolf with ties to the Wild Eight? Why would I believe that?"

"Is that so hard to believe? You saved my life after all." He grinned.

She growled. The man was infuriating. She had no doubt he could run circles around her with words and wit. He was constantly trying to push every one of her buttons, but infuriating as it was, there was charm in his dark, playful game. She *liked* their verbal sparring, which only ruffled her feathers even more.

"Come with me to Wolf Pack Run. I'll sign the paperwork to remove the price from your head myself."

She had no doubt he held that kind of power, but she knew better. Alpha males were all the same. "And what do you get out of this, Commander?"

He reached into his saddlebag, retrieving an apple nestled inside for his horse. The animal sniffed the apple, brushing his lips over the skin and making it inedible for Colt before turning his nose up at it.

Colt scowled. "Did you have to lick it if you weren't going to eat it?" he grumbled at the beast.

Belle couldn't help but stifle a grin.

He placed the apple back in the saddlebag. "I already knew the vampires were up to something, that they planned to take Grey Wolf soldiers captive, though I didn't know I was their target. During active wartime, the Grey Wolves and the Seven Range Pact act as one. Now that I know the vampires' intent, I'll need the Pact's approval in order to eradicate them and stop this scheme of theirs in its tracks."

Belle recognized where he was going with this, and she didn't like it one bit.

"And for that, I'll need proof," he said, "Eyewitness proof."

She was shaking her head as soon as the words left his mouth. "No. No."

"You'll need to play the role of prisoner—for now—then plead guilty to the charges outstanding against you, show your remorse, and testify about what you overheard from the vampires to the Seven Range Pact."

She was no Wild Eight. Not really. She'd only stayed because if she hadn't…

She shoved past him. With the strength he'd

demonstrated thus far, he could have held her in place, but he let her go.

"You can tell Maverick your story. He's a reasonable man, Belle. If you help us, he won't put you back in a cell. Not if I have anything to say about it."

"I swore an oath to save lives, no matter the personal cost." She spun to face him again. "I don't regret a single one of the lives I saved—Wild Eight or otherwise. Not for a second."

He'd never understand that. This cowboy wolf had everything. He could never understand her plight. She'd been dealt the worst kind of hand in life, born a Rogue and then being forced into an unwanted pack affiliation she'd been too terrified to escape, until...

She thought of Dalia, and guilt seared through her.

No. She would save herself. She didn't need some cowboy to come into her life and sweep her off her feet as he saved her. She'd already saved herself from Wyatt. "I'm not remorseful," she repeated, inhaling a long breath. "I'm not sorry for the things I've done, because in my mind, they weren't really crimes at all."

It was more than that. The real truth in her hesitation remained unspoken, and she intended to keep it that way. It was a tempting offer, but she turned away from him and started to walk back toward the cabin.

His horse stomped a front hoof as if in agreement. At least *someone* was on her side.

Colt followed her. "What would you do with your newfound freedom, Belle?"

She kept walking, refusing to turn back toward him. "I don't see how my future has anything to do with you."

"The life of a Rogue is a lonely one."

She gaped at him. "A pack wolf giving a born Rogue a lecture on what it's like to be a Rogue? You really are arrogant, aren't you?"

"The life of an outlaw is even lonelier," he said.

"I'll take my chances."

"This is your best option, Belle."

Her mind was reeling, terrified of the possibility, yet deep down…she knew he was right. As she considered the true weight of his offer, an ounce of hope sparked there. If what he said was true, if she fulfilled her promise, she could have her life back. Her job. The rodeo. Her freedom. Once and for all. With no price on her head, no having to watch her back constantly. She might not have been guilty of the crimes they accused her of, but she was guilty of others, and what difference would it make if she didn't have her freedom?

The life of a Rogue is a lonely one, but the life of an outlaw is even lonelier…

She'd already spent far too much of her life alone.

"And if I do this, you'll guarantee that I walk away free? No more price on my head? You swear to it?" Something told her he was a man of his word.

A satisfied smirk curled across his lips. He had her, and he knew it. "I'll sign your release paperwork myself."

She had no other choice. Not if she wanted true freedom.

He extended his hand toward her. "Do we have a deal, Belle?"

She hesitated. If she did this, she'd need to tread carefully to keep herself safe. "Fine," she said, shaking his hand. "You have yourself a deal, *Colt*." Not Commander. She refused to use his title.

He grinned at her obvious jab, and from that look alone, she couldn't help feeling as if she'd just made a wager with the devil himself.

"Good," he said coolly, still gripping her hand in a firm hold that prickled heated awareness across her flesh. By the grip of their hands, he yanked her toward him. Before she knew what was going on, his hands were suddenly on her waist. He hoisted her up into the saddle before she could protest. Within seconds, he'd mounted the horse, sitting behind her. His large, muscled arms wrapped around her as he reached for the reins.

He nudged the beast forward with the heel of his cowboy boots, and the horse started to trot. "You won't regret this, Belle," he said as they started down the mountainside.

She'd been telling herself that same thing since the moment she'd decided to save him back in that clearing, and somehow, despite her logic telling her she was making yet another horrible decision, her intuition and heart told her that he was right.

Chapter 5

COLT HAD *ALMOST* LET HER WALK AWAY.

That thought haunted him as they rode down the mountainside atop Silver. The snow-covered pine trees and surrounding scenery passed in a steady blur. Or maybe he was too distracted by the enticing scent of a certain beauty's dark hair inches from his face. She smelled of spring, of lemon verbena and sweet wildflowers, despite the cold winter air surrounding them. It was a warm, intoxicating mixture that made his cock ache.

What had he been thinking? If he'd let her go, Maverick would have been beyond pissed, but that paled in comparison to what really vexed him. It was the thought that if he'd let her walk away, that would have meant he couldn't guarantee her safety. This woman was an enemy to him, but all things considered, the thought of leaving her open to potential attack was torturous. He never showed an enemy mercy, yet he *wanted* to help her.

And he hated it. He fucking hated it.

The last thing he needed was this woman thinking he was some knight in shining armor. He was no prize. Just a man who paid his debts, whose past wouldn't allow him to abandon a woman to danger and violence, and if she confessed to the Seven Range Pact as they planned, it would give him what he needed to protect his own life and the secrets that came with it, *and* the excuse he needed to set her free.

For good…

And then he could wipe his hands clean of the debt he owed her.

Until then, that left him with plenty of time to kill with this she-wolf under his charge. Plenty of time for the scent of her hair to torture him.

He imagined how she would taste on his tongue. He guessed like strawberry wine and berries. Already, she'd gotten under his skin, which meant she was an itch he needed to take care of. A man couldn't force this kind of desire away. He needed to address it, or it would do him one worse and become a weakness.

And Colt couldn't afford weakness, especially not now.

Even a hazel-eyed woman whose irises reminded him of the first emerald grass that broke through the brown earth come spring.

Never had a woman's scent called to him this way.

It went against every fiber of his being. Let alone over a she-wolf who growled at him and held his own knife to his throat like the viper-tongued little minx she was. He usually preferred his women a little less…prickly, and this woman might as well have been a cactus.

True, he'd developed a reputation for enjoying women over the years, but that had been mostly *before* he'd become commander, when he'd been a young ambitious soldier, rising in the ranks under his father's command. Before women had been capable of being temptations that would cloud his mind on the battlefield.

It was his one and only vice. His escape. Because for the short time he held a woman in his arms, he was able to lose himself, to forget who and what he was—the monster beneath the lie.

He tipped the rim of his Stetson to keep the blinding sun reflecting off the snow from his eyes. Come hell or high water, he had no intention of diving down that rabbit hole, at least not now. He needed to focus. Home in on his plans. Matters would move quickly once he had the Pact's approval, and he'd need to strategize. Easier said than done, considering that, at the moment, that round, ample ass of hers was pushing against the bulge in his jeans, courtesy of the continuous sway of Silver's saddle.

A deep, rumbling growl sounded inches away from Colt, enough to cause Silver's ears to rise in alert. He pulled on the reins, slowing the beast to a sudden halt.

He raised an eyebrow. They'd been riding more than a few hours now and were drawing close to the Missoula ranch, but that couldn't have been this woman's stomach, could it?

"You hungry?" he asked.

She opened her mouth to protest when her stomach growled again. A light shade of pink flushed her cheeks. He hadn't seen her eat at the cabin, and neither had he. Hell, she likely hadn't had a truly decent meal in days if she'd been locked up in the cells. They kept the prisoners fed, but it wasn't ideal fare. She had to be more ravenous than he was, and the least he could do before he handed her off to the guards to play prisoner was put some hot food in her belly.

"I'll take that as a yes," he mumbled.

He seized the opportunity to hunt wholeheartedly. Being cooped up inside the cabin had made him feel idle. He knew himself well enough to know that idle hands truly were the devil's workshop. Already he itched with the need to work, to keep his thoughts from swirling down into the dark abyss of his past. Post-attack, the vampires had likely retreated to regroup, and there was still enough light left to the day so they'd be holed up somewhere—for now. The sun may not have been death to them, but it weakened them considerably. As much as he wanted to ride straight through to get the news to Maverick, it would be wise to take a meal break.

They rode a short way down the mountainside and deeper into the forest, stopping in a small patch where the trees were less dense. Colt dismounted first, and she followed. He removed Silver's bit, allowing the horse to go forage nearby. When finished, he turned back toward Belle and pointed to a large rock.

"Stay here." Lifting the rim of his shirt, he stripped the material over his head.

"What are you doing?"

He shot a glance over his shoulder toward her. She was scanning over the planes of his back, her eyes wide at the sight of his battle scars. His body, though pure muscle, was a testament to the hard life he lived. He'd been training to be high commander since the night James had taken him in, and he carried the brutal wounds to show it.

"Hunting for food." He cast his shirt onto a nearby rock. "I could use some grub, and from the sounds your stomach was making, clearly you're hungry, too." He reached for the button of his jeans.

Without so much as a backward glance, he shifted. Bones cracked. Muscle stretched and fur grew. The painfully sweet release sent a burning sensation through his skin as if he had just burst forth from a constricting hold as he darted into the woods.

Twenty minutes later, he trotted back to camp with two dead hares clutched between his jaws. Dropping the hares on the ground, he quickly shifted back into human form and pulled on his clothes before he set about building a fire.

He gathered and piled nearby brush, then lit it with the lighter he kept in Silver's saddlebag. "Stoke the flames." He passed her a long stick.

She frowned at the command, but she didn't question it. As she stoked the fire, he retrieved the hares, laying them out on a nearby rock and using his switchblade to start the skinning process.

When he glanced up from his work, her nose was wrinkled in disgust.

"Don't tell me you're a vegetarian." Just what he needed. A she-wolf who wouldn't touch meat. He wasn't sure which side of him it would offend more—the carnivorous wolf, his true nature, or the tried-and-true rancher who raised beef to market. It was an honest, fair way to make a living in these parts, and the Grey Wolves depended on their ranch for income.

Her frown deepened. "No, I'm not a vegetarian."

"Your issue then?" His eyes darted down to the bloodied rabbit in front of him.

"You're skinning it all wrong. If you do it like that, you won't be able to use the hide," she scolded.

He chuckled darkly. "And what would a city-slickin' Wild Eight know about skinning an animal?"

The Wild Eight had made their home in downtown Billings. The ranchlands and mountains outside Billings were what the Grey Wolves claimed as territory, along with several subpacks farther north near Missoula, one near Helena, and several more down near Bozeman.

Colt hacked another slice, purposefully haphazardly to rile her. He was going for efficiency, not preservation. If he were to preserve the hide of every animal he killed in these woods, he'd have enough fur to clothe all his men.

Her lips tightened into that angry pucker. "I'm no city slicker." She jabbed the stick at the fire's embers, a little harder than necessary.

Apparently, he'd struck a nerve. No matter. He wasn't here to make friends. All she had to do was go along with his plan.

When he'd finished skinning the hares, he rigged them up on makeshift spits he created from some branches and set them over the fire. They sat in silence, waiting for their dinner to cook. Finally, when the hares were finished, he passed one to her and took one for himself.

The gamy meat filled his mouth as he chomped down into the leg.

"You're not going to put me back in the cell, are you?" Her voice broke the heavy silence between them.

He glanced up from his food and swallowed the bite he was chewing. "No. I can't risk you being in with the other prisoners." Not if he wanted to be able to sleep at night. The thought of any of those grubby monsters putting their paws on her made his stomach churn. "You'll stay in one of the guest houses with soldiers posted outside the door as long as I can trust you won't slip out the window with a friggin' bobby pin again."

He wasn't about to get further into the mechanics of how she'd be treated as a prisoner. He would save that until after they'd finished eating. He had about five of the Grey Wolves' most elite men with him at the Missoula ranch and the dozens of young cowboys he'd been training under his charge. Between them, he'd ensure she'd be treated fairly, but having guards watching her every move was the only way. He couldn't free her without reason, not unless he wanted his own loyalties questioned.

"Did you learn that little trick from the Wild Eight?" he asked, referring to her escape.

"No." She finally took a bite of her rabbit. A small, satisfied groan escaped her lips.

Colt fought down an aroused growl. Had she made that sound when she'd been pressed naked against him in the clearing…

"I know from your file you were with them three years," he continued, forcing his thoughts elsewhere. "You expect me to think you didn't pick up a thing or two?"

"I learned how to pick locks on the ranch growing up. We lost a key to a padlock on the stable gates. We didn't have much cash to spare, so I learned how to pick the lock. It became a hobby from there. We were busy out on the ranch, but for a young girl, it's not the most exciting life."

"We?"

He couldn't stop himself from asking. Once they both fulfilled their ends of the bargain, that would be it for them. No need to get attached, yet somehow he found he *wanted* to know more. How could he not?

Because when her gentle hands had caressed him, she'd made him forget who he was, what he was. Not the valiant Grey Wolf warrior everyone thought him to be, but one of the most hardened, violent, lethal wolves among these mountains—a product of both his ambition and the circumstance of his birth. And for a brief moment, for once in his life, he'd felt worthy.

"My mother and I." She glanced down at the rabbit but didn't take a bite. "I never knew my father."

That made two of them. The only time he'd met his birth father had been the night he'd lost his mother, the night James had taken him in. It was an experience he would happily forget.

"So where was that ranch you called home?" He took another large bite of rabbit. He wasn't typically the kind to make small talk, but he needed to keep the conversation moving freely. Eventually, he'd need answers from her, and that would come easier if she trusted him.

"Florida," she answered. "We owned a small cow-calf operation, mostly local buyers."

She'll be right at home at Wolf Pack Run. Colt frowned as soon as the thought crossed his mind. No. He could not go down that road.

This was *definitely* an itch he would need to scratch. Before this got out of hand. But on his terms…with his rules, if only she agreed.

"The Sunshine State, huh?" He supposed that explained the ever-present smell of sun and salt on her skin. Even as ivory as she was, it was as if she'd carried the sunshine and the sand here with her.

He cursed under his breath. He was known for his ironclad will, his strict self-control, even as he took his pleasure. It was how he'd managed to avoid the complexities of a relationship for so long. One night and one night only, and no women from the main ranch at Wolf Pack Run. Those were his rules. And yet, this woman, he couldn't seem to resist…

Either he was way more desperate to get laid than he thought, or this woman was trouble, plain and simple.

Pushing the thought aside, he swallowed the bite of rabbit he'd been chewing and forced himself to focus on their conversation—and not the way those perfectly round breasts felt pushed against his bare chest.

"Florida, where the old go to die and the young run from the law," he joked.

When he glanced up at her, she tried to glare at him, but he saw the amusement tugging at the edge of her lips.

"Yet you ended up here in Montana?"

She shrugged. "I traveled a lot once I got out of med school. I thought I wanted to settle down here. Now I'd give anything to go back to what I had before."

"Which was?"

"The rodeo," she said. "I was an orthopedic surgeon on a couple different circuits." She grinned. "Still think I'm a city slicker?"

He gave a small tilt of his Stetson. "I stand corrected."

She took a bite of her rabbit, chewed, and swallowed. "I don't know why I'm talking to you about this."

"That makes two of us." At least he wasn't the only one sensing the strange tension between them. It was as if some invisible force were pushing them together. He took another chomp of hare, a bite with heavy sinew that he had to tug apart with his teeth.

When he finished chewing, he shrugged. "In any case, we're on the same side now."

Her dark eyebrows shot toward her hairline. "Are we?"

"You and I want the same thing, Belle."

He tossed the leftover bones and gristle of his rabbit into the flames. The fire crackled and spit a burst of embers as he placed his hands on his knees. "You almost finished?"

She nodded.

"Good. There are a few finer points of our agreement we need to go over." Colt moved to stand, but as he did, a sharp hiss tore from his lips. He clutched his chest where the wound from his blade was still healing.

"Stubborn cowboys. I was afraid that was going to happen," Belle mumbled in between bites of rabbit. "You all think you're near invincible when it comes to pain. I knew you were going to overexert yourself. Riding down the mountainside post-injury was bad enough, but then hunting."

"Why didn't you say something?" he grumbled.

"Would you have listened?"

"Likely not," he admitted. "Though I should have."

"I appreciate a man who can admit when he was wrong." She threw what remained of her rabbit into the fire, causing the flames to roar again. Crossing to Silver, she splashed some of the water from his canteen over her hands before pouring some for Silver to lap his tongue at. The horse whinnied appreciatively. If Colt didn't know better, he would have thought she was *still* trying to steal his horse.

"Don't get used to it," he grumbled.

She smiled a tight-lipped grin. "I wouldn't dream of it." Clutching his arm, she guided him back down to where he'd been seated and reached for the hem of his shirt. "I'm going to make sure you didn't reopen the wound."

He gave a curt nod, but he was watching her with eyes like a hawk.

Slowly, she peeled his shirt up, revealing several ripples of abs until she reached where his still-healing wound remained. Not far beneath his solar plexus. Much higher, and the blade would have pierced the ventricles of his left lung or, worse, his heart. Much lower, and it would have hit his intestines. Either could have proven fatal. He'd been lucky.

When she peeled the material away from the inflamed flesh, he realized the bandage was missing. It must have fallen off when he'd shifted.

"Let me grab the gauze and adhesive."

She released his shirt and headed toward Silver.

"I don't have any," he said.

When she had Silver's saddlebag, she reached inside. "I packed some in here while you were asleep. I've cared for enough cowboys to know that as soon as you were up and walking again, you were going to tear out of that cabin like a bat outta hell, so I planned ahead."

"Yet you think *I'm* a control freak." He watched her make her way back toward him, supplies in hand, as he enjoyed the sway of her full hips.

"There's a difference between controlling and being thorough. I take the care of my patients very seriously." She set the supplies down on the log beside him. "So you were saying something about our agreement?"

He nodded. "We'll return to the main ranch at Wolf Pack Run in two moons. Once there, you'll remain in custody until the Seven Range Pact convenes and you deliver your testimony. In the meantime, there are some ground rules you'll need to adhere to."

She knelt in front of him to reach his wound, sitting between his spread knees. "Such as?"

"Rule number one: Never breathe a word of this agreement to anyone. Do you understand?" His gaze narrowed in a hawklike stare, impressing the seriousness of that order upon her.

She reached for the canteen, unscrewed the cap, and poured some of the liquid on the gauze. When the gauze was good and damp, she reached for him.

A low grumble released in his throat as she began to wipe the fresh blood from the edges of the wound. Thanks to his true nature, it had begun to scab over, but it would still bleed if he overexerted himself.

"What's rule number two?" she asked.

"You didn't agree to rule number one."

"It's never a good idea to enter a contract, verbal or otherwise, without the full details. As a commander, I think you would know that, Colt." She wiped at the blood. "What's rule number two?"

"Rule number two is you need to behave like a prisoner. Be convincing."

"That sounds harder than rule number one."

Colt shook his head. No surprise there.

"And rule number three?" she asked.

He narrowed his gaze again. "Don't speak a word of this to anyone."

"That's the same rule as number one."

"It's so important, it bears repeating. If rule number one is broken, I won't be able to protect you any longer. All our agreements will be null and void."

"Is that what you're doing, Colt? Protecting me?" She braced her hand against his bare chest as their gazes locked.

"Yes," he said. It may have been the first full truth he'd spoken to her. Not wrapped in teasing, challenge, intimidation, or any of the other bullshit armor he wore to protect himself.

"And when this is over?" she asked.

He hesitated. "You'll be able to leave Wolf Pack Run and never look back."

Her chin drew into a tight line, and for a moment, he almost thought he saw her lip quiver, but then it was gone. Maybe this woman was far better at hiding her emotions than he thought.

"Is that what you plan to do with your freedom, head back to the rodeo?" he asked.

She discarded the bloodied gauze in the fire and reached for a fresh piece and the adhesive, careful to be gentle as she covered the tender skin. "It is. I think it will make me happy. There was a time when I loved it." When her bare fingertips touched him without the guard of the gauze, he tensed. She cocked her head to the side slightly as her hand lingered against his bare flesh. She was still kneeling between his thighs. "Does it hurt when I touch you there?"

"No, Belle." His words were a near purr. "That was a different kind of growl."

"I…" She started to speak, then paused.

As they lingered there, the tension between them heightened. A steady thrumming ache built in his cock, heady and visceral. He needed to take care of this once and for all, stop this madness before it got out of hand. One night. That was all it would take. Then this hunger would be tamed and he could go back to focusing on his work. She cleared her throat, but he caught the scent of desire on her. He knew it was there without a doubt.

"You never answered, Belle. Do you agree to my terms?"

"I don't see I have much of a choice."

"Do we have ourselves a deal then?"

She released a weighted sigh. "I think we do."

"Good," he said. "That leaves us time to discuss another negotiation."

She raised a brow, pushed herself to standing, and crossed the clearing to return the spare adhesive and gauze to his saddlebag. "And what would that be?"

As she faced toward him again, a wicked grin crossed his lips. "The night we're going to spend together."

Chapter 6

"Excuse me?"

He'd surprised her when he'd let slip that he wanted to *protect* her. *Help* her. But...Belle couldn't have heard him correctly, could she?

"I want to make it clear that our prior agreements still stand, and they have no relation to your decision. Regardless of my position, you have a choice, of course."

Maybe she *had* heard him correctly. He couldn't possibly be serious. She gaped at him. Yes, there was heat between them. Tension. She sensed it, too. But she wasn't about to admit that. Definitely not to him. She couldn't risk another relationship with an alpha wolf—no matter how attractive and brave he might be, or how tempting the offer. No matter how much she wanted to see that softer side of him again.

No. She needed to nip this in the bud before it got out of hand.

She settled on being saucy. It worked with him, and that seemed to be the only way they could converse without her simultaneously wanting to pull her hair out and feeling weak in the knees whenever he looked at her. "Do you often try to piss off women who saved your life?"

"Only when I've already seen them naked."

She knew he was teasing, but still she forced a snarl.

Those intense gray eyes locked onto her, causing her stomach to fill with traitorous butterflies. "Is that what I do you to, Belle? Piss you off?"

The question was so to-the-point that it caught her off guard. She wasn't certain she could define how he made her feel. Yes, there was frustration, but there was also something...more. Something complicated.

At her lack of response, he smirked. "I didn't think so."

"What's that supposed to mean?"

He shrugged. "Only that you wear your emotions on your sleeve. You can glare and pucker those full pink lips at me like you've tasted something sour all you want, Belle, but your eyes give you away."

She raised a brow. "Oh really? And what do they say?"

His gaze locked with hers. "They say that our verbal sparring doesn't really piss you off at all. In fact, I'd go so far as to say you not only like it, you crave it."

She laughed. "That's absurd. I barely know you."

"You don't need to know someone to be attracted to them."

"Me? Attracted to you?" She crossed her arms over her chest. "Not a chance."

"You enjoyed when I held you naked against me—in the clearing." He said it with such utter confidence, as if he knew it without a doubt. "You can't deny that."

She *could*, and she *would* for that matter, even if it wasn't true. "Don't flatter yourself, Colt."

He chuckled darkly, pushing from where he sat on the log to stand. At his full height, he was all the more intimidating, towering over her. "I don't need flattery. Most women find me attractive. It's a matter of fact. Some are better at hiding it than others." Those steely eyes fell to her. "But you're not one of those women, Belle. You can't hide your emotions, even when you try."

She was hiding more from him than he'd ever know. "I'm not like most women."

"No, you're not," he agreed. Colt's eyes narrowed, and he stepped closer to the fire, staring into its depths. The flames burned bright, casting a dim orange glow on his face and creating shadows that hollowed the sharp lines of his cheekbones. "Most women bat their eyelashes, smile, and giggle when they find a man attractive. You, on the other hand, do the opposite. You narrow those pretty hazel eyes, pucker that little mouth, and let that viper-tongued wit fly, but it's a defense mechanism. I'm a commander, Belle." His gaze flicked toward her. "I know a defense tactic when I see one."

"You think you have me all figured out, don't you?"

"No." He chuckled. "I know a challenge when I see one, and you work hard to be a challenge, Belle. But if the look in your wolf eyes is any indication, you may be a challenge, but you're not as difficult to solve as you think. Not for me."

She scoffed at him. "You're not my type at all."

It wasn't true. Not in the slightest. But she needed to try to keep him at arm's length. Her experiences with Wyatt had taught her that. It didn't matter that she wanted otherwise. Before Colt, Belle hadn't been certain she had a type, but with each passing second, she became more certain that if there were a reference book of her life, under "Belle's type," Colt Cavanaugh's picture would be the definition. See synonyms for reference: worst fear, here comes trouble, and The Devil Wears a Cowboy Hat.

There was that wolfish grin again. He saw straight through her. "Could have fooled me." He turned away from the fire and drew closer. "I saw your desire in the clearing, felt the way you melted into my arms."

Her hands clenched into fists. She was quickly losing this battle. "I was faking it."

He shook his head, that grin still curving his lips in the slightest tilt as he prowled toward her. "You're lying."

He stood in front of her now, less than a foot away. She retreated until her spine pushed flush against one of the mighty pines behind her. The width and breadth of his shoulders dwarfed her, but still she fought to regain control. This was no more than one of his power plays.

"Then prove it." The words slipped from her lips before she could stop them.

Those metal-gray eyes burned a molten liquid steel. "There are two things you need to know about me, Belle. The first is that I hate to be defied. As a commander, I'm more than used to getting my way. In fact, I damn well expect it. The second is that I never back down from a challenge"—his next words were a near growl—"because I always win."

Her eyes narrowed. "Do your worst, Commander."

Something sparked in his eyes, and within seconds, he was on top of her, caging her between the hard muscles of his body and the bumpy bark of the tree. He clasped his hands overtop hers, pinning them above her head as he leaned in. His lips were so near, they brushed against hers as they spoke in a series of fluttering caresses, so hot and brazen, she could hardly breathe.

"I don't think you realize what kind of fire you're playing with, sweetheart," he purred.

"I think I know *exactly* what I'm doing," she challenged. Unwittingly, her tongue darted out to wet her lips, and slowly, his gaze fell there. Belle's breath caught, and she felt the anticipation building in her chest. His mouth was so close, she could feel the warmth of his breath on her chin. Her pulse quickened, and a slick wave of heat blossomed between her legs.

His eyes flashed gold. His lips were on hers then, taking hold in a kiss that could only be described as a claiming. It was a delicious, dangerous declaration of war…and she couldn't get enough. He laid siege upon her mouth, kneading until her bottom lip was caught between his teeth. He sucked on the gentle flesh—hard. She gasped, surging forward into his arms. He seized the brief opening of her mouth to his advantage, expertly parting the seam of her lips until she opened completely for him, the taste of him filling her mouth. He tasted of dark spices and male.

The scruff of his beard brushed and teased against the sensitive skin of her cheeks as their tongues clashed in a hot, fevered dance. As he took full advantage of his conquest, his hands explored, doing unimaginable, ungentlemanly things as he cupped the bulk of her ass in one hand and fisted the locks of her hair in the other.

She wasn't a small woman, but he leveraged her weight with ease. Pulling her toward him, he used his knee to nudge her legs open, and then he pressed her against him. The hard, long length of his cock strained against his jeans and pushed between her thighs, finding her center and grinding against it in a tantalizing caress. The sensation, coupled with the onslaught of his kiss, made her shudder. And before she could form a coherent thought and realize that he'd won their battle, she waved the white flag of surrender…and moaned.

Abruptly, he released her. A satisfied smirk curled on his lips as he stepped back from the tree and surveyed his work. She knew what she must look like with plump, freshly kissed lips, hardened nipples, and legs splayed wide in need.

He had won. They both knew it from the look of satisfaction in his eyes and the uncontrollable desire making her heart race. He had made his point.

Still, she tried to fight it, tried to push him away to protect herself, even though she wanted him to draw nearer. She straightened, closing her thighs and brushing herself off as if the kiss had done nothing, meant nothing to her. "See. Not affected at all."

His grin was near sinister and so sexy, it hurt. "Whether you like it or not, you blossom for me, Belle. There's something between us, and you know it." His eyes fell to the hardened peaks of her nipples, and he grinned. Not the award-winning smile she'd been wanting, but a gorgeous, white-toothed grin nonetheless, and she decided then that she hated the pure temptation that was Colt Cavanaugh. Everything about him made her want to go against the promises she'd made herself, the things she'd never do again. Everything from that hardened-warrior exterior to the softness she knew lay underneath. The bravery, the courage, the charm. Every last smug, arrogant gorgeous inch of his being.

Yes, even those inches…

She pushed past him to stand beside the fire and stare into its depths. She couldn't get involved with another alpha wolf, especially one who held so much power over her. He may have saved her life, but she'd sworn she wouldn't place herself in such a vulnerable position again. There was no excuse for the way she'd reacted to him in the clearing or now. She should know better than that. He had kissed her to prove a point. It was a power play. Everything was with him. Nothing more.

She gazed into the flames, trying to convince herself that was true, that it was nothing but lust between them, but she couldn't. Contrary to the image he projected, he was merciful, caring. He could have taken her captive without offering her a deal and forced her to testify to the Seven Range Pact, but he hadn't. He was trying to help her.

"I wouldn't be standing here if it wasn't for you," he finally said, breaking the silence between them.

His words forced her to look up. There was unfettered gratitude in his eyes, and her breath stopped short. Almost…kind, the tenderness from him she craved. If he kept that up, he'd have her hook, line, and sinker.

Immediately, she tried to push him away. She couldn't get further entangled with this cowboy. She couldn't. "You don't fool me, Colt. You can try to warm me to you all you want, but I know your reputation. You bed women like it's sport. One night and done, and you never call in the morning. So those smoldering eyes won't work on me." She'd heard the rumors from the Wild Eight females. Normally, she didn't put stock in such things, but in this case, it was all the more reason not to trust her feelings toward him.

When she did venture into a relationship again, she wanted passion, tenderness, caring. Not a one-night stand that would lead nowhere.

She crossed to his horse, which had taken to moping and looking rather neglected with all this talk and none about him. She reached into the saddlebag and removed the apple Colt had offered earlier. When she extended it toward the beast, the horse happily bit into the juicy skin of the green Granny Smith.

"Traitor," Colt grumbled at Silver. He glanced back toward Belle. "Would you be so judgmental of my sexual history if I were a woman?" he asked.

As she finished feeding Silver the apple, she cast a glance toward him. "What do you mean?"

"It means that I think your problem has less to do with the number of partners I've slept with and more with the fact that I don't call them in the morning."

Call her old-fashioned, but she struggled to see what was wrong with that. "How horrible of me. How dare women expect men to care about them, to at least *consider* a relationship."

"I make my expectations known from the start, and the women I'm with agree to those terms. It's not my fault if they think they can change me. I'm very clear from the beginning. I don't do relationships. In my position, they're a liability I can't afford."

Relationships as a liability? she thought. *What a miserable existence.*

"So that would be your terms?" she asked.

"Yes."

That one word held such a dark, sinful promise that her nipples tightened and her breasts grew heavy with need. She fought to keep her voice level. "I'm not even your type."

A man like him would be interested in leggy blonds

or, at the very least, alpha females, Grey Wolf women worthy of his station. Not a dark-haired Rogue with ties to the Wild Eight who fought to tame the flyaways of her curls every morning and whose figure could be at least ten pounds trimmer. Belle had her positive attributes, but she'd never counted her looks as one of them. She was smart as a whip and a helluva surgeon to boot. But in her experience, it was not brainy, bookish, and busty who was the belle of the ball. It was tall, leggy, smiling, pretty, and amiable. Decidedly not... What was it he'd called her? Viper-tongued.

"I think I'll be the judge of that. Change can be refreshing," he answered.

His reassurance did little to abate her thoughts.

"So do we have ourselves an agreement, Belle? One night together? That's all I can offer you, but I think you know as well as I do that it would be good between us." He paused. "Better than good."

She shook her head. "I can't agree to that."

No matter how tempting the offer...

"A shame." He shoved his hands in his pockets. The fire had burned down to little more than embers, and he used his boot to stomp out the remaining few. "We need to keep moving. We've lingered here long enough, and I need to return to my work." He crossed to where she stood beside Silver and placed his foot in the stirrup.

"That's it?" She gaped at him. "You ask me to spend one wild, hot night with you, and then we drop the topic suddenly, as if it's nothing?"

Colt swung up into the saddle. "No means no, sweetheart. You may think I'm an arrogant rake, but even *I* know there are lines that cannot and should not be crossed." He extended a hand down toward her. "But if you change your mind…"

"You'll be the first to know." She took his hand, placing her foot in the stirrup and climbing into the saddle in front of him.

They rode for another hour in silence. Ever since their conversation in the clearing, there had been a subtle tension between them. In Belle's mind, that tension worsened with each passing minute as they drew closer to the Missoula Grey Wolf territory.

Keep your eye on the prize, Belle. When all this is over, you'll have your freedom. True freedom.

When Colt pulled back on Silver's reins, Belle knew they were close. Silver slowed to a halt, and Colt quickly dismounted. Belle's wolf smelled and sensed the nearness of the pack. Awareness prickled through her, raising the fine hairs across her arms and down the nape of her neck.

"Do you remember the rules?" he asked.

After she dismounted, she gave a nod.

"Good." He must have sensed her unease, because he gave her a pointed look. "Your guards will be my most trusted soldiers, Belle. You may be our enemy, but you're no monster like your packmembers, and as commander, I have little tolerance for violence against women. You'll receive no ill treatment. I promise you."

"I'm trusting you're a man of your word, Colt."

"Your trust isn't misplaced, sweetheart." He tipped his hat toward her. "Showtime."

Belle's stomach clenched.

Colt took another step forward, crossing an invisible boundary line, then threw back his head and released a long, echoing howl.

A moment later, a chorus of responses echoed back. The howls that emanated throughout the forest were ones of relief and elation at his return. Belle felt a lump form in her throat as the continuing howls drew nearer. What she wouldn't give to have a pack that cared for her like that, that presented her with unending loyalty and love.

But that had been her mistake, thinking that a Rogue like her could have those things. The Wild Eight had taught her that. The life of a pack wolf, at least a pack the likes of the Grey Wolves, wasn't for a Rogue like her, and it never would be.

Stepping behind her, Colt removed the handcuffs from Silver's saddlebag before coming to stand in front of her again. This time, he placed her wrists in front of her, allowing that intense, steely gaze to sear into her. At the feel of the cold metal against her skin, she gasped. The edges of his temple creased with concern, but she shook her head at him. She'd promised to make this convincing.

He leaned down and whispered into her ear. "It will be all right."

The warmth of his breath tingled down her spine, bringing her back to the feeling of being in his arms in the clearing, of that kiss that had torn her to pieces as much as it had put her back together again.

His intentions had been clear from the start. Long before he'd known who she was, and even now, as his enemy, they were clear as day.

I'll protect you, he had said. *You have my word.*

She had no doubt about that truth.

He stepped back, placing several paces between them. Suddenly, the first of his men burst forth from the trees, two massive Grey Wolves, nearly as large and agile as Colt. Shifting from wolf into human form within seconds, they stood nude before them. As a Rogue, that was one aspect of pack life Belle was certain she'd never get used to.

"Colt," a dark-haired Grey Wolf breathed, clear relief across his handsome face at the sight of his packmate alive and well. "Are you injured?" He had a thick, heavy drawl to his voice that sounded straight from Texas, and the brown shade of his skin hinted at Latin descent.

"Austin," Colt greeted him. His eyes darted to the other wolf present, the one who appeared to have a permanent scowl etched across his face. He'd be handsome if he didn't appear so harsh.

"Malcolm," Colt said.

Malcolm gave a grim nod. "We thought you were—" He stopped short as his eyes tracked to Belle and the handcuffs locking her wrists.

Several other packmembers emerged from the trees. Even with a quick glance, from the way they'd addressed Colt by name and their sheer size, she recognized that the first two must be elite warriors. Everyone knew the Grey Wolves had an elite team, the best of the best, in their fighters. Not that it made the other packmembers any less intimidating. Most of them she'd never seen before, but she recognized one of the guards. He'd led her cellblock. At the sight of her, he blanched.

Colt turned his gaze toward the guard, his eyes promising he'd deal with him later. "Austin and his team will assume responsibility for Miss Beaumont. She'll be testifying before the Seven Range Pact. Until then, she'll be in your charge. Take her to the guest cabin. She'll be kept separate from the other prisoners."

Colt's eyes flicked toward Belle expectantly. He didn't even need to speak the order aloud.

Within seconds, Austin was directing two of the men in his charge toward her. They gripped her by the arms with a firm, commanding hold.

"In exchange for her cooperation, I expect humane treatment." Colt's gaze combed over his men, lingering for the briefest moments on each one of them. "If any of you so much as move a single hair on her head out of place, you will answer to me personally. Do I make myself clear?"

"Yes, sir."

"And you'll be gettin' hell from me, too," Austin drawled. "I won't be stitchin' up any of your messes. I may be a medic, but no one's injured on my charge, especially a woman. Got it?"

"Yes, sir," the soldiers answered back in unison.

Colt nodded. "Good. Return to the ranch immediately. We have a lot of work to do, gentlemen."

The soldiers gripping Belle led her forward, urging her into step with them as everyone started to head back to the ranch, but Colt stepped into their path.

His gaze raked over her, distant and assessing, as if he barely knew her. It was so convincing, even she had a hard time believing otherwise. He was good. Damn good.

"Should you change your mind, my previous offer still stands, Miss Beaumont." He ducked down to whisper in her ear, so low that she knew only she could hear. "I may not promise to call the next morning like a gentleman, but you wouldn't forget a night with me."

She was certain he was right.

Her cheeks burned hot as he pulled away, but she

kept her gaze lowered. With the tight cinch of her lips, she hoped her reaction came across as anger to his soldiers, rather than the way he actually affected her.

"Consider it." Colt stepped out of the way in order to let them pass. "I won't ask again."

As his soldiers led her away, she glanced over her shoulder. Those steeled eyes watched her, cold, calculating, and searing straight through her. Every part of her prickled with awareness, the same deep feeling of instinct she'd felt in his arms and again when he'd kissed her. Power play be damned, and somehow, though he'd sworn this would be the last *he* would mention it, she knew without a doubt that this wouldn't be the last of their negotiation.

Chapter 7

"YOU SEEM DISTRACTED." DEAN STOOD INSIDE THE MISSOULA ranch barn beside Colt, a clipboard in one hand and a pen in the other as he took inventory of the ranch's supply stock.

Distracted was putting it lightly. Colt had spent the morning on the subpack's small training field running drills. Considering the Missoula ranch was only about a quarter the size of Wolf Pack Run, their training field was less than what he was used to. The Missoula ranch, though fully operational and similar in function to Wolf Pack Run, didn't boast Wolf Pack Run's underground training facilities and an additional training field like his men were used to, but they were soldiers and cowboys, so they'd make do.

Even with the field cramped with men, the monotony of drills had left his mind far too much room to wander. After a short lunch break, when they'd regrouped for sparring, it'd become clear to Colt that, for once, his head wasn't in the fight. Luckily, he'd been able to hand the remainder of his duties over to Austin, the Grey Wolves' resident Texan and medic, and Malcolm, the dark and hardened Grey Wolf executioner—the Healer and the Destroyer, respectively, both fierce warriors on the battlefield.

Colt hated passing the buck, but Austin and Malcolm were among the ten elite Grey Wolf warriors who led the pack. Well, nine elite warriors. They'd lost two men at the beginning of the war, and only one among their pack's finest had been replaced with a new appointment. Maverick had yet to name the last. Colt knew Austin and Malcolm were capable of completing the remainder of the day's training, and he'd taken the opportunity to volunteer for some ranch work.

That was what he truly needed. Time in the open mountain air to clear his head, breathing in the bitter cold and working with his hands. The wild abandon of the vast, sprawling land and the life of a cowboy had always called to him.

Little had he known he'd be stuck on inventory duty.

In a few weeks, it would be calving season, and it was high time they took stock of their supplies and ordered more sweet feed, powdered colostrum replacer, nursing bottles, blankets, and other necessities. Calving season was their busiest and most stressful time of the year, and its success largely determined their future profits.

"Nothing on my mind, just zoned out," Colt replied. He leaned on one of the wrought-iron stall gates.

Sure, he was zoned out, thinking of a certain gorgeous, viper-tongued she-wolf. He would *not* continue to think about a woman who was not only his enemy, but who also had rejected him outright. It was her choice, plain and simple, and he respected that, but that didn't mean he had to like it. Silver hadn't fared much better. The horse, who was tied to a post outside the barn, released a long sigh. He'd been more than a little melancholy and just a tad dramatic about Belle's absence.

But Colt had done his due diligence when they'd returned to the Missoula ranch, looking up Belle's file and gathering information on her. His recollection had been right. As far as they knew, she'd never actively engaged in battle or disobedience against the Grey Wolves. She'd simply been the Wild Eight's physician. The odd part was that there was no record of her being involved with the renegade pack prior to three years ago, just before Wes Calhoun, now Grey Wolf second-in-command, had stepped down as Wild Eight packmaster. Something about the timeline didn't sit right with Colt. He was missing a piece of the puzzle, he was certain.

In any case, there was nothing further to discuss with Belle until it came time for her testimony tomorrow. They would drive his truck back down to Wolf Pack Run.

Dean grinned. "Does zoning out mean you no longer notice when you step straight into a cow patty?"

Colt glanced to the heel of his boot and swore. "Shit."

"That'd be about right." Dean chuckled.

While Colt busied himself with scraping his heel through the wood chips and hay covering the barn floor to rid his boot of muck, the Grey Wolves' front-of-house director scanned the supply shelves and added another checkmark to his list.

The dark-skinned cowboy oversaw the ranch's business operations as they pertained to the outside world— both at Wolf Pack Run and with a team of men out at the subpacks. Born a Grey Wolf but having grown up in Oklahoma before relocating to Wolf Pack Run, Dean was used to living among humans. It was his responsibility to coordinate bringing the pack's cattle to market, as well as dealing with their human business associates and suppliers. To the nonshifters who did business with Wolf Pack Run, Dean was the face of the ranch. The cowboy and Grey Wolf warrior worked hard to turn a profit while keeping his true nature hidden.

"Where's the spout around here?" Colt grumbled. He'd need to stick his boot under some water to get this level of mess off.

"If you weren't so caught up in your own head, you would have heard me when I told you the spout froze over." Dean gave Colt a side-eye glance as he combed through the supply shelf, counting how many nursing bottles they had in stock. The bottles were a contingency plan to keep calves alive if they encountered a heifer who refused to nurse or lost one of the mothers during birth.

As cold and wet a winter as they'd had this year, along with the fact that there was still snow on the ground, the coming spring wouldn't be as warm as usual, which meant they were in for a rough calving season. Timing was best when the spring calves hit the ground in warm, dry weather, favorable conditions for the young's survival. When it was cold and damp with many animals huddled inside, the barn became a breeding ground for potential infection and the death of the calves if the pack didn't stay vigilant.

Montana weather was fierce and unpredictable, particularly in the winter and early spring, but the northwest side of the state was always in for the worst. Even though the Missoula ranch and the main ranch at Wolf Pack Run outside Billings were only a few hours apart, the difference in weather between the northwest and south/central areas had to be taken into account.

"Did you put that on the list already? To check the pipes out here when the weather warms?" Dean asked.

Colt glanced down at his own clipboard, finding it blank. "No." He placed his hand on his hip as he released a frustrated huff. "Maybe I do have a lot on my mind," he admitted.

"A woman?" Dean raised a brow.

Colt refused to meet Dean's eyes. Was he that transparent? It'd been only two days, yet he couldn't help replaying every detail of his and Belle's interactions in his head. He barely knew the woman, but he found he actually *missed* their verbal sparring. To make matters worse, he also struggled to consider the pending threat the vampires posed against him and their kind without his thoughts turning to her. He tried to tell himself that it was because the topics were related, but even he recognized it was a piss-poor excuse. He was all manner of fucked.

…Or *not*, in this case.

At least he'd be rid of her soon. Once she was no longer in his territory, he'd have no choice but to stop thinking about her. Upon delivering the news to Maverick, the packmaster had immediately requested a convening of the Seven Range Pact to decide how to deal with the conflict. Colt and Belle were due to return to Wolf Pack Run tomorrow so she could deliver her testimony. Once Maverick received the Pact's approval—which Colt had no doubt they would receive—he could begin to gather the information and evidence they needed to launch a counterstrike against the vampires.

Those filthy bloodsuckers would think twice about ever targeting him or the Grey Wolves again.

"It's always a woman," Dean drawled. "That's the only thing that can bring a cowboy to his knees, that or the broadside of a bull's horns."

Colt imagined himself with a choice of taking on either Belle Beaumont or an angry bull. Horns and all, he'd choose the bull.

"Not with me." He brushed Dean off.

Dean chuckled again. "Oh, 'scuse me. I forgot. There's no such thing as female troubles for Commander Casanova…"

Colt winced at the nickname. Only the other elite warriors dared call him that, but the jab still irked him.

Grabbing his canteen, Colt finally settled on dumping the contents over his boot. It would have to make do until he could give it a true clean.

Dean eyed him, waiting for Colt to continue. The man could make patience a near-torturous art.

"I can't seem to wrap my head around this development with the vampires," Colt confessed. It wasn't far from the truth.

Silver let out a haughty huff in response as if to say *Yeah, right.* Similarly, Dean gave him a look that said he agreed with Silver. Neither of them believed Colt for a second.

"Seems pretty simple to me. If those bloodsuckers find a way to feed off us, that changes the whole game." Dean moved a box of blankets down from the shelf. "But you know that already." Dean pegged Colt with a hard stare. "There's something you're not saying."

"Why me?" Colt asked.

Dean snorted. "Don't tell me you're going soft all the sudden, Colt," he joked. "'Why me?' Shit." Dean chuckled.

Colt grumbled. "You know what I mean. Why am I the target? There has to be a reason. Why not Maverick, Wes, or even you for that matter?"

"Likely because Maverick may be packmaster, but it's you and your commanding strategies, your war tactics and intelligence gathering that are responsible for their losses. Not to mention, you're more accessible than Maverick, for good reason, and less of a loose cannon than Wes. Why *not* you is the better question." Dean started counting the folded blankets in the crate in front of him.

Dean might be right, and Colt knew the other Grey Wolf elite warriors, the select few who were clued in to the situation, likely thought the same. But Colt had a suspicion it was more than that. Betrayal wasn't taken lightly among the Grey Wolves, and that was what Colt's secrets would amount to, even though he'd loyally served their pack.

There was only one way the vampires could know his secret, and Colt wasn't even certain such a document existed. But if it did, there were only two people he could speak to who might know of its existence. Asking Wes Calhoun was out of the question, tantamount to admitting the truth outright, which left him only one other option…

"I have to go." Colt dropped his clipboard on top of the blanket box and headed for the open barn door.

"You're just gonna abandon me like that?"

"I wasn't much help anyway." And he likely wouldn't be until he took care of this.

"Damn straight, you weren't," Dean grumbled.

Colt would find a way to make it up to his packmate. Until then, he had a few questions for a certain viper-tongued she-wolf.

———

The door to Colt's private cabin burst open, allowing the cold to blow in. The fire in the hearth flickered, the flames briefly dimming to a steady burning ember before roaring to life again. Colt stared into the fire, his thoughts racing. The cold at his back sent a chill down his spine, but it wasn't the wind that caused him to still. It was the feminine voice that accompanied it.

"You wanted to see me, Commander?"

It had only been two days, but her voice sounded throatier, deeper in timbre than he remembered, the kind of voice meant for late-night phone calls and meetings in dark corners of a hotel lobby.

Austin held her by the arms. Her wrists were bound again, though he knew she'd been roaming around without handcuffs inside the guest cabin that served as her house arrest. She watched him with incredulous eyes, as if he'd had nerve to summon her. He'd missed that cheekiness, stubborn woman that she was.

His eyes darted to Austin. "Thank you."

"Course." Austin nodded as he made his exit. The door to the cabin clicked shut behind him, leaving Colt and Belle alone.

Colt crossed the room, circling behind her. With one of the keys at his belt, he unlocked her cuffs. When the metal fell away from her wrists, she released a breathy, relieved sort of moan. The sound stirred something low in his belly. What he wouldn't give to hear her make that sound with her pressed naked against him again. He was grateful her back was to him so she couldn't see the desire burning in his now-golden wolf eyes.

"You have no idea how good it feels to have those off," she breathed.

He stepped out from behind her, returning to the fireside, and he felt his eyes fade back to their usual color. He placed his hands on the mantel, resting his weight there. The warmth of the flames licked away the remaining cold in the air as the fire cast shadows about the cabin. It was well past sundown.

"Why'd you bring me here, Colt? We agreed I had to behave as a prisoner. I figured that meant acting as if we were strangers."

"And that agreement still stands. You're here as a prisoner." He cleared his throat. "Last we spoke, you agreed to testify to the Seven Range Pact, but I need another favor. I need you to tell me everything you know."

Belle raised a brow. "About what? I already told you what I overheard in the clearing."

"Not about that. About the Wild Eight, the other four remaining members' whereabouts and motivations, how that pertains to the vampires' plans, and"—he paused, reluctant to place his next request—"and anything you may have heard from them about me."

She didn't seem to notice the gravity of that last statement or what it had taken for him to ask it. "You? The only thing I've heard from the Wild Eight about you has little to do with the vampires."

"What is it you've heard about me?"

She crossed her arms over her chest, and her hip jutted out to one side slightly as if her patience with him was limited. "That you're as loyal to the Grey Wolves as you are deadly to your enemies."

So the truth…

"And?" he prompted.

That you're not a Grey Wolf… He waited for those words to pass her lips.

She hesitated, but finally she answered, "And that

you're as much of a rake in the bedroom as you are a lethal warrior on the battlefield."

He chuckled. Nothing he hadn't been accused of before. "And do I live up to my reputation?" Curiosity got the better of him, and he couldn't help but ask.

A blush warmed her cheeks. "I can't really speak to that."

Yet. He fought down an aroused growl. Changing the subject, he crossed over to the nearby bookshelf and feigned scanning the titles. He'd always been a reader. The classics, those were his favorites, but as of late, he hadn't had the time. "And my other questions?"

"I don't have answers. I'm not involved with the Wild Eight anymore," she said.

"This kind of attack isn't done spur of the moment. The vampires had to have been planning this for some time, and you know they were heavily involved with the Wild Eight at the start of the war. The planning would likely have taken place shortly before you left."

From the corner of his eye, he saw her shrug. "If so, I wasn't clued in."

He drew closer to her, using his size and position to intimidate. Maybe she'd prove more forthcoming if he reminded her of the power dynamic here. She was his prisoner after all. Deal or not. But as he prowled toward her, she didn't so much as blink an eye. "If you give answers like that to the Seven Range Pact, you're never going to convince them, Belle, and then I won't be able to help you."

Her brows drew low as her eyes narrowed. "I can't answer something I don't know."

He didn't believe that for a second. "You can't tell me you spent three years with them and don't have a single bit of useful information. Think, Belle. Is there something, anything you can remember?"

She was quickly losing patience with him. He could see it from the flush on her neck. This was what he'd missed, the sight of her flustered and on the verge of wanting to throttle him. Passion was what their little word wars brought about in her. He could see it as clear as day. Belle Beaumont was practically bursting with restrained, unused passion.

"I told you. I don't know anything."

"Spoken like a true Wild Eight," he shot back. He said it as much to rile her as he did because it was true. It was clear where her loyalties lay.

She stepped toward him, the two of them nearly nose to nose. Her hands clenched into fists. Her features twisted with anger and resentment, and to Colt's surprise, tears gathered in her eyes. "I'm not Wild Eight. I've *never* been Wild Eight, and I am nothing like them." She turned away to hide her emotion.

He'd never intended to make her cry. He glanced in the mirror above the fireside mantel. Staring at his reflection, his gaze traced over the hard features of his face. He looked so much like his birth father in that moment that it pained him. More than usual. It was in the shape of his eyes, the line of his chin, the straight edge of his nose. And if making an indelible powerhouse of a woman like Belle Beaumont cry didn't prove he was just as much of a monster as the man who'd sired him, he didn't know what did.

"You wouldn't believe me," she whispered. Her back was turned toward him, and her shoulders trembled. "No one ever believes me."

He'd never seen such a pained, visceral reaction from a prisoner in response to simple questioning, not in all his days. Wolves were violent, enraged, predatory when cornered and threatened with a loss of their freedom, but she didn't appear to be any of those things. Yes, she was angry, but she also looked sad, defeated, like a woman who'd been broken one too many times.

He'd seen that look before. In the eyes of his mother. Not Sonya, but his *real* mother, before her death. When she would come home from time spent with his monster of a sire. She'd pay the babysitter, then tuck him into bed, and when she thought he was good and asleep, that he couldn't hear her, she'd lock herself in her room, crying herself to sleep.

The sounds still haunted him at night.

"Try me," he urged.

Reluctantly, Belle took a deep, calming breath, but she still refused to look at him. "They forced me to join. I was a Rogue."

A Rogue. Like his mother had been. The confession instantly softened him to her plea—and Colt never softened. Not for anyone.

The missing pieces from her file fell into place. That was why there was no record of her. When she said she'd worked the rodeo, he thought that must have been a brief absence from her pack life with the Wild Eight, but there was no record of her anywhere in the Grey Wolf files before three years prior, which meant she hadn't been born Wild Eight. She'd been taken in, and if what she said was true, she'd been taken into the pack by force.

From his childhood, he knew firsthand the way the Wild Eight had taken advantage of Rogue wolves desperate for a pack, pulling Rogues into their ranks, making them dependent like the true abusers the Wild Eight were. Rogue she-wolves were the most vulnerable. Though stronger than humans, most were physically weaker than the males of their species and far less violent. Easy targets. The memories of his early years were riddled with dark, painful images of how much the Wild Eight could hurt and manipulate a woman, the things they would do to break her.

And how brutal the punishment was when she didn't obey. He'd learned that lesson the hard way the night his mother died, the night James took him.

"You were their captive?" he asked.

"They didn't keep me in chains, if that's what you mean, but I had no choice but to stay."

He waited in silence, hoping she would elaborate.

She released a shaky breath. "They would have come after me if I left...and...and there was an old she-wolf there, Dalia."

"Dalia Maxwell." He nodded. Wyatt and Eli Maxwell's ancient great-aunt. The woman was no enemy of his, just unfortunately a relative of two of the Wild Eight's members. She'd only been involved in the pack when she'd become so sickly that the charge of her care fell to her asshole nephews. As far as the Grey Wolves knew, the old woman had been bedridden for years. No threat to the current Grey Wolves, but still Colt knew of her. He'd memorized the name of every member of his enemy pack before they'd fallen.

Belle nodded. "She...she was in really poor health. She should have been in hospice, but they didn't care for her the way they should have. She was kind to me, and

I never knew my own grandmother. If…if I'd left, she would have…" Belle's voice cracked.

Her sniffling was answer enough. Colt forced himself to look away. The sight of her quivering lip made him hurt, deep in places where he hadn't even known he could feel pain anymore.

"I didn't stay for me," she whispered. "I stayed because I couldn't stand the thought of them neglecting Dalia, abandoning her to die alone."

She could be lying to save her own skin, but he believed her. It went against everything in him to trust a woman who was supposed to be his enemy, but he did.

"I believe you," he breathed. He couldn't understand it even as he said it.

"You do?" Her eyes grew wide as she faced him. Her question was so full of raw hope that Colt knew she was telling the truth. *Fuck.* This would have been easier if she were a true member of his enemy pack, but it wasn't that cut and dried. The hope that quivered in her voice both made his chest ache and filled him with contempt at the thought of any man threatening an innocent woman.

"It wouldn't surprise me that they'd take advantage of a Rogue she-wolf—or treat an old woman badly for that matter. The Wild Eight were monsters." He knew that firsthand. In more ways than he cared to admit. He lived with that reality every day. "Being a physician would make you a desirable target."

She stepped toward him. Even with her eyes red and puffy from crying, she was still breathtaking, so beautiful, it nearly hurt to look at her. To make matters worse, if his childhood had taught him anything about women who had been hurt as badly as she'd been, that meant she had no idea the power she held in just that single look. She didn't have a clue what she was truly worth, because likely no one had ever told her.

And that was even more dangerous.

Because Colt wanted to tell her, to make her see. "I'm not your enemy," he said.

The desperation and surprise in her features was clear.

Realization flooded over him. Deep in his instincts, maybe somehow, he'd known from the start. From the moment he'd realized who she was, his instincts had been trying to tell him she was innocent, and he'd missed the memo. He'd done this woman wrong without knowing it.

And he couldn't live with that. Not when he already owed her a debt for saving his life. He'd already wronged one Rogue female in his lifetime. He wasn't about to repeat that mistake. He'd never be able to atone for his sins, but treating Belle right, no matter the consequences, was a close start. Which meant he needed to do what his gut and his heart had been telling him all along.

"In that case..." Unhooking the handcuffs from the belt loop of his old ranch jeans, he tossed them to the cabin floor in front of her feet. The metal clanged against the hardwood, sharp and loud.

Her eyes darted between the cuffs at her feet and him.

He inhaled a deep breath. "Consider my debt discharged."

Belle gaped at Colt. For once, she found herself at a loss for words.

He believed her...when no one else ever had. That

thought was enough to undo her. The tears came fast, pouring down her cheeks. They were a mixture of relief, gratitude, and regret that she hadn't told him sooner. She'd never expected anyone to believe her, let alone the Grey Wolf high commander. And now...

"You can't possibly mean?" She whispered the words. It felt as if speaking at a normal pitch would cause the possibility to evaporate into the ether.

Colt gave a hard nod. His jaw was drawn tight. "That's exactly what I mean. You're free to go."

"What about my testimony to the Seven Range Pact?" she breathed.

"I'll think of something."

Her eyes grew wide. He would do that? For her? "But it can't be that simple. They're expecting me to testify. If I don't show, the search for me will be renewed."

Colt shook his head. "Don't underestimate the power I hold in the Grey Wolf Pack, Belle. I'll help you sneak past the guards, then I'll tell the Pact and my men that you escaped. They won't question me. You're not number one on our priority list for threats to the pack. They won't come looking for you."

"And your counterstrike? Your packmaster?"

"I'll deliver your testimony secondhand. It's a risk I'll have to take, and don't worry about Maverick. I'll handle him. He won't be pleased, but I'll deal with the blowback."

She inhaled a sharp breath, fear shaking her as she asked her last question. "And the price on my head?"

Colt nodded. "Consider it taken care of. I'll tell Maverick I interrogated you myself, that you were innocent. Give it some time, and I'll be able to move you off the watch list."

He was putting everything on the line. For her. Risking it all.

A weight lifted off Belle's chest. Even on that night when she'd done the unthinkable in self-defense, she had thought that she'd never truly escape the Wild Eight and what they'd done to her, to Dalia, to so many others. That feeling had been a part of her for so long, she hadn't realized how it had choked the life from her.

She felt Colt's eyes on her. That dark, steely gaze blazed a trail of heat over her skin. Every time he looked at her, she felt the heat that had passed between them when he'd kissed her, when he'd felt her. His body had been warm, strong, and virile as he'd pressed against her, and the way his length pressed against her most intimate places during that kiss had made her cheeks burn hot with desire. She hadn't wanted that moment to end.

She wasn't supposed to like him. They were enemies. But how could she not? Sure, he was as arrogant as she had expected of a Grey Wolf commander, but he also defied her expectation at every turn. Even in their initial agreement, she had recognized she was getting the better end of their bargain, but now she understood what lay beneath all that bravado. Arrogant and hardened as he was on the exterior, Colt Cavanaugh had a clear place in his heart for mercy, for kindness.

And he believed her when no one else ever had.

She glanced up to find those steel eyes watching her, and her breath caught. Colt's gaze held all the tenderness she'd seen from him that first night in the clearing. The vulnerability had drawn her in. This was a man who'd seen and waged wars, but who still felt—deeply—and if the look in his eyes was any indication, who felt deeply *for her*.

You and I want the same thing, Belle. His previous words shook her.

He'd been protecting her, caring for her from the start, though he was too hardened, too stubborn to allow her to see it. Until now…

"I'll need to wipe the files, so it may take a few days until the clearance comes through. You'll need to lie low until then. Hole up in a motel in the middle of nowhere."

"Thank you." She hoped those two simple words brimmed with the gratitude she felt.

"Think nothing of it. You saved my life." When he didn't say anything further, she realized he was giving her the opportunity to leave.

"I guess this is goodbye then."

He gave a curt nod, refusing to look at her as he crossed back to the mantel. He placed his hand over the marbled edge and stared down at the fire. Once again, he didn't allow her to see his pain, but she knew it was there. She felt it.

As her hand connected with the smooth, round brass on the doorknob, she hesitated. Her chest ached. This would likely be the last time she'd ever see him, and that pained her more than she'd anticipated…

And she could tell it pained him, too.

Her hand fell away from the door handle. "Before I go, I should probably look at your wounds again. Just to make sure they healed properly." It was an obvious stalling tactic.

Maybe if she had a few more minutes to process, she could find the words to tell him how she felt.

He glanced up, his brow furrowed in mild confusion. "Sure," he muttered.

Crossing the room toward him, she stood in front of him. He gestured to the buttons of his shirt, and from the smirk that curled his lips, she realized he wasn't going to make this easy on her. She gripped the hem of the material, tugging him toward her with confidence as she started in on the top button.

As she worked her way down, he cleared his throat. "Why did you leave?" he asked.

She was about to admit that she wasn't quite ready to leave when he clarified, "Why did you leave the rodeo?"

It was a personal question, but after the kindness he'd shown her, she felt compelled to answer. "I had some good people in my life, and I enjoyed my work, the travel, but I...I moved around so much, I didn't have any close friends." She opened the sides of his shirt, revealing the bare chest beneath. Her fingers danced over the skin where the wound had been. It was barely more than a puckered scar now. It would likely be smooth in a few days.

"I wanted friends, a family, and a..." A lump formed in her throat. She could barely speak around it. The truth was difficult to admit to a Grey Wolf cowboy like him. "And a pack," she finally managed. "That's how I fell into the Wild Eight's hands. I wanted that kind of life so badly that I...I didn't even see the way they were using me. Not at first." She blinked away her gathering tears and forced a laugh. "Boy, was I stupid, huh? As if a Rogue could ever have any of those things..." With his wound clearly healed and no more excuse to stay, she moved to turn away, but Colt caught her chin in his hand.

"Don't." His command was firm yet gentle as he forced her to meet his gaze. She couldn't have looked away if she'd wanted to. The steel of his eyes had melted, leaving a warmth and a depth that bored straight through her. The burning glow of the fire reflected in his gaze.

"Don't tear yourself down like that," Colt said. "You may be a Rogue, but everyone deserves a family, a pack, happiness. And I can tell by the way you cared for me, saved me—all when you thought I was your enemy— that you're more than decent, Belle Beaumont. You're a kindhearted woman, and you deserve happiness. Don't ever deny yourself that."

He released her chin and she lowered her head, searching for some way out of the raw, vulnerable feeling in her chest. She'd never felt so open, so bare, even when she'd been standing nude before him in the clearing, and in that moment, she wanted to believe his words were true with every part of her, so badly it made her ache.

"Thank you," she whispered, still blinking away tears.

"Few people want anything more than to be accepted for who they are. I'm certain of that." His voice was graveled at the edges, like he held back emotions of his own. He sounded as if he spoke from experience.

Had Belle been a braver person, she might have asked, but she didn't dare. This man was off-limits for her in so many ways. Instead, she reached toward his scar, running her fingers gently over the surface. Inches away, she felt the steady thrum of his heart.

"It's healed," she whispered.

Her fingertips brushed against the warmth of his skin, and he growled.

Her hand lingered against his bare flesh. Colt's eyes blazed the gold of his wolf's. Fierce, powerful, and hungry.

"I…" She didn't know what to say.

The tension between them heightened with each passing second. Belle felt her own eyes flash to the golden of her wolf's as the fresh scent of sandalwood and soap on his skin overpowered her senses. She wanted him, plain and simple.

Gently, she eased away, fleeing toward the safety of the door. She felt his eyes follow her as she went. Nerves and indecision churned in her stomach. Once again, she felt like the timid woman she'd always been. The way she'd been before she met him. Unable to form words in the face of a stranger, at least when she wasn't donning her lab coat. Escaping from the Wild Eight had changed her, forced her to harden.

But this cowboy was quickly becoming more than a stranger to her, and she found she didn't want to go back to the tender woman she'd been before, the one who'd allowed countless other wolves to hurt her, take advantage of her. She wanted to be the kind of woman who took her destiny into her own hands, who made her own decisions, who didn't define herself by what she should or shouldn't do.

By what was forbidden to her.

Steadying herself with her grip on the doorknob, Belle inhaled a deep breath.

"Colt," she said without turning to look at him.

"Yes, sweetheart," he drawled.

"When we were in the forest, you said you thought it would be good between us?"

His tone lowered. "I did."

"And do you still think that?"

"Yes, Belle." His voice was graveled, growing strained. "I *know* it would be good between us. Better than good."

She nodded even as her hands shook. She swallowed, hard.

"I do, too." She sighed. "One night never hurt anything."

The aroused growl that rumbled behind her was all the confirmation she needed.

Chapter 8

COLT PROWLED TOWARD BELLE, CROSSING THE CABIN IN three quick strides. Her back was turned toward him, and he knew she hadn't prepared for his onslaught. He caught her shoulders in his hands, and she stilled beneath his touch, bracing a hand against the door for support.

Slowly, his hands slid over her, one resting on the delicate skin of her neck and the other cupping the side of one breast. She inhaled a sharp breath, and he eased her closer. The full curve of her ass pushed against the throbbing erection behind the fly of his jeans, and he growled, low and deep.

His words were a fevered whisper against her ear. "I want you, Belle Beaumont. I've wanted you from the moment I laid eyes on you, naked and about to steal my horse."

She opened her mouth to protest, but her words caught on a gasp as his canines brushed against the delicate skin of her throat. He caressed her breast, massaging and kneading until the hardened peak of her nipple pressed through her shirt.

Slowly, the hand at her neck descended lower. He felt the warmth rising in her, saw the flush on her neck, the way her breathing quickened.

As his hand reached the soft curve of her navel, the pads of his fingertips, rough from years of work on the ranch, grazed the bare skin beneath the waistband of her jeans. A wave of her scent flooded him, and he smelled her arousal, felt the eager beat of her pulse.

He eased his hand beneath the waistband of her jeans just above her mons. He wanted to feel her, touch her. But he needed to be certain.

"Just say the word, Belle. Say the word, and I'll stop," he whispered. He wanted her, but he needed to hear she wanted this, too.

"Please…" she panted. She gripped his hand, urging it lower. "Please don't stop."

Colt growled. That was all the encouragement he needed. He pushed his hand further down, cupping her soft mound in his hand as his fingertips parted her, quickly locating her clit at the apex.

She pushed into his hand, grinding that sweet bead against his fingertips as he rubbed her.

"That's it, baby," he purred.

A wicked grin crossed his lips as she ground against him, releasing a throaty moan at the rhythm he created against her cunt. Her breathing quickened, turning into hot and heavy panting as her pleasure grew with each stroke. From the way her back arched and her breasts tightened, he knew she was close. He dipped his fingers lower, probing the wet, tender flesh. She was practically dripping for him.

He couldn't take it anymore.

He intended to make her come so hard, she forgot her damn name.

Releasing her, Colt spun Belle to face him. He popped open the button of her jeans, wrenching them down to her knees, before she kicked off her cowgirl boots. Gripping her by the waist, he lifted her into his arms, one hand supporting the weight of her bare ass as he pressed her against the doorframe. She straddled him, open and splayed. He pushed his other hand between her legs, his fingers slipping inside her with ease. She cried out, pushing and rubbing against him as she rode his hand.

"Come for me, Belle," he growled against her neck. "Come for me, baby."

He located the spot deep inside he knew would drive her wild and rubbed—hard. She seized, coming apart in his arms on a wave of pleasure. She cried out, but he caught the sound with his lips, claiming her kiss in the way he'd wanted to from the start.

She was like sugar on his tongue. All delicious, sinful indulgence and longing. She tasted like everything he wanted. And everything he could never have…

Temptation personified.

For a moment, that was all he knew. The taste of her lips, the feel of her against him. He lost himself in her.

As they tasted each other, a fire lit between them, heated and electric. The force of their desire was so strong, it was damn near magnetic. The length of his hardened cock strained against the fly of his jeans. As she straddled him, the hardened bulge rubbed against her center, pushing against that sweet spot between her legs. She groaned against him, the very moan he'd been fantasizing about earlier.

He wanted her naked and bare beneath him again. This time, he wouldn't let her go. Not by a long shot. He'd take his time until she was begging for release.

Still kissing her, he carried her into the bedroom. He refused to pull his lips from hers, even when he lowered her on top of the bed.

The mattress released a moaning creak. They were all

hands, each desperate and hungry for more. He tore her clothes until she was nude.

Releasing her lips from his, he used his mouth to explore, leaving a trail of kisses down the slender curve of her neck until he reached the swell of her breasts. He cupped one in his hand, pushing it upward. He sucked that little cherry of a nipple in his mouth, and she cried out. He swirled his tongue around the taut peak, teasing until he tugged it gently between his teeth. He paid equal attention to her other breast, fingering her other nipple in kind. She writhed beneath him, squirming and arching her back at the feel of his tongue against her.

When he released her, he trailed his mouth lower, pausing to kiss the curves of her hip bones before he spread her legs open wide before him and laid a single kiss at the top of her mound.

She gasped and pushed up onto her elbows, closing her legs slightly. "What are you doing?" Her eyes were wide with what he interpreted to be more wonder than fear.

He ran both hands over her ankles, up the length of her legs to settle on her thighs. "I was planning to eat that wet, hot cunt of yours." The words were vulgar, and he knew it. A soldier's lingo, but he wanted to see her reaction.

She sucked in a small gasp of air.

He arched an eyebrow. "You're not a virgin, are you?"

At his question, she laughed. The curls of her hair bounced slightly. "No. Definitely not, but I've never had a partner who was willing to..." She left the sentence hanging there.

"Who was willing to eat your pussy?"

"Yes," she said, slightly more breathless than she'd

started. "My first few times, I was too nervous to ask, but with my last partner…he said he wouldn't like the taste and the…"

"Scent?" Colt finished for her.

A deep blush filled her cheeks, but he saw the glossy sheen in those entrancing hazel eyes as she said it.

He didn't know what prompted him to ask his next question, but he did. "Belle, has anyone ever made you come before? Aside from me just now?"

She gave a small shake of her head. "Until now, I've always finished myself," she whispered.

Anger filled him. The thought of any other man with her was maddening enough, but whoever the fucker was who'd been with her before, who'd put that look of shame in her eyes about her own body and failed to pleasure her? Colt could have gutted the man with his blade without blinking.

He didn't care if it took all night. Whatever he did, he wouldn't leave this cabin until she came multiple times.

Slowly, he eased her thighs open, and she melted into his touch. She was wet, glistening for him. He leaned in, brushing the soft skin of her folds with the tip of his nose. "The smell of you makes my mouth water." He dipped a finger inside her, gathering her sweet nectar and licking it from his finger. "The taste of you makes my cock stiff." His eyes flashed to his wolf's, and he smiled a sinful grin at her. "And I plan to make you come so hard, you forget your own name."

Belle shivered as Colt ran a hand down over her thighs. She was nude, spread wide before him, but he was still fully clothed. His gaze blazed a trail of heat through her as he admired her. As if she were a breathtaking sight *down there*.

And the lights were still on...

He could see every detail of her in full color. It should have mortified her, but she couldn't bring herself to look away. He seemed entranced by her, as if she were a moving work of art meant for him to touch, feel, taste. The surge of power that thrummed through her in response was addictive. He was going slowly, which she knew was solely for her pleasure; she'd felt how ready he was. He idly ran his fingers between the lips of her pussy. The movement was so casual yet intimate that she felt the build of arousal rising in her chest again. He touched her as if she were his, as if there were no restrictions between them and he found pleasure in every part of her.

It'd never been like this with any other man.

She trembled as his forefinger and thumb lazily parted her lower lips.

"Haven't you already done that?" she asked, her voice breathy and full of need in a way she didn't recognize. "Made me..." She couldn't bring herself to end the sentence. Even naked and open before him like this, she couldn't form the words.

"Come?" He dipped a finger inside her entrance, wetting the digit as he caressed her.

A blush warmed her cheeks. She'd never been very good at talking dirty. Thanks to all her medical training, she'd never been able to move beyond anatomically correct terms in the bedroom. If she was honest, she'd always lacked the confidence. Talking dirty felt unbearably naughty.

But the orgasm he'd given her had been mind-blowing.

She hadn't thought she was capable of that kind of pleasure, especially not with a partner, and she wanted to ask
for it, to tell him what she wanted.

Though something told her a man like Colt already
knew exactly what she wanted...

She inhaled a shaky breath. Lord, the way he played
with her. She rolled her hips, easing into his touch, and
he let out a low growl.

"I have," he answered. "But that won't be the last time."

She tensed, unsure how to tell him that she wasn't
sure she could.

He must have caught on to what she was thinking,
because a naughty smile curled his lips. "It's possible,
Belle. With a partner who knows what he's doing, it can
be that good. I promise you."

"And you're a man who knows what he's doing?"
Her voice sounded disembodied, throaty, sexy.

He chuckled. "You've said yourself I've had my
share of experience." A wicked grin crossed his lips. "I
said it would be good between us."

"Better than good," she corrected.

"There's that sexy little minx you keep hidden." His
grin widened.

Capturing the bead of her clit between his fingers,
he gently rolled the sensitive flesh in a sensual circle
that caused her back to arch and her legs to shake. She
moaned. With him touching her like that, she had no
doubt that he'd deliver on his promise.

She felt her arousal building, barreling toward
another peak.

"Surrender to me, Belle," he whispered, his voice a
dark temptation that vibrated through her.

"I thought I had," she teased. She could barely pant out the words.

He dipped his fingers inside her, touching that spot that had made her wild only minutes ago. Her whole body seized with growing anticipation. She bucked her hips against his hand, pushing him deeper.

The deep-golden color of his wolf eyes flared. "If it were up to me, sassy-mouthed she-wolves would be properly punished." He smoothed his palm over her bare backside in a teasing promise.

Lord, did she want to give this man everything he wanted and more.

"Those are my terms, Belle. One night of complete surrender."

Slowly, she nodded, and the spark in his eyes roared into a heated fire. As if he'd been waiting for her further consent, he gently gripped the outer lips of her pussy, pushing them together as he rolled her clit beneath. The indirect contact was just what she needed after the sensitivity of her first climax, and her muscles tightened until she reached her breaking point.

She shattered in his arms all over again. Her second orgasm was somehow more powerful than the first. Waves of pleasure rolled through her, drowning her in ecstasy until she saw spots in front of her gaze. The sensation raked her whole body, leaving her breathless.

Colt grinned from between her thighs, his smile equal parts satisfaction and I-told-you-so. She gave a playful growl in response, and his grin widened.

Stripping off his shirt, Colt pulled the top sheet off the bed, twisting it into a series of knots. He prowled toward her, his movements every bit those of the feral wild animal she knew him to be.

"What are you doing?" she breathed. A thrill of excitement rose in her.

The grin that crossed his lips was downright delectable, and he ran a hand through his hair, leaving a ruffled, delicious mess in his wake. "You thought I was kidding about surrendering?" That wicked grin widened, and he caught her left wrist in his hand with ease. His touch was firm yet gentle, belying all the strength she knew he possessed.

"I warned you I'm a control freak." Something dark flared in his eyes, and it stirred something deep in her womb.

"Clearly." She eased toward the headboard, but he refused to loosen his grip. He captured her chin in his other hand, forcing her to look at him.

"Do you trust me, Belle?" The words were a gentle purr that wrapped around her. She'd never thought her lady parts were capable of quivering before, but beneath Colt's heated gaze, they did. And he'd already made her orgasm—twice.

"Yes," she breathed. Despite the sinful promise in his eyes, she trusted this man without question.

"Good." He looped the knotted sheet around the headboard, circling the other end around her wrist. He gently gripped the other within his hands, moving so fast, he seemed to be a blur. In seconds, she was tied to the bed. The placement of the tied sheet allowed her just enough room to wiggle, but not enough to escape him. Not that she wanted to.

He dipped his head down, drawing the taut peak of

her nipple between his teeth as he licked and sucked. She moaned, arching into him, until he released her.

He licked his lips. "As I was touching your wet, hot cunt, I was memorizing, testing your responses, figuring out what gave you pleasure."

She could barely comprehend what he was saying. Not with her head so clouded with desire.

He blew on the puckered wet flesh of her nipple, and the sensation sent a delicious chill through her. "I approach sex the same way I approach war, Belle. They're both an art of strategy, endurance, and patience."

"You weren't kidding about being a control freak," she teased.

His smile was dark and painfully sexy. "What you need is someone to make you recognize the power you hold, how sexy you can be while still in control."

She wasn't certain where he was going with this. Ducking down to her breast again, he tugged gently at the skin with his teeth, and the ache between her thighs deepened. She wanted him inside her—now.

When he released her, his words were a hungry, devilish purr. "I'm not going to do a damn thing to you, Belle." He grinned. "Not unless you tell me to."

"What?" Belle's eyes grew wide, and she surged forward against the ties.

Colt had no doubt that if she'd been untied, she would have throttled him. It took every ounce of his strength and control to move this slowly, to ease her into it, but he needed this to be good for her. He wanted to take her rough and hard right now, pumping into her until the bed frame banged against the wall, but this was about her, not him.

"That's so unfair," she breathed. Her hazel eyes narrowed into a glare as she shook her head at him. "You have to realize I have a hard time talking about… about *that*."

That was the whole point. Belle needed to push her boundaries. He'd seen that in her from the very first time they'd met in the clearing. She didn't care much for rules, especially the ones he set. It was what had drawn him to her from the start.

But when it came to her sexuality, she was timid, almost shy, though he could tell she didn't want to be. And he intended to help her remedy that.

"This is another one of your power plays."

He lifted a shoulder, then dropped it again. "Maybe… except you're the one in power here, Belle. I won't do anything unless you tell me to."

"And you'll take pleasure in that?"

His cock jerked in response. He wanted to take her now. The anticipation was sweet torture.

"You bet, sweetheart. Every time I say anything vulgar, that creamy skin of yours flushes pink, and I can't resist. I want to see you flush all the way down to your gorgeous nipples, if I have anything to say about it." He flashed a wicked grin at her. "And better make it dirty, Belle. Absolutely filthy. I'm a soldier. I expect nothing less than your most vulgar language."

She stared at him, eyes narrowed in frustration, but she couldn't hide from him. He saw the spark of intrigue at what he'd asked of her. She had the worst poker face.

"I'm waiting, Belle."

"I…" She fumbled over the words. He watched as she chewed on that plump lower lip. "I want you to take off your pants."

"Fair enough." An easy place to start. Gripping his leather belt, he undid the buckle and stripped the belt from its loops. He unbuttoned the old, worn ranch jeans he wore and lowered the zipper, easing them down until his erection sprang forth. He didn't make a habit of wearing underwear, and Belle's eyes grew wide in surprise as she took in the impressive length and width of him.

"Don't worry. It'll fit," he teased.

She smiled and shook her head at him.

"What should I do next, Belle?"

"I…" She hesitated, her hungry gaze oscillating between his cock and the rest of his body. "I…I think I want your mouth on me."

He growled. He'd been hoping she'd say that, but he wouldn't let her off that easy. He licked his lips. "You want my mouth…*where*?" He was going to make her say it.

"On my…" She blushed so pink that his cock stiffened. "On my pussy," she breathed.

That word on her lips shot through him like a live wire. His cock jerked eagerly, his balls growing tight with need. *Fuck.* She was driving him wild. He could barely stand it. "And what do you want me to do when I put my mouth on your wet, hot pussy, Belle?"

"I want you to…" She hesitated. "I…I can't say it."

"You can, and you will, Belle," he urged.

"I…I want you to lick me," she panted.

"Mmm," he groaned. "Lick you, huh? Reminds me of a lollipop." Lowering himself between her legs, he brushed the prickle of his beard against one of her thighs as he urged her open for him. "I'll give you some leeway this time, Belle, because I'm so eager to have the taste of you on my tongue, but next time, I'll accept nothing short of tongue-fucking."

She gasped, and his mouth was on her, his tongue circling her clit until she bucked against him. Every time she did so, he released her in favor of probing deep inside her. With each onslaught and release, he edged her closer, heightening her pleasure with each brief deprivation. With Belle, the absence made her crave it more as her sweet nectar coated his tongue. She was so wet for him, dripping, and he lapped up her pleasure.

He gripped her ass cheeks in his hand, feasting on her as she made fucking sexy sounds. The noises she made were so full of pleasure, he could barely contain himself.

"I want you inside me," she demanded. "*Now.*"

He didn't need to be asked twice. Releasing her from his lips, he positioned himself outside her entrance. With one swift push, he sheathed himself inside her, and she cried out.

"Fuck," he moaned.

She fit him like a glove. Every bit as tight and sweet as he'd imagined. Clutching the curve of her hips, he buried himself in her, thrusting until he was balls deep. She took every thick inch of him, her moaning growing louder as he pumped into her until they were both sweating and rutting like the fucking beasts they were.

He felt her legs shaking as her walls wrapped around him, growing tighter with each passing second.

"Come for me, Belle," he growled. "Come for me, sweetheart."

The muscles of her pussy clenched. "Colt..." She moaned his name as she found her release.

He was right behind her, his own climax barreling through him like lightning. Lowering himself into missionary, he spent himself inside her, filling her with his hot seed as he captured her lips with his. As he stared down into her gorgeous hazel eyes, he forgot himself. The darker sides of his past blurred and disappeared, and for a brief moment, he was Colt. Only Colt. Not high commander of the Grey Wolf armies, not the violent monster his position and his birthright forced him to be, but just a man who'd found peace in the arms of a strong, beautiful woman. She made him feel open, raw, alive, because for once in his life, he was worthy.

Because she made it so...

As the last shudders of climax tore through them both, they lay tangled in each other's arms with Colt still buried deep inside her as their tongues clashed in a passionate kiss.

They lay there like that for what felt like hours. Finally, she broke the kiss, gasping for air. He eased out of her, rolling onto the bed beside her as they both relaxed into the rumple of sheets.

Belle released a long sigh. "That was the best you've got?" she challenged. He watched a sly little grin tilt her lips.

He quickly untied her. Gripping her by the hips, he rolled her on top of him until she was riding cowgirl. Her eyes grew wide in surprise at the feel of him hard again so soon.

"We've barely gotten started, sweetheart."

They spent the next several hours exploring each

other's bodies, until they both felt thoroughly and completely spent. They lay back onto the bed together, satiated, with their limbs tangled together, both of their chests still panting heavily with exertion. Normally, this was the part where things went downhill, where he started to get bored, when the thrill of the chase was over and there was nothing left but same-old, same-old sex. But with Belle it was different. Everything about tonight had been different.

As Colt rolled onto his side to look at her, he intended to tell her that after a few minutes of recovery, he had plenty more in store for them, but as she turned those large hazel eyes on him, his breath caught in his throat. Because in an instant, he realized he'd made a mistake. The emotion that stirred behind her eyes clenched at his heart, and the fact that instead of recoiling from it, he wanted to draw closer, told him everything he needed to know.

Belle Beaumont was dangerous, and he needed to get the hell away from her. Pushing off the bed, he padded toward the bedroom door without so much as a glance over his shoulder.

"Where are you going?" she called after him.

Clearly, she'd been expecting to see the same emotion reflected in his eyes, and Colt had a feeling if he'd stayed, she would have. But he couldn't. He couldn't allow that to happen, to open up fully even if he wanted to, not without risking everything.

Wrenching on his jeans, not even bothering to button them, he unlocked the door. "I need some air," he grumbled before pulling the door shut behind him.

Chapter 9

COLT STEPPED OUT ONTO THE CABIN'S WRAPAROUND PORCH, easing the door closed behind him. The silhouettes of the pine trees cast dark shadows over the shimmering white snow, promising an unknown world within their depths. The forest wasn't the only unknown laid out before him. His mind drifted to the sight of Belle lying naked on his bed, her legs tangled in the sheets and a look of pure, sated bliss on her face. It'd taken everything in him to walk out of the cabin and leave her to her own devices.

But he needed to clear his head—and fast. He'd never had any trouble walking away after sex, but as he'd retreated out to the silence of the cold night, he'd had to fight to put one foot in front of the other. That'd never been a problem before. His break post-sex was ritualistic in nature, putting distance between him and whatever partner he happened to be with. It was the way it'd always been for him, even back before he'd become commander and he'd stupidly given the whole relationship bit an honest try.

He'd never indulged in intimacy. From the very first time he'd had sex as a young, horny teenager and all the way through the years of his adulthood, he'd never understood the want after he was already spent.

Until now.

An ache of longing tore at his chest. That single thought was enough to scare even him senseless.

"It's a beautiful night." Belle's voice sounded from behind him, instantly cutting through the cold and wrapping around him like a warm blanket. Her voice was breathy in a way that reminded him of how she moaned.

"Yeah," he answered.

She came to stand at the porch railing beside him. She had a quilt wrapped around her, shielding her nakedness. Though if she was feeling anything like he was... His blood was still burning so hot from the electricity between them, he could have jumped into the Arctic Ocean without a shiver.

Belle leaned into the railing, one of her curls falling into her face. "Stargazing post-sex. If your reputation holds true, you must be an expert at finding constellations."

He chuckled. "These days, it's far less frequent than you'd think."

"Running out of willing females, Commander?" A teasing smile tugged at the corners of her lips.

He shook his head. "No, just fewer who catch my interest these days." His gaze raked over her. She was delectable, every inch of her, and he planned to take her plenty more times before night's end.

"I'm honored."

"Stargazing's better than my post-sex cigarettes of years past."

Turning away from him, she scanned the darkness before her gaze darted toward him again. "You know smoking is horrible for you, right?" She stared down the line of her slender nose at him, and that single black curl bobbed and danced, begging for him to wrap his finger around it.

The look she was giving him was every bit the

intelligent, chastising physician. All she needed was the lab coat and a pair of sexy, dark-rimmed glasses to peek at him through, and she'd be sexier than any "doctor" in any adult film he'd ever seen. A gorgeous mixture of both beauty and brains.

"It was a post-sex indulgence only, but I quit long ago and have no thoughts of resuming the habit. Though, correct me if I'm wrong, Doc, but even back when I was a smoker, cigarettes didn't cause too much damage before my true nature could heal it. I'm no human."

Werewolves weren't nearly as fragile as humans, and as such, they could indulge a bit more freely in the vices of the world. Smoke, booze…even sex held less of a risk.

Belle frowned. "Technically, yes. But as a physician, I still can't condone it."

"Why not?"

"Well, one of the things we're sorely lacking in our world is peer-reviewed scientific studies of our kind. We really don't know much about our health other than anecdotal evidence and the similarities we bear to humans. For all you know, those cigarettes from years ago could have caused your testicles to shrink and lessened your chance of procreation with each puff, but since we've never studied it, such effects would be unknown to you. It's something that someday I'd like to remedy."

"Shrinking balls?" he teased.

She tried to frown, but he could see the edges of a smile tugging at her lips.

"So considering you've just seen my balls within the last hour, what's your prognosis, doc?"

She blushed a deep shade of pink, as if he hadn't just been buried deep inside her. It was a regular occurrence, her blushing, and it'd started to become a game of sorts in seeing whether he managed to make that flush extend down to the soft mounds of her breasts.

"I'm no urologist, but I'd say in most matters of that area, you're a bit…above average."

He chuckled. "Right. Horse cock."

The flush in her cheeks deepened.

Turning his attention back out toward the night, his eyes combed through the edges of the darkness. For a brief moment, the gentle sway of the trees in the night wind transported him. They'd moved with the same shuddering grace on another cold night like this. The night his mother died. In vivid detail, he recollected drawing closer to James as they'd fled the Rogue house where he and his mother had been squatting at the time. He'd been young enough that he was still terrified of the dark, and something about the sway of the trees, despite the horrors that had burned fresh in his mind, had caused him to cling to James's hand tighter.

"Where'd you go?" Belle asked, drawing him back.

"Nowhere," he said, returning his focus to the present. He scanned the forest again. Aside from the trees, it was unusually still. The last few nights he'd been on the Missoula ranch, he'd come out here to take in some fresh air and watch the bright stars that lit the vast Montana sky. Usually he noted at least one of his men prowling through the underbrush as they made their rounds. He must have missed them. No doubt they'd circle back around soon enough.

"'Nowhere' doesn't cause someone to get that far-away look in his eyes," Belle said.

He grunted in acknowledgment but didn't elaborate.

There was no way he was going down that road with her—or anyone, for that matter. The events of his mother's death and the circumstances of his birth were filed away in his mind under *fucked up shit that never needs to see the light of day*. Belle waited a moment, clearly hoping he'd open up to her, but when it became clear he didn't intend to discuss the matter, she changed topics.

"So no cuddling and snuggling after sex?" she asked.

He leaned onto the railing. "Do I strike you as the cuddling type?"

A bark of a laugh escaped her lips. "No. No, not at all." She released a sigh. "Is that part of your whole 'no relationships' thing?"

He nodded. No point in beating around the bush. She knew what she'd signed up for.

"Most men I've been with promptly fall asleep post-sex," she said.

"I don't *sleep* with women. That never ends well."

"You have nightmares?"

The question caused him to stiffen. Of course, she would realize. She'd seen it back at the cabin, and she was a physician after all. She'd recognize the side effects of PTSD when she saw them. It was a point of contention for him, a weakness and embarrassment he didn't feel the need to discuss with most of his partners.

"Yeah," he breathed. The word dissipated on an exhale. He hadn't planned on elaborating, but something about the chill of the night air—or maybe the way Belle was looking at him—made this time different.

"They come to me at night," he confessed. "The people I've killed, the wrongs I've done, the lies I've told." He spoke the words without thinking. He couldn't have stopped the confession spilling from his lips if he tried, not with the way she was looking at him, so full of acceptance and care. "If my lack of control scares me, my actions and choices, the things I do have control over, terrify me even more."

He'd never told anyone this. Not Maverick, Wes, or Sierra—the handful of people he would consider himself somewhat close to. He'd never come anywhere near confessing his fears to any of them.

He chanced a look at her, and it was the worst kind of mistake. The tenderness in her eyes as she watched him tore him to pieces, broke through every armor he'd ever used to protect himself.

She lifted her hand to reach for him, but the warning in his gaze stopped her short.

He couldn't bear another moment of this. "I don't deserve your pity. Not by a long shot." He shook his head. "I don't know why I'm telling you this."

"It's a doctor thing," she said. "Especially female doctors. People feel comfortable telling us their darkest secrets. Maybe because they know we'll take care of them and never tell a soul. You know, patient confidentiality and all."

If that was case, she was even more dangerous than he'd anticipated. It didn't matter that she wasn't a true Wild Eight. If Belle Beaumont made him want to share his secrets, she was as toxic as any enemy. Straightening to his full height, he squared his shoulders. He needed to ask her to leave. Though he hadn't nearly had his fill of her and he had more than a few ideas for how he wanted to spend the rest of the night, he knew that would make an already bad decision worse. He never should have let her stay.

Prolonging the inevitable would only make this more difficult, and if the way his heart thumped like a jack-rabbit against his breastbone was any indication, she was an itch even he wasn't able to quite scratch. And that was a rough road he had no intention of traveling. The desire brewing inside him had barely been tamed by their nighttime rendezvous, and he had a feeling it would only grow worse from here.

He needed to get her out of here, and fast.

As he opened his mouth to say as much, Belle interjected with "Do you smell that?" Her nose wrinkled in disgust.

As she said the words, Colt caught the scent on the breeze. It was the sickly, sweet scent of death. Of vampires. Colt's hand eased onto Belle's shoulder, gripping tight as he gave her a pointed look. Without any sudden movements to alert their enemy, he scanned the tree line. This wasn't some random bloodsucker on a suicide mission. They were surrounded, which meant this was a coordinated and planned attack.

And now that he knew their motivations, he knew exactly what they were here for.

They'd come for him.

"Belle," he breathed.

Immediately, Belle caught the change in his demeanor, and her eyes widened in terror.

He squeezed her shoulder in reassurance. "There's a major gap in their formation to the southwest side of the cabin. Nine o'clock." He indicated the spot with the flick of his eyes. "When the first of them show themselves, I want you to run in that direction, and I don't want you to stop running until you reach the stables. Take your pick of the horses. Don't stop until horizon breaks, long after these fuckers will be back in their covens hiding from the sun. You understand?"

Belle gulped, but she gave a small nod. "What about you?" she whispered.

Colt shook his head. "I'm going to hold them off while you get out."

"Colt, you can't. With this many, they'll…" Her voice trailed off.

Take you alive. It was unspoken, but her message was clear. He knew it. That was these bloodsuckers' plan after all. But he wasn't about to see this woman get hurt. Not by a long shot. And Colt Cavanaugh, high commander of the Grey Wolf armies, never backed down from a fight. Never. It wasn't his way.

Tears streamed down Belle's cheeks, whether from fear for her own life or his, he couldn't be certain.

He pegged her with a hard stare. It was intended to fortify her, strengthen her, but it only caused the tears to fall faster. "No crying, Belle. Just action. Do you understand?"

"We didn't even get to say goodbye."

He sensed the subtle movement in the darkness. The vampires were closing in, preparing for their attack.

"Usually women are angry *because* I said goodbye, not crying because I didn't." He shook his head. "I'm not worth your tears, sweetheart." He reached out and twisted the single curl across her cheek, gently tucking it behind her ear. "Run, Belle, and don't look back," he growled as the first of his enemies tore through the tree line.

Belle shifted into her wolf and bolted toward the tree line. Colt ripped his concealed blade from his boot, then vaulted over the patio railing. He landed in the snow with a thud before he charged toward his enemies, blade swinging. In his peripheral vision, he watched Belle run to her escape before he launched himself into the melee. The first one to reach him lunged from his right. Colt spun away from the attack, slicing his blade across the vampire's throat. It wasn't enough to kill the beast, but it would leave it temporarily maimed. When another attacked at his left, he met it blow for blow, engaging in a lethal killing dance until he staked it straight in the heart.

He managed to take out five before they overwhelmed him by sheer numbers. Tackling him, they pinned him to the ground. He continued to struggle, even once a pair of silver handcuffs was clenched around his wrists.

Karma's payback for his treatment of Belle, he guessed.

Dragging his head up by the hair, they eased him to his knees, and Colt wasn't surprised in the slightest to find himself face-to-face with Lucas again. Only this time, the bloodsucker had enough backup, which meant some of Colt's men had likely lost their lives.

He growled.

"Commander, good to see you again." Lucas grinned, his sharp fangs protruding to make his delight as sinister as it was ugly.

"I'll bleed you myself, Lucas," Colt snarled.

Lucas's eyes transitioned to their bright, glowing red. "We'll see if you feel the same way when you're strapped to my experiment table." With a quick nod of his head, Lucas's men gripped Colt by the arms, hauling him kicking and fighting into the woods.

As they dragged Colt into the darkness, his only reassurance was that even if they killed him, Belle had made it out alive. He'd given her the freedom he promised. And for a man like him, who'd faced death more times than he could count, for now, that was enough.

Chapter 10

IF COLT DIED HERE TONIGHT, IT WOULDN'T BE IN VAIN. HE couldn't remember the last time they had given him water, and his limbs ached with dehydration. Nausea churned his stomach. Metal clanged against metal as he rattled the chains that held him in place. It had become a game of sorts, a reminder to his enemy that he'd yet to give up.

Not even with the tip of the vampire's silver blade shoved against his windpipe.

"I'll ask you one more time, Commander." The deep voice echoed against the steel walls. His enemy eased the blade ever closer to Colt's jugular. "Will you surrender to me?"

It was the game they played. The sick fuck favored slow, sadistic methods intended to break a wolf.

Colt wasn't any wolf.

Summoning the last bit of fight left in him, Colt closed his eyes, leaning into the searing pain of the blade without fear. In the freezing air of the dungeon, even with his body broken in ways he couldn't have begun to fathom, it didn't take much imagination to bring himself back there to the memory, fresh and new in his mind. To the silent, snow-covered forest. To her.

She was a vision, naked and writhing beneath him. His hands fisting and tangling the dark curls of her hair as he drove himself into her. She was dripping for him as she wrapped her legs around him and moaned with pleasure that he felt all the way from his balls to that thumping organ in his chest he dared call a heart.

Staring up at him with heavy-lidded eyes, the hazel starbursts of her irises shone all the more emerald from the pale cream of her cheeks and the just-kissed pink of her swollen lips.

"I see you, Colt. I see all of you," her eyes seemed to say.

And did he revel in it—like a refreshing burst of spring water to his shriveled desert of a soul. He'd been consumed by the desperate ache. She filled a deep need inside the cavern of his chest in a way he hadn't realized he craved until she stormed into his life. And for that moment, it was enough to keep him going, to refuse to cave to his enemies for another day.

His death would mean something, even if he died here now. Not for Maverick, not for the Grey Wolves, the pack that loved him and called him their own. The very same pack that would shun him if they knew what he truly was. No, if he died tonight, it would be for her.

For her protection. For her life. For the bliss she'd gifted him, a gleaming diamond gem in an otherwise dark life.

Even though the promise in her eyes wasn't true. As much as he wanted it to be, deep down, he knew it. Despite the night they'd shared, she hadn't seen the real him, the monster beneath the carefully crafted warrior exterior.

But on that cold silver table, death hovering like a ghostly promise over him, with his enemy's blade at his throat, for a brief moment, he allowed himself enough delusion to believe it.

And that delusion fueled his resolve.

"Kill me then." Colt opened his eyes, his irises glowing the fierce gold of his wolf as he turned his gaze toward his enemy. The snarl that tore from his throat was laced with lethal intent. "But I refuse to break."

Lucas smiled with malicious intent. "Well, in that case…"

Colt jolted awake, his heart pounding and his breathing labored. Despite the cold sweat running down his torso, he didn't need to take in his surroundings. He knew he was lying safely in his bed, in his apartment, inside the main compound of the Grey Wolves' ranch at Wolf Pack Run, yet his heart raced as if he were back there again in that godforsaken cell.

They hadn't killed him as the memory promised, though they'd tortured him until he'd barely remembered his own name. He'd healed from the injuries, but the memories still tormented him. God-awful nightmares. He'd had dozens of them in the handful of weeks he'd been back home on the ranch, but still they remained clear, so vivid he could practically taste his own blood when he woke.

He sat up in bed, checking the clock on his nightstand. Just before sunrise, which meant it was high time for him to get some breakfast before he headed out to the pasture. Calving season was due to start any day, and the cattle weren't going to bring themselves in near the barn. He also was eager to get the work done before Maverick and Wes returned from their meeting with the Seven Range Pact this afternoon. If he wasn't finished by then, the torment of waiting a moment longer for the final news of the Pact's decision would kill him.

Rising from bed, Colt showered, then dressed and made his way down to the mess hall. After chowing down on more than one round of bacon, eggs, and hash browns, he rode one of the ATVs out to the stables, met up with the other Grey Wolf ranch hands he was working with, saddled up Silver, and rode into the pasture.

This time of year, the cattle weren't far out. They stayed close to the barn where they'd been fed most of the winter instead of venturing out where the grass was still sparse. Moving them in near the fences made for easy, enjoyable work, and the day passed by in a blur. The work distracted Colt, allowing him a refuge from his thoughts, from the guilt and blame and the rage that had niggled at the back of his mind since his packmates had rescued him from the vampires. And her...

It was early afternoon by the time they finished. Having brought the herd in and separated out the pregnant cows about to drop calves, Colt rode Silver back to Wolf Pack Run. Maverick and Wes would be back shortly, and since he planned to ride back out to the pastures to operate the hay baler until dinner, he didn't have the mind to take Silver back to the stables.

When they reached the main compound, Colt tied Silver to a quartering post, a development that caused Silver to huff in distress. Colt tried to appease the beast by retrieving an apple for the horse from his saddlebag.

He held the apple out, but after giving the Granny Smith a tentative sniff, Silver nudged the apple out of Colt's hand with a distasteful grumble, knocking it to the ground.

Colt frowned. "You're damn wasteful, Silver." Apparently, nothing but Honeycrisp would do for the equine prima donna.

Silver had been downright moody and despondent since Colt's return, but honestly, Colt thought it had more to do with the absence of a certain she-wolf than Silver being angry about Colt's enforced absence. He patted a hand through the beast's mane. Even his horse preferred her.

Retrieving the apple and returning it to his bag, Colt headed to Maverick's office. He'd give the Granny Smith to one of the other horses in the stable later. Then maybe *his* horse would be a bit more appreciative.

Situated in the center of the main compound and attached to an adjoining security room lined with the pack's latest technologies, Maverick's office served as the Grey Wolf Pack's command central. Colt passed his own apartment on the way in. Aside from Maverick's private office, the main compound housed the apartments of the pack's ten elite warriors, including Colt's, along with their security offices, several conference rooms, and a rec room.

Colt knocked, then entered. He stepped inside the office to find the back of Maverick's leather desk chair facing toward him, a clear sign that the packmaster had yet to return from his meeting. The chair sat behind a custom wooden desk, the burled edge artfully carved from the trunk of a massive oak. Colt sat down in one of the chairs in front of it and waited.

A few moments later, the door to Maverick's office swung open, and the Grey Wolf packmaster stepped inside.

Upon his entrance, Colt immediately stood. "Packmaster," he said. "I have the status reports for the day and I—"

"Cut the 'packmaster' bullshit, Colt. We've known

each other since we were kids. I've never once told you to call me packmaster outside of formal ceremonies, and we both know why you're here." Maverick crossed behind his desk and set down the large stack of files he'd been carrying. "The front lines have been a ghost town since you returned. All quiet on the western front." He glanced up at Colt. "You're here about the Seven Range Pact vote."

"Am I that transparent?" Colt asked.

Maverick smiled, but it didn't quite reach his eyes. "Only since I've known you so long." The smile faded, and he released a hefty sigh. The Grey Wolf packmaster wasn't one to pull any punches. "The vote was a no, Colt."

For a moment, Colt didn't say anything. He just stood there, contemplating the ramifications of the Pact's decision.

When he'd escaped the vampires' torture, he and his packmates had returned to Wolf Pack Run and recounted the horrors to Maverick. Every gruesome, hairsplitting detail from the moment he'd laid eyes on Lucas in the clearing up to the moment his fellow elite warriors had arrived to rescue him.

The only detail he'd left out was his torrid affair with a Rogue she-wolf, who also happened to be the former physician of the Wild Eight. Colt was a man of his word, and when he'd promised Belle to never speak of her to any other Grey Wolf as thanks for saving his life, he'd meant it—even if it meant lying to his packmaster. He knew he'd never see her again, but that didn't matter. As soon as he'd returned to Wolf Pack Run, he'd wiped her name from their files, disposed of all information on her, and told Maverick that the Belle Beaumont he'd had captive at the Missoula pack headquarters had been killed in the melee. For all intents and purposes, Belle Beaumont no longer existed...

Despite that minor lapse in truth, Colt had outlined his suspicions that the vampires were plotting to find a way to feed off werewolves. He had no proof of this for the Grey Wolves other than his word and the eerie fact that they'd taken several vials of his blood while he was in captivity.

Maverick had promised to take the issue up with the Seven Range Pact. The goal was to get a counterintelligence strike, manned by Colt, approved to gather further intelligence before they launched a full-fledged attack. Maverick had expressed his concern that the Pact might not deem retaliation for the sake of one still-living commander worth risking the lives of their most elite troops on a covert mission for which they had little definitive proof, but Colt hadn't actually anticipated they'd vote against him.

As he tried to hold in the anger growing inside him, Colt's hands balled into fists. His anger shook him to the core, like a bucking bronco he could barely contain. "How did you vote?"

"Colt," Maverick said.

Colt raised his voice. Not at all the usual reverence he gave his friend and packmaster. "How did you vote, Maverick?" he asked.

"That question is uncalled for. You—"

"How did you vote?" Colt snarled. He couldn't hold the anger in any longer. Packmaster or not, he couldn't. Not this time.

Maverick held his gaze, his emerald eyes burning

with an emotion Colt couldn't identify. If Colt's insubordinate tone angered him, he didn't show it, or at least he was willing to tolerate it, for now. "I voted against it," he said.

Without warning, Colt turned to leave. He couldn't do this. Not now. Not without telling Maverick exactly how he felt about him and his fucking Pact's decision. Colt had been loyal to this man his whole life, but his loyalty to the Grey Wolves went far beyond Maverick.

"Colt." Maverick spoke his name with a mix of concern and censure in his voice that only fueled Colt's frustration. It was like pouring hot oil on already burning flames.

Colt kept his back turned, his voice barely above a whisper. If he spoke any louder, he knew his rage would get the best of him.

"You weren't there, Maverick," he said. "You weren't there in that room. You didn't hear their taunts, feel their silver blades against your skin, smell the scent of their coppery breath as they leaned over you to torture you one more time. You. Weren't. There." He punctuated each final word with every ounce of his anger.

"You're right," Maverick said from behind him. "You're right. I wasn't there. But I know the facts, Colt. By all accounts, the Pact's scientists say it's not possible. This was some twisted mental game the vampires wanted to play, and if we hadn't gotten you out of there when we did, they likely would have killed you. That was their end goal. Nothing more. We even searched for the missing bobcat and cougar you mentioned, but we didn't find anything. Even if they had access to your blood, it wouldn't be possible for them to feed from werewolves.

That would mean they had found a way to alter your DNA or theirs. All our techs say it isn't feasible."

Maverick was wrong. Colt knew it without a doubt.

"I can't possibly know what you've been through, but I think you would realize that I understand the depth of your hatred for them." Maverick spoke indirectly of the death of his former mate, killed at the hands of a vampire shortly after he'd become packmaster. The packmaster's tone softened. "I understand the need for revenge."

Colt shook his head. This wasn't about him or his need for revenge. "It isn't about me. I told you their request before the Missoula attack, about what I overheard. It's not personal."

"And you don't think that was a ploy to rile you? An attempt to cloud your judgment before battle? You're the high commander of the Grey Wolf armies. Aside from myself and Wes, you're the sole man responsible for all the deaths of their coven members and allies. The pack is under my leadership, but *you've* led our troops, *you've* won the battles. They purposefully approached at a time when they knew you would take the meeting, and then they took you captive and tortured you with the intent to kill. Thank God, they didn't get that far."

Maverick's frustration grew with each passing word. "I am man enough to admit that if anyone bears the responsibility for what you went through, I'm that man. I never should have allowed the situation to begin with. It was an error in judgment, and I'm sorry for it."

Colt inhaled several deep breaths, keeping his breathing level. He refused to address Maverick's apology. He wouldn't even give it any validity. "They're plotting something against the pack and I know it,

Maverick. Allow me to conduct reconnaissance, to find out the truth."

"You know I can't do that, Colt. During wartime, the Seven Range Pact acts as one. Their decision is my decision. It's out of my hands."

"I need to protect the pack."

"It's not like you to challenge me like this. Is this about protecting our pack or protecting your ego?"

Colt stiffened.

"We both know that any man who endured that kind of torture would want to seek revenge, but as packmaster, I can't allow your personal vendetta to supersede the needs of the Pact. I understand you think you need this, but—"

Colt finally spun to face Maverick. "This isn't about me, damn it!" he yelled.

It was about them, all of them. All the lives that had been lost in that battle and every battle before. All the lives that would be lost if he didn't fix this.

The room seemed to freeze. Maverick stared at him, the air between them fraught with tension as neither dared to move. Colt had never raised his voice to Maverick, even when they were kids, yet here he was, yelling like he wasn't in perfect control of himself and his emotions, as if he didn't strive to be of loyal service to this wolf who was also his friend. Though he wasn't certain about anything anymore, was he? He hadn't been certain since he'd nearly died on the vampires' godforsaken silver table, knowing he'd failed his men. Yet as he'd lain bleeding, all he'd been able to think about to keep himself going had been a beautiful, naked she-wolf with an untamable head of dark curls.

A woman he could never have, who he'd never see again.

"Colt, you can't possibly think you're to blame for this."

It was an absurd statement, because Colt didn't think that. He lived it. "Why can't I?"

Maverick gaped at him. "How could you have prevented this?"

When Colt didn't respond, Maverick stepped around his desk. "Haven't I always been the first to tell you when you've screwed up, when you've failed me?" He placed a large hand on Colt's shoulder. "This isn't one of those times." He dropped his hand to his side. "Regardless, the Pact's decision is final, and you'll have to live with it, as we all will."

Maverick tugged open a desk drawer and reached inside to remove a different file. "I promised the coyotes I'd return to the conference room for a private discussion. You know the way out."

He stepped past Colt, file in hand, before he paused in the doorway. "And, Colt, if you pursue this against my orders, there will be repercussions."

Maverick walked down the hall toward the conference room. It was several seconds before Colt even thought to move, and he didn't do so until the sound of another familiar voice came from behind him.

"You don't always have to listen to him, you know."

Colt turned to find the icy blue-green eyes of the Grey Wolf second-in-command staring at him. Wes leaned in the office doorway, his face shadowed as he removed the pale Stetson from his head, revealing a mess of untamable blond hair.

A wild, near-feral wolf, Wes Calhoun, former packmaster of the Wild Eight and legitimate son of the nefarious Nolan Calhoun, one of the deadliest wolves in history, was now loyal to the Grey Wolves. Wes even looked like a younger version of Nolan.

Like father, like son, Colt thought.

Having surrendered himself to the pack several years earlier, Wes had been spared by Maverick, the Grey Wolf packmaster and a wolf he'd once called his sworn enemy. But even now, several years later, Wes was still as much of a troublemaker as his former title suggested.

Though they were cut from the same cloth and fierce but often oppositional friends, Colt and Wes were as different as night and day. Colt was known for being a man of discipline and loyalty, for following every order to the letter, while Wes was well known for defying pack laws and conventions at every turn. It was a luxury Colt envied but never allowed himself.

The repeated incidents of Wes's rebellion had decreased only now that he'd found another distraction: his fiancé, a human rancher named Naomi Evans.

Colt sat down again, propping the edge of his boots on Maverick's desk. "That's easy for you to say. No one expects you to follow orders. If they do, they're fools."

Wes's mouth pulled into a smirk. "You're likely right on that count. But you don't fool me, Commander." He gave Colt a knowing look. "You paint a nice picture, Mr. Perfect Grey Wolf Soldier, but we both know you don't always play by the rules."

From anyone else, Colt would have stiffened in fear that his secret, the truth of his birth, had been discovered. He wasn't the perfect Grey Wolf soldier in more ways than Wes would ever know. But Colt knew exactly what Wes referred to.

Several months earlier, Colt had played a key role in his friend's appointment to second-in-command. Though they hadn't spoke of it since, it had been a secretive, strategic move on his part that undermined Maverick's direct orders.

Everyone had expected the position of second-in-command to be his. Colt was driven, determined, and his ambition for rising in the pack ranks until he'd become high commander was well documented. Being the next highest-ranking member of the Grey Wolf warriors, he *was* the natural choice for second-in-command, and he'd played right into the pack's expectations. What they still didn't realize, save for Wes, was that Colt hadn't wanted the position all along.

Being second-in-command would have meant that in the event of Maverick's death, Colt would have been named packmaster. If he felt like he lived as an imposter every day as the Grey Wolf commander, he would never escape the feeling if he led the pack. Not to mention, it would have opened his past history to political scrutiny in a way he couldn't allow. At least with Wes, everyone knew he wasn't born a Grey Wolf. Of course, there had been other motivations for Colt as well.

Reasons Colt would rather take to the grave than admit to anyone, even Wes…

"Only when it suits my purposes." Colt lowered his boots and stood, prepared to leave the conversation there.

"And this doesn't?" Wes asked.

He had a point.

"There's no one who wants to know more what those bloodsuckers are up to than I do, but if Maverick and the Seven Range Pact forbid it, then my hands are tied."

It was a bold-faced lie, and Wes likely knew it. Regardless of whether his actions were officially approved by Maverick and the Pact, Colt's loyalty was first and foremost to the Grey Wolves, even above their packmaster, and he wouldn't rest until he knew exactly what the vampires were planning. All Maverick's orders meant was that now Colt had to find a way to gather the information he needed without Maverick knowing he was doing so, at least not until he had ample evidence. It would be a dangerous move, risking his station and pack censure, but he'd risked it before for far less.

Wes narrowed his eyes as if he saw straight through Colt. "You don't expect me to believe that, do you?"

"Believe what you want." Colt turned to leave, but Wes's next words stopped him in his tracks.

"The wedding is tomorrow," Wes said.

Colt knew this, of course. He was Wes's best man, but the way he said it gave Colt pause. "You getting cold feet?"

"Fuck no," Wes muttered. "I've never been more certain of anything in my life. I know I still owe you, but—"

Colt placed his Stetson on his head. "You don't owe me anything, Wes." If anything, it was the other way around.

"Regardless, I need a favor." Wes's eyes darkened. "Naomi deserves a perfect honeymoon, and…"

Colt didn't like where this was going. Wes wasn't one to beat around the bush. "And?"

Wes shook his head. "And I need you to watch Black Jack."

Even as Wes uttered the words, Colt was shaking his head. It *was* a helluva favor, more than was fair to ask any sane person. The mustang's reputation throughout the pack was almost as nefarious as that of his rider. The horse might well be the single most ornery beast Colt had ever had the displeasure to encounter. Black Jack put poor pretentious Silver to shame.

"I'm already serving as your best man," he offered.

Wes didn't seem to hear him. "If he bites another one of the stable hands, they might stage a walkout if I don't house him in a separate stable. I wouldn't ask if I hadn't exhausted all other options. You know as well as I do that no one wants to care for that bastard while I'm away, and Naomi doesn't want him along on the honeymoon."

"I can't imagine why," Colt muttered.

"I'm asking you this as a friend, as a—"

Colt raised a hand, cutting Wes short. He knew what Wes was about to say.

As a brother...

But Colt couldn't stand to hear the words.

They were truer than Wes would ever know.

Colt released a long sigh and peered at Wes from beneath his Stetson. Sometimes Wes looked so much like Nolan Calhoun that it hurt, and then there were times like this when Wes was so much of a friend to Colt that he could almost forget that Wes and Nolan were cut from the same cloth.

"Fine. I'll watch your horse."

Wes clapped Colt on the shoulder. "I can't say you won't regret this, because you likely will." He chuckled darkly.

Didn't Colt know it. He turned to leave again, feeling the call of returning to the ranch work, where the darkness of his thoughts and past were easily chased away. But he paused, glancing over his shoulder at his friend, his brother. "You really love her, don't you?" he asked.

Wes held his gaze, not a bit of shame in his eyes. "You know I do."

Colt nodded. He couldn't help but think of Belle, of the violent circumstances of their parting. He knew they never could have been together, but he still wondered what could have been if the circumstances had been different.

Maybe his birth father had been wrong. Wes had lived a more violent life than most, but he'd still found love, which meant maybe it wasn't something in Colt's blood that made him undeserving of the emotion.

Maybe it was only Colt…

"Put your foot on the gas pedal, Belle. That's all you have to do."

Belle muttered the words to herself while she idled at the side of the road in her old beater pickup truck. Silence from the empty cab answered, and the warmth of her breath swirled around her face as she exhaled. She glanced down at her cold knuckles turning white against her tightened grip on the steering wheel. The air in the cab chilled her despite her heavy Carhartt. With the dampness of the melting snow in the air as spring arrived and the old truck's heater broken yet again, it was colder than any born-and-bred Florida girl should ever have to endure. Springtime in Montana was never kind as far as she was concerned.

And neither were those butterflies buzzing in her stomach.

Her grip tightened further. It was now or never. She needed to know that he was alive, and she needed to tell him. She pulled out the burner phone she'd purchased and lit up the screen. The calendar date stared back at her. She blinked, still in disbelief, wondering if the numbers might come into better focus in front of her eyes, telling her that she wasn't seeing what she thought she was. But still the numbers remained.

Somewhere in the back of her mind, she'd been aware of the day's date, of course, but in the melee, she had lost track. Now, as she stared down at the date on the phone's calendar, reality sank in. Her period was nearly a month late. Post-clearance of her name, she'd been preparing to return to her old life when reality had struck her. She'd been late before. But never *this* late.

And after sleeping with a certain virile Grey Wolf commander. She groaned. What had she been thinking?

Unconsciously, her hand drifted to her stomach as if she could somehow sense the potential life there, but all she felt was the soft tissue of her abdomen. Despite her fear of the future, a part of her was hopeful. She'd always wanted a family, and while this might not be how she'd intended, she would have that family all the same, if it really were the case.

She'd need to find another werewolf physician for an examination to confirm all was well, but...

She removed her foot from the brake pedal and pressed down on the gas. The old truck clunked over the rocky bumps of the open dirt road. The turnoff she'd taken from the main stretch of highway reached for miles without so much as a soul or a building in sight, yet somehow, even this far from the Grey Wolf ranch, she still felt as if she were being watched—which chances were likely, she was.

She rode like this for what felt like a good twenty minutes before she finally reached the small hut of an outpost station. She was still miles from the main compound at Wolf Pack Run, but the two wolves stationed at the outpost met her with wary eyes nonetheless. One of them stepped out as she pulled up beside them. His hand rested firmly on a gun at his belt, probably loaded with silver bullets.

She rolled down her driver's side window. "Hi, my name's Elizabeth—" She planned to give an alias.

"Pack affiliation?" he asked, cutting her off midsentence.

She gaped at him, struggling to find a response. "Uh…like I was saying, my name is Elizabeth Beautane, and I…"

"Pack affiliation?" he asked again. A hint of impatience filled his tone.

She hadn't expected to get hit with the hard questions before she even passed through the gates. She clutched the steering wheel for support. "I don't have one," she answered. "Not currently." To her credit, her voice didn't hold so much as a hint of the dread swirling in her gut.

As she'd anticipated, at her admission, the guard's eyes narrowed with that familiar sense of distrust she'd been treated to her whole life. Everywhere she went, whenever discussions of pack affiliation rose—which they inevitably did, and quickly—it was always the same. Otherwise friendly conversations immediately turned sour, akin to if she'd announced she were best friends with Charles Manson or the little sister of the Unabomber or some other awful pariah, rather than a young female wolf who'd simply been born without a pack. All the more reason they needed someone like the Rogue advocating for her kind.

But to these wolves, she *was* a pariah. A Rogue, just like her mother before her, and wouldn't that always be the case? She'd learned that much about other wolves. As natural pack creatures, they were fiercely loyal to those within their pack. To those outside it, they were downright clannish, unaccepting of all outsiders. She'd never met a pack wolf who'd been truly relaxed in her presence.

Well, all but one.

The voice of the Grey Wolf guard immediately snapped her back to the moment. "The packmaster doesn't take meetings with Rogues. If you'd like to speak to someone about joining the pack, you can speak to our enrollment chair and request a meeting with Mav—"

"I don't give two flying craps about joining your pack," she challenged. "And I don't need to speak to Maverick. I'm here for Colt." Wasn't that always the assumption? That a Rogue wolf must naturally be either evil or in desperate want of a pack? As if she needed to be a part of a group who currently looked down on her as less-than due to the circumstances of her birth.

"I can't allow you in without a meeting. Your options are—"

"You don't understand. I need to meet with Colt. Immediately." That familiar sense of panic crept in. A part of her might have been excited, hopeful even, at the thought of having a child to call her own, but how was she going to break the news to him? They'd sworn only one night together. It would likely be one of the most difficult things she'd ever done.

The guard stepped back, his hand clearly placed on his gun. "Miss, I'm going to have to ask you to step out of the vehicle."

She shook her head. "No, I'm here to meet with your commander, and I'm not going anywhere until I do. I'm no criminal. Why don't you ask *him* if he'd be willing to see me?" Colt might have his rules, and she didn't expect much in the way of a relationship, but something told her that if she was expecting, he'd do right by her and their child.

The guard reached for her door handle. In that moment, Belle didn't think. She simply reacted. So naturally, she did the only thing a defiant, desperate woman with her foot on the gas pedal could do.

She floored it.

The old truck raced forward. Her pulse beat like a jackhammer as the truck careened down the dirt roadway in a flurry of dust and debris. The sound of shouting from the outpost rang through the open window, and for a brief moment, despite her fear and adrenaline, she smiled in satisfaction. Let them try to catch her on wheels when the most they had to work with were four paws or a horse.

But such pleasure disappeared the instant a league of cowboys riding on ATVs burst forth from the nearby trees, brandishing handguns and a variety of other weaponry. They surrounded her vehicle within moments, blocking the road.

It took Belle all of two seconds to realize she'd made a terrible mistake.

She slammed on the brakes, and the truck screeched to a stop. Unless she wanted to add vehicular manslaughter to her rapidly growing list of offenses against the Grey Wolves, she had no other choice. Before she could raise her hands in surrender, someone ripped the driver's side door of her truck wide open and wrenched her from the cab. They shoved her onto the hard mountain ground, causing her to eat dirt as sure as if she were a toddler making mud pies. One wrenched her arms behind her back. A small click of a lock, followed by searing pain across her skin, signaled the silver handcuffs at her wrists.

At least she was familiar with them at this point.

She spat out the mouthful of dirt as the guards pulled her to her feet again. "Let me go," she shrieked. She flailed beneath the guards' grasp as they began to haul her toward one of the ATVs. "I want to meet with Colt," she yelled.

"Don't they all?" one of the guards snickered. "Another one who can't stay away. Commander Casanova strikes again."

Commander Casanova? Ugh. Really?

They probably thought she was some crazy ex desperate for his attentions. Belle snarled. Let them think what they wanted. She wasn't here for some ridiculous booty call.

"Just take me to your commander," she snapped.

"It's your lucky day. You'll get to meet more than the high commander; you'll meet the packmaster himself." One of the guards pushing her forward growled low near her ear, "When he orders your execution."

Chapter 11

FERAL, MALE, AND UNFORGIVING, MAVERICK GREY WAS every bit as formidable as legend and legacy painted him to be. Belle knew this from the moment the massive wolf stepped into his office. Her breath staggered at the power that rolled off him, filling the room with such thick masculine virility, she could have choked on it. But it was his eyes that were truly haunting, giving a glimpse of unspeakable violence, both seen and lived. The eyes of a warrior.

Only one other pair of eyes had ever chilled her so before.

His gaze fell to where Belle knelt on the floor, or really, where she'd been tossed by his guards. A small scar slashed through his left eyebrow, drawing attention to the pale green of the iris. *From a knife wound*, she guessed from the smooth nature of the scarring. A claw, talon, or other lethal instrument would have left something more jagged.

The guard who'd handcuffed her spoke first. "Packmaster, she drove onto the ranch without clearance. She nearly mowed down several of our men with her tru—"

"If they hadn't swarmed my vehicle, I wouldn't have needed to slam on the brakes," she said. Despite the fear in her gut, she lifted her eyes to meet Maverick's. "Please," she pleaded.

That smooth scar drew lower as those intimidating eyes narrowed. The voice that followed was so deep and graveled, it seemed to vibrate through her. James Earl Jones had nothing on this guy.

"Leave us," he ordered.

Without another word, the guards retreated. As the door shut behind them, Belle regretted wishing for their hasty exit. She was alone with the most powerful werewolf packmaster in America, arguably the most powerful in the world, and she was handcuffed.

"What's to stop me from killing you?"

I'm pregnant with your friend's baby.

"Basic decency." Her response came out far more defiant than she'd intended.

Those pale-green eyes narrowed further.

She scrambled to explain herself. "I haven't hurt anyone. I may have caused a ruckus, but only because of your guards' behavior. It was foolish, but I need to speak with Colt."

"Colt?" He raised a brow.

She fought down a groan. This was not going well. "The high commander," she corrected.

"And how do you know the Grey Wolf High commander, Miss Beautane?"

"I…" Hell. She hadn't thought this through.

He took me captive, then let me go, and then we had a hot one-night stand that resulted in me being pregnant. Crap. Crap. Crap.

"He…he saved my life," she finally managed. Vague was likely her best bet at this point.

Maverick examined her with careful eyes. "You're either incredibly brave or incredibly reckless to come storming in here—though, by my estimation, I think you're both." Slowly, he began to circle the room, waiting to listen to her plea. "You have two minutes. Say your piece."

What piece?

"Umm…a month ago, I was attacked by vampires in the northern Grey Wolf territory."

If she didn't have Maverick's attention before, she held it now.

"The Missoula Massacre?"

Massacre. What a fitting title. She'd been far too isolated from all other supernaturals since then—waiting for the clearance Colt had promised her to go through—to have heard it termed such, but she knew they spoke of the same event. It had been one of the darkest, most terrifying nights of her life. She'd done as Colt had told her and run without looking back, knowing that he'd been taken, thinking that he'd died for her. She'd never felt such pain.

It had felt as if her heart had been sucked inside a black hole.

To make matters worse, she'd also known there was a chance the clearance wouldn't go through when he'd been captured, that she would spend her life on the run, but when news of his subsequent return several days later had made its way through the Rogue circuits, she'd felt such a keen sense of relief that he was alive and well, and that she would have her freedom after all, that she'd cried for days.

He may have been a known ladies' man and a warrior with an established reputation for violence, but he was a man of his word. She knew that much.

A month was merely a drop in the sea of time, and in the constant adrenaline of not knowing his fate or her own, time had blurred. It felt like yesterday that she had been there. In the forest. Hearing the distant sounds of screams and fighting, and then running, running away as they...

She shuddered at the thought.

"We believed there to be no civilian survivors. Only our most elite warriors and a handful of soldiers lived. We probed the whole territory. I prowled every inch of that goddamn forest myself, looking for..." Maverick's voice trailed off.

"I fled and went into hiding."

"A wise choice. Vampires don't leave survivors. Not unless it's to their advantage." As Maverick spoke the words, a faraway look glossed over his eyes. It was clear his mind remained elsewhere.

He glanced up at her. "Why not come here? To Wolf Pack Run?"

She wasn't sure how to answer that.

Sensing her unease, Maverick crouched down in front of her, meeting her at eye level. If she'd thought he'd been intimidating as he loomed over her before, it was nothing compared to being this close. She saw every sharp line and fierce hollow of his face, those green eyes drilling into her with staggering intensity.

"I..." She stuttered over her words.

The door to his office creaked open. She didn't bother to glance over her shoulder and see who had stepped inside. Until a familiar, smooth baritone cut through her stammering.

"I'll take it from here, Maverick." Colt strode into the

room as if he owned the place. Maverick stood, and Colt clapped the packmaster on the shoulder as if they were old friends. He didn't so much as glance in her direction.

"This woman claims to know you." Maverick posed it as more of a statement than a question.

"She does?" Colt's cold, steeled gaze fell on her for a beat, only long enough to acknowledge her presence. "Yes, I'm familiar with Miss..." His gaze shot to her again, clearly prompting her to supply further information.

"Beautane," she offered. "You might not remember me, Commander, but you saved me during the Missoula Massacre. I wanted to come and...uh...formally...thank you." It sounded like a horrible excuse, even to her own ears, but she couldn't very well announce the truth in front of the Grey Wolf packmaster himself.

Both Maverick and Colt looked at her as if she were insane.

"Helluva way to make an entrance." Maverick's eyes were narrowed in suspicion. "And for only a thank-you..."

Colt lingered slightly behind him, out of the packmaster's line of sight. He glared at Belle as if screaming *This is your mess!*

Belle scrambled for an adequate explanation. Man, she was going to butcher this. She was a terrible actress and an even worse liar. "I was...uh...just so overcome with...uh...feminine emotion..."

Feminine emotion, Belle? Really?

But she was committed at this point. She couldn't stop now.

"...at the thought of not being able to thank him for saving me," she continued, "that I sort of...lost it."

"Feminine emotion?" Maverick looked every bit as suspicious as she sounded. She might as well have been Lucille Ball on *I Love Lucy*. She used to watch old reruns on late-night television with her mother, laughing at Lucy giving ridiculous excuses to Ricky for the millionth time. Except that Maverick Grey was no gullible Ricky Ricardo, and there was no way in hell he believed a word of this. She saw it clear as day on his face.

Colt's mouth drew into a flat, unamused line. "Lost it," Colt repeated. "Right." From the look he was giving her, he too seemed to think that she'd lost it.

A deep, embarrassed blush filled her cheeks.

Maverick's gaze darted back and forth between the two of them for a long moment. She knew without a doubt both she and Colt looked guilty as hell. She'd made the high commander her unwilling partner in crime, the Ricky to her Lucy. Maverick's gaze raked over Belle one last time, lingering however briefly on her curves as he quirked a brow.

It was as if his eyes said *You're not his usual type*.

The red in her cheeks deepened.

"Right." Maverick cleared his throat. "I'm late for a meeting." The packmaster made his way toward the door, then paused, turning around. His attention settled on her. "But there's one thing I still don't understand. You told the guards you didn't have a pack, yet you were attacked on Grey Wolf territory?"

A lump formed in her throat. *No, don't do it. Don't ask.*

"What were you doing there?"

She gaped at him.

"She meant she lost her pack in the Massacre," Colt interjected. He answered without missing a beat, supplying the lie for her as if he'd rehearsed it a hundred times before. "Miss Beautane is a subpack Grey Wolf," he clarified.

"Really?" Maverick quirked a brow, assessing Belle's reaction.

She hung her head, hiding her face as if in grief over the loss of her packmembers. She was going to hell for this. She was certain.

"My apologies for your loss, Miss Beautane." The phrase was tentative, testing. "Any Grey Wolf always has a home here. Though it's standard protocol, given your little…entrance, that you pass a security clearance before you're free to come and go as you please." She heard the rattle of the handle as he gripped it. "Welcome to Wolf Pack Run."

The door closed behind the packmaster a moment later, and Belle breathed a sigh of relief. Lifting her head, she stared at Colt for a long moment, taking in the sight of him here before her and, more importantly, alive. He was exactly as she remembered. She suspected his face had been full of boyish charm in his childhood, but life had twisted him into something far harder, from the stubbled beard that lined his jaw to those haunting gray eyes.

It was as if he saw right through her to all her fears, her mistakes, her lies. They were the eyes of a drill sergeant who'd trained all his life to see through every inch of his soldiers' bullshit.

It didn't help matters that he knew what she looked like naked.

"Thank God for meetings?" It was the only thing she could think to say.

"Maverick may be packmaster, but he knows when to let me handle my own mess." The tight line of his jaw showcased his annoyance. "There was no meeting, Belle." Pausing, he raked his gaze over her. "Or should I call you Elizabeth Beautane now?" He smirked. "Next time you pick an alias, sweetheart, choose something a little further from Elizabeth Beaumont, don't you think?"

Instantly, she prickled. She'd forgotten how much he ruffled her feathers. That smirk of his was infuriating. "I didn't figure it mattered. As you know, Belle Beaumont died while in Grey Wolf custody during the Missoula Massacre."

It was the story he'd concocted. Thankfully, she wasn't well enough known among the Wild Eight that many would recognize her picture. Even if someone noticed a resemblance, few would likely question the validity of her death since it had come directly from the Grey Wolves.

"Did you really have to kill me off?" she asked.

Maybe the pregnancy hormones were causing her to be emotional, but something about that had irked her when she'd first heard it. She'd been eating dinner alone in a supernaturals-only bar, a relocation of the once-raided Midnight Coyote Saloon, when she'd heard several shifter patrons gossiping about the news. Even among Rogues and non–wolf shifters, the elite Grey Wolves and the details of their pack lives were akin to many Americans' obsession with British royalty, nosy and gossip filled. As she'd sat there, sipping her cola and picking at a basket of french fries while she'd eavesdropped on the details from the next booth over, it had felt as if she hadn't meant anything to him—which likely she hadn't, considering his reputation. But she hadn't wanted the reminder, especially not when, with each passing day, her period became later and later.

He shrugged. "You wanted your freedom. I gave it to you. It was the most effective way."

Silence passed between them.

He cleared his throat. "What are you doing here, Belle?"

The tight line of his jaw indicated his annoyance. Not that she blamed him. She'd stormed the place, causing a commotion, but in her defense, his guards hadn't left her much choice. This was nothing like how she'd planned to tell him. Some part of her had hoped he'd be happy to see her, to know she was safe, but he didn't appear to be either of those things.

She tried to find the words. No sharp retort or quick quip of their usual banter could make this level of communication easier. She inhaled a deep breath, trying to give herself strength, but it proved impossible with his steely eyes searing into her. Last time she'd seen this man, he'd been buried so deep inside her, she hadn't known such pleasure existed. He'd heard sounds come from her she'd never made before.

And now she was carrying his child. After only one night together.

She'd been a fool, taking no precautions to protect herself—though he was equally responsible in that regard, even though sexual diseases weren't a consideration among their kind.

"I don't know how to tell you this, but…I'm…I think I might be…" She swallowed down the lump in her throat, but as she did so, her face suddenly grew warm. Uncomfortable heat gathered in her cheeks. It felt like the sun itself had taken up residence inside her face as the weight of everything washed over her.

Belle's breath grew shallow as she struggled to draw air and anxiety gripped her. It was too much. Every bit of it. She struggled to breathe, and her knees buckled. In the distance, she thought she heard Colt curse as her eyes rolled back in her head, and then she was falling...

———

Colt carried his fair share of ghosts. Each night, the silence and darkness of his own mind broke down the careful barriers he'd erected, laying siege until each morning he awakened drenched in sweat. The reassurance that he would always wake, unharmed though haunted, kept him sane. Knowing his ghosts could only reach him in the vulnerability of his sleep provided him with a waking refuge. He held no such reassurance now. Because this ghost was all too real.

And apparently, he'd be carrying this particular ghost literally, since she was crumpling to the floor before his eyes.

Shit.

Colt dove for Belle, catching her midfall. Sweeping her into his arms, he cradled her against him. As soon he did, she startled, grabbing on to him as she came to as quickly as she'd fallen.

"I'm okay. I'm okay," she rasped. Immediately, she tried to ease away from him. "I can stand on my own," she protested.

No way. She wasn't lifting a finger. Not if he had anything to say about it. He lifted her with ease, ignoring her weak protests as he kicked the door to Maverick's office open and headed down the hall.

"Where are you taking me?" She sighed, giving up on fighting him, whether for lack of energy or resignation he wasn't certain.

"My apartment," he answered.

He carried her down a series of hallways until they reached his private rooms. His apartment decorations were sparse. Stark black and white. Modern. Clean. He may have been a cowboy, but that didn't mean his decor had to be western, too. He laid her out on his black leather sofa, gently lowering her onto the cushions. Without a word, he retrieved a pillow and propped it behind her head, then promptly did the same with her feet. He fetched her a glass of water from the tap and passed the glass to her. She eased up slightly, enough to take a sip. She looked pale, a little green around the gills.

Unlike her, he was no intelligent doctor, but he could at least make her comfortable. Sitting down on the edge of his coffee table across from her, he plucked the water glass from her when she was finished and set the empty glass on a nearby coaster.

"First time I've ever given a woman the vapors, I'll say that much," he drawled. "You wanna tell me what the hell that was about?"

She watched him with tired eyes. He remembered all too well the way her smile could light up the room. Whenever he'd made her grin, he remembered it feeling like a ray of sunshine in the middle of the cold, gray Montana weather. He would give anything to see her smile like that again, and that was too dangerous for his liking.

"Nerves. We just lied to Maverick and..." Her voice trailed off.

"What are you doing here, Belle?" he asked.

He leaned his weight on his knees. Though it'd only been a month since he'd last seen her, a horrific lifetime had passed for him. How many nights had he spent longing for her, hoping that the outcome between them could have been different...

And living with the harsh reality that it never would be.

"I...I thought you had died..." she finally managed to whisper.

His gaze captured hers. Whatever she saw there must have intimidated her, because she tore her gaze away.

"I did," he answered. "Twice. But they revived me. It was a game they played. My packmembers saved me." He left it at that. He would never scar her with the dark details of what had happened to him. He knew the guilt it would bring her—though it was unwarranted. It was his duty to protect her, and he took pride in that service, in his position.

Even if it suited him because he was a monster.

A beat of silence passed between them. Colt rarely found himself at a loss for words, but he didn't know where to begin. What did you say to a woman whose face had kept you alive on the brink of death?

I didn't save you. You saved me.

She placed her hand on his pectoral, overtop the steady thrum of his heart as if she were counting the beats of his pulse beneath her trained fingertips to reassure herself he was alive.

As her hand connected with the material of his shirt, that distant electricity he remembered jolted through him, charging his limbs like a live wire as no other woman's touch ever had. It made him ache in places he didn't know he could hurt. Far worse than any physical pain the vampires had caused him. The kind of pain that didn't lessen with time, but only grew more acute. Instantly, he recoiled from her touch. No. He couldn't go there again. Not now. Not ever. No matter how much he wanted to. One night. That was all they'd promised. He wasn't allowed more. He'd never be allowed more, even if the loss of her would nearly kill him. She could never be his.

Not with the secrets he kept.

He stepped away from her. He had to fight to force the words from his lips, to distance himself. In truth, all he wanted to do was to draw her close. If only circumstances were different…

He cleared his throat. "I want to make this clear from the outset: there can be nothing between us."

The curt detachment of his words seemed to catch her off guard.

She blinked. "Excuse me?"

"As much as we both can agree we enjoyed our…" He struggled to find the word.

Lovemaking. Passionate night. Intimacy. Best night of my life. Fuck.

"Tryst…" he finally offered.

Tryst? What the hell was that supposed to mean? The words they'd whispered, the intimacy they'd shared, all chalked up to a word meant to describe some fun one-night stand. Who even used the word *tryst* anymore? With every phrase he uttered, the pain inside him grew sharper. But he knew what had to be done.

End this now. It will only grow more difficult with time.

"It's for the best that we stay away from each other."

She was glaring at him, her lower lip quivering with hurt. The color returned to her cheeks as she slowly sat up. "Tryst? You call that a tryst?"

The hurt in her eyes cut him in two. *Shit.* What the hell was she doing here? He was never supposed to see her again, so when the vampires had tortured him, he'd allowed his mind to question, to wonder…to dream.

To hope for what could have been, if he were a different man.

Dreaming of her had been safe then. But now she was here and all too real…

As real as his lies, the dark side of his past that needed to stay hidden, which meant he needed her gone. If she didn't leave soon, he'd break every rule he'd ever set for himself, every promise he'd ever made to his family, his pack, to James…

And then he would lose everything. His pack, the only family he knew.

As hard as he'd tried to resist it, there had been more than heat between them that night. Given time, he knew there could be more there, and he'd never felt that way with anyone. Not in all his years. And he *couldn't* feel that way with anyone. He would never be afforded that luxury.

His tone deepened as he forced out words he didn't mean or want to say. "No, I wouldn't call it a tryst," he said. "I'd call it fucking." It was as vulgar as he'd intended. Meant to wound and, more importantly, to protect him and his secrets, his lies. "I thought I'd save you the army language. Even a commander's vocabulary is hardly better than a foot soldier's."

"Or a sailor's, for that matter," she snarled.

His gaze flicked toward her. There was that viper-tongued pistol he'd missed…

"And what makes you think I'd even want another night with you?" Hurt shone through her eyes, and she hurled the question at him with every ounce of her pain.

He froze. Her attack stung, and if the smug look on her face was any indicator, she felt proud of that. She should have been. Few things ever caught him off guard. He was a man who made his living keeping his guard up. The largest and strongest werewolf army ever to have existed hinged upon him keeping his guard up.

Except on a rare night in the snow-covered Montana mountains when he didn't…

She stood, brushing herself off before she pegged him with a hard stare. "You were good. But not that great."

He chuckled dark and low. It sounded forced through the pain, but he didn't care. She was challenging him. Plain and outright, which meant she was angry. He could withstand her anger. It was the hurt he couldn't bear.

When he didn't rise to the bait, her hands clenched into fists. "Is that all I was to you? Some silly tryst?"

A lump crawled into his throat. He couldn't address what she was to him. Not now. Not ever. Not even he was that good a liar.

She stomped her foot, her frustration with him mounting. "Answer me," she begged. "Please." The hurt was back in her eyes, and it flayed him open. She was shaking her head. "Give me something, anything, Colt. Throw me a bone here, even if it's just physical. At least tell me you enjoyed what we had."

"Is that what you came for? Something purely physical?" His words were harsh, distant.

She shook her head. "You know that's not true, but if that's all you'll give me, I'll take it."

He watched her, suspended in indecision between what he wanted and what he knew he couldn't have. He needed to make her see. To show her that he could never be what she needed from him. To leave her wanting more. So then she'd realize that allowing this to go further would only cause pain for them both.

Fuck.

One taste. To prove his point. That was all he would allow himself.

In an instant, the dynamic between them switched. His eyes flashed to his wolf's, and he could practically see her nipples tightening beneath her blouse. "So that's enough for you, is it, Belle?" Slowly, he prowled toward her with the smooth gait of a predatory animal.

"Colt," she warned. She backed away until she bumped into the far wall of his living room.

"Yes, Belle?" His words were a sultry purr.

He eased closer, and she sucked in that little intake of breath, the one she did every time she anticipated him touching her. Lowering his head to her neck, he inhaled the scent of her curls. She smelled divine. Like sex and sunshine and everything he'd ever wanted.

And more.

His lips grazed the beat of her pulse, hovering beneath her ear in that spot he knew drove her wild with need. "You came for the feel of my mouth on your skin..." he breathed.

He trailed a single hand up the side of her curves,

the wide swath of her hip, the narrow band of waist, the soft mound of her breast, until he was brushing over her shoulder and gently twisting his fingers into her curls.

"The feel of my hands in your hair."

Her breathing hitched.

He was rock hard and aching for her.

His other hand drifted down her side, toying with the edge of her jeans, until he dipped his fingertips beneath the edge, grazing the line of her undergarments. "The feel of my hand between your legs."

She leaned into him, rocking her hips forward. He was dying to feel how wet she was. But he couldn't. He wouldn't be able to stop himself.

"Or the length of my cock buried deep inside you," he whispered against her lips. He could practically taste her on his tongue. Her lips were like candy…

And he didn't mean her mouth.

"And nothing more?" With that last word, he pulled away from her. It took everything in him to ease back, placing some much needed distance between them. He was torturing himself as much as he was teasing her.

"This can't happen," he reiterated as he slipped away from her. "We both know it's not enough for you."

For either of us…

"Fine," she near growled. "I'm enough of a woman to admit it. But I'm also not the only one who wants this." She stepped forward. Her small hand shot out, cupping the hard length of his cock through his jeans. Her hand barely covered the girth of him, but the feel of her palm pressed against his aching shaft would be enough to give him blue balls for days. *Fuck.* He had a feeling his own hand wouldn't be much use for this ache.

He growled.

"Tell me I'm wrong." A challenge blazed in her eyes.

He loved it when she was like this. Saucy, brazen, wild. He loved that he brought those things out in her. She had him there.

"You're not wrong," he admitted.

Releasing him, she stepped back. Instantly, he wanted her touching him again. He ached for her hand, wrapped around him and rubbing up and down the length of his cock.

Shit.

His attraction to her was fucking magnetic. Faint or not, bringing her back to his apartment when he knew they couldn't be together topped his lists of not very bright ideas, right alongside his twenty-first birthday in Vegas and that one time he'd stupidly let Blaze use his Amazon Prime account.

Never again.

End this now. It's only going to escalate from here.

Already he was envisioning bending her over his bed and taking her roughly from behind. He wanted to leave her aching for him. And he had a feeling that round ass of hers would look just as pleasing when pink as the gorgeous shade on her cheekbones.

"So you want to give me the real reason this can't happen, Commander Casanova?" she said, breaking the tension between them.

He stiffened. He didn't bother to ask where she'd heard that god-awful nickname. Likely one of his idiot soldiers when they'd hauled her in. They'd be running extra laps during training for weeks as a result. Normally, the nickname barely irked him, but on Belle's

lips, it pissed him off with rage he struggled to contain.
He didn't want to be Casanova to anyone.

Not anyone but her.

Colt settled on the best excuse he could find. He
couldn't ignore her. Not unless he wanted her to try to
prove her own point again…which he did, if he was
honest. To think this was the same woman who couldn't
so much as utter the word *cock* without turning fifty
shades of red. Their night together had changed her. Filled
her with confidence in her sexuality. He could see it.

"I make it a point never to be seen fraternizing beyond
normal work relations with the females of our species,
at least not at Wolf Pack Run. More importantly, there
are extra considerations because…" He hesitated on the
next words, trying to find the right phrasing.

"Because I'm not a Grey Wolf," she finished for him.
"Because I'm a Rogue with ties to the Wild Eight."

He saw the disappointment in her eyes. "Because *I'm*
high commander of the Grey Wolf armies," he finished.

It wasn't about her or being a Rogue. If only she
knew how familiar he was with that life. But he saw
the sheen of tears in her eyes, and as much as it killed
him, he knew it was better this way. This was the closest to the truth he could give her. Not without revealing
everything he'd worked his whole life to hide.

Couldn't she see him for what he was? The monster
he'd been born as? If she looked closely enough, she had
to be able to see him. The real him. The truth beneath the
Grey Wolf commander facade. His stare bore into her,
urging her, willing her to see.

But she turned away from him in her hurt.

"Those were your words, not mine." He wanted to

make that clear. "Belle, I understand what it's like to be standing on the outside looking in at something you want but can never have. Believe me when I say I know the feeling more than most."

He lived that reality every day. As a child, he'd lived it when he'd been separated, excluded from his birth father's pack—the bastard son of a monstrous man who couldn't have given two shits about anyone but himself, even though Colt had been naive enough to want him to. And his mother, so caught up in her own nightmarish relationship with his sire that she failed to choose what was best for them both. Her death had been decades ago, yet his heart ached for her, for the ways he'd never know her now that she was gone. The Grey Wolves were his pack, his family. He loved them as his own flesh and blood, but they'd never truly be *his* family, *his* blood. No matter how hard he wished it.

Even as he stood among them, he'd always be the outsider looking in, his hidden truths keeping him forever separate.

And now, separate from Belle, too…

The pain in Colt's eyes tore Belle in two, making her question all the truths he left unspoken, but what he *had* said vibrated through her, awakening her reason like a tuning fork. She couldn't tell this cowboy she was pregnant with his child. Not when he viewed her as an outsider, thought so little of her, all because she'd been born a Rogue.

I thought you were different. She wanted to scream it at him from the mountaintops.

A familiar ache filled her whenever she looked at him now—a deep-seated longing. It started in her chest and resonated down to the heavy feeling in her womb. He was right, though she'd never admit it. Choosing to have a child might not have been a mindful decision, but she'd always wanted a family, children, and a partner to call her own and a pack to belong to, but as a Rogue, she'd never have those things, not even with this wild, feral Grey Wolf who made her feel things she hadn't known she could feel. For a brief time, she'd thought she would find that sense of belonging in the Wild Eight, but it had all been a lie. She'd made the mistake of trusting them. It was her biggest regret.

And now…

She recognized she had no one to rely on but herself. She'd made this mistake before, and she wouldn't make it again. She would wait until she was certain the pregnancy was progressing normally, beyond the first twelve weeks when the risk of miscarriage was high, and if that time came, then she'd give him the option of fulfilling his role as a father, but she'd be prepared to do this without his help. She had a friend, a fellow werewolf female she'd met in med school who'd become an obstetrician for humans. She could reach out to her, make her twelve-week appointment. And until then… this would be no one's burden but her own.

"Don't pretend that's not what you were about to say, Colt. I'm a Rogue. I've heard that from pack wolves my whole life."

"Why are you really here, Belle?" he repeated.

The stiff frustration in his tone meant he wouldn't allow her to skirt the answer this time. But she wasn't ready to tell him the truth. She had been when she'd arrived. She'd had the best intentions, but that was before she'd realized she didn't mean anything to him.

"What about your family? Your friends? Your freedom? Hell, even the rodeo?" His questions flew at her like knives, cutting straight to the core and reminding her of everything she was missing.

Her hands clenched into fists, and she trembled. She felt light-headed and flopped onto the couch, sinking into the cushions so he didn't have to catch her again, for the sake of the baby.

Oh God...

"My mother passed away years ago. She was all I had. As for friends, I thought I had one here"—her lips drew tight—"but clearly, I was mistaken." Pushing herself to stand, she moved from the sofa toward the door. "I'll see myself out."

Colt shook his head. "No. You still haven't answered me. Why are you here, Belle?"

She settled on the first thing that came to mind. "I swore to you that I would testify to the Seven Range Pact. After you saved my life—again—it seemed right to pay my debt. Even as Elizabeth Beautane, I can still do that." It hadn't been her original intention, but it was true. He may not want her, at least in a romantic sense, but she considered him a friend all the same, and what the vampires had done to him sickened her.

She wanted revenge for him as much as he did. The way they'd hurt him...

It brought out a violent streak in her she hadn't realized she had.

"I...thought I could help you," she said.

"You thought wrong."

He might as well have told her she didn't mean a thing to him.

"After the massacre, I told the Pact what you overheard. I said they should consider it postmortem testimony. It was a lie, but it served a purpose. You got your freedom, and I had my counterstrike, or so I thought…"

Belle gaze softened. "What do you mean?"

"The Seven Range Pact voted against me."

Belle's stomach churned. After what the vampires had done to him, it was like throwing salt on an open wound. "Why would they do that?" she breathed.

He shrugged, but she knew it was a matter of life or death to him. "Lack of proof. Even though the vampires drew my blood when they held me captive, the Pact's scientists think the serum is impossible. They say it was an intimidation tactic to throw me off my game."

Belle was shaking her head. She'd overheard the conversation herself. It had never been meant for Colt's ears. Intimidation tactic, her ass. "What about the other missing shifters?" she asked. "The bobcat? The cougar?"

Colt shook his head. "Both the bobcat pride leader and the cougar pride leader reported none of their packmembers missing."

"Maybe not packmembers…" Belle's eyes widened in realization.

Colt raised a brow.

"When I fled after the massacre, I found another Rogue house and—"

Colt scowled as he interrupted. "I thought I warned you about getting involved with the likes of that vigilante bastard. He's dangerous. He—"

"Would you listen and not lecture, Commander?" she snapped. "There was a note. In the house. It was a warning note from him."

"From the Rogue?" Colt's Adam's apple jerked. "Not a Rogue, but *the* Rogue?" His eyes widened in disbelief. "No one knows who he is, Belle."

Belle nodded. "I know, but it was signed with his alias. It wasn't handwritten. It was a copy, but he was warning other Rogues that there'd been disappearances among our kind. To watch our backs, to stay vigilant. Maybe the Pact couldn't find any packmembers missing because their targets weren't packmembers at all."

Colt clutched his chin, staring down at his boots. "It's possible," he muttered.

Belle nodded. "If you tell the Seven Range Pact, maybe they'll reconsider. Maybe they'll—"

Colt raised a hand to stop her. "No, Belle. They won't."

She gaped at him. "Why not? If Rogues are going missing, then—?"

"Because no packleader keeps a roster on Rogues." Colt was still shaking his head. "They're not..."

Packmembers, she mentally finished.

She stiffened. Which meant not only could they not go missing, as far as the Pact was concerned, but they didn't exist at all. Her stomach churned. Most Rogues were that way by choice, but what about shifters like her who'd been born that way? What about them?

She didn't care what a dark, violent, and dangerous vigilante the Rogue was. At least he recognized what the Grey Wolves and other packs failed to see. Shifters like her existed, and their lives mattered.

Colt was still shaking his head. "I know it's not right,

but they won't see it the way you do, Belle. I can't change centuries of prejudice toward your kind in a single meeting. Their decision is final, and even if they hadn't voted against it, placing you right under Maverick and the Pact's noses wouldn't be a logical decision."

"I see." She swallowed the lump in her throat. "Well, my mother always told me never to linger where I wasn't wanted." She reached the door handle in several strides. She needed out of here.

Colt's hand slammed against the frame. "You can't walk out of here."

"Why not? I'm not your prisoner. Not this time." First he pushed her away, and now he told her she couldn't leave? The man was more up and down than a roller coaster.

Don't pretend the unpredictability doesn't thrill you, Belle. She never knew what was coming next with him, the next emotion, the next touch, the next line of banter. It was mesmerizing, thrilling, and terrifying all at once.

"We lied to Maverick," he said, holding the door closed with massive weight. "We told him you're a Grey Wolf. He wasn't convinced."

She snorted. "That's an understatement."

"So if you jet out of here now," Colt continued, "before you've barely even stayed a few hours, he'll *know* you're not a pack wolf. Any Grey Wolf who'd been even a month without their packmates would be itching to be among them. Stay less than a week, and he'll know you're not one of us."

She tried the handle again, but the pressure he exerted on the door threatened to break the frame—and he was barely trying. "What does it matter? You killed me off."

"And Maverick is the only man who has the power to

resurrect you." His gaze fell to her, frustratingly distant. "Nothing fully disappears from our databases, Belle. You heard him. After that little stunt you pulled, you'll need to go through a security clearance. I can take care of that. It's my usual duty anyway, but if Maverick gets suspicious, if he decides to dig deeper and goes looking for your information himself, not only will he find you, but he'll know I lied from the start, and then…"

"Then you'll never get revenge on the vampires," she finished.

"It's more than revenge. I need to protect my pack. I owe it to them. The Seven Range Pact may have voted against it, but I have other plans." The seriousness of his tone made it feel as if the situation meant life or death. She supposed in some ways it did. Other plans? Why wasn't she surprised? When this man set his mind to something, nothing stood in his way. Not mountains or packmasters or Pacts. Not even hotheaded she-wolves.

"One week?" she asked.

He nodded. "One week. You lie low. Keep your head down while I take care of your security clearance. Don't draw attention to yourself, and when the time has passed—"

"I leave and don't look back." She may not have understood why he was pushing her away. It may have hurt that he clearly didn't want her, but she cared for him all the same, and she wouldn't endanger his entire pack for the sake of her pride.

"One week," she agreed. "Only until the clearance goes through. You'll barely know I'm here."

Her vision blurred, and she retreated to the couch again, resting on the cushions. She needed a moment to process this.

Colt didn't spare her such mercy. "I'll send someone in to show you around." He wrenched open the door. He was halfway through it before he paused. "Oh. And, Belle?" he threw back over her shoulder. His tone was frustrated.

And sexy as all hell.

Those golden wolf eyes burned hot over her skin. Her breasts grew heavy with need. A heavy ache curled low in her belly, and she felt herself slicken. She half expected him to prowl across the room toward her, to finish the heat he'd started between them moments ago.

"Yes, Colt?" she breathed.

He knew exactly what he was doing to her, and he was enjoying it. *Damn him.*

He flashed her a wicked grin. "It's Commander to you now."

Her eyes narrowed, and he closed the door, leaving her as spitting mad as she was aroused.

Chapter 12

BELLE RESTED ON COLT'S COUCH, FUMING FOR WHAT FELT like hours. With each passing minute, her frustration with her current situation mounted. Why had she ever thought it would be a good idea to come here? It had been an ill-planned choice.

Like some other ill-planned choices. Her hand drifted to her belly.

No use crying over spilled milk now. There wasn't much she could do about the pregnancy other than take care of herself, because she had no intention of ending it. This was her chance to have a family of her own—with or without Colt.

She leaned into the sofa cushions with a sigh.

He'd changed. The man who had shown her mercy on the mountainside was no more, or at least he was buried deeper under the hardened exterior of a cowboy turned warrior. But how could he not be? After what they'd done to him.

I did die. Twice. His words tore through her.

She shuddered at the thought.

The door to his apartment burst open, and she grumbled her displeasure, expecting the "Commander." She snarled at the thought of calling him that. Instead, a young woman, a female Grey Wolf who by appearance was a handful of years her junior, stood in the doorway.

"I'm sorry. I thought you were…" Belle's voice

trailed off. Best not to announce that she'd been growling at the mere thought of the Grey Wolf high commander.

The she-wolf slipped through the door. She pushed it shut behind her, and the latch closed with a click as she leaned against the frame. Her eyes, large and green, fell on Belle and stayed there. "You thought I was my brother?"

Could this be Colt's younger sister? Belle didn't think so. They didn't look anything alike. Whoever she was, she was a spritely little thing. Slightly upturned nose, large eyes, and delicate bone structure. She was small in stature with an almost boyish figure, despite the feminine features of her face.

"Elizabeth, right?" the she-wolf asked.

Belle watched as the little sprite of a she-wolf made her way closer to the couch. She walked right up, seeming unconcerned that Belle could be a potential threat.

She supposed this woman thought her to be a Grey Wolf, which meant she had to play the part.

The young she-wolf reached for Belle's hand, offering to help her up, but Belle shrank back from her touch. The look in the she-wolf's eyes softened. "Someone's hurt you before." She said it with absolute certainty, as if she saw straight into Belle's soul. "I hope it wasn't my brother. Maverick and his friends are too harsh, if you ask me."

"Maverick." Belle's eyes widened. She saw it now. They had the same green eyes, like jade with flecks of emerald. She hadn't recognized it at first, but she did now. The intensity was the same, too, only on Maverick's little sister, the gaze was full of kindness, a wise sort of knowing that would look out of place on the hardened packmaster.

"The one and only." She reached for Belle's hand again.

This time, Belle didn't shrink away.

The young she-wolf helped her to her feet.

The warm feeling of another wolf's touch gave instant and immediate relief. She was almost disappointed when the contact between them broke.

You just have to pretend to be a pack wolf. Not actually act like one, she chided herself.

For Colt's sake. One week, and then she was done.

"Thank you." She gave a smile to the woman, which was instantly returned.

"My name's Maeve," the she-wolf introduced herself.

"Maeve Gray?" Belle raised an eyebrow. She recognized the name. How could she not? The she-wolf had been born into *the* original Grey Wolf bloodline. Maverick wasn't yet mated. As his sister, that made Maeve one powerful and influential female. Despite that fact, Belle felt instantly affectionate toward her—Maverick's little sister or not.

"Nice to meet you, Maeve."

"Likewise." Maeve headed for the door. Halfway there, she glanced back. "Are you coming?"

Belle stared at the woman with wide eyes. "You mean I'm really free to go? Shouldn't I stay here?" Colt had told her to lie low.

"Boy, my brother really did a number on you with his scare tactics, didn't he?" Maeve's slender brows scrunched down in a look of concern. "Or was it Colt? We're not actually related, but he might as well be my brother, too. I grew up chasing his and Maverick's coattails, and I'll have his ass if he hurt you."

Belle didn't answer. Maverick was far from the worst of it, but she didn't say as much, and Colt may have hurt her, but she wasn't about to share the intimate details.

Maeve waved a hand in dismissal. "Don't concern yourself with them. Come with me. I'm going to give you a tour around the ranch."

A tour? As if she were a guest, not a prisoner or a pariah who their packmaster might recognize. Maybe she was such a minuscule blip on his radar that he would never know. Either way, she was here for now, and she might as well enjoy the freedom while it lasted.

Hooking her arm through Belle's as if they were instant friends, Maeve led Belle out of the apartment, tugging her along with surprising strength, considering Maeve's minuscule size. Somehow, Belle knew without a doubt that given time, if Maeve had her way, they would be friends. And if she could win over the packmaster's little sister, how hard would it be to earn the packmaster's mercy?

Maybe she had made the right decision coming here after all.

An hour later, Belle still wasn't regretting her decision.

"Was it your brother who stuck you with the job of showing the new girl around?" Belle asked as Maeve led her out of the infirmary. Belle had spotted the still-under-construction building off in the distance, and Maeve had offered to show it to her.

As they'd wandered through the small center, Belle had marveled at the stunning new equipment. Brand-new CT and EKG machines and even a portable in-office arthroscopy system gleamed shiny and new as if the plastic wrapping had only recently been removed. Her fingers had itched to take the new orthotic 3-D printer technology for a test run. Everything appeared pristine. Maeve had explained that the facility was newly expanded. Apparently, Maverick had thought it pertinent to increase their medical facilities in preparation for the bloodshed of war, though doctors of their kind were hard to find. As their medic, Austin would get a boost from having up-to-the-minute equipment, and in a pinch, others could be trained to assist him.

As a physician, she knew firsthand that wolves with medical training were few and far between, considering the training required attending medical school alongside a bunch of humans, a risky move. But as a Rogue, Belle had lived among humans long enough to know their minds would substitute any excuse before they accepted the reality that something *other* lived among them.

Belle had been the other her whole life, whether among werewolves or humans.

"He didn't make me give you a tour." Maeve's answer brought Belle back from her own thoughts. "I volunteered. I need to find things to keep myself busy around here. He means well, but my brother practically keeps me under lock and key. He was already ten years old when I was born. He helped change my diapers, so he's always been fiercely protective. He treats me like a delicate flower."

"That must be nice." As an only child, Belle would have given her left arm to have a sibling. Even an overprotective elder brother. The ranch where she grew up, though small, had been lonely with just her and her mother.

They reached the exit door.

Maeve shook her head. "It's miserable. I want

something exciting in my life—wonder, hope, adventure."

She hit the metal bar on the double doors and pushed it open. They stepped outside, the sprawling acres and hills of Grey Wolf ranchlands spread before them. They stood at the edge of a veritable village of buildings and homes, all centered around one massive major compound complex. In the distance, the ranchlands stretched as far as the eye could see. They had to be sitting on more than one hundred thousand acres of land. Belle's cowgirl heart ached with desire.

A state-of-the-art hospital on acres of sprawling Montana ranchland. Man, what she wouldn't give to work in a facility like this. On the Grey Wolf ranch with fellow wolves, a place where she could both use her skills and make a life for herself without being in hiding. A place where she could have friends like Maeve. Create a home on the ranch, among the pack.

A place to belong.

Her thoughts immediately turned to Colt and the little spark in her belly, and she blushed before the thought soured.

She'd never have anything like this.

"Miserable?" she asked Maeve, pushing the ache in her chest aside. She couldn't imagine much on this gorgeous ranchland being miserable.

"You have no idea how much it sucks to be treated like you're some princess." Maeve unlaced her arm from Belle's, beckoning for her to follow as they walked toward the other buildings. The bustle of pack life up ahead was already apparent. Male and female packmembers going about their day-to-day activities shot curious glances their way.

Somehow Belle's feet managed to follow Maeve, despite her brain's growing anxiety and need to retreat from those prying stares. She wasn't exactly comfortable around packs, having always been the outsider. "Well, aren't you?"

Maeve shot her a confused glance.

"Like a princess?" Belle elaborated. "I mean, you're the sister of Maverick Grey, the Grey Wolf packmaster, the strongest and most powerful wolf in North America. You were born into the original line of Grey Wolves. Doesn't that make you a little something like royalty?"

Maeve rolled her eyes, but a smile quirked at her lips. "Sure it does, but who wants to be a princess when she can be a cowgirl?" she quipped.

They continued in this companionable manner for the better part of another hour, Maeve wandering around Wolf Pack Run and showing Belle all their facilities. Aside from the small, newly built hospital, the Grey Wolves also boasted a massive compound that housed their elite warriors, their central command, and Maverick's private offices, as well as a plethora of scattered cottages that housed the families and single wolves who made up the rest of the pack, plus a dozen or so guest cottages perched up within the mountains.

A kitchen the size of a small stadium was attached to a mess hall that kept the hungry wolves well fed, and both an open-air training field and an underground training center for the fighters, along with the daily activities of ranch living, kept them in peak physical condition.

And Maeve hadn't even begun to show her any of the actual ranch operation yet. According to the spritely she-wolf, they were primarily a cow-calf operation, but they also raised yearlings and cared for some of the state's wild horses.

In the midst of their ongoing conversation, when Belle confessed that she'd grown up on a ranch and had a fierce love of horses, Maeve promptly announced that she absolutely needed to see the Grey Wolf stables. Belle gathered the impression that the Grey Wolf female would take any excuse for something to do, and if she was reading her right, Maeve enjoyed their fast and easy friendship as much as Belle did.

This is only temporary, Belle.

They rode out over the pastures on one of the pack's ATVs, past an enormous barn and acres used for crops and vegetation in the warmer weather, until they reached the stables. If by stables, one meant massive, equine care center.

Belle's jaw dropped as they stepped inside. What the Grey Wolves called a simple stable housed over fifty horses. "This is incredible."

Maeve smiled, following Belle's gaze. "I suppose it is."

They walked through the building, the stable hands casting occasional glances their way, but not questioning their presence. Belle petted several of the horses, stroking their manes as Maeve outlined the details of the Grey Wolves' ranching practices to her. They largely worked the same as any other major Montana operation. Unless someone dared to venture out onto the huge expanse of their private lands—and she'd seen firsthand how far that had gotten her—no human would ever be the wiser to their true nature. They hid in plain sight.

Belle was listening intently until she spotted a familiar equine face.

"Silver." She smiled.

The horse flicked his tail excitedly at the sight of her and let out a joyful whinny. Immediately, she crossed over to his stall and stroked a hand through his pale mane. The horse nuzzled into her shoulder affectionately as if they were old friends.

"I see you two know each other." Maeve chuckled.

Belle nodded but didn't elaborate. Maeve would likely think she'd met Silver when Colt saved her during the Missoula Massacre. It kept in line with their story.

As Belle showered Silver with the affection he craved, she glanced into the next stall. Inside, the horse stood cockeyed. Belle watched it with careful, assessing eyes as it lay down in the hay, favoring its front right leg.

"He's gone lame," a feminine voice said from behind them.

Belle twisted toward the sound. A dark-skinned woman, around these parts likely Native American, stood with her hands on her hips, watching them. She wore cowgirl boots and a Stetson, and if the dirt and hay on her clothes were any indication, she'd been working out here or in the pasture for the better part of the day.

"Elizabeth, this is Naomi," Maeve said, introducing the woman. "Naomi, this is Elizabeth. She's new here."

Naomi reached out a hand to shake hers. "Pleasure."

Belle took it. The other woman's grip was strong, yet not like the strength of a...

"You're a human." The words fell from Belle's lips before she could stop them. She hadn't caught the woman's scent before, thanks to the smell of hay and freshly mucked manure permeating the air of the stables, but now that she'd caught it, she couldn't mistake it.

"The only one you'll find on this ranch," Naomi answered.

"And you're here willingly?" Belle's eyes grew wide. Naomi nodded.

Belle eyed the woman, flabbergasted. "That's a story I'm interested to hear."

Maeve took that as her cue to pipe in on the introductions. "Naomi's engaged to the Grey Wolf second-in-command. They're getting married tomorrow." She let out a small, enthused squeak and clapped her hands.

Belle hadn't heard the Grey Wolves had appointed a new second-in-command. Their previous second, Bo, had been killed in battle roughly six months earlier. The rumors of it had spread through their world like wildfire, even among Rogues, who, sporting a natural pack mentality, were the worst kinds of gossips.

"Congratulations," Belle said.

"Thanks. I think Maeve's more excited than I am." Naomi laughed. "My future husband and I are already mated." She shrugged.

Mated? How could a human and a werewolf mate? Belle shook her head. She didn't want to pry, but from the look of pure happiness in the human woman's eyes, Belle had no doubt it was true.

Maeve rubbed her hands together in anticipation. "It's not every day one of our elite warriors walks down the aisle, and I actually get to *be* in the wedding and wear a gorgeous dress to boot. The last time that happened, I was a teenager and they made me the flower girl. Can you believe that? Fifteen and a flower girl. You should have seen that poufy monstrosity." She shuddered. "Thanks to Naomi, I get to wear a dress that

makes me look like I have a hint of curves this time."
She gestured to her boyish figure. "It's going to be a
huge occasion." Maeve's eyes took on a dreamy quality.
Whether the wedding was the occasion she referred to or
the chance to have a womanly look to her figure, Belle
wasn't certain.

Not a princess. Sure.

Belle followed Naomi's gaze back to the ill horse.

"He's favoring his front right leg a lot," she offered.

Naomi nodded. "I'd noticed."

"Likely an abscess under his hoof. It's a pocket of
infection in the lamina. Usually, it starts with a small
puncture wound, maybe a misplaced shoe nail or something sharp he stepped on, and it progresses from there.
The hole allows the bacteria in, and bacteria love dark,
damp places like that."

"I called Austin—he's our farrier and takes care of
all the medical husbandry around here—but he's still
out at the Missoula ranch, so I'll have to call someone
else soon. He's also the Grey Wolves' main medic and a
soldier to boot. The man's so overworked, it's not even
funny," Naomi said.

Belle gestured to the stall. "I'm a physician, but I
have a fair amount of animal husbandry experience. I
grew up on a ranch. I can handle removing a shoe and
draining the abscess."

Hell, she'd performed surgeries that repaired fragile
human bones from shattered, fragmented pieces. She
was more than confident she could handle this.

"You grew up on a ranch, huh?" Naomi smiled. "That
makes two of us. If you're confident you can do this, I'm
more than happy to let you try."

Together, the three women led the stumbling horse from his stall, careful he didn't topple over and crush any of them with his weight. When they had him secured, Belle instructed the other women on the tools she'd need.

Once everything was sanitized and she'd donned gloves, Belle made quick work of paring away the shoe on the affected hoof. She balanced the horse's leg in a bucket of ice to lessen the bruising and slow the rapid blood flow. Removing the shoe confirmed her diagnosis. The area beneath the horse's hoof was tender and causing him clear pain. Belle drained the abscess, being as gentle with the beast as she could.

When she was finished, she stood. "Try to keep the area clean to avoid reinfection. Let's soak his hoof in Epsom salts and warm water, and that will help draw the rest of the infection out. Once we do that, we'll bandage him up, but you'll need to repeat the process for a few days while it heals. You may want to give him an anti-inflammatory shot to keep him out of pain."

She glanced up at her companions, who were looking at her with identical smiles on their faces. She could have sworn she heard one of them whisper Colt's name, but she was likely just being paranoid.

"What?" she asked.

Maeve grinned. "So you and Colt met on the Missoula ranch, huh?" she asked. The question seemed to hold more meaning than Maeve was letting on.

Belle gave a stiff nod, as Maeve and Naomi exchanged knowing glances. It was a clear look of *Are you thinking what I'm thinking?*

Naomi was nodding as she gave an assessing look to

Belle's curvaceous figure. "Sierra's lean, but all muscle. I bet you could let it out in the right places, and it would be perfect," Naomi said to Maeve. "Then Sierra gets her way and doesn't have to wear a dress, and she could be free to move around while doing the photos."

Belle raised a brow. "What are you two talking about it?"

The mischievous grin across Maeve's face widened. "Elizabeth, how do you feel about satin?"

Belle eyed the other women warily. She could see some sort of plan forming, and despite her dread at that thought, for a moment, Belle almost forgot that these budding friendships were temporary.

Chapter 13

"YOU LOOK LIKE A HELLS ANGEL WEARING A TUX." COLT yanked at the satin material of Wes's tie, straightening it for the umpteenth time. He wrinkled his nose in disdain as he examined his friend and fellow packmate standing before him. Wes Calhoun looked about as right in a suit and tie as a pig did in a tutu, and thanks to Maeve's latest pet antics—a "teacup pig" she'd affectionately taken in and named Tucker—it hadn't been that long since Colt had seen such a sight.

Wes grumbled as Colt straightened his collar. "Coming from you, that's rich."

Colt knew he wasn't much cut out for the suit-and-tie business either. He was far more at home in his old ranch jeans and a T-shirt, or on the occasion he was feeling fancy, a button-down or a flannel. At least the bride had allowed them to don dress Stetsons, though the groom's appeared to be MIA at the moment, revealing a mop of messy blond locks.

"At least my hair looks like I run a comb through it," Colt shot back.

Wes's hair nearly reached his chin, and comb or no comb, he never looked freshly groomed. Wild was more like it.

"Naomi says it's sexy bed head." Wes grinned.

Colt rolled his eyes. "Of course, she does." He reached for the nearby plastic container that housed the groom's boutonniere and accompanying pins. "I'm sure that's why she insisted on the dress Stetson to match the suit."

A wry grin crossed Wes's lips. "She may have mentioned I needed to tame it for the ceremony, but she was sure singing a different tune last night."

Colt shook his head. "Say no more. You're supposed to be a gentleman today. I know you don't know the meaning of the word, but rule number one is gentlemen don't kiss and tell."

"And you know about being a gentleman, Commander Casanova?"

Colt grunted. "Not you, too."

Wes shrugged. "Wolves talk."

Colt worked the pin through the back side of the small flower arrangement. Yellow gerbera daisy. Every bit as charming and country chic as the bride herself. "Don't humans think it's bad luck to see the bride the night before the big day?"

"It's on the wedding day that's bad luck, and I'm no gentleman, nor a sucker for tradition." Wes chuckled. "Which means up until midnight last night, we were—"

The door to Wes's apartment burst open, saving Colt from the mental image of Wes rolling in the hay with his human bride-to-be—*literally* in the hay, based on what the stable hands had told him. It'd been less than twenty-four hours since a certain viper-tongued she-wolf had arrived at the pack, and he'd been considering doing the same. Probably best that she'd been doing an excellent job of lying low. He hadn't seen her since, though somehow Silver had. He knew because the horse had been in a considerably better mood. It was better this way, not seeing her. It meant Colt hadn't had the chance to defy his own rules.

He had a feeling he was starting not to like rules. At least when it came to her.

At the sudden intrusion, Colt's hand slipped, missing the mark with the pin so he jabbed his finger instead.

"Shit," he swore, bringing the digit to his mouth. But once his eyes turned to the door, he didn't have much time to bitch about the unexpected arrival. What stood in the doorframe was... Well, Colt wasn't entirely sure what he was seeing.

"What in the blazing fuck is that?" Wes sneered, his gaze raking up and down their fellow packmate's attire as his nose wrinkled in disgust.

Blaze-ing fuck being about right. Blaze, the Grey Wolf chief of intelligence and tech expert, stood in the doorway. The fuchsia-pink suit he wore was covered in small, black silhouettes of palm trees, accompanied by a dressy white undershirt and a tie that matched the suit. When Colt squinted the right way, Blaze looked like a muscular hot-pink flamingo. Aside from palm trees, considering flamingoes were another common motif in Blaze's outrageous clothing choices, that aesthetic might have been what he was shooting for.

Blaze sauntered into the room, looking every bit at home in the ridiculous getup. "You like it?" He smoothed a hand down his lapel.

He knew perfectly well that Colt and Wes would likely burn the garment in one of the ranch's late-night campfires as soon as they had the chance.

"What are you doing here, Blaze?" Colt grumbled at their packmate. If Blaze wanted to look like a pink peacock, so be it, but on Wes's wedding day, Colt knew the other wolf was doing it to rile Wes. Not that pissing off the Grey Wolf second-in-command was very difficult. He wasn't known for having a calm temper.

But as best man, it was Colt's job to get Wes to the altar in one piece, and considering the way Wes looked as if he was ready to throttle Blaze, that challenge was proving increasingly difficult.

"I came to congratulate Wes," Blaze answered.

Wes snarled.

Colt shot Wes a hard stare that may as well have said *Don't take this idiot's bait*. "That's all fine and dandy, but what are you doing in"—Colt wasn't quite sure what to call it—"that suit," he finally managed. He said *suit* as if it were a dirty word. Even to Colt, who didn't give two licks about fashion sense, calling such an atrocity a suit seemed plain wrong. It was *un*suitable in every way possible.

"How often do I get the occasion for formal wear?" Blaze shrugged.

"You call that formal wear?" Wes growled.

Colt was shaking his head. "You're not even in the wedding party, Blaze."

Wes's bride-to-be, a true cowgirl at heart, hadn't wanted her wedding day to be a tux and gown affair, so only the wedding party and Maverick, who was conducting the ceremony, would be in semiformal attire. Even the bride herself planned to sport a pair of bright-red leather cowgirl boots beneath her short, white wedding gown. It was intended to be a fun western-themed occasion, and considering the happy couple were getting officially married—official by human standards—in a traditional ceremony with only Naomi, her future husband, her brother, Jacob, and her fellow tribal members at the Crow tribe res in a few days' time, dressing up hadn't been the highest priority.

Blaze flashed Wes a playful grin. "Your future wife gave it the okay."

"My wife has a soft spot for kitschy things," Wes snarled. "But I don't."

With that, Wes turned back toward Colt, gesturing at the boutonniere.

Wes didn't have two legs to stand on when it came to making Blaze take the suit off. Wes may have been one of the fiercest wolves among these mountains, but even he was an occasional pushover when it came to butting heads with his gorgeous bride.

If you asked Colt, seeing Wes put in his place was a refreshing change of pace.

"Why do you feel the need to tie the knot anyway? You're already mated," Blaze asked.

As Wes told it, they had been since the night Naomi had become their most recent—and only human—packmember.

"Congratulations, huh?" Colt gave Blaze the side-eye as he finally pinned the daisy to Wes's suit.

"She's human. It is important to her," Wes added.

Colt brushed off Wes's collar. "There. That's about as decent as you'll ever look. Minus the hat."

Wes retrieved his dress Stetson from a nearby hook and tipped it onto his head. "It better be. She deserves more than decent."

Blaze made a fake gagging noise. "Oh, good Lord. Save it until the honeymoon."

As Blaze gave another pretend retch in the corner, Maverick strode into the room. The packmaster in formal wear looked even more out of place than Colt and Wes did. Several of his midnight-black ceremonial tattoos—which covered the majority of his tanned torso, all the way from his wrists to the line of his neck—peeked from beneath his suit coat.

Wes chuckled. "And you said *I* looked like a Hells Angel."

Maverick shot Wes an impatient glare. "I'm only doing this at your wife's request."

"Future wife," Blaze corrected.

Maverick's gaze fell to Blaze, and the packmaster's usually unreadable demeanor twisted in a look of obvious distaste. "Take that thing off." It was the tone he reserved for direct orders. Like Colt, Maverick rarely made requests.

"I won't," Blaze quipped.

Amid grumbles of protest about wardrobe policing being a blatant abuse of power, Blaze sulked from Wes's apartment, closing the door behind him as a satisfied grin crossed Wes's lips. A moment later, the door flew open again, revealing Maeve in her bridesmaid's gown, cradling a squalling bundle of pink flesh that, upon quick glance, might have been a swaddled baby nursing from a bottle, but on closer inspection was none other than Tucker the teacup pig.

"Doesn't anyone knock around here?" Colt questioned.

Maeve stormed into the room like a force of nature, despite being barely half the size of every other person present and carrying an animal that belonged among the ranch's livestock. Sierra, Maeve's best friend and Colt's younger sister, trailed behind Maeve. Sierra clutched a seriously expensive professional camera in her hands. Colt noted she wore a dressy blue pants suit and flats rather than the spring-yellow bridesmaid's gown and heels she was supposed to be wearing.

"The bride's almost ready," Maeve announced to the three of them, as if this were unexpected, joyous news. Considering the ceremony was scheduled to start in approximately fifteen minutes and Naomi's two overly enthusiastic bridesmaids were likely to fuss over her so much they'd make the bride fashionably late rather than on time, it *was* surprising.

"We still need to go over what I've written," Maverick said.

Maeve looked at Maverick as if he'd grown two heads, and Sierra immediately defaulted to the glare she reserved solely for Maverick. Despite having followed him around like a lovesick puppy for most of her girlhood, as soon as Sierra had reached her late teens, her obvious feelings for Maverick had taken a sudden and abrupt turn. Nowadays, Colt was certain there wasn't a man on this green earth who Sierra hated more.

"The bride waits for no one," she said. Coming from Sierra, it was far more threatening than from Maeve.

Maverick growled in response. Sierra was lucky she was Colt's sister. From anyone else, he wouldn't have accepted such disrespect.

Without giving the packmaster a second glance, Sierra made her way toward Colt. "You don't clean up half-bad, brother." She slugged him in the shoulder in a manner that was far more cowgirl than ladylike.

Colt grunted as he fought not to wince. Sierra's

strength was in part a gift of James and Sonya's pure Grey Wolf genetics—the previous commander's blood-line was among the purest of their kind, except only for the Grey family themselves—but Colt supposed *he* was in part to blame for honing her fighting skills. With his training, Sierra had become the pack's finest female warrior, able to hold her own even among the most elite alpha males of the pack.

Meanwhile, Maeve rounded on Maverick, laying into him as only she could. Their bickering quickly deterio-rated into background noise.

"Not even Naomi and Maeve could manage to get you into a dress and heels, huh?" Colt asked Sierra. He wasn't the least bit surprised.

His sister shrugged. "I finally convinced Naomi it wasn't the best idea." She gave the DSLR camera around her neck a small shake.

Wes nodded. "I told her I'm not the most photogenic, but Naomi insisted."

"I'll make sure I catch your less snarly, scary angle," Sierra teased.

To think that Wes Calhoun—Colt's former enemy, of all people—was concerned about being photogenic. Oh, how the mighty had fallen.

Colt glanced back and forth between the two of them. "If Sierra's taking photos, Maverick's walking Maeve down the aisle, and Jacob's giving Naomi away, who am I—?"

His question was immediately cut off by the echoing stomp of Maeve's heel against the hardwood floor.

"Maverick," Maeve chastised, "you were supposed to go over your reading with Wes weeks ago!"

Maverick sighed. "I've been busy running the pack, Maeve."

"That's no excuse," she snapped before she released a long sigh. "You better make it good then. There's no time now."

Maeve's attention shifted toward the piglet in her arms. Tucker had released the bottle he'd been suckling on and was grunting and sniffing at Maeve with his milk-damp snout.

"Tell me you're not bringing that thing to the ceremony," Maverick said.

Maeve frowned. "Of course not. But he needed to be fed and rocked to sleep beforehand. He can't go to sleep without it." She cooed at the wiggling pink beast in her arms.

Maverick swore. "He's a damn pig, Maeve. He's happiest in a pile of—"

"Enough, you two," Sierra scolded. "I better see all of you in your places in the next five minutes so I can take pictures before the bride arrives, or it will be the end of you." Sierra barked out the order, waving them toward the door.

In response, the whole group followed her lead, the packmaster included.

And to think their father had raised *Colt* to be the commander.

Maverick was shaking his head. "She's still convinced there's such a thing as a 'teacup' pig," he grumbled at Colt as they moseyed out into the hall.

"You'll be sorry when he stays all adorable and tiny and wants nothing to do with you," Maeve shot back. Her voice was followed by a high-pitched, keening pig squeal.

"I doubt that," Maverick said.

Colt grinned as he followed along behind them, but as they reached the door, he hesitated. He caught Wes by the shoulder and pegged his packmate with a hard stare. "You ready for this?"

Wes grinned. "Why wouldn't I be?" He glanced at his boots and placed his hands on his hips, refusing to look at Colt. "But if it wasn't for you, I wouldn't be—"

"Save it until after my speech." Colt raised a hand. "Now, I'm only going to say this once, so listen close. I'm happy for you." He slapped hands with Wes, pulling the other wolf into a hug.

"Soft doesn't suit you." Wes chuckled.

"Or you." Colt grinned. "So we're even."

Colt broke the brotherly embrace between them as he clapped Wes on the shoulder. "Go get her, you mangy mongrel."

He may not have been a true Grey Wolf, but Colt loved his crazy packmates all the same, and the thought of his true identity being exposed, of ever being forced to give them all up, to give up this life, knotted his insides. Even if that meant giving up a woman who crumbled the armor he'd placed around his heart.

Chapter 14

TEN MINUTES LATER, COLT WAS SERIOUSLY REGRETTING the preliminary nature of that thought. All the pack was in attendance. Hundreds of Grey Wolves sat in folding chairs decorated with white satin covers and yellow silk bows, waiting for the ceremony to begin. The wooden trellis under which they sat was decorated with twinkling lights and arrangements of gerbera daisies and sunflowers. The air bustled with anticipation.

Everyone appeared happy, content, excited. Everyone except the two men standing beside Colt. He stood next to Wes and Naomi's brother, Jacob Evans, a hulking, human ex-Marine and cowboy, who from the scowl plastered across his face was every bit as thrilled with his sister's pending nuptials as he was with the fact that her groom was a werewolf.

Wes didn't look that much better.

"Apparently you didn't succeed in talking her out of it," Wes smirked.

"No." The answer from Jacob made it clear he wasn't interested in discussing the matter further, especially not with Wes. From what Colt had heard, Naomi's revelation of Wes's true nature to her brother several weeks ago hadn't gone well.

"If you ruin this for her, I'll gut you myself," Wes grumbled.

Jacob's lip curled in response. If looks could kill…

In Wes's defense, he had tried to get Jacob to like him. Well, as much as Wes Calhoun cared that *anyone* liked him.

Colt raked a hand through his hair. Just what he needed. To break up a brawl between the groom and the bride's brother all of five minutes before the bride arrived. Why had he ever agreed to be best man?

"Take your place," he muttered to Wes. One rough shove between the shoulders, and he was urging Wes down the aisle. Best to separate him from Jacob while they were both still breathing. Colt cued Blaze to hit the music.

Pachelbel's "Canon" pumped through the speaker system, and Colt gestured Maeve and Maverick down the aisle. But then he saw her.

Belle was standing arm in arm with Maeve on the opposite side of the aisle while Sierra snapped pictures of the two of them. The flashing strobe of the camera lit her creamy skin from within, highlighting the pale-pink blush of her cheeks, and for a moment, she was so breathtaking, Colt couldn't bring himself to look away.

What was it about this woman that tore to shreds all the walls he'd erected to protect himself? Every time he looked at her, a deep ache filled his chest, a longing he hadn't felt before. One night should have been enough, but it wasn't. It would never be. Not with her.

He sighed. She'd been here less than twenty-four hours, and already Maeve, Sierra, and Naomi had pulled her into their ragtag group of females. They were all troublemakers, the whole lot of them.

Colt stalked toward her without a thought about who was watching. As he reached her, her eyes grew wide, and she let out a little *eep* noise that reminded him far too much of what she did when the prickle of his beard tickled between her thighs.

"What are you doing?" he growled. He placed his hand on her lower back and guided her away from Maeve and Sierra. The other two women stared after them curiously. "What part of lie low don't you understand?" he whispered.

Belle's lips cinched into that familiar pucker. "I tried, but if you don't understand how this happened, apparently you don't know Maeve or your own sister." She scowled at him.

He *did* know them, and he wasn't in the least bit surprised they'd railroaded her.

"Try to keep your distance from me then."

"More romantic words have never been spoken." She huffed. "But that'll prove difficult."

"Why?" he asked.

"Because we're walking down the aisle together."

Which meant he'd also have to dance with her at the reception.

This reeked of a setup.

Colt shot a glance toward Maeve and Sierra. Immediately, Maeve grabbed Maverick's arm and headed down the aisle with him, leading the start of the wedding party, but his sister only smiled a cheeky grin as if to say *sorry, not sorry*, before she snapped a shot of Colt and Belle. The flash left multicolored dots swimming through Colt's vision. When he got Maeve and Sierra alone, he'd give each of them a proper dressing-down about the consequences of meddling in people's love lives.

"I think that's our cue." Belle nodded toward the aisle.

With no other choice, Colt extended his arm toward her. As Belle's hand wrapped around the bulk of his bicep, even through the suit coat, his body immediately responded to her touch. He'd been with plenty of women, but never before had his wolf responded so eagerly. All it took was one brush of her hand, and he was ready to throw her over his shoulder like a caveman and carry her off into the nearby woods.

It was damn unnerving.

Colt led her forward, but when they reached the start of the aisle, Wes and the other members of the bridal party waiting for them at the end, Belle clutched his arm with all her strength and attempted to spin him in the opposite direction.

Colt refused to budge. "What are you doing?" He kept his voice low as they made their way down the aisle.

Belle's eyes were the size of saucers. "No one told me the groom was Wes Calhoun," she whispered.

Of course, she would recognize Wes. During the first few months she'd been with the Wild Eight, he would have been her packmaster. Colt's gaze shot toward the groom. Wes's eyes flicked from Belle to Colt, and he cocked a single *what the fuck* brow.

Colt shrugged. Leaning back toward Belle, he whispered. "It'll be fine. He's harmless."

The longer Belle stared at Wes, the more the color drained from her face.

"You've spent the night with me, Belle. You've braved worse than a wedding with Wes Calhoun as the groom." With that final word to her, they parted. Belle took her place behind Maeve, and Colt stood next to Wes.

"Don't ask," he mumbled when Wes looked at him.

Everyone stood, rising in expectation of the bride.

And then…they waited.

Eventually, Blaze had to pause the music. Wes appeared to be more anxious by the second, starting to pace at the altar, and Belle was so pale at this point that she could pass out at any moment.

Colt leaned across the aisle toward Maeve. "I thought you said she was going to be on time."

Maeve shook her head. "She said she was going to be. I don't know what—"

The sound of a horse's pounding hooves broke the silence. Everyone turned toward the noise. Naomi rode up on Black Jack, Wes's ornery beast of a horse, looking every bit the country cowgirl bride. The hem of her white dress was speckled with mud, and she was wearing her bright-red cowgirl boots.

She dismounted, hopping down from the massive beast with a thud, before she plastered a large smile on her face. "Sorry I'm late," she announced. "This asshole decided to break out of his pen at the last minute." She cast a sidelong glance toward Black Jack, who gave a sneering huff.

Hooking her arm on Jacob's, Naomi grinned. "Let's get this show on the road."

―――⁘―――

At least she didn't have to wear heels. Belle crossed her legs at the ankles, thankful for the comfort of the crafted brown-leather cowgirl boots she was wearing. She'd been trying to imagine all the ways the evening could possibly be worse, but at this point, the heels were about all she could think of.

Following the sunset ceremony, the wedding party and guests had been led to an outdoor reception area for dinner and dancing. A wide garden trellis covered in hundreds of glittering lights lit up the night and the dance floor. Tables with white linen tablecloths and bouquets of giant yellow sunflowers provided seating.

Belle slumped down in her chair and tried to shrink behind the table's centerpiece, but she knew she was failing—miserably. Every time she moved, the halter neckline of the too-tight bridesmaid's dress pushed the large expanse of her cleavage forward, placing her breasts front and center.

As if she'd needed any help in that department.

Though Naomi, Maeve, and Sierra had insisted the dress's empire waist and flowing material would accommodate Belle's ample curves, that had only accounted for her lower half. And considering her already large breasts were a bit fuller of late, the effect was only exaggerated.

If it hadn't been her newfound friend's wedding night and if the females of the Grey Wolf Pack weren't so persuasive, she might have strangled all of them.

In any case, she prayed everyone was too focused on the bride and groom on the dance floor to notice her. Her eyes fell to the groom in question, and her stomach turned.

The groom.

As if she could have forgotten. She shrank even lower behind the centerpiece. Grabbing her champagne glass, she longed to down the bubbly contents in one large gulp, but she couldn't. Belle had been shocked enough to be walking down the aisle arm in arm with Colt, who was apparently Sierra's older brother. But when she'd laid eyes on Wes Calhoun, nefarious supernatural

outlaw and former packmaster of the Wild Eight, now
Grey Wolf second-in-command and Naomi's newly-
wed husband, she'd nearly fainted. It'd been years since
she'd last seen the former packmaster in the flesh. He'd
left the Wild Eight only a handful of months after she'd
fallen headfirst into Wyatt's trap, but they had met on
more than one occasion.

She only hoped she wasn't significant enough for him
to remember her. She'd only been Wyatt's girlfriend at
that point, not their official physician yet. She hadn't
been worried about Colt giving her true identity away,
but seeing the Grey Wolf second-in-command was a different matter entirely.

When the bride and groom's dance ended, a chorus
of cheers and wolf whistles broke out among the guests
as Wes pulled Naomi into a deep kiss so heated that it
caused Belle to blush. Seizing the moment of distraction,
Belle dashed out of her chair, bringing the champagne
glass with her. With any luck, she could leave the party
without being noticed, head back to the temporary cabin
they'd assigned her, and wait until the party was over.
Maybe then she could skate beneath attention.

She slipped through the crowds of people to the edge of
the reception area. As she reached the shadows of the surrounding night, she stopped and scanned the party as she
unceremoniously poured the champagne into the grass.

Suddenly, a large hand grasped her wrist, pulling
her into the darkness. Her small shriek of terror was
drowned by the loud sounds of country music blaring as
guests took to the dance floor. Her wolf eyes immediately adjusted to the darkness. Colt leaned over her, so
close, it made her skin burn hot.

"Do you have something against champagne?" His wolf eyes flashed gold. "I believe you were looking for me."

Wearing a dress Stetson and a well-fitted suit that highlighted the breadth of his shoulders and the lean muscles of his hips, he looked far too delicious for any woman's good. But with his wolf eyes glowing liquid gold in the pale moonlight and the rim of his Stetson casting further shadow on his handsome features, show-casing just the hint of his wicked grin, she knew he was anything but a gentleman.

A reminder of all the things he'd done to her, the ways he'd made her moan, seared through her. She struggled to draw in a breath.

She wasn't sure how he interpreted her silence, but he eased back, the shadows shifting until his face came into clear view. "I thought I told you to lie low, not make yourself noticeable. You'd been doing a decent job until tonight."

"I was trying to do that until you decided to man-handle me. I was about to head to my cabin." Her words were harsh, totally unlike her, but that was what he did to her, wasn't it? He unleashed some sort of fire in her that she couldn't even begin to understand.

The side of his mouth quirked in an unapologetic grin. They both knew he hadn't manhandled her. Every time he touched her, there was a tenderness that belied his unyielding strength. The gentleness and restraint were so out of place with a hardened cowboy like him that it melted her insides to mush.

"How could anyone not notice you in that getup? You look stunning, Belle." His eyes swept downward, lingering for a moment. The memory of his mouth on her breasts, the heat of his lips as he'd gently tugged on her nipples with his teeth, flashed through her mind, and she flushed.

He must have known what she was thinking, because his grin widened.

"It was your friends' idea. Naomi and Maeve can be very persuasive." It was the only excuse she had to offer. "And your sister, Sierra, is no better."

From the gleam of heat in his eyes, she had a sudden suspicion being good at persuasion was a common trait among the Grey Wolf pack.

"You looked very much at home among the Grey Wolves. You're blending in well."

She almost laughed. "Then I was doing a good job of acting, considering I was trying not to pass out or vomit on the groom's shoes." She shuddered. "You could have warned me Wes Calhoun was the new Grey Wolf second-in-command."

"I didn't think to, but don't worry about Wes. He won't give you away. I'll see to it."

"I thought you wanted me to stay away from you."

"I didn't say that was what I wanted. I said that was what you *should* do." That mischievous grin crossed his lips. "If you know what's good for you."

Silence passed between them, awkward and full of tension.

"What do you want, Colt?"

He nodded toward the dance floor. The shadow cast from his Stetson hollowed his cheekbones further. "A dance with you. The wedding party is up next, and I intend to take full advantage of it."

"I already told you I was leaving." She didn't think

she could stand another second of him looking at her like that, like she was beautiful and worthwhile, not after what had passed between them in his apartment. Not with what she was hiding. Hurt seared through her. She pushed past him, heading out into the night.

"Belle," he called after her.

There was something in the tone of his voice that stopped her in her tracks.

She felt him approach behind her, padding across the grass. The gentle spring breeze blew through her hair.

"I was harsh before. The way I treated you. It was..."

The muscles of Belle's shoulders tightened as she fought not to turn toward him. She'd never heard him hesitate before.

"It was uncalled for," he continued, "but you caught me off guard." He paused again. "I'm sorry if I hurt you. I can't say that wasn't my intention. I thought it would make pushing you away easier, but it didn't, and I regret it."

His sincerity caused a lump of emotion to clog her throat. The graveled, strained quality of his voice told her it'd been hard for him to say. Alpha males like Colt Cavanaugh didn't make a habit of apologizing.

"I would have said you never let your guard down."

"I have a rougher time keeping my guard up when it comes to you." There was a hint of pain in those words. She faced him.

"Please." Those gray eyes softened from steel to the color of the Montana sky during a thunderstorm, breathtaking and conflicted. "Just one dance. Let me make it up to you. I'll grovel and tell you what a dick I was being and everything."

She fought down a chuckle. It made her angry that he could make her smile again after he'd been so cruel before, but she couldn't help it.

Removing his Stetson for a moment, he ran his fingers through his hair before placing the hat back on his head. As he did so, his armor snapped back into place. The walls he'd erected to keep out the rest of the world had been raised again, clear as day. All she ever saw of the true Colt Cavanaugh were little glimpses. Enough to keep her intrigued and coming back for more.

He tipped his Stetson down low. "If you do it right, dancing may as well be a precursor to sex."

She bristled. So much for any sign of tenderness. "So that's what you want? To sleep with me again?"

"No, I'm saying that's why I haven't danced with anyone else."

Colt Cavanaugh might have been a valiant warrior willing to risk his life for her—on more than one occasion—but he wasn't going to ride her off into the sunset on the back of Silver. She'd known that from the start.

So why did it still disappoint her so much?

"I have a rule against sleeping with the women at Wolf Pack Run. Too much potential for complication," he said.

"You have a lot of rules."

He swept a hand over his tie, straightening it. "I appreciate order."

She nodded. "Right. Control freak."

So that was the only reason. Not that he didn't want to dance with anyone other than her. Of course that would be the case.

You knew who and what he was when you went to bed with him, Belle. No point in crying about it now.

"I know what you're thinking, Belle, and no, that's not the only reason." He read her like she was a novel he'd long ago memorized. "The more important reason is I find my tastes have been somewhat singular as of late." He eased closer, and a blush crept up her neck.

"I know the fact that I'm a Rogue makes me a pariah among pack wolves like you and your packmates, and you've already made it clear you don't want me, but you don't have to rub it in. I know your type, Colt. You said it yourself. We've had our one night together. I may as well be used goods to you." The truth of how she'd been feeling this whole miserable evening spilled forth like an uncontrollable wildfire. Her voice was raised, but she knew with the country reception music thumping, no one could hear her.

Colt's features hardened, and he practically snarled his response at her. "No." He was shaking his head, and his jaw drew so tight, it seemed as if his teeth might crack. "If you think I have such a low opinion of you, then you know nothing about me at all." His hand shot out, and he grabbed hold of her wrist gently yet firmly as he tugged her back toward the party.

"What are you doing?" She pulled back slightly, but it was clear he wasn't letting her go.

"Staking my claim," he answered.

There was no use arguing. He'd made up his mind, and she knew when he did, the man was immovable. They were at the edge of the reception area, and he led her out onto the dance floor. The next song was cueing, and a slow country ballad blasted over the speakers.

Before she could stop him, he'd tugged her into his arms, pulling her against him. His large hand cupped her lower back, and he pulled her flush against his chest. The top of her head barely reached the height of his shoulder, and then they were swaying. He led her around the dance floor with ease.

Of course, he would.

"Staking your claim?" she whispered. "Like a dog pissing on something?"

He eased back enough to glance down at her. "Well, I am a wolf, but even I'm not quite that kinky."

Belle threw back her head and laughed. She couldn't help herself. She needed a good chuckle if she expected to make it to the end of this song. When the last of her laughter shook through her, his eyes were still on her.

"Do you see that?" he asked.

"See what?"

"The way they're all looking at you."

She scanned the crowd. He was right. Many of the Grey Wolves were glancing their way. "It's because I'm not one of them."

Colt spun her into a smooth twirl and then caught her again. "That may be true for some of them, but it's more than that. When you laugh, Belle, that delicious blush fills your cheeks and you light up the whole room."

"Coming from the man whose grin puts Tom Cruise to shame."

He turned that exact grin on her. All white teeth and charm. "You're not the least bit undesirable, Belle. Second only to the bride, you've been the belle of the ball all night, and that's only because no woman ever looks better than on her wedding day."

"Belle of the ball. Aren't you punny?" she joked.

He grinned. "You know what I mean." His hand slid to the curve of her spine.

She shook her head. "It's because you're making me look desirable."

"Maybe so, but I couldn't do that if I didn't believe it myself."

Heat pooled between her legs.

"I thought you said there could be nothing between us."

He twirled her and then caught her again. He was an expert dancer. The same way every movement, every word of his was practiced, except for those occasional glimpses of the real him.

"And there can't be, but that doesn't mean I'm going to let any of my packmates have you either. I refuse to share."

She misstepped and nearly landed on his foot, but he caught her. "So let me get this straight: You don't want me, but no one else can have me?" She rolled her eyes. "That makes perfect sense."

"I never said I didn't want you, Belle." He tore his gaze away from her, staring out into the crowd. "There are things even I can't share, because of my position."

"That's cryptic." Her heart thumped hard in her chest at the prospect of him wanting her, and she fought to ignore it. She looked up at him. "Can't share or won't?"

He held her gaze, refusing to look away. "Both."

"And that's supposed to be enough for me?" The music slowed, starting to fade out, but he didn't seem to notice.

"It has to be. I never promise anything more." He hesitated. Something in his eyes softened. "Even if I want to."

"But that was before." She gazed up at him, willing him to understand the words she left unspoken.

Before we had a connection, before it was clear there was something between us. Before I thought you may have died, and it tore me to pieces.

...before you meant something to me.

His Adam's apple bobbed in his throat as he swallowed down the emotion. He knew exactly what she meant. She saw it in his eyes, which meant he'd felt it, too.

"Do you know what happened to me when the vampires took me captive?" he asked.

She had no idea, but she had her fears. "No."

A darkness overtook his whole demeanor. "They tortured me, but I refused to surrender to them."

Her heart ached for him. He might have been stubborn, irritating; he might have hurt her, but no one deserved that. "I'm so sorry, Colt."

His lips twitched, fighting a snarl. "You know I don't like pity, Belle. That's not why I'm telling you this." They were still swaying. "Every time I'd feel like breaking, there was one thing that would give me the strength to keep going."

"What was that?"

"The memory of the night I spent with you." His eyes captured hers, searching her soul for answers. "We barely know each other."

"We've been through more together than most people have in a lifetime."

"Maybe you're right, but we've only spent one night together, yet every time I thought I was about to die, it was your face I would see and that's what kept me going. Why is that?"

Butterflies fluttered in her stomach, threatening to leave her speechless. "Maybe because we're friends?"

He chuckled. "Friends. Is that what you'd call us?"

"Wouldn't you?" She blinked.

"Friends," he mused. Lowering his voice to a whisper, he leaned into her ear. The heat of his breath tickled over her earlobe and neck, sending shivers down her body. "I've never met a friend I've wanted to fuck more." He pulled away. "But that doesn't change anything."

She was struggling to draw breath. "Colt, everyone is staring."

He was looking at her as if she were the only other person in the room. "I already told you, Belle. How many times do I need to say it? You're breathtaking, and I don't do dances. Of course, everyone is staring."

"No. That's not what I mean."

He raised a brow.

"Colt, they're staring...because the song ended several minutes ago."

And yet he was still holding her.

Chapter 15

BELLE COULDN'T QUITE REMEMBER HOW SHE AND COLT separated. He might have muttered some vague excuse to release her as someone called out his name, but the next thing she knew, she was standing alone on the dance floor. Her head was still as clouded as if he were still in front of her.

"May I cut in?"

The question came from behind her. Before she could answer, she was in someone's arms again, and they were definitely not Colt's.

"Wes," she breathed.

"Belle," he acknowledged, sweeping her onto the dance floor at arm's length.

Her stomach churned. Caught up in a dance with him, there was no way to escape. And she knew full well that had been his intention.

"Shouldn't you be dancing with your bride?" she asked. It was a pathetic attempt, but she had to try.

He nodded to where Naomi was dancing with a man who was clearly related to her. "She's dancing with her brother this song, and considering he didn't manage to talk her out of marrying me, now that the deed is done, he's likely pushing for an annulment."

She couldn't imagine why. Everyone knew Wes Calhoun was a man no one crossed, and if someone did, well…they didn't live to tell the tale. "He's a brave man."

Wes chuckled darkly. His gaze drifted to his wife and lingered there appreciatively. "I've grown more patient over the years. Besides, he'd lost that battle long before I met him. Naomi and I were already mated." His attention shifted back toward her. "So should I call you Elizabeth Beautane, since that seems to be the alias you're going by these days?"

"It's not entirely an alias. That is my legal first name."

"The devil's in the details."

Or dancing with me, she thought.

"So how does my former pack's physician show up in my wedding party under an alias, claiming to be a Grey Wolf, only twenty-four hours after she arrives at the pack?"

She shrugged as best she could while keeping pace with him. "The wedding part was your wife and her friends' doing. As for the alias and the Grey Wolf part, you'll have to take it up with Colt."

"Colt." He smirked. "Not Commander, though I'm not surprised after that little display. Seems like you have Commander Casanova's full attention."

Commander Casanova? Oh God, they *all* called him that?

She feigned innocence. "I don't know what you mean."

Wes shook his head. "Don't play coy with me after crashing my wedding, Belle. How do you and Colt know each other?"

I had a wild hot night with him, and now I'm carrying his baby...

"It isn't crashing if your wife invited me, and like I said, you'll need to take it up with Colt." There was no way she was getting into this with Wes freaking

Calhoun. Not now. Not ever. The only person on this green earth she found more terrifying was perhaps Maverick Grey, and it was a toss-up.

"I will. After the wedding." His eyes found Naomi again. "Tonight, it's all about her. But in the meantime, Belle, you should know that Colt is a brother to me. I knew when we met before that you were harmless. Wyatt had you so wrapped around his finger that you couldn't see what you were getting yourself into."

"But *you* knew." It was an accusation, plain and simple.

Something in his eyes darkened. "It wasn't my job to babysit some Rogue she-wolf who wanted a taste of living on the Wild side, and I had my own demons to contend with."

"Where are you going with this, Wes?"

"The Wild Eight changes people. I know that first-hand. I won't say anything to Maverick—running to our packmaster isn't my style." He stopped dancing abruptly, lowering his voice to a low, threatening whisper as he released her. "But if you hurt Colt, I won't hesitate."

Belle stiffened. Stepping away from her, Wes navigated his way across the dance floor, leaving Belle standing stupefied in his wake. She watched from a distance as he approached Colt. Wes leaned in to whisper something to the commander, and the two men grinned.

Belle watched Colt and Wes with their faces side by side. They looked eerily similar. Typically, one wouldn't notice it. Colt had gray eyes and dirty-blond locks so close to brown that his beard was, in fact, brown, while Wes was as golden blond and blue-eyed as they came, so their coloring was entirely different. If the two men had been across the room from each other, she would have said there were only minor similarities, but seeing them so close together, she realized how wrong that was. There was a slight difference in facial structure and coloring, but the shape of their eyes, the way they crinkled at the edges as they smiled, the masculine curve of their noses, and most notably, the wry, mischievous nature of those wide, white-toothed grins were nearly identical.

Wes's words echoed in her head.

Colt is a brother to me.

Not *like* a brother but *is* a brother. That minor distinction changed everything.

Belle froze. She ceased to hear the music or sense the movement around her, the party stilled in her mind as the weight of her realization flooded over her. Her heart thumped in her chest, her pulse racing. It all made sense now. Why a Grey Wolf high commander would give any thought to the innocence of a Rogue she-wolf with ties to the Wild Eight.

She thought she'd escaped the Wild Eight, but it was only taking a new form.

She needed to get out of here right now. She couldn't deal with this. After Wyatt, she'd sworn to herself she'd never go down that path again.

You don't know anything for certain, Belle. Calm down, she chastised herself.

But she couldn't, because just as she was about to flee the party, Colt's cold, steely eyes found hers, and she knew in an instant her suspicions were correct.

Colt Cavanaugh, high commander of the Grey Wolves, and the man who'd saved her life, wasn't a Grey Wolf at all. Maybe he was now, but he hadn't been born to the pack.

As Belle stared into his eyes, she knew. Wes was Colt's brother, which meant Colt was a son of Nolan Calhoun. And he was no Grey Wolf.

He was Wild Eight through and through.

Belle turned on the heel of her boot and ran.

She didn't stop until she reached the cover of the nearby forest, panting and struggling for breath. Until a large hand clapped over her mouth.

"What did you say to her?" Colt snarled at Wes.

Moments earlier, he'd watched Belle run from the party like someone had lit a fire beneath her boots. Something had spooked her, and considering Wes had pulled her into a sudden—albeit brief—dance moments before that, he had an idea exactly who the culprit was.

"Nothing awful. Just told her if she crossed you, I'd turn her in myself."

Colt glared at Wes as if he were about to rip his head off.

Wes frowned. "She's Wild Eight, Colt. That's my game, and you know it. What do you want her for anyway?"

Since the Wild Eight's dissolution, Wes had been in charge of the few prisoners who'd surrendered themselves to the pack. They were attempting to reintegrate them as Grey Wolves, but it would be a long process before they were fully involved in pack life.

Lifelong allegiances didn't disappear overnight.

Colt growled. "Nice one, asshole. If anything, you should be more worried that I hurt her, not the other way around." Colt shoved his recently drained champagne glass into Wes's hand. "Do me a favor, Wes, and stay the fuck out of my love life."

Wes quirked a brow. "Love life?" He let out a long, low whistle.

Colt snarled in response. "Just keep your mouth shut and stay out of my business, Wes."

"Oh, man, you're done for." The groom chuckled. "Been there, done that, brother, and look where I am now."

Wes was still laughing at Colt's expense as Colt prowled across the dance floor. He'd deal with Wes later. They may have been sons of the same monster of a man, but that didn't mean Colt wouldn't tear Wes a new one.

Colt plowed after Belle, searching through the darkness for her. He was several meters outside the reception area when he heard the scream. If he hadn't decided to go after her, he might not have heard it, but he'd know that sound anywhere. He recognized it from when the vampire had attacked her in the clearing.

"Belle!" he shouted.

Racing toward the trees, Colt shifted midrun, bounding toward the source of the noise. His pulse thrummed into overdrive. He needed to reach her, protect her. He followed the sound and her scent a short way into the woods. Running faster than he ever had in his life, he burst through the pines and found Belle surrounded by Dean and the other wolves assigned to the evening's patrol. They'd clearly arrived only moments before he had. She was lying at the base of a massive oak, her whole body shaking as she curled among the gnarled roots of the tree.

Colt shifted back into human form, immediately rushing to her side. "What the hell happened?" he ground out.

Tears streamed down Belle's face, and she was shaking from head to toe.

Dean shifted into human form, throwing his hands

into the air. "We found her like this. You know as much as we do."

Gripping Belle's shoulders, Colt forced her to look at him. Her face was red and blotchy from crying, and her eyes were so wide and scared that it took everything in him not to howl in anger.

"What happened?" he demanded.

"S-someone grabbed m-me from behind."

Colt turned back toward his men. "Search the woods," he ordered. When they didn't move, he snarled. "Now."

The men scattered, fanning out in search as Colt drew Belle into his arms. She was trembling harder than if she'd been dunked in ice water.

"They…they covered my mouth," she continued, "and then I bit them, so they uncovered it, and I screamed. I…I thought I was going to die, but then they heard you yell and they…disappeared."

"Who was it, Belle? Vampire? Werewolf?"

She shook her head. "I don't know. I know it sounds crazy, but even though only one set of hands grabbed me…I smelled…both." She collapsed against him, sobbing.

He drew her in to him, cradling her against his chest as if he could shield her from the cruelty of the world. Whoever had attacked her, he would bleed them.

"What did they say, sweetheart?"

"They said"—Belle inhaled a shaky breath—"'You're no Grey Wolf, you Wild Eight bitch.'"

—◆◆◆—

Colt paced across his apartment again. It was likely the hundredth time he'd done so in the past fifteen minutes. Much more, and he'd wear a hole in the floor.

Belle huddled on the sofa, an old quilt Sonya had once made for him wrapped around her shoulders and a mug of Earl Grey sweetened with honey in her hands. The mug, a previous Christmas gag gift from Sierra, read *At Least I'm Good Looking...* He may not have spent more than his first five years with his birth mother, but he knew from when she'd come home from meeting with Nolan that there was little that wasn't made better by the soothing qualities of a blanket and a steaming beverage in hand.

Colt had instructed his men to search every inch of the Grey Wolf lands. Luckily, the music had drowned out the ruckus and they were able to use the guards on hand, so the incident hadn't interrupted the wedding, and thankfully Belle wasn't injured, just shaken up.

His men had covered the immediate area where Belle had been attacked, yet the search proved fruitless. Whoever had attacked her was skilled enough to ghost a mission when plans derailed, and they'd done so without a trace. Nevertheless, Colt wouldn't allow the Grey Wolf soldiers to rest until they exhausted every possibility.

"You're certain you can't recall anything else? Any indicator of who could have done this?" Belle's shaking had subsided, and they needed to get to the bottom of this.

"I told you already. It was all a blur. It happened so fast. I smelled both vampire and werewolf, but there was one set of hands on me. That's all I know."

He'd been hoping she'd recollect the details once the initial shock waned, but that didn't seem to be the case. Not that he blamed her. Eyewitness accounts were notoriously unreliable, let alone in a dark forest and when attacked from behind. But what irked him was what the bastard had said to her.

You're no Grey Wolf, you Wild Eight bitch.

Colt snarled at the thought. That single phrase left him with more than a passing suspicion about why she might have been targeted. But he couldn't articulate that truth to her. Not without revealing his own darkness.

"This reeks of Lucas and his men. It would be just like them to target someone they thought they could overpower easily."

He'd anticipated a counterstrike after his escape. Perhaps they'd seen Belle as she'd escaped from the cabin and recognized her? The pattern among Lucas's choices wasn't lost on him. First him, the only Wild Eight fully hidden among the Grey Wolves, and now Belle, another Wild Eight hidden among the Grey Wolf pack—and they'd chosen to attack her on the night of a known Wild Eight leader's wedding, no less. They were threatening to expose him for who and what he was, but how did they know? He wagered the exposure was all for revenge, but the question remained: Why did they need Wild Eight blood specifically for their sick experiment in the first place?

"Do you have any other enemies, Belle?" Sure, this reeked of Lucas, but if Colt was going to protect her—and he was—he needed to cover all bases.

"You mean besides the Grey Wolves?" Belle stared into the depths of her tea mug. The dark liquid inside nearly sloshed over the edges, but the way she examined it, she might as well have been reading the dregs of the tea leaves.

"This wasn't a Grey Wolf." He trusted the pack more than that. They might be wary of outsiders, but no Grey Wolf would have done this, especially since they all thought she was a Grey Wolf—save for Wes, who had a stable alibi at the time and wouldn't have lifted a hand against a woman.

Belle shook her head slightly, barely acknowledging him. She was hiding something. He'd known when they first met that she'd been on the run, though the fact that she didn't trust him enough to tell him the truth stung. She'd been right earlier when she'd said there was something between them. He couldn't bring himself to consider what it was, but even a known rake like him couldn't deny it.

Everything about her had been different from the start. Every touch, every grin, every intimate moment heightened. In a way that meant something, made it matter.

Made *her* matter, as if some invisible force had pushed them together from the start.

He shoved the thought aside. No. It didn't matter, because they couldn't be together. That was the basic truth of it. Glancing toward her, he watched her sip from the steaming mug. Maybe she feared repercussions from her attacker if she told the truth. Maybe reassuring her of her safety was the best recourse.

"First thing come sunrise, we'll go to the Missoula ranch with a small group of my best warriors. Austin and Malcolm are still there, holding down the fort. They'll help, and keep your identity quiet, if I ask them to."

At this, her attention snapped toward him.

"If whoever attacked you decides to try again, we'll be there to protect you, and being away from Wolf

Pack Run where the other civilian packmembers could become casualties in any potential blowback is another consideration. The Missoula ranch is the best option. Plus, since the massacre, they've only had a skeleton crew working their ranch. With calving starting any day now, they'll need a few extra hands."

"Why help me, Colt?"

He didn't know why, but the look she gave him made him feel as if they were strangers all over again. "It gives me the excuse I need to run a recon mission on the vamps. I can't do that right here under Maverick's nose when he's given direct orders against it. Once I have the information I need, he and the Seven Range Pact will have no choice but to launch a counterattack."

It was true. He'd been formulating the idea since Maverick first told him the news of the Pact's decision, long before Belle had been attacked or even arrived at Wolf Pack Run. It was a thinly veiled excuse.

And she knew it.

"Bullshit," Belle muttered before she drew another sip from the tea mug. She set it down on his coffee table with a little more force than necessary. The surface of the liquid threatened to spill. "You may not like it, Colt, but at this point, I can see through the mask you wear, and I call bullshit."

Colt's shoulders tensed. She'd been cutting through his armor from the start, but he didn't contradict her.

She pegged him with an expectant stare. "What's the real reason? Why are you being so kind to me?" Belle's eyes narrowed as she watched him, as if he were from some alien planet, a creature she'd never seen before. He knew firsthand that for a Rogue female like her who'd fallen into the hands of the Wild Eight, kindness wasn't plentiful, but this seemed different.

"First you saved my life in that clearing and nearly got yourself killed in the process," she said, "and then you set me free, and now you're offering to help me again. Why?"

"Because it's the right thing to do..." It was the only explanation he had to offer. He wasn't sure he knew why himself. The image of his mother came to mind. He would have given anything for someone to have helped her escape the clutches of the Wild Eight.

"And you always do that? The right thing?" Her tone dripped with accusation, but he had no clue what she was getting at. Clearly, she was pissed, hurt even.

"If this is about what I said before, I'll say it again, Belle. I'm sorry. I'll say it till I'm blue in the face. I know that doesn't negate the pain I caused, but—"

"It's not that." Belle was shaking her head. She reached for her mug again, taking refuge in it. She took a long sip. "I'm just pointing out you're not the perfect altruistic hero you paint yourself to be."

Had those words come from anyone else, he could have believed them, but from Belle, he almost laughed. She'd seen more of the real him than perhaps anyone ever had. "That I paint myself to be, huh?" He threw the question back at her. "I've never claimed to be a hero, Belle. I've been saying that from the start. You, on the other hand, are one to talk."

She glared at him. "What's that supposed to mean?"

"You act as if everything you do is saintly, self-righteous. Saving the lives of the Wild Eight? That was the right thing to do, too?"

"If you're trying to make me feel bad about what I've done, Commander, save your breath. As I told you already, the Wild Eight may have been monsters, but I don't regret any of the lives I saved, not for a second. I swore an oath. As a physician, it's my duty to value life, not to pass judgment and determine who's worthy of my care."

"And they were worthy of your care, the Wild Eight?"

"No more or less worthy than you are."

He froze. "You'd liken me to those murderous scum?" So she *did* see him for what he truly was. A monster born of blood and violence.

She laughed. "Coming from the man who has been lying to me from the start? I know the truth, Colt."

"What the hell are you talking about, Belle?" Whatever it was, clearly, tonight's events had brought it to the surface.

She didn't answer, but he wasn't letting this go.

"What were you running from when you left the party, Belle? Why were you out in the middle of the woods?"

"Because I was trying to run away," she answered. "I was planning to leave Wolf Pack Run."

He'd told her before why that was a poor decision. It would draw suspicion, but she knew that, which meant apparently something had negated that consideration. He drew closer. "Why? Because of what Wes said? He's all bark, no bite, Belle. Not anymore. And I know him. I promise he—"

"This isn't about Wes!" she yelled. She was shaking again.

But he couldn't understand it. He was offering to help her, to protect her, yet she was treating him as if he'd wronged her from the start.

Now that she was talking, she couldn't seem to stop. "It's about the fact that you haven't been truthful with me from the moment we met." Her eyes were full of hurt and anger as she lashed out. "I should have known there was a reason a Grey Wolf commander would be so kind to a Rogue like me. It couldn't have been out of the kindness of your heart, could it? But I was stupid enough to believe it, just like I was stupid enough to believe all the promises of the Wild Eight!"

She was standing now, shaking from head to toe.

He raised both hands in the sign of surrender. "Belle, I have no idea what you're talking about, unless you tell—"

"I know the truth, Colt!" she yelled.

Colt froze.

No. She couldn't possibly know. There was no way. She...

Her chest heaved in and out from her labored breaths, as if it took everything in her to speak aloud. "I realized it when I saw you and Wes standing next to each other. It's why you've made every choice you have from the start."

Colt's pulse raced, thrumming in his temple until he nearly heard it echoing in his own ears. "And why's that?" He needed to hear her say it. It'd been well over twenty years since the words had been spoke aloud. He and James had agreed never to discuss it.

"From the moment you met me, you haven't been truthful." She shook her head. "You're not a Grey Wolf, Colt Cavanaugh. You're as Wild Eight as they come."

—◦◦◦—

"Who told you?" Colt snarled.

Anger radiated off him, feral and palpable. The

tension between them was so thick, Belle could have cut it with the knife at his belt.

"Who told you?" he growled again.

"So you're not denying it?" Her worst fear was confirmed. A complicated swirl of emotions hit her. Anger, hurt, fear, pain. How could he have been lying to her this whole time?

"I may not have been forthcoming from the start, Belle, but I'm no liar." The vein in Colt's temple ticked a strained beat. He looked ready to tear into something, to maim, to kill.

She didn't know how she hadn't seen it before. The violence in him he barely contained, the rage of an alpha male. It was so Wild Eight; he reeked of it.

"No one living knows about this. Not Maverick. Not Sierra. Not even Wes, and the man's my brother."

Belle harbored more than a passing suspicion he was wrong on that last point, considering it was Wes whose word choice had tipped her off, but that was family business she had no intention of springing on him, not when he already looked as if his anger was strong enough to rip the world in two, the ground beneath them crumbling all the way to the earth's core beneath only his bare hands.

"No one needed to tell me. I put the pieces together myself." Her hand fell to her belly. She tried not to think about what that meant for their potential child. "That's why you were willing to help me from the start. Must be a hard life as a double agent, lying to all the people who love you. My guess is you were using me to pay some sick debt to your birth pack. Was that it?"

As soon as the words left her mouth, she regretted

them. She was being ridiculous, yet she couldn't stop the emotion. She was doing exactly what he'd done to her, attempting to push him away when things got too real, instead of facing the fact she'd broken every promise she'd made never to get involved with the Wild Eight again.

Even now that she knew the truth, she couldn't lie to herself. She cared about Colt, Wild Eight or not, and after what she'd been through with Wyatt, that fact terrified her.

Colt's jaw clenched and his upper lip curled in rage, but to his credit, he didn't so much as raise his voice at her. His tone was cool, calm...distant. "I'll say it again, Belle. If you think so little of me, then you don't know me at all. I may be one of those monsters, but I've been loyal to the Grey Wolves since before I knew the full meaning of the word."

He exhaled a long breath. Whatever he was about to say, it pained him.

Deeply.

"How could I ever be loyal to the Wild Eight? I may have been sired by Nolan fucking Calhoun himself, but any loyalty I had to him flew out the window the night he murdered my mother."

Belle's heart stopped. A lump crawled into her throat as she realized the implications of what she'd done, of how deeply she'd hurt him.

A watery quality glassed over Colt's steely gray eyes, but he didn't dare shed a tear. Life had hardened him so much that she saw he couldn't even allow himself that simple refuge.

"I was only five years old when I watched him

murder her," he whispered. His breathing was ragged, scattered, and at the sight of his raw pain, tears poured down her cheeks. His pain was so clear, it tore straight through her. He'd been hurt by them, too, far worse than she had ever been.

Oh Lord, what have I done?

She wanted to go to him, but she knew better. If she reached for him now, he would only push her further away, and rightfully so.

"James Cavanaugh, then high commander of the Grey Wolves and the man I now call my father, found me that night, sobbing over my mother's corpse." He spoke the words as if in a trance. Though he was looking right at her, he was somewhere else. Lost in a distant nightmare that *she* had forced to the surface.

"That night, the Grey Wolves were trying to target Nolan when he went to visit his mistress, that being my mother. Nolan was officially married to Wes's mother at the time but keeping my mom on the side. It's my understanding that Wes's mom died shortly thereafter too, though whether at Nolan's hands or not, I've never asked."

Belle swallowed the lump in her throat. "Is that why he killed her? Because the Grey Wolves were coming?"

Colt didn't answer. She could see he was still too lost in the hell he'd lived through.

"James and his wife, Sonya, took me in," he confessed. "James told everyone I was his son from an affair he'd had with a Grey Wolf woman before he and Sonya were married. Everyone believed him. They had Sierra shortly thereafter."

"Does Sierra know?" she asked.

Colt shook his head.

I know what it's like to be on the outside looking in. His words echoed back to her. Every bit of it made sense now. She knew what it was like to be born an outcast, but even she had her mother to love her, to accept her, someone she could depend on. How must it feel to become a lie he'd been forced into and then live that lie every day, hoping and praying that the family he now called his own didn't find out? To fear that they would hate him? Cast him out?

This powerful alpha standing in front of her might have been a formidable force of a man, but he'd never known true love, acceptance. Not even from his own family.

Belle ached for him. His own adopted sister didn't know the truth, yet she had wanted—no *expected*—him to tell her, and unknowingly compared him to those who had taken everything from him. When really all he'd been was afraid to show his real self to anyone.

She'd never forgive herself. She had to fix this. Had to make this right.

She eased toward him. "Colt, I didn't know. I—"

"Don't." He drew back from her as if she had him cornered. "It's my deepest secret, Belle. James died years ago, and on the night he took me in, I swore to him that I'd never sully the Cavanaugh's pure Grey Wolf bloodline or his memory by ever telling a soul. I owe my entire life to the man, so you can understand why I didn't tell you, and why…" His voice trailed off.

…And why we can't be together.

She understood that now. With her ties to the Wild Eight, willful or not, if anyone ever found out, he'd lose everything. His position, his family's reputation, the pack he now called his own...and the family that had saved him.

Tears continued to pour down her face. They wouldn't stop. "I'm so sorry, Colt. I—"

He raised a hand, tearing his gaze away from her as if he couldn't stand to look at her. "Don't, Belle. We're even now."

The admission that she'd hurt him tore her in two.

Prowling past her, he headed for the door of his apartment, still refusing to look at her.

"Colt," she pleaded.

"We leave for the Missoula ranch first thing come sunrise." Without another word, he closed the door behind him, leaving her standing there desperate for how she could ever make this right.

Chapter 16

THE RAIN COMPLICATED THINGS. COLT LEANED ON THE OPEN barn door, staring out at the pasture as the sky opened. He'd ridden in only moments earlier, barely escaping being drenched from head to toe. The gentle patter of the fat raindrops hitting the ground echoed inside the barn, and the scent of damp spring grass hung in the air. At least they'd managed to get most of the ranch work done. The rain would cause minor issues with visibility on the recon mission tonight, and the damp evening wasn't favorable calving conditions, but he enjoyed the sound all the same.

A sharp whinny drew his attention. Colt turned to find Wes's horse, Black Jack, baring his teeth at a goose who'd taken refuge in the barn. Silver was watching the other horse with disdain, his tail raised high and haughty as if Black Jack's petty antics were beneath him.

"Leave the goose be. It's more his home than yours," Colt grumbled at Black Jack. He'd had it to the end of his rope with the ornery beast. He wished he could say the four bites healing on various parts of his body, which Black Jack had caused over the past six days, were love nips or because the horse was homesick and missing his rider, but Colt knew better. Black Jack was an asshole, plain and simple. It was no wonder Wes was pissed off all the time.

Since Black Jack and his own prima donna of a horse

maintained an ongoing feud, Belle had mainly been caring for Silver and serving as his rider since they'd arrived at the Missoula ranch, which meant at least Silver was pleased as punch. It gave Colt plenty of excuses to avoid being alone with her, on account of the fact that Black Jack and Silver might rip each other a new one. But that feat grew more difficult with each passing day. Sure, he and Belle had had plenty of interaction, but it had been cordial and only in the presence of his men. And his men weren't much help on this front. They were so friggin' charmed with her that it bordered on obnoxious.

He couldn't blame them when she was constantly flitting around, lending an extra hand with the ranch work, tending to minor wounds, and even making lunch for them on occasion. It was obvious she was trying to make herself useful, and the soldiers loved it. The real kicker had come yesterday afternoon when she'd not only taken a shift monitoring the calving shed, but also somehow still found time to cook a delicious pot-roast dinner with peach cobbler for dessert.

When Austin had announced the warm, gooey dessert was orgasmic and he might be in love, and Dean had responded by offering to battle Austin for her, Colt had nearly throttled them both. The pie was the most delicious thing he'd ever tasted—aside from the woman herself— but that didn't matter. Being charmed by her was hard enough, especially now that she knew his secrets, but seeing how his soldiers adored her made it worse.

"Won't be much longer," he muttered to himself.

Silver moseyed over and rested his head on Colt's shoulder as if he too understood the struggle. Colt patted the beast's cheek. Though he was fairly certain Silver's struggle had less to do with women and more to do with a certain ornery mustang. At that moment, Black Jack decided to kick open his stall gate and all-out chase the goose out of the barn, snapping at its heels as it ran, flapping its wings and honking. Colt shook his head, and he could have sworn Silver did the same. He had no idea what Wes saw in that bastard of a horse.

Thoughts of Wes and his ornery horse turned Colt's thoughts to the pack and their safety. His men had been gathering intelligence on where the vampires stored their scientific data, and tonight was the night they would retrieve it. According to the intelligence Colt had bribed Blaze into gathering on his behalf, Lucas was still operating out of a coven not far outside the Missoula ranch. All they needed to do was get in there and find any incriminating evidence they could, and then get the hell out. Colt had mapped out the schematics, so now it was just a matter of following through with the plan.

Once they did, they could quickly launch their counterstrike. With Lucas engaged in battle with the Grey Wolves, Belle would need to go.

It's better this way. She can't stay.

At least, that was what he kept telling himself.

By nightfall, the rain had drenched the ground, creating heavy puddles and pockets of water out in the pasture, meaning the pregnant mothers were coming into the calving shed thoroughly soaked. As the temperature dropped with each passing hour, they'd need to stay vigilant and use the heater to keep the calves healthy and free of infection. And the visibility for their mission wasn't much better, but they would manage.

"Are you ready?" Colt asked.

He and Blaze were positioned in front of the several computer screens Blaze had rigged up to serve as their command center. When the time came and the controls flipped on, they'd be able to see everything through the lenses of Austin's goggles—a nifty little bit of technology Blaze had replicated based on data he had conveniently "stumbled on" while "perusing" the Dark Net and which bore a striking resemblance to the latest U.S. Army technology. When Maverick had discovered where the design originated several months earlier, he hadn't been pleased. But Blaze had gotten away with it because having a brilliant technologist and hacker on their side was integral to besting their enemies and staying off human radar. It didn't help matters that Blaze was also an alarmingly talented warrior for someone who spent most of his time perched in a desk chair.

Blaze cracked his knuckles and neck in a show of preparedness. He flopped down into his computer seat and twisted toward Colt. After dinner, his packmate had forgone the god-awful Hawaiian shirt he'd been sporting all day in favor of his pajamas—a T-shirt that read *If you don't like tacos, I'm nacho type* and a pair of lounge pants covered in little pineapple houses and SpongeBob SquarePants figures. "I was born ready," Blaze said with an exaggerated wiggle of his eyebrows.

Colt rolled his eyes. "Sure you were." He glanced at the clock. It was two minutes before sundown, which meant they had approximately an hour before the vampires rose, when it was still shadowed enough to slip past their security. While vampires weren't cursed to roam the night and sleep in coffins, the sun did weaken them with extended exposure, so they remained mostly nocturnal.

Colt's cell phone vibrated in the back pocket of his jeans, and he reached for it.

As Colt pressed the receiver to his ear, Austin's drawling voice confirmed, "All men in place."

Colt nodded toward Blaze. "Patch them through," he ordered.

Colt locked his phone into the station dock and pulled on his headset. It wouldn't be his first time commanding a mission from a remote location, but he didn't prefer it. He considered himself a boots-on-the-ground leader, and his men rarely conducted missions without him. The way he saw it, if he wasn't regularly risking his life for the pack right alongside them, he was little more than a battle-educated figurehead. But in this case, it would have been counterproductive to the mission. He was one of the vampires' targets. Having him burst in there, guns blazing, would play right into the vampires' plans, in the event the Grey Wolves were discovered and taken captive.

Colt leaned over Blaze's station, one hand on the back of his packmate's computer chair and the other on the desk. With their combination of careful planning, superior technology, and Colt's memory of the coven's layouts from his capture, he would be able to run this mission as if he were there. He'd planned out every detail in depth.

"Can you hear me, Austin?"

"Loud and clear," Austin answered.

"Roger that," Blaze responded. "Enter from the east entrance. When you get there, scan the lock and Blaze will hack the alarm."

"Yes, sir," Austin answered. They were already on the move.

They'd drilled their plans in detail for the past several

days before Colt had allowed them to move in. Austin, Malcolm, and the others had this memorized so thoroughly that they could likely complete it in their sleep.

"Scannin' the system." Austin's voice sounded over the headset speakers.

The image of the security keypad loaded onto Blaze's screen. Blaze's fingers flew across the keyboard, enlarging and analyzing. He might be a major pain in the ass with terrible fashion sense, but even Colt had to admit that the wolf was a veritable tech genius.

"Got it," Blaze said.

On the screen, the lock clicked open.

"Damn fine work," Austin replied.

Blaze grinned. "It's sexy. I know."

"Don't stroke his ego any more than necessary," Colt instructed. "Head in. Keep right down the hall."

The soldiers slipped into the building, their night-vision goggles penetrating through the darkness. In his periphery, Colt scanned the adjacent monitor. If their scanner was correct, the three vampire guards were in place, as anticipated.

"Three vamps," Colt directed. "The first is up ahead on the right. Take him out in a choke hold. We can't have him alerting the other guards."

Colt watched on the screen as Austin lifted his hand in front of his goggles in an okay symbol. Austin shifted his attention to Malcolm and the other soldiers, directing the camera there as he went. He communicated their next move with hand signals. Colt's pulse pounded, his muscles tightening in anticipation of the kill as if he were there himself. What he wouldn't give to bleed every one of those fuckers dry…

The first kill went smoothly. Austin and the team followed Colt's instructions, taking out the first bloodsucker. They snatched the beast from behind, pulling him into a silent choke hold before staking the monster straight through the heart. The second kill didn't go quite as smoothly. The vampire noticed them as they rounded the corner, but the monster barely had time to let out a threatening hiss before Malcolm improvised, impaling the vamp's vocal cords with an arrow straight to the throat before staking him in the chest. A single vampire was no match for several well-trained Grey Wolf soldiers at once. It made the task far too easy, barely a challenge. As they approached the third and final kill, the vampire shifted on Colt's monitor screen.

"Don't move," Colt ordered. "Hold position." It was headed in their direction, but from the looks of it, it was likely to take a different turn. For some reason, the vamp was abandoning its post. "Prepare for fire and hold."

Austin lifted his gun. The forty-five fitted with a silencer wouldn't kill a vamp, but it'd give it pause, enough to slow it down until one of the soldiers could either stake it or cut off its head.

"Blaze, get me eyes on that fanger," Colt ordered.

Blaze's fingers raced across the keyboard until a second screen popped up, allowing Colt's attention to turn between Austin's view and wherever the stray vamp was headed. As Colt anticipated, the vamp turned in the other direction, leaving the path ahead clear for the team. But where the hell was the bloodsucker headed?

"Resume progress," Colt directed. "Target is up ahead to the left." It was a straight shot in. All they would need to do was reach Lucas's computer and insert the jump drive Blaze had given them. Then the were-wolf would be able to work his magic, downloading all the vampires' files from their private and protected server to the pack's own. With any luck, there would be incriminating evidence there, more than enough detail about the vampires' plans to convince the Seven Range Pact to launch a counterstrike.

The Grey Wolf team rounded the corner, easing down the hall toward the final destination point. After watching a moment of Austin signaling for Malcolm to pick the lock and their struggle with the key pins, Colt watched on the screen as the door swung open.

"We're in," Austin whispered through the intercom.

They made quick work of placing the drive in the computer's USB port. As soon as it connected, Blaze's fingers were racing across his keyboard in a fury, combining buttons and creating commands as code flashed in green letters across his screen.

"T-minus fifteen seconds," he said.

"Cut the Jason Bourne shit." Colt growled. But that was when his eyes fell to the second screen, to where the stray vamp guard had disappeared—and the crowd of half-turned he'd unleashed.

Headed straight in the team's direction.

"Shit!" Colt's instincts shifted into high alert. "Get outta there, Austin!"

Colt watched in horror as Austin ducked out into the hall. In the line of Austin's night vision, several of the half-turned charged toward them. Colt's heart thumped against his breastbone. His gaze darted to the monitor. The place was now swarming with the half-turned—bigger, stronger, and far more lethal bloodsuckers.

"Abort mission," Colt growled. "Now."

"No!" Blaze shouted. "Five more seconds, and I've got it."

"Colt!" Austin yelled through the confusion.

"Get the fuck out of there now, Austin!" Colt hollered. "That's a direct order." Evidence or not, he wouldn't deliver his men a death sentence.

"I've almost got it," Blaze muttered.

"Go!" Austin yelled to his men. He ripped the jump drive from its port with two seconds left to go. Blaze roared a pissed-off groan, but there was no time. The soldiers needed to get out of there—fast. The camera attached to Austin's goggles shook and vibrated as he ran, before one of the vamps jumped straight into his line of sight.

"Shit!" he and Colt swore in unison.

Within seconds, the camera went black.

"Where'd they go, Blaze? Where the fuck did they go?"

Blaze hunkered over his keyboard, slamming in various commands. "I don't know. I'm trying to get them back, but the diagnostic isn't responding. It's—"

"Fuck!" Colt slammed a fist onto the desk. Something had tipped them off, but he had taken every precaution, dotted every *i* and double-crossed every *t*. Now his men were in hot water—thanks to a miscall in his judgment. And for all he knew, they could be dead because of it.

Time slowed as Colt paced the front porch of the cabin they were all staying in. If those bloodsuckers got hold of even one of his men, he'd never forgive himself. Twenty minutes later when the black van tore into the drive, the tires let out an earsplitting screech. All seven soldiers unloaded from the van, carrying

Austin. Even in the darkness, Colt saw the blood staining his black clothes and speckling the gravel of the driveway. They carried him into the cabin amid a chorus of shouts. At all the commotion, Belle was running down the stairs within seconds, struggling to tie a cotton robe around herself.

"Belle," Colt breathed. For the first time in days, he locked eyes with her, pleading with her to save his packmate.

In an instant, her eyes seemed to convey everything he knew she'd been trying to get him alone to say. All the pent-up emotion of the last week. *I'm sorry. I didn't know. I didn't mean to hurt you.* And the one that slayed him the most.

I still care for you.

She knew exactly who and what he was, yet still she wanted him. All of him. He wanted to haul her into his arms and kiss her for everything she was worth, but it still wasn't that simple. She gave a single nod, with a promise in her eyes of *We'll talk later*. Charging past him, she became the perfect ray of calm and focus in the storm.

"Out of my way," she shouted, pushing through his men. They cleared a path, and she went straight to Austin's side. Immediately, she began assessing the wolf's wounds. With her wolf strength, she ripped Austin's shirt open, revealing a gaping wound where it appeared a vampire had taken a large chunk out of him.

Colt swore. Belle, on the other hand, didn't so much as flinch.

"I need scissors, a clean washcloth, thread, a needle, tweezers, and alcohol for sterilization, stat," she ordered.

When his men didn't immediately pay attention to her, Colt snarled.

"You heard the woman!" he barked.

Everyone rushed to fulfill Belle's requests as Colt lingered on the other side of the couch, allowing Belle enough room to tend to Austin.

Austin's eyes flickered open. "Colt," he rasped. "They were everywhere. They... We didn't get..." Austin reached for him.

Colt clutched the other man's hand in reassurance. "I know. It was my fault. I—" But there was something clutched inside the other man's fist. Colt eased the item from Austin's hand, holding it up. The USB drive.

"Give that here," Blaze demanded. He'd been standing at the edge of the room with his laptop clutched near his chest. "I may still be able to get something off it." He tore the USB from Colt's hands and immediately shoved the drive into his computer, cursing the entire way about only having needed two seconds longer.

Colt shifted his attention back toward Belle and Austin as several of the soldiers returned with her supplies. Shoving a towel into his hand, she directed him with ease. "I need you to hold this. Put pressure on the wound to slow the bleeding."

He did as she instructed, aware that doctor or not, she was the only person in the world he not only welcomed but wanted to hear order him around like that. From her, he'd accept anything she was willing to give him, because she saw him, truly saw him. In the way he'd longed for when he'd been strapped to the vampires' table. And yet...

His gaze circled back to his bleeding packmate. "Will

he be all right?" He thought he already knew the answer to that, but he needed to be certain.

"Yes, he'll be fine," she reassured him. "Just keep that pressure steady, Colt."

Colt. Not Commander.

In that moment, he swore to himself never to allow her to call him Commander again.

Chapter 17

BELLE WRAPPED HER JACKET AROUND HERSELF AS SHE EASED out into the dim lighting of the porch. The pale-yellow glow of the overhead light cast the covered wooden wraparound in shadows, and several flies buzzed near the porch light. Save for the cold of the Montana spring nipping at her hands and feet, the rustic, country feel reminded her all too much of the low twangs and smooth talking of the South she'd once called home.

Save for the virile and handsome cowboy leaning against the porch railing with his back to her.

She drew her jacket tighter around herself to brace against the chill. With Austin cared for and stable, she'd put her bloodstained nightgown and robe in a bath of cold water in hopes of getting the blood out, and then she'd changed back into her clothes. The screen creaked shut behind her.

"I expected you'd be asleep by now," Colt drawled.

It was only a few hours until sunrise, and she'd been making a habit of going to bed early the past few days. In part, it'd been because she wanted to rise and help with the ranch work in the morning hours when they needed the most hands, but it was also because she couldn't bring herself to linger post-dinner when it was clear Colt had no desire to converse with her.

"Most of the men are asleep," she said, explaining her

presence. "Blaze is the only one still awake. I heard him in there still swearing as I came out here."

Colt grumbled. "I suppose that means it's my shift for the calving shed, then." The cows had started dropping calves shortly after they arrived, and the number of delivering mothers increased with each passing day. As a result, the calving shed needed to be checked every two hours to ensure the deliveries were progressing and the calves being birthed maintained a stable condition. Oftentimes, a mother didn't have the wherewithal post-birth to lick them clean as she should, stimulating their breathing and heart rate, or the mother on occasion was unwilling or unable to nurse.

"Actually, it was Austin's turn, but he's obviously unable at the moment. Malcolm and Dean both volunteered, but they all looked so drained after the mission that I said I would do it."

"How's Austin doing?" Colt asked.

She smiled. "Same as the last time you asked. Stable. He'll heal in a few days. Nothing a few stitches couldn't take care of, though he'll have one hell of a scar. That vamp really took a chunk out of him."

Colt nodded, turning to stare out into the darkness of the night again. "They favor you, you know. The soldiers. You've been kind to them."

"They're more cowboys than soldiers, the way they behave." She chuckled.

She saw a hint of a smile tug at his lips. "You're likely right, but they love you all the same."

"There's only one cowboy's love I'm interested in." Her smile faltered. She'd been trying to get him alone all week, to tell him how sorry she was, to explain herself. But he didn't appear interested.

The muscles of his shoulders stiffened beneath the taut material of his suede jacket. He turned toward her, his gaze searing into her as if he were searching the depths of her soul. "You can't possibly mean that, Belle."

She crossed her arms over her chest, shielding herself. "I can, and I do." She met his stare, holding a stiff upper lip even though everything in her made her want to cry, to sob with the weight of all the emotions she'd been holding in. She stepped toward him.

"Belle," he warned.

"I'm sorry, Colt." The words rushed forth as if she'd lifted the dam off a raging river. "I never meant to hurt you like that. I was shocked and hurting myself because I felt like you'd lied to me, but once you told me the truth, I realized how unfair I was being, and I—"

Colt was shaking his head. "Save your apologies, Belle. I'd already forgiven you the moment it happened."

She gaped at him. But if he'd forgiven her, then why had he...? "I thought you were angry, so angry you didn't want to speak to me. I was worried you'd never want to talk to me again."

"I can't say I wasn't hurt, but I couldn't blame you for making the assumptions you did, especially not after the way I behaved when you showed up at Wolf Pack Run. Had I been in your position, I would have thought the same myself. And..." His voice trailed off as he tipped his Stetson off his head, running his fingers through his hair in that way that gave him the most delicious kind of bed head.

He was so handsome. All kinds of perfect western charm.

"Hell, how do I say this?" He swore under his breath before he finally looked at her. "Belle, I've already forgiven you for any wrong you'll ever do me a thousand times over. How could I not?" There was a deep sadness in his eyes that made her breath catch. It was everything she'd hoped to hear in one single look.

I want you. I care about you, and nothing's going to change that.

He didn't need to say it aloud.

"You saved me," he said.

She forced a laugh. "Colt, you've saved my life more times than I can count. You don't still think you owe me for when I patched you up after that vampire—"

"No." He cut her off with the shake of his head. "That's not what I mean." He worried the brim of his Stetson in his hands, struggling to find the words. "When the vampires held me captive, it was the thought of the night we spent together that kept me going. And I...I can't begin to tell you how much I'm grateful for that."

It was the most romantic thing she'd ever heard, so full of emotion, it made her heart ache. And she'd never been more relieved. Tears poured down her cheeks. She couldn't stop them now.

He placed his Stetson back on his head. "Sweetheart, don't cry." He stepped toward her, and that was all the invite she needed.

She rushed to him, throwing herself into his arms without hesitation. She wrapped herself in him, burying her face in the hard muscles of his chest as she curled her arms around his middle. He was strong and warm, and he smelled like warm spices and the hard work of a male, and she could drown in it. A steady ache thrummed in her heart, radiating all the way down to the tightness in her womb.

She wanted to tell him, but she had no idea how. She supposed the best place to start was with the truth.

"Colt, I—" She let out another sob as he cradled her against him. "There are some things I need to tell you."

He rubbed slow, steady circles on her back that made her melt into him further. He was so gentle for a man she knew wielded so much power. "I already told you, Belle. You don't need to apologize or explain—"

"But I do," she interjected. She eased away from his embrace. "There are things you need to know." Inhaling a deep breath to draw strength, she gathered every bit of determination she held deep down inside her. She'd start with the easiest parts and move forward from there. "When we first met, I…I lied to you."

Colt tensed, but she continued.

"You asked if I knew anything about the death of Wyatt Maxwell. You mentioned the Grey Wolves wanted to know who killed him. You asked me if I knew anything, and I…I lied." Her hands clenched into fists as she struggled to speak the truth. "When I first joined the Wild Eight, Wyatt and I were dating. Things quickly went south, and when I tried to leave, I found out being with a monster like him meant I wasn't allowed to walk free. We fought and fought, and eventually I managed to leave him—but I couldn't escape the Wild Eight. There was another wolf, an older woman, Dalia. I mentioned her to you before, but there's more to the story than I initially let on. I couldn't abandon her to his ill use."

She inhaled a deep breath. "I thought I could protect her from him. He viewed her as a burden. Wyatt didn't care for anyone who wasn't a benefit to him, but I didn't think he'd go so far as to hurt her. She would sometimes get confused come evening. She had sun-down syndrome. It's a symptom of dementia that gets worse as the day winds down into evening, causing nighttime confusion. He gave her some pills, and then I found her…" Her lip quivered. "I confronted him, and you know Wyatt. He wasn't about to take any lip from a woman. He came after me. I was certain he would kill me. He had me on the floor. He was hitting me sense-less. I was scared he would kill me, but I managed to get ahold of his gun, and I…"

"I should have told you," she breathed, "but I was scared, and I…" She forced herself to meet his gaze. "That's why I reacted so strongly when I found out you were Wild Eight. I should have known better than to lump you among their numbers after you saved me and after we…"

After we made love.

It was no tryst. To either of them. She knew that much.

Tears filled her eyes. She knew he couldn't possi-bly understand what she was crying about, but at the sight of her tears, something in Colt's hardened, cold features softened.

As if he cared. About her. A Rogue. A prisoner. A fugitive.

As if she wasn't all the nasty labels that life's unfor-tunate circumstances had stuck her with, but instead, a woman who desperately needed help. Not that he knew all those things about her, but that somehow failed to matter.

Before she knew what was going on, he pulled her into his arms again. His warmth wrapped around her, as if he could shield her from the outside world.

"I won't hurt you, Belle, and I won't tell a soul. You're safe with me."

His words shocked her, but she heard the sincerity there.

"Why?" she sobbed into his chest. "Why would you bother to help me? All this time, I haven't been truthful, and I…" Another sob raked her.

"That bastard deserved to die more than most." Colt's tone held a hint of violence, as if he regretted he hadn't been able to do the honors himself. "I tried to kill him myself a few times," he admitted, "and you may be full of sass, Belle, but if a gentle woman like you resorted to doing what you did, I have no doubt he deserved it. Any man who lays a hand to a woman does." He hesitated, and even though she couldn't see his features from where she'd buried her head into his chest, she heard the pain and vulnerability in his words as clear as day. "And no one deserves to live their life in fear that others will find out who they really are."

He reached down and, with a gentle hand, tilted her chin until she met his gaze. Her breath caught.

"Why are you scared, beauty?" he whispered.

That single question undid her. No one had ever bothered to ask her that single all-important question: Why?

Why she was so afraid? Why she was running? Why had she killed Wyatt?

No one ever dared ask her why.

Until this dark, mysterious cowboy. A wolf who had saved her life countless times, as if it were something worth saving.

She opened her mouth to speak, but his eyes flashed to his wolf's. Something predatory and feral glimmered in their depths. She would have told him everything then, confessed it all.

She'd been in want of a pack. The mountains of Montana had called to her, offering her a home in her wolf's native lands, but when she'd arrived in Billings, she'd been so desperate for the acceptance from her fellow wolves, a privilege she'd never known, that she'd fallen into the wrong hands. Wyatt had been kind to her at first, welcoming her into the Wild Eight with open arms. She'd served as their physician. But as time passed and she'd realized the nefarious dark nature of the Wild Eight wolves, she'd tried to leave.

But she couldn't. Wyatt wouldn't let her.

For years, he'd controlled her in a way that she was ashamed to admit, because she *should* have been stronger, but she wasn't. She hadn't been strong until the night she'd confronted him, until she'd defended herself and Dalia.

She couldn't have known that a mere week later, the majority of the Wild Eight would be wiped out in a battle with the Grey Wolves, only a handful of surviving members being taken captive and even less, herself included, remaining at large. She also couldn't have known that her reputation as their physician, as a key member of their pack, despite being forced to stay with them under threat of her life, would follow her all the way to the Missoula ranch where she ran for refuge, where they had heard of her crimes and made their accusations.

Traitor.

Murderer.

She hadn't thought of it that way until they'd said it. If you asked her, the act was self-defense, her one last chance at escaping Wyatt's clutches.

In that moment, she would have told Colt Cavanaugh, high commander of the Grey Wolf armies, all this.

If he hadn't chosen that exact moment to capture the nape of her neck in his hands and kiss her. He'd kissed her before, but this was different. This kiss was filled with everything between them that had previously been restrained. The fullness of their emotion, their desire, their need. It was a kiss that didn't shy away from the truth, that offered full acceptance, even when they were both at their most vulnerable.

As their tongues mingled and he gained entry into her mouth, she melted into him, her body seeming to mold into his. They kissed so long and deeply that she felt as if they were there for hours, him holding her against him as they explored each other.

When he finally released her, she rested her head against his chest, reveling in the warmth of his arms.

"I know I said there shouldn't be anything between us, but I..." He fell quiet, leaving the words unspoken, but she knew.

She shook her head. "I understand now."

He wanted her, far beyond a one-night stand. She knew that now, but she also understood why they couldn't be together, how being with her would force him to give up his pack unless he wanted the truth exposed, yet she still had hope...

Butterflies stirred in her belly. A reminder of what was at stake.

"There's something else I need to tell you," she whispered. Now was the right time, even though she was terrified of his reaction. She feared he might push her away, but she knew it was a risk she had to take. She'd always felt it was right to tell him. So much had gotten in the way of that.

He chuckled low and deep as he nuzzled the bristle of his beard across the top of her head. "After that revelation and the hell of a night we've had, I think I've had about all the truth I can stomach for now. Can it hold till morning?"

She didn't want it to, but she supposed she could wait one more day. She didn't want to shock his nerves for the night any more than necessary, even though she had a feeling Colt was made of far tougher stuff than even a rough night like this. "Only if you promise that I won't have to wait longer than that. I should have told you long before."

"Morning," he agreed. "I promise."

Easing away from her, he leaned against the porch, adjusting his now-skewed Stetson. She'd nearly knocked it off his head as she'd thrown her arms around his neck when his lips met hers.

A beat of silence passed between them, the air fraught with tension.

"You go on to bed," he urged. "I'll take care of the calves. You did a fair amount of work already on Austin. Get some sleep."

"After a kiss like that, I don't think I could sleep, even if I tried."

That wry grin crossed his lips as if he was thinking of more that would keep her awake. "Well, in any case, someone has to go out and check the shed, and after that attack at Wolf Pack Run, I don't like the idea of you out in the pasture alone in the middle of the night."

Thirty minutes later (even though it was no more than a six-minute ride), they'd managed to wrangle Black

Jack into submission after several bouts of bucking and snapping every time they tried to place a boot in one of the stirrups on his back. Belle had suggested they just bite the bullet and walk, but Colt had been intent on mastering the ornery beast.

"Wes said this asshole of a horse prefers when he rides bareback, but I'm not giving this bastard any leeway after how much he's bitten me this week," Colt had said. "I'd just as soon leave his ornery ass in his pen, but you saw the tantrum he pulled when he thought we'd take another horse over him."

Belle chuckled. There really was no winning with the mustang.

"I'm never agreeing to watch that beast for Wes again," Colt was saying as they entered the calving shed.

A distressed-sounding *moo* interrupted him, and they both exchanged a knowing look as they picked up their pace. Heading to the end of the stalls, they found one of the cows lying in her fresh hay, making a horrible keening sound.

"Who did the last check?" Belle asked.

"I did." Colt eased into the pen with her.

She passed him one of the arm-length gloves, and he checked the cow's progress. "She's about at the same point she was before. I think the calf's stuck." He muttered curses under his breath.

But Belle was already pulling on her own arm-length glove and easing past the stall gate. She moved past him. "Allow me."

Colt was crouched down beside the cow. "You think I haven't done my fair share of getting one of these critters unstuck from the birth canal?"

She shook her head. "No, but who would you rather have with an arm up your vagina? A cowboy or a trained physician?"

"Neither." He chuckled. "Not that I think she much cares either way." He nodded to the ailing beast. "I'll try to keep a good hold on her."

Belle eased down to the lower half of the cow's body, checking what she could see from the outside.

"I can't believe you said the word 'vagina,'" Colt muttered.

Considering she was staring straight into the cow at the moment before reaching up to check the calf's position, the comment struck her as ridiculous, even though she knew what he meant.

"Don't be such a jerk," she said, laughing. "It's a medically accurate term. Even *I* can say that."

"But not 'pussy'?" he teased.

Had she been in any other position, she likely would have blushed, but she was a bit preoccupied. "I did say it," she said, but only under sexually delicious duress.

The calf was hooked on the mother's pubic bone. Once Belle reached its hooves, the mother could finish the delivery. Her hand wrapped around one of the calves' ankles.

"On three," she said, counting down. "One. Two. Three."

She gave a hearty yank. The cow let out a long, distressed *moo* as the calf slid further down into the birth canal. Belle eased back. Already she could see the mother pushing to birth the calf.

"You're not half-bad at that," Colt said as she stripped off her gloves.

"There was a time when I considered being a

veterinarian, but orthopedic surgery pays better." She shrugged. "Plus, I have a softer spot for cowboys than I do for animals."

Colt grinned.

They stayed a bit longer, waiting until the mother delivered her healthy calf before they put it under the heater to dry off, then checking on the others who were in the shed but hadn't yet progressed into the full labor. When they finished their chores, they tried to rope Black Jack, but the horse wasn't having a second of it. They ended up walking back in companionable silence as the first hints of the sun peeked over the mountain skyline. When they reached the cabin, Belle sat on the old bench porch swing and beckoned for Colt to sit down beside her. He did, and they sat together for a while watching as the sky started to light up with streaks of orange overcoming the deep, midnight blue.

"It's amazing, isn't it?"

"You mean the view?" he asked.

She nodded, though when she glanced at him, she realized he hadn't been looking at the sunrise. He'd been looking at her.

Heat filled her cheeks, and she pulled her gaze away. "Yeah," she said. "The sunrise, but I also meant the cattle giving birth. It may be messy and difficult, but every time I see it, there's still something amazing about new life being brought into the world, don't you think?"

It was the truth, but she was also curious, feeling him out to get his impressions. She knew watching cattle deliver a calf wasn't the same as a woman giving birth, especially if it was your own child, but she wanted to know what he thought about it all the same.

"Yeah, I suppose it is." He left it at that, and even though she'd agreed she wouldn't unload the full truth on him until they'd gotten some rest, she couldn't stop herself from pushing a bit further. "I'm assuming that means you want kids of your own someday?" He watched her from the corner of his eye.

She grinned. "Oh yeah. Tons of them. A whole house full if I had my druthers."

He chuckled and leaned back into the seat, slinging an arm around her shoulders. "You know, even though you're a Rogue, that doesn't surprise me in the least."

She raised a brow. "And why is that?"

"You like caring for others. That's what makes you a good doctor, and it's also why they're all so crazy about you." His gaze flicked to the doorway as if to indicate his soldiers. "For a Rogue, you sure do fit right in to pack life."

A deep ache opened in her chest, making her feel raw. "I've always wanted a pack," she admitted.

His gaze snapped toward her, and he looked a bit confused. "I thought you said you didn't need anyone. That—"

She shook her head. "I know I said that, but it wasn't the truth. I said it to protect myself. A pack is the one thing I can never have, and I…" She struggled to speak around the lump in her throat. "If I pretended I didn't want one, I thought that would make it hurt less." She drew air into her lungs, yet somehow it hurt to breathe. "I guess that's why I want such a big family. If I can't have a pack, then maybe I can find another wolf to help start a pack of my own, you know?" She swallowed down the massive lump in her throat. "Do you want kids?"

She knew it was unfair to ask when he had no idea

what the question meant to her, but she couldn't bring herself not to.

"No."

The answer was short and curt.

"My role as commander isn't suited to it, so I've never considered it a possibility. A mate and a family would be a liability, something our enemies could exploit, and I wouldn't want to put someone in that position. And well...I mean...you know the truth. I don't think I could be with a woman who didn't know, but if she did, then she..."

"Then she wouldn't be a Grey Wolf," she finished for him.

He'd never be with her. She'd known that from the moment he'd confessed his true identity, and she wasn't about to ask him to leave his pack, the one thing she'd always longed for, and the only thing he'd ever had, in order to be with her, even if she was pregnant with his child. Even as much as that hurt.

She couldn't do that to him.

"No." He shook his head.

When she didn't look up at him, he gently gripped her chin. "Belle, look at me."

Her eyes were watering, filling up with tears, but she looked up anyway. When she did, what she saw there shocked her. His normally steely eyes were so soft and gray that they reminded her of rolling thunderclouds. "I was going to say because she wouldn't be you."

Chapter 18

COLT'S GAZE FIXATED ON HER LIPS. ONE SECOND, HE HAD been thinking about capturing Belle's lips with his own, and the next, her lips were on his, her mouth gentle and probing against the hardened set of his jaw. Her smooth, creamy skin brushed against the rough scratch of his whiskers. *She* had kissed *him*.

Colt growled, a low and aroused grumble as he buried his hands in the soft tangle of curls at the nape of her neck. He wanted to draw that sweet tongue of hers deep into his mouth, tasting until his cock throbbed with need and he lost himself enough to bury himself deep in the heat between her legs. But he couldn't.

He broke the kiss between them. Her breath came in short, ragged pants against his lips. His own breathing wasn't much better.

"Belle," he purred. Their lips were so close, he could feel the tender flesh brush against him as he spoke. "Belle, you know we can't do this again."

"Why not?" she pleaded, easing closer.

The raw need in her tone shook him, causing the ever-growing ache in his cock to pulse. He leaned away from her, putting some much-needed distance between them. "You know we can't be together. More than one night, and we both know we'll get too wrapped up in this to want to end things. It's already hard enough as it is. I don't want to hurt you more."

"Bullshit," she said.

Colt blinked at her.

"Bullshit," she repeated. "When we were at the cabin, you told me that all the women you've slept with, that they knew what they were getting themselves into, knew you didn't do relationships yet they chose to be with you anyway. How is this any different?"

His upper lip twitched in frustration. How could she compare herself to any who came before her? "Because you're different. You mean something to me, Belle. Those other women, they never wanted me, not the true me. They wanted my reputation, my position, for me to be another notch on their bedposts that they could brag about." He fought back a snarl at the rumors his love life had created. "Commander fucking Casanova, remember?" he grumbled. "I couldn't have cared about those women beyond one night, not the way I do with you. I've told you that much, and I won't take advantage of you."

That was the end of the discussion as far as he was concerned, but she wasn't having it.

"It's not taking advantage of me if I want it."

She was testing every limit he had. He wanted her so much. Wanted to take her hard and rough right here on this porch. Why did she have to make this so difficult?

"What do you want from me, woman? I've already broken every rule for you, shown you parts of myself I never wanted to show another living soul. Every day, I struggle not to be like the wolf who sired me. I won't start now by using you for my own pleasure when I can't promise you more. We've had our one night. We'll leave it at that. It's already caused us enough trouble as it is."

"Is that what I am to you? Trouble?" she asked.

"No, Belle. That's what *I* am to you. One night together, and already I can see you've got your eyes on forever. But my circumstance won't change." He shook his head. "Making love to you again when I know you want more wouldn't just be cruel. It'd show you exactly how much of a monster I am, and I have no intention of doing that."

He moved to stand, but she caught him by the arm, urging him back down onto the bench of the porch swing.

"Nolan Calhoun may be your father, Colt, but from the moment I met you, I've yet to see any of this monster you think you are." She gripped what she could of his bicep. Her hand barely wrapped halfway around it. "You want to know what I think?"

He was still shaking his head. "You'll likely tell me either way, so go on."

"I think you use Nolan as an excuse."

He stilled, watching her from the corner of his eye. She had no idea what she was getting herself into. But part of him didn't want to warn her. Part of him wanted to let the pieces fall where they may.

"He may have been your birth father, but he wasn't the man who raised you. I'd wager you're more like James than you've *ever* been like Nolan. You may say you're a monster, but you do that to push people away, keep them at arm's length. But I know the truth…" She placed a hand on the whiskers of his cheek. "You may be Wild Eight, Colt Cavanaugh, but you don't have a single monstrous bone in your whole body."

"That's where you're wrong."

She was so wrong. Horribly, terribly wrong.

Gripping her by the hips, he wrenched her into his lap, shoving her legs open until she was straddling the rock-hard length of him. She let out a breathy little moan as he rubbed against her. His words were a dark, sinful promise. "You want to see what a monster I can be, then fine," he purred. "I'll show you." He fisted her hair, pulling her down as he ground against her. She practically whimpered with want of him, her eyes pleading.

"I may care for you, Belle, but I'll never be the kind of man who calls in the morning."

"I'm not asking you to be." She bit her lower lip, drawing his attention there in a way that made his cock throb. "Take me," she whispered. "Touch me. Fuck me."

He growled. He knew she'd chosen that dirty word just for him. "You deserve more than what I have to offer."

"I don't care," she breathed, leaning against him. The soft mounds of her breasts pushed flush against his chest. "I want you, Colt. All of you."

If she wanted him at his worst, his darkest and dirtiest, then he'd give her exactly that.

His order was dark and feral. "Get on your knees."

Belle's eyes widened. A hint of an amused smile curled on her lips as she blinked at him. "Excuse me?"

"You heard me." He leaned forward, lifting her from his lap to set her firmly on the porch in front of him. She stood, watching his every move.

"Get on your knees, Belle," he purred again.

He saw her immediate urge was to resist his commanding tone, but that hint of a grin told him a part of her was thrilled by it. He wasn't requesting her submission—he was demanding it. And from that spark in her eyes, she loved it.

She eased down in front of him, reaching for his belt buckle. With painfully slow movements meant to torture him, she undid the clasp, loosening the button and lowering the zipper of his jeans until the length of him sprang forth.

She gripped him at the base, and an aroused moan rumbled in his chest. A bead of moisture gathered at the tip as she stroked his shaft. Dipping her head down, she swiped off the salty drop with a flick of her tongue.

Colt's head fell backward, and he let out a satisfied groan. The feel of her mouth on him was exquisite. He buried his hands in her hair, tangling the dark curls in his fingers.

Her soft lips grazed over the tender flesh, kissing and nuzzling against the thickness of the head until he was barely able to control himself.

"I love this darker side of you," she whispered against him as she trailed delicious kisses over the length of his cock. "Just as much as the gentleness I know you're capable of."

She held him at the base again, drawing him fully into her mouth. Her tongue was hot and wet against him, the heat of her mouth doing wild and unimaginable things to him. Her tongue massaged the tender underside of the head, hitting that spot that drove him crazy with want and made his balls tighten in anticipation.

He watched her as she worked over him, drawing him in and out of her mouth until he was the one bucking with need. The porch swing acted as a horrible temptation, allowing her to glide easier down the length of his cock as she drew him all the way back near her throat.

When he started to think he couldn't take anymore,

she drew back, blowing a gentle burst of cool air across his moist skin. His dick jerked in response.

"Does this make you feel powerful? Like some big, bad alpha wolf?" she asked. Her voice was low and aroused.

He gave a barely perceptible nod. Her submission did make him feel powerful, strong and feral. She grinned at him, staring up at him with those large hazel eyes lined with thick, dark lashes.

"That's where you're wrong." She grinned. She circled her tongue over him, licking him like he was the most delicious thing she'd ever tasted. He let out a deep-throated groan.

"I'm the one in power here, Colt," she whispered, "and I intend to use it to the fullest."

The things this woman could do to him. Drawing him into her mouth again, she worked the length of his shaft until he was teetering on the brink, so close to spilling his seed into the wet heat of her mouth that he couldn't take it.

"Come here," he growled.

Lifting her with ease, he pulled her up, ripping at the button of her pants until her jeans were around her ankles. She kicked off her boots, and he used the heel of his own boot to shove the jeans the rest of the way off as he tugged her into his lap. He sheathed himself inside her and she cried out. He pumped into her, rubbing against the bead of her clit as she rode him. She was tight, so much tighter than even her delicious mouth had been, and so wet, he could barely stand it. The thought of his cock in her mouth causing that heat to blossom between her legs sent him over the edge.

He spilled himself inside her, crying out as he came.

Another few strokes of his thumb over that hot bead between her thighs, and she followed him, finding her climax in a burst of ecstasy that left them both panting.

She collapsed against him, burying her face in the crook of his neck as she nuzzled him, kissed him. Every inch of his skin felt charged and alive.

"See," she whispered against his ear. "I can talk dirty, even without the naughty words." He felt her grin against his skin.

He chuckled.

Suddenly, the creak of the porch's screen door opened, and someone padded outside. "What the hell is going on out here? Are you guys—? Shit."

Colt pulled Belle closer, attempting to shield her from view.

Blaze swore. "I can't ever unsee that," he groaned loudly, tearing back into the house.

When Blaze was good and gone, Colt eased Belle back. She'd had her head buried into his shoulder. He expected her to be mortified, though in Blaze's defense, they had been rutting like animals out in the open air of the porch. Hardly somewhere private.

A beat of silence passed between them. Belle's cheeks burned a blazing red, but before he could apologize, she started to laugh, full-bellied giggles that were infectious. Pretty soon he was laughing, too, the two of them collapsing into each other.

"Did you see his face?" Belle asked, wiping tears of laughter from her eyes. "Oh, I would have given anything to see the horror there." Another fresh round of giggles shook her.

Colt let out another chuckle. "It won't kill him.

Walking in on your packmates is practically par for the course in pack life, so he better get used to it, particularly if a lot of them are mated."

At that word, a stiff sort of silence fell between them, cutting their laughter short. The mention of mates made his heart hurt as it never had before. He'd never had a woman in his life he'd wanted to consider as a mate, but when he thought of that possibility with Belle...

Well...it made life feel really fucking unfair.

But Colt wasn't ready for their night together to end. Not yet.

"Let's take this upstairs," he suggested, "before anyone else hears us."

"I think the whole cabin likely heard the noises you were making," she teased.

Colt shrugged. "Serves them right for all the times I've had to hear them."

Pulling their clothes back into place, they made their way up to Colt's bedroom, where they made love long into the early morning hours, long past when they should have. When they were both finally spent, they heard the sounds of some of his men moving around downstairs, preparing breakfast. The scent of bacon and eggs wafted up the staircase. But they stayed hidden away, nestled in the comfort of the blankets and sheets.

Colt rested his head against the pillow, tucking Belle against the length of his body. She grinned. "I thought you didn't do cuddling."

"I don't. Not usually," he said as his eyes caught hers. "Only with you."

Their time was quickly coming to an end, but he wanted to prolong this moment as much as possible.

"So I'm not used to this cuddling-after-sex thing. What do people do?" he asked, casting a glance toward her.

Belle shrugged. "I don't know. Sometimes you just lie there. Other times you talk, make conversation about pretty much anything, sometimes the sorts of stuff you wouldn't talk about otherwise. You know, intimacy, secrets. Often the man falls asleep." At that last bit, she frowned.

She stroked her fingers lazily over his chest, tracing a handful of scars there. One he'd gotten from a battle with a Rogue cougar when they'd been helping another shifter pack with an issue they'd been having.

"Tell me about your childhood," he whispered.

She raised a brow. "Why?"

"Well, I have no intention of closing my eyes and falling asleep. Not when I could be enjoying you instead," he said. "So if that leaves conversation, why not start with the early years."

She smiled. "I grew up on a ranch in Florida with my mother, simple as that. My father wasn't in the picture, so my mom was my everything. She was an amazing mother, loving and caring, but firm when she needed to be."

"Like someone else I know," he said.

Belle grinned.

"And your mother? She was a Rogue, too?" he asked.

Belle shook her head. "By choice, yes, but by birth, no. She was a pack wolf, but she…she didn't like to talk about it. She'd run away from her pack when she was still young. I'd always hoped that some day she'd tell me who they were, but she never did, and now she's gone." She released a long sigh. "Well, the way she told it, I wouldn't have wanted to be a part of that life anyway."

He nodded. "That happens sometimes. Even to the Greys themselves."

She quirked a brow. "You're kidding."

"Nope. Maverick had an aunt, his father's sister, who ran away from the pack and never looked back. To this day, nobody knows why. It was a whole big scandal when we were kids. Too young to really understand why she might have wanted to leave."

"That's a shame." Belle rested her head on his shoulder.

A beat of silence passed. Someone was laughing downstairs in the kitchen.

"What about you?" she asked. "Tell me about your mother. What was she like?"

Colt stiffened. The thought of his mother was still a pain so fresh, he struggled to speak about it. In part because he'd never truly worked through the grief. He'd had to shove it down deep inside himself so he could be the Grey Wolf he really wasn't.

He cleared his throat. "My mother was a Rogue by birth, and she wasn't the kind of parent you could describe as amazing. She was a mess, to be honest. So wrapped up in Nolan, she couldn't see straight. It messed with her head. She didn't always take care of me the way she should have, but I loved her. There's a lot of guilt when I think of her because I…"

His voice cut off. He didn't know if he could say it. He'd never told anyone this. Not even James.

"It's all right." Belle caressed the skin of his chest and arms. "You don't have to tell me."

"No," he said, the word coming out more forcefully than he'd intended. "I want to tell you, Belle. I…I need to get this off my chest." It was such a relief to have someone know who he was and care for him anyway. He wanted to share this with her, not because he had to, but because he wanted to. Because he trusted her.

"I told you Nolan killed my mother," he said. "But what I didn't tell you was that it was my fault."

"Colt..." She reached for him.

He let her touch him, but even she couldn't take this pain away. "Don't try to tell me it isn't my fault, because it is." He drew in a sharp breath. "My mother was Nolan's mistress. He was married to Wes's mom, and from my understanding, it made her real upset to think about another woman sleeping with her man, so Nolan and my mother only met in secret. I was five years old, and I'd never met the man. I knew who he was. I'd seen photos of him, but that wasn't enough. I wanted to see him for myself.

"So one night when my mother had fallen asleep after she'd gotten home from being with him. I snuck out. I retraced her steps. I may have been small at the time, but I had a whole plan, a system I'd been working on for months."

Belle's hand flew to her mouth, but she didn't dare make a sound. Already she could see where this was headed.

"I snuck into the Wild Eight clubhouse, just to get a glimpse of him. I thought I was so stealthy and cool. Five years old and breaking in like I was some kind of bandit. Needless to say, I was discovered. Not just by Nolan, and the moment his wife saw me, she knew instantly who I was. I looked enough like him, even back then. I was so terrified that I ran. I managed to get out of there, but Nolan was so mad that his wife had discovered he'd not only still been sleeping with my mother, but had sired another son—a son who could someday try to thwart Wes's rightful place as packmaster—that...he took that anger out on my mother."

Belle gasped, her eyes full of empathy. Colt swallowed the massive lump in his throat, unable to continue. She could fill in the details from there.

"You can see why I've spent my whole life trying to avoid anyone getting close to me. Even now, as a Grey Wolf, my position as commander puts anyone I care for in jeopardy, and after losing my mother, I can't put myself in the position..."

To let it happen again.

Belle threw herself on him, wrapping him in her arms as if squeezing him as tight as she could would somehow heal those decades-old wounds. "I know you told me not to say this, Colt, but it wasn't your fault. None of it was your fault. You were just a curious little boy who wanted to know his father. It was Nolan who was the monster. Not you."

If only he could bring himself to believe that. What she didn't see was that he'd spent every day since becoming as much of a monster as Nolan had been. Sure, he was on the better side now, but he'd still spent his life waging war, fighting battles, killing his enemies without remorse, exactly like his sire before him. And how could he expect any woman to place herself in the midst of that?

They lay tangled in each other's arms until, ironically, Belle was the one who finally fell asleep, tuckered out from their night together. Colt lay there for a long time, listening to the sounds of her steady breathing as she snuggled against him. Eventually, he forced himself to ease out of the bed, rising and putting on his clothes. After the results of last night, there would be plenty of work today, and he needed to find out if Blaze had managed to recover any of the leftover data.

As he eased the door to his bedroom open and started to slip out into the hall, he glanced back over his shoulder. This woman—the only person on the planet who knew everything about him and accepted him, who cared for him anyway—was perhaps the closest thing he'd ever had to a true friend, even closer than his packmates. He cared for them, too, but it wasn't the same. Not when they'd never known the truth.

As he stood there, watching her, the voice of himself as a child rang as a distant memory in his head.

I swear to you.

He'd promised James that he'd never sully his family name by admitting he wasn't a Grey Wolf, and he intended to keep that promise. But at the moment, it didn't feel like that promise was saving him, protecting him as James had. It felt as if it were tearing him in two.

Because if he'd known back then that swearing that promise to the man he now called his father would mean he'd have to choose between his pack and this woman, he would never have given his word.

He would choose her over everything in an instant.

Chapter 19

BELLE AWOKE MIDAFTERNOON. AS SOON AS SHE SAT UP, realized what time it was and that Colt was no longer beside her, her mind began to race. She needed to tell him. He'd asked her to wait until this morning, and now the time had come.

As she dressed, her hands shook with nerves. Just as she was about to head to his office, the door to his room burst open.

Belle jumped. "Maeve?"

The Grey Wolf female glided into the room, not bothering to knock. Her sudden arrival at the Missoula ranch was a surprise.

As if she could see right through her, Maeve's jaw dropped in openmouthed glee. "I knew it! You slept with him." Belle's blush deepened, and Maeve's hands flew to cover her mouth.

"Shh," Belle hushed her. "If you announce it any louder, every wolf in the cabin will hear you."

Maeve's mischievous grin widened. "I can practically smell his scent on you. Every male on this ranch will already have a clue." She waved a hand in dismissal. "Everyone has to know already."

The door behind Maeve pushed open, as if her weight against it was little consequence, which it likely was. The woman couldn't weigh more than one hundred pounds soaking wet, despite the intensity of her hugs.

Sierra eased through the crack in the door. "Don't know what already?" she asked, clearly having overheard part of the conversation.

Belle groaned.

Maeve's grin grew all the more wicked. "Elizabeth slept with your brother," she announced. The use of her full name, as an intended alias, reminded Belle of what a tricky situation this was.

Belle cringed. *Better to rip it off like a Band-Aid, I suppose.*

"Oh, that," Sierra said, her tone unimpressed, as if Maeve had just announced the sky was blue or the grass was green. "I knew it was only a matter of time as soon as he danced with her at the wedding. Colt was clearly taken with her, more than usual." Sierra grinned in amusement.

Maeve squealed. "My plan worked! I'm officially a matchmaker!"

It was Belle's turn for her jaw to drop. "You planned that horrible dress on purpose?" she gasped.

Maeve clapped her hands excitedly. "It was partially Naomi's idea, too."

As if that somehow made it better.

Sierra was laughing, clearly mighty amused at this exchange.

"You were in on it, too?" Belle asked.

Sierra's laughter stopped abruptly, and she wrinkled her nose in disgust. "Ew. No."

Maeve whipped out her cell phone. "I have to text Naomi. I can't believe we were so right about the two of you. On my first matchmaking attempt, too. Even I'm impressed."

Belle frowned. "We had already slept together at that point." She said the words without thinking.

"What?" Maeve's excitement dissipated.

Sierra burst out laughing. "And the plot thickens."

Belle raised both hands to stop the other two women. "Before you two start further inquiries into my love life, what are you doing here?"

Maeve leaned in to whisper to Sierra. "Did you notice she said 'love life,' not 'sex life'?"

As if Belle couldn't hear her, standing two feet away, no less.

"We're here to take you back to Wolf Pack Run," Sierra said.

"What?" Belle gaped.

"Didn't you hear?" Sierra asked. "The guys broke into the vampires' security system last night. The Seven Range Pact approved a counterstrike on the vampires an hour ago, which means whoever from the vampires was after you will be shaking in their boots. You're free to go. Colt called us this morning and had us drive up here. You'll need to come back to Wolf Pack Run and sign some more forms before you're fully released from official protection, but then..."

"I'll be free," Belle finished Sierra's sentence.

Colt had done it. He'd kept his promise. She'd confessed everything to him, and still he'd let her go, forgiven her, trusted her. And for the first time in years, she was fully and totally free. Free from the Wild Eight. Free from the darkness of her past, free from Wyatt, and free from...

Her heart sank.

Free from him...

Oh, Colt.

No, no. That was never what she'd wanted. Just as she'd begun to hope that maybe...

Her hand fell to her stomach as bile rose up in her throat. Belle dove for the nearby trash can. She retched the empty contents of her stomach into the bin. Sierra rushed to her side, holding back Belle's curls.

"I'll get a cold washcloth," Maeve called as she ran to retrieve it.

A few minutes later, when the wave of nausea and anxiety had subsided, Belle tried to stand, but Sierra lifted her, easing her onto the bedside and supporting her weight as if she weighed little at all. She'd known the other she-wolf was pure muscle, but her strength was really impressive. Maeve returned a moment later and laid the cool, damp cloth across Belle's forehead.

"Are you okay?" Sierra asked.

Maeve placed a hand on Belle's in concern. "Do you need anything?"

Belle was so grateful to the two women that she couldn't bring herself to be annoyed at their meddling. Without a doubt, she knew there would never be a time in which she wouldn't call these two her friends.

Friends. The word echoed in her mind.

Belle sat up. Her friends gripped her to offer support, but her bout of nausea had quickly dissipated. It had been a fierce reminder that she and Colt were long overdue for a chat.

"I need to talk to him." She moved to stand.

"Don't you think you should rest after—?" Maeve started to ask, but Sierra shook her head.

"No, let her go. She can handle this." Sierra stood,

pulling Belle into a gentle but fierce hug before she whispered, "Go give my idiot brother hell."

———⌇⌇———

Belle found Colt in his temporary office inside the cabin. He didn't turn toward her when she entered. He was standing over his desk, his hands on the polished wood and his back toward her as he stared down at a stack of papers. She watched as his shoulders shifted and tensed, each movement highlighting the sinew and muscle that lay beneath his shirt.

She closed the door behind her. When the latch clicked shut, Colt turned toward her. She was already shaking her head at him.

He frowned. "I see Sierra and Maeve told you the news."

"They did." She nodded. "I was surprised you didn't deliver it yourself."

He cast the papers in his hand onto the desk. "It seemed like it would be easier if I didn't."

"Easier? For you or for me?"

Colt watched her for a long beat before making a show of scanning over his paperwork. She wasn't sure whether he was trying to brush her off or struggling with what to say.

"Blaze managed to recover some of the data," he said, changing the topic. "There was more than enough evidence of Lucas's plan to synthesize an injection that would allow vampires to consume werewolf blood— recorded data, charts. You were right. They gain power from it, and the purer the blood, the better. Though that still doesn't explain what they wanted me for."

He inhaled sharply. "I forwarded all of it to Maverick

this morning. If we don't address this, the fate of the species could be at stake. I've already started planning."

He paused. "We've both known all along it would end like this. It's always been temporary. We knew that from the start."

She sighed. "That doesn't mean I want it to be."

The muscles in his shoulders tensed again. He slipped his hands into his pockets and leaned against the desk. "I know."

Belle wrung her hands together. She had his attention now. It was now or never. "There's...there's something I need to tell you. Something I should have told you from the start." Sweat gathered on her palms, and she had to work to keep herself from shaking. "When I came back to Wolf Pack Run, I didn't come to help you win over the Seven Range Pact. I didn't plan to help you," she admitted.

Colt's brow furrowed. "I don't understand…"

"Well, I *did* want to help you," she amended. Oh man, she was already royally messing this up. "But the help was secondary. The real reason I came is because I…I wanted to tell you…" She inhaled a deep breath. Anxiety gripped her like a vice. "Colt, I'm pregnant."

In an instant, the color drained from Colt's face. She hadn't seen his tanned skin look so pale since he'd been about to drop dead from blood loss after the vampire had attacked him. The Adam's apple in his throat gave an uneasy bob as he gulped.

His gaze fell to her belly, searching for a difference there.

Belle stared down at her hands, willing them to quit trembling. "I have an appointment with an obstetrician to make sure everything is progressing well. She's a wolf, too." Well, that was neither here nor there. She chanced a glance at him.

The color was slowly returning to his cheeks, and he looked resolved, calm even. "I suppose that changes things then…"

For a moment, her heart swelled with hope.

He cleared his throat. "I'll need to return to Wolf Pack Run with you, announce my resignation to Maverick."

All the relief and hope she'd felt in the past moment dropped away. "Announce your resignation?" She gaped at him.

His demeanor was calm, distant, like he'd been when they first met. The image of the cold, calculating commander. Everything she knew now was a mask, a shield to keep the real him hidden from the world. Hours ago, those gray eyes had been full of emotion, and seeing them so chilled tore at her heartstrings. He might as well have ripped the still-beating organ from her chest.

"I can't ask you to live your life pretending to be a Grey Wolf when you're not, Belle. I know what that's like, and I won't do that to you, and even more importantly, I won't do that to my child. But I also can't continue lying to my packmaster. Not forever. The only choice is to leave the pack and renounce my position."

"But you've worked your whole life to follow in your father's footsteps. You told me that yourself. I won't ask you to give up your pack for me."

"I know you're not asking, Belle, but I'll give it up for you." His eyes fell to her stomach, and even with his stare cold and distant, she warmed there. "For our child. I have to."

I have to. As if she were an obligation, not a choice.

"Why not tell Maverick the truth?" she asked. "He loves you, Colt. They all do. They'll accept you as you are…"

"No." That single word cut through her in its finality. "No, I can't do that."

"So you'd rather have them think you're walking away than let them see who you really are?"

"I made a promise to James," he said. "And besides, there's nothing willful about it."

And there it was. The truth of the matter. She wasn't his choice. She and their child were an obligation. Nothing more.

"Colt, do you love me?" She swallowed hard. Based on the way he was looking at her, she wasn't sure she wanted to know the answer.

"Belle, I…" He hesitated.

No. She couldn't bear to hear him say he didn't. His pause was answer enough. She shook her head. It occurred to her that when she'd first returned to the pack, she hadn't expected a relationship with him. Little more than a cordial agreement about parental rights. But now…

She wanted so much more.

"No, I can't accept that."

"Belle." He stood from where he'd perched on the desk and stepped toward her.

"No!" She warned him away with a growl. "Child or not, I won't be with a man who has to be forced into choosing me."

Still, he eased toward her, backing her closer to the door. "You know it's not like that, Belle. You know how much I care for you, but—"

"But you don't love me! Not like I love you," she yelled.

Colt stilled. For a long, pulsing moment, they stood

there, staring at each other. The weight of her confession hung between them, filling the air with tension. It was so thick, she felt as if she could choke on it.

"Belle…" he breathed.

"No." She lashed out, defending her hurting heart. Her lower lip quivered, and her eyes welled with tears. "Don't try to tell me how I feel, Colt. I love you, but I won't spend the rest of my life with you unwillingly chained to me. If you loved me, if you had chosen me, it would be different. But if I let you walk away from your position, your pack, your family, you'll resent me. It may not happen at first, but over the years, it will, and I won't live the rest of my life with a partner who will grow to hate me." Belle charged toward the door.

"Where are you going?" He tried to follow her, but she waved him off.

He knew better than to push her. Not when she was so barely held together that she felt as if one touch would cause her to shatter.

"To Wolf Pack Run. To finish my paperwork." She gripped the door handle.

"And then?"

"I don't know," she shot back as she pulled the door open.

His hand grabbed hers. The feel of his skin brushing hers shattered her. The tears came hot and fierce. She refused to look at him.

"It's my child, too, Belle," he whispered. "If you refuse to be with me, even though I've offered to give up everything for you, you still can't keep me away."

"You know I wouldn't." The fact that he thought that of her hurt even more. No matter how much it destroyed her, she would never deprive their child of a relationship with him. Never. "Giving up everything hardly means much when you're being forced against your will."

She would run straight to Maeve and Sierra, ask them to take her back to Wolf Pack Run immediately. Because she needed to be away from here, from him. She still couldn't look at him. "As for the baby, my first doctor's appointment is on the fifth." She tore her hand away from his as she fled from the room. "I'll call you in a few weeks."

She couldn't bring herself to look back to see his face.

Chapter 20

THE BREEZE FROM THE OPEN AIR RUFFLED BELLE'S HAIR AS she gazed out the window. She was sitting in the back seat of Sierra's F-150. The windows were rolled down, and the air from the open highway blew into the cab. They'd been on the road for the better part of an hour as they headed back down to Wolf Pack Run in the foothills of the Beartooth Mountains outside Billings.

After Belle had left Colt's office, she'd run to her room and packed her things. Sierra and Maeve had found her like that, red-faced and eyes puffy from crying as she shoved the few amenities she had into an old backpack. Neither of the Grey Wolf females had asked what happened or attempted to pry further. They'd simply helped her pack, loaded her up with tissues and hugs, and ushered her out to the car. The only words spoken were Sierra's occasional mutterings under her breath about how her brother "was a damn fool" and how she'd "skin him alive" as soon as she had the chance.

Belle leaned back into her seat. She felt raw with pain, almost numb as she watched the vast blue sky roll by. White puffy clouds floated in the distance.

A small ding sounded from the dashboard as the gas light came on.

"We'll need to stop soon," Maeve said. She was sitting in the front seat, and Sierra was driving. It had taken less than five minutes for Belle to gather that Maeve was always the back-seat—or in this case, front-seat—driver.

"I know," Sierra said, glancing into the rearview mirror. "But I don't want to yet."

"Why not?" Maeve asked. "The price is only going to go up as we get closer to Billings."

Sierra's eyes flicked to the rearview mirror again. "Yes, Maeve," she said, slightly exasperated. "I know, but I'm waiting until these assholes quit tailgating me."

Belle glanced out the window behind her. A large white van with black tinted windows trailed them, periodically pulling closer and closer to the truck's bumper.

"They've been trailing us since shortly after we pulled out of the Missoula ranch," Sierra said. "It's giving me a bad feeling."

"Pull off at this next exit," Maeve suggested. "You don't have to stop at the gas station. Just let them go by, and we'll get back on the highway. Once they're gone, then we'll get gas."

"Good idea," Belle agreed. "And roll the window up," she suggested.

Sierra did so before she changed lanes, promptly pulling off at the next exit, but the van followed.

"No way that's a coincidence." Maeve craned her neck to get a better view of the vehicle. "Do you think they're following us?"

"I don't like this," Sierra growled.

Belle's pulse kicked into overdrive, and she checked that her seat belt was securely fastened. They were quickly approaching a yellow light about to turn red.

"I'm going for it." Sierra jammed her foot down onto the gas pedal. The truck lurched forward, and they sped through the light as it turned red. The van hit the brakes to stop as they barreled through the intersection and back onto the highway ramp.

"They're gone," Maeve said, checking in the rearview.

"Nice." Sierra grinned as they headed back onto the highway without the van trailing them.

Belle sat a little easier in her seat.

"Uh…Sierra," Maeve said, her voice taking on a note of panic.

Belle twisted in her seat to look behind them. The van had pulled off the ramp, racing at full speed toward them. Whoever was in the van, they were *definitely* following them. Belle's blood ran cold.

"Shit," Sierra swore. She floored the gas pedal again.

Maeve let out a little squeak as she scrambled to grab her cell phone. "I'm calling Maverick."

Sierra weaved in and out of traffic, attempting to throw the van off their trail.

"They're gaining on us," Belle warned.

"I'm going as fast as I can," Sierra barked.

Maeve was already on her cell phone. "Maverick, it's me. We're on the highway back from the Missoula ranch, and there's this white van following us."

Suddenly, the front end of the van connected with the bumper of the truck in an obvious tap.

"Shit!" Sierra yelled.

"Scratch that," Maeve squeaked. "They're trying to ram our car off the road."

The van slammed into them again, this time causing them to swerve. They narrowly missed colliding with a nearby Volkswagen Beetle.

"Maverick says to floor it and not to stop," Maeve said.

"Thanks, Packmaster Obvious," Sierra snapped. She steered the truck with precision, as if she'd been in a million car chases before, but still the van gained on them.

It slammed into them a third time, so hard the back of the truck fishtailed. Maeve and Belle screamed, and Maeve's cell phone clattered to the floor. Sierra fought against the momentum, wrenching on the wheel to regain the balance, but the van slammed them again. The truck went flying, turning over in midair.

Belle's body became weightless, anchored only by the security of her seat belt. Broken glass flew through the air in a sparkling shower. The truck landed upside down with a massive crash, the screeching sounds of crushing, crunching metal piercing her ears until Belle blacked out.

When she came to, she was hanging upside down by the seat belt, and someone was tugging on her.

"Elizabeth. Elizabeth!" It was Maeve. She was free of her own seat belt and crawling through the glass and debris into the back of the cab to reach for her. Sierra was slumped partway out the broken window of the cab from where Maeve had clearly removed her from her seat belt, but the she-wolf was unconscious. Blood ran from her temple, where her forehead had hit the steering wheel. The truck's airbag had failed to deploy.

Belle undid her seat belt, collapsing onto the roof of the car as she reached for Maeve's hand. She gripped the other woman's palm, but Maeve's eyes grew wide and she screamed. Someone had ahold of her ankle and was wrenching her from the car. Belle slid from the vehicle along with her, unable to fight after the blows from the crash.

"Leave the other," a familiar-sounding voice ordered. "She's one of their warriors. We can't have her waking up and trying to let her friends out."

Someone yanked Belle to her feet. As she lifted her gaze to their attacker, she expected to see the same face she'd seen glaring at her from the shadow depths in the clearing, just before Colt had been stabbed, but it wasn't.

"Eli," she gasped.

One of the final five remaining members of the Wild Eight, four if she wasn't counted, and, more importantly, Wyatt's brother.

Immediately, he gripped her by the throat. Belle struggled to breathe. "Don't look so surprised, you murderous bitch," Eli hissed. "After you killed my brother, you really thought I wouldn't come for you?"

Belle struggled for air, unable to speak. If she could have, she would have told him what an abusive fuck his brother was, but it wouldn't have mattered, because Eli's eyes blazed with revenge and evil intent.

There were several other wolves with him. Hired Rogues by her guess. They'd be little help to her. Black spots swam in front of her eyes, and Eli tossed her to the ground.

"Throw them in the back of the van," he ordered. "Take them to Lucas."

Belle's eyes widened. So Eli and that monster were working together. No wonder she'd smelled both vampire and wolf when she'd been attacked. It'd been Eli who'd tried to abduct her. They'd been looking for a vampire, when it was a werewolf working for him the whole time.

"And make sure you duct-tape their mouths real

good." Eli cast her an evil grin. "This one's likely to bite when she's cornered."

———

It had been a little over an hour since Belle stormed from his office, yet Colt hadn't managed to get any work done. He had tried to rid his mind of her, but he was failing miserably. He'd even abandoned the counterstrike plans and gone out to the calving shed to muck out the stalls and lay down some fresh hay to clear his head. Nothing like cleaning up cow shit to make a man put his own bullshit into perspective, but it was no use.

He was still struggling to wrap his mind around the part where Belle had confessed she was pregnant with his child. Shit, he wasn't certain he was ready to be a father, but the thought of having a family with Belle filled him with hope for the future—even as he mourned the inevitable loss of his pack.

He jabbed the shovel he was holding into the hay, digging and lifting another pile into the wheelbarrow.

And she'd told him she loved him.

Colt hadn't said those three words to a woman other than his sister since his mother had died. Did he even know the feeling in the romantic sense? Until now, he'd never allowed any woman close enough to come near to loving her.

Except for Belle…

Colt wasn't prepared to answer that question, but as he moved to drive the shovel into the muck again, his cell phone rang. It was likely Sierra, calling to update him on their progress back to Wolf Pack Run or, more likely, chew him out for making Belle cry. He was already beating himself up inside over that. He didn't need the extra help.

He glanced at the phone. Instead of Sierra, Maverick's name flashed across the screen.

"Hello?" he answered.

"Colt." Maverick's voice was tense.

Colt dropped the shovel he was holding.

"What happened?" he breathed.

"A white van followed the females after they left the Missoula ranch. Maeve called me. The line went dead. The GPS on Maeve's phone is showing up just outside mile marker 316 in the Bozeman Pass on I-90."

"I'm on my way." Colt pocketed his cell phone and tore out of the calving shed toward the main house as if his life depended on it. He was shouting orders to his men from the moment he reached the door.

He didn't remember any of the details of the ride, but as he saw Sierra's truck lying in a ditch, a swarm of human police officers surrounding it, Colt stiffened. For a moment, he couldn't breathe, couldn't think, and it was as if his heart suddenly stopped beating within his chest.

Both his sister and Belle.

No.

No. No. No.

He didn't even wait for the car to stop before he was running through the traffic cones toward the accident.

"Colt!" Sierra shouted to him from the back of an ambulance, where she'd clearly been fighting against being treated. It wouldn't take much for the human paramedics to discover there was something different about her.

She ran to him. He caught her in his arms. She was bleeding from the head. "They attacked us, Colt. Wild Eight. But I heard them say they were going to Lucas. They took Elizabeth and Maeve, but they—"

Colt didn't hear the next words Sierra spoke. His mind was already making the connections, drawing the parallels. All he heard was the sound of his own pulse thumping inside his temple. His vision turned red at the edges. But he forced it down, locking his rage away with the ironclad control James had taught him. He was already formulating a plan, calculating the best routes of entry and means of attack. He would make Lucas's death slow and torturous. By comparison, what they'd done to him would be mere child's play, and he wouldn't rest until every last member of their coven met their true death.

But first, he needed to find her. Save her.

Because he loved her...

———···———

Belle wrapped her arms around her knees and huddled in the corner of the vampires' cell. After Eli and his hired Rogue wolf thugs had abducted them from Sierra's truck, they'd thrown Belle and Maeve into the back of their van. They'd duct-taped their mouths and bound their hands and feet, leaving them no escape. Belle's stomach had churned in fear with each turn of the van's wheels, bringing them closer and closer to the vampires' coven, but that was nothing compared to the fear she felt now.

As soon as they'd arrived, the vampires had separated them. Which meant those bastards had Maeve alone.

Belle's heart thumped as her pulse raced. She'd never forgive herself if Eli hurt Maeve.

She hung her head. "It's me you want revenge against, you bastard. Leave Maeve alone," she whispered. She'd screamed it for nearly the first hour since they'd locked her up, but it'd quickly become clear she'd take her own beating if she didn't stay quiet.

Suddenly, the door to the next cell swung open with a whining creak, and Belle's head jerked up. Maeve stumbled into the next cell over, eating the concrete face-first from where the vampire guard had shoved her.

"Maeve." Belle scrambled toward her, reaching through the bars between them as the cell door slammed shut with an echoing clang.

The she-wolf was already pushing herself to her knees. "I'm okay," she squeaked. "I'm okay." But from the quiver in her normally enthusiasm-filled voice, Belle knew Maeve was putting on a brave face.

She eased closer to the bars between them, close enough they could touch. Belle brushed Maeve's short brown locks from her face, revealing road rash across her cheek from where she'd hit the pavement. It was then Belle noticed the way Maeve cradled her arm. Belle reached for the other woman, carefully moving the limb to test that it wasn't broken, but it was then she noticed the trail of blood at the crook of Maeve's elbow. Not two pinpricks of a vampire bite, but one tiny, bruised puncture wound.

From a needle.

"Maeve, did they...?"

Maeve nodded.

Belle's eyes grew wide. Of course. Colt's blood wouldn't

have given them what they expected since he wasn't a Grey Wolf. The vampires she'd overheard in the clearing had said the purer the blood, the more strength the serum gave them. Which meant even if Colt and the rest of the Grey Wolves found them before it was too late, the vampires would have exactly what they needed. Not from Colt, but from Maeve.

"We need to get out of here," Belle whispered, gripping Maeve's hands. The two of them alone wouldn't be able to take on all the vampires, but they might be able to slip out undetected. Belle reached to the nape of her neck, removing the bobby pins she'd kept permanently hidden there since she'd escaped from the Missoula Grey Wolf cells. They'd saved her once before. Maybe they would again.

"What are you doing?" Maeve whispered.

"Picking the lock."

"Where did you learn to do that?" Maeve asked.

Belle ignored Maeve's question and crept over to her cell door. She'd free herself and then Maeve next. The guards had all but abandoned them, expecting that there was no way for them to escape. She had a feeling their presence was to lure Colt here and little more; they'd gotten what they wanted from Maeve. The only reason they hadn't killed them outright was they likely had plans to use Maeve against the Grey Wolf packmaster himself.

Belle repeated her trick, using one of the bobby pins to slip into the housing on the lock and twisting. But several minutes later, she still hadn't managed to work it open. These locks were industrial, but she'd never encountered an average lock she couldn't pick.

She swore under her breath.

"I think I can be of assistance." A deep voice sounded from the cell adjacent to Maeve's.

A figure seemed to unfold from the shadows, his movements so eerily smooth and full of power they reminded Belle of a predatory cat. But the eyes that glowed back at them in the darkness were pure wolf. A scraggly beard obscured the view of his face, as if he'd been here a few days.

Belle's breath caught. She didn't know how she hadn't sensed him there. She glanced toward Maeve. Maeve's eyes had grown to the size of saucers, and she was staring at the man as if she'd never seen a male of their species before.

"Who are you?" Belle asked, a hint of a warning growl in her voice. She allowed her wolf eyes to shine back in a clear show of aggression. She couldn't have fought this massive alpha if she tried—*tried* being the key word—if it came to that.

He answered with a grin. Whoever he was, he was a handsome devil, and from that devious, wicked smile and the fiery darkness of his eyes, Belle had no doubt that *devil* was an accurate descriptor. His size, matching that of any of the elite Grey Wolves, would have been enough to intimidate, but it was that penetrating stare that stilled her. Not captivating like Colt's, but terrifying in its intensity.

But it was the spark of fire, of recognition in his gaze as it fell to Maeve, that caused Belle to snarl.

"And what's your name, princess?" he purred in Maeve's direction, though Belle had a feeling he already knew.

"Maeve Grey."

"Maeve," Belle whispered in warning. She shot her friend a look of *Don't answer this creep*, but Maeve wasn't paying her any mind.

Sidling up to the edge of the cell's silver bars, he peered at them. A pair of cold, icy blue eyes stared back. Belle wasn't sure why, but something in those eerie eyes stopped her in her tracks.

"Pass me that pin of yours, and I'll have us out in no time," he whispered.

"You're a criminal." The words fell from her lips before she could stop them. She didn't know how she knew, but she did. This man was trouble, danger. Maybe not to her, but to others.

A devious smile curled on his lips. "By Grey Wolf standards, so are you, I'd wager."

Belle stiffened. *How did he...?*

She was still reeling when Maeve stood and eased toward the torchlights on the other side of her cell to get a better look at his face.

"Maeve!" Belle snapped.

A thin, strong arm shot between the silver bars, careless of the burning pain the silver caused, and gripped Maeve hard by the wrist. She froze. His grip on her remained tight enough to hold her still, but gentle enough not to hurt her. Those blue eyes blazed pure fire.

"I'll make it worth your while," he whispered to Maeve.

"Maeve," Belle warned again.

"How?" Maeve asked him, oblivious to Belle's warnings.

Belle knew how. Maeve might have been too innocent to recognize what he meant, but Belle saw it in the depths of his burning gaze. This was a man who dealt in blood and death, in fire and brimstone, and as much as the prospect of freeing him caused her knees to shake, she didn't want him as her enemy. Somehow, she knew intrinsically that was what she would be to him. Either friend or foe, no in between.

"There's a back entrance," he said. "I can take you both with me."

Belle didn't like the sound of this. She didn't trust this wolf.

"You don't even have to labor yourself," he purred to Maeve. "Just slip me that little pin of yours, princess, and I'll be in your debt. I'm a master with locks. I'll have it open in half the time." His voice wrapped around them like smooth velvet.

Maeve was watching his face, refusing to look away. "Give me a bobby pin, Elizabeth."

"Maeve," Belle scolded.

"I know what I'm doing," Maeve said. She could easily pull away from this man's hold, but she hadn't. Belle had a suspicion that Maeve knew something she didn't.

Reluctantly, Belle passed one of the pins to her through the cell bars, and immediately Maeve slipped it into the Devil's hand. Snatching it away with greedy excitement, he released Maeve and shifted his attention to the lock of his cell. Belle only managed several paces of her own cell before his swung open.

He hadn't lied. He'd picked the lock in record time. He prowled forth, suddenly more intimidating than Belle had initially imagined. He had the lock on Maeve's cell open just as fast. As Maeve stepped from the cell, the alpha suddenly seized her again, pulling her against him.

Maeve struggled, her eyes flashing gold. Belle snarled.

"Quiet," he growled back, dragging Maeve back into the shadows with him.

That was when Belle heard it. The sound of the guard's steps quickly approaching. Maeve's eyes widened as if she'd heard it, too. He tossed the bobby pin back to Belle. It fell just outside her cell, but within reach.

"I'm not leaving without my friend." Maeve struggled against his hold.

"If you hurt her…" Belle warned.

His grip on Maeve tightened, and his eyes turned toward Belle. "Even I know better than to tempt the anger of Maverick Grey. She'll be delivered safely back to her big brother. You have my word." He flashed Belle a wicked grin. "You know as well as I do that a Rogue's word is worth more than a pack wolf's."

In an instant, Belle knew exactly who this wolf was. Like hell she was leaving her friend with this vigilante. But Belle didn't get the choice, because at that moment, one of the vampire guards rounded the corner just as the Rogue and Maeve slipped into the darkness, disappearing as smoothly as he'd appeared—and leaving Belle no other choice. She snatched the bobby pin from the floor outside her cell and hunkered down to wait.

Chapter 21

THEY FOUND THE ABANDONED VAN SEVERAL MILES OUTSIDE downtown Billings. On occasion, Blaze's ability to tap into the local police force's radio scanners had its advantages. From there, it wasn't difficult to realize that Eli and Lucas had taken Belle and Maeve to the main coven located downtown.

Eli and Lucas…what a bizarre team.

With Sierra's tip that Belle and Maeve's abductor was Wild Eight, Colt figured that Eli was the culprit. Considering what Belle had confessed about putting down Wyatt like the vicious dog he was, it was easy to pinpoint why the former Wild Eight member wanted revenge. Colt had no clue whether Eli and Lucas had been working together from the start, but it was of little consequence.

The Billings coven was housed in an underground fortress that boasted superior security. A battle there would cause serious casualties, but it was a risk Colt was willing to take.

Because he was going to get Belle back in one piece—her *and* Maeve—even if he had to give his own life.

Maverick stood beside Colt, directly outside the entrance to the coven, gun in hand. Maverick hadn't blinked when Colt confessed the truth of Belle's identity to him. He'd likely suspected she wasn't a Grey Wolf, even if he hadn't known the full truth. Colt had known from the start that Maverick hadn't fully bought his and Belle's story.

The reprimand would come later, once the females were safe again.

"You ready?" Maverick asked.

The plan Colt had formulated was simple. He and a small group of his men were going to charge in as if he were on a solo revenge mission, which was likely what Lucas expected. They'd take out as many of their enemies as they could in the first round, shooting and fighting for maximum bloodshed until they were taken captive—which they inevitably would be. Once the blood bags were occupied with them, Maverick and the Grey Wolf elite warriors—minus Colt, and Wes, who was still off on his honeymoon in the Galapagos of Ecuador—would sneak in. Maverick's team would silently locate Belle and Maeve, releasing them before all-out chaos ensued.

With a nod, Colt cocked back the hammer of his forty-five. Using a silent hand gesture, he signaled his men and they took their places. Two Grey Wolf soldiers moved forward, prepared to pummel the door with a battering ram, when suddenly the door eased open of its own accord.

Every weapon was raised in anticipation. But instead of a vampire, Maeve stumbled out of the coven, bruised in a few places and bleeding a thin trail of blood from the crook of her elbow. They'd taken her blood, too— but she was alive and safe.

"Don't shoot!" Maverick ordered.

Maeve rushed into his arms.

"Maeve, where's—?"

"She's still inside. Lucas has her," Maeve sobbed. "There was some alpha wolf there, and he helped us pick the lock. He—"

That was all Colt needed to hear. He signaled to his men, who took their positions as Maverick, Maeve, and the elite team fell back into the shadows. They would stay hidden until the first attack calmed down and their enemy least expected them.

Colt charged in, rushing through the halls of the coven, searching for Belle. When he crossed paths with the first vampire, he fired, his bullet hitting the blood-sucker straight in the head. The vamp fell, struggling to regenerate as its blood pooled on the floor, but Colt wouldn't let that happen.

Drawing his stake from his boot, he plunged the lacquered wood into the vampire's beating heart. The vamp exploded in a spray of blood. It was satisfying, yet too easy. Lucas would prove the real challenge.

Colt and his men plowed forward, guns blazing. They'd taken out seven bloodsuckers by the time they reached Lucas's lab. By that point, Colt and his soldiers had separated down the labyrinth of halls in various directions. The whole coven had been alerted to their presence, and the shouts of vampire guards echoed in the distance as they came searching for them, but Colt was going to reach Lucas first. Belle would be close by, and Lucas likely intended to use her to his advantage.

Colt's irises flashed to the golden of his wolf's before he threw back his head and howled to draw the attention of all the guards. He sensed he was getting closer to her now. If he had trusted those same instincts all along, he would have known from the start this woman was his mate. She was meant for him, without a doubt. The feral growl of an angry she-wolf sounded down a nearby hall, not far from the cells. Colt rounded the corner, heading toward the noise, gun at the ready. When he reached the cells, he found Eli gripping Belle by the hair, his blade pressed to her jugular.

"This is for trying to escape, you bitch," Eli growled.

Colt's heart dropped, but he remained focused. He wanted to tell her he'd choose her over everything. He'd feared that she would be a weakness for his enemies to exploit, but she already was his weakness. His weakness and his greatest strength.

At the sight of him, Belle struggled harder. "Colt."

Eli snarled, pressing the blade harder against Belle's jugular. The hateful look in his eyes said he didn't think twice about hurting a woman. "Surprise. Surprise. Look who's here to save the day," Eli mocked.

Colt held his gun steady, trained on Eli's forehead. Neither wolf nor vampire could survive a .45 to the skull.

"Don't fight him, Belle." His gaze caught hers.

I'll protect you. Think of yourself and the baby.

Belle gave a barely perceptible nod.

"Put the blade down, or I shoot," Colt warned Eli.

"Not a chance," Eli growled. "You want to bet I can slit her throat before you take your shot?"

Colt snarled. He would bury this fucker six feet under even if it was the last thing he did.

Within seconds, the vampire guards swarmed the hall, surrounding Colt with weapons raised.

"Commander, you finally join us." Lucas emerged from the crowd, a twisted smile on his face.

"Tell him to lower his gun," Eli demanded.

Lucas nodded. "You heard the man."

Colt shook his head. "Not unless I get something in return."

"I don't think you're in a place to negotiate, Commander," Lucas hissed.

"Really? Because last I checked, my gun is aimed straight at your errand boy's head."

Lucas cast a side-glance toward Belle. "Eli will let her go if you answer me one question, Commander."

"You said the bitch was mine as soon as you had him." Eli gave Belle's hair a hard yank, and she gasped in pain.

Colt's finger itched to pull the trigger. Maverick and the other alphas would be closing in now. It'd only be a matter of minutes. He just needed to keep Lucas talking.

Lucas gave an amused nod. He clearly thought Eli was about equivalent to a bug beneath his shoe. "And you'll have your fun once I've had mine."

"What the fuck do you need her for? You have him here. Now the bitch is mine," Eli growled.

Lucas ignored him. "How'd you do it?" he asked Colt.

One of the vampire guards had disappeared into the hall and hadn't returned, and Colt had a feeling his pack-master and the Grey Wolf elite alphas had something to do with that. Maverick moved with all the silence of a large cat or a leopard, yet he was twice as lethal.

"Don't play coy with me," Lucas hissed. "You're pure-blooded Grey Wolf. The sample should have been perfect. How did you circumvent my serum?"

Colt schooled his features. So that was what this was about. Not revenge for his escape or a target on the remaining Wild Eight wolves. Belle had been no more than a ploy to get him here. He hadn't been the target because of his identity. He'd been a target because of his lie, the mask he wore as a Grey Wolf soldier, and then his blood hadn't worked. Of course it wouldn't.

"I think you'll find I'm a bit of a disappointment, Lucas," he said.

Colt sensed his packmates closing in. He needed to hold Lucas's attention a beat longer. Colt's heart pounded, throbbing in his temples. He knew what he needed to do. He needed something that would anger Lucas, deflate his ego, throw him off guard.

He met his enemy's gaze, speaking the truth aloud even though he knew Maverick and his fellow warriors could hear him. "Because unfortunately for you, I'm not a Grey Wolf."

Lucas's red eyes narrowed as Maverick drove his blade down into one of the guard's backs. The guard screeched, his blood exploding everywhere. Eli jerked toward the noise just as Colt pulled the trigger. His shot rang out, releasing an all-out melee. The bullet landed straight in Eli's forehead. The bastard crumpled to the ground, dragging Belle down with him. Colt tried to run to her, but Lucas lunged for him, knocking him to the floor and sending Colt's gun skidding across it.

From the corner of his eye, Colt saw Dean ushering Belle toward safety. Which left him to focus on fighting Lucas.

Lucas's fist drove into Colt's jaw, but Colt rebounded, delivering a powerful throat punch that left the bloodsucker gasping for air. They met each other's hits blow for blow. The vampire was strong, fast, cunning, but no more so than Colt.

Without warning, the bloodsucker reached for

his knife. He brought it down in a powerful arc. Colt blocked the blade as it hovered inches over his heart.

If only he could reach the stake at his belt, he would have this bloodsucker right where he wanted him.

"Colt!" one of his packmates shouted.

In the midst of his own battle, Blaze kicked Colt's gun toward him, but Lucas was too focused on the thrill of his strike, his blade inches from Colt's chest, to notice. Colt reached for the gun with his free hand. If his fingers would just go an inch farther...

"Any last words, Commander?" the vampire hissed.

"Yeah." Colt nodded, his words near panting as he strained with all his strength to hold back the vampire. His hand made contact with his .45 as he met Lucas's gaze. "Fuck you."

Colt bashed the butt of his gun upside the vampire's head, knocking the bloodsucker off-balance while gripping the vamp by the throat. Lucas lifted his blade again, but not before Colt reached his stake, pulling the vampire down toward him as he plunged it into the bloodsucker's back, piercing his heart. Lucas's blade clattered to the floor. A moment later, Colt stood, chest heaving. The bastard was dead.

When Colt lifted his gaze, Maverick was staring at him, panting at having won his own battle against one of the vamps. As he looked toward Colt, his face twisted with confusion and anger. "What the fuck do you mean you're not a Grey Wolf?" he snarled.

But Colt didn't have the time to answer the packmaster's question. Just behind Maverick, Eli rose to his feet, barely alive but clutching Lucas's blade in his hand. He was pale and swaying on his feet, but the spark in his eyes said if he couldn't have Belle's life, the Grey Wolf packmaster would do.

"No!" Colt shouted. He shoved Maverick out of the way, placing himself in the line of fire. A sharp, stabbing pain pierced his chest, and Colt was vaguely aware of the feeling of his body hitting the cold stone floor of the dungeon before everything went black.

Chapter 22

COLT AWOKE TWENTY-FOUR HOURS LATER IN THE PACK'S NEW infirmary to find all eight of the elite alpha warriors, the packmaster included—along with Maeve and a few others—standing over him.

"What's going on?" he rasped. He eased up in the bed, scratching at his beard. He couldn't remember how he'd gotten here. "Did we manage to kill…?"

Maverick nodded. "Lucas is dead. As for his work, that's uncertain. They drew Maeve's blood when they held her, and since she's pure Grey Wolf…"

There was a chance another vampire could carry out Lucas's twisted scientific legacy. It would likely take time for someone to pick up his work where he left off, but still.

"Not to mention that bastard got away," Malcolm snarled.

Colt raised a brow.

"Apparently, the vampires had managed to take the Rogue captive. You know I'm never a fan of vamps killing shifters, but in that case…" Maverick snarled. "We don't know how the bastard managed to get out."

Maeve shrank into Maverick's shadows, suddenly looking flushed and also a little panic-stricken.

Colt wanted to tell Maverick about the missing Rogue shifters Belle had told him about, but that was a conversation for later.

It was all coming back to Colt now. Belle, Lucas, Eli, the blade.

And before that, him confessing the truth to stall Lucas.

His eyes darted around at all his packmembers. "Why are you all here?" he breathed. He had the feeling he already knew the unfortunate answer to that. His stomach churned.

"This is an intervention," Maverick said, confirming Colt's worst fear.

Colt winced. *Shit.* He'd known this was coming.

He hung his head, extending his wrists toward Maverick. "Whether you're going to kill me or cast me out, please make it quick."

Maverick scoffed at him before Blaze interjected, "Not an intervention to kick you out, dumbass. An intervention to tell you to stop being such a pussy."

"Shut the fuck up, Blaze," Dean growled.

Colt lifted his head, his eyes darting between them all again. "What's going on?"

Maeve gave a whimsical sort of shrug as she sighed. "Word's gotten out that you're not a Grey Wolf."

Maverick frowned, clearly unamused. "Apparently we have more than one elite warrior who's Wild Eight."

Colt's jaw fell slack. "You mean you're not going to kill me? To cast me out of the pack?"

The packmaster bristled. "I may be angry enough to want to beat you into an ever-loving pulp for not telling me sooner, and I can't believe I'm having to give you this sappy, shitty speech, Colt Cavanaugh, but you're as fucking Grey Wolf as they come. None of us could give two shits about your bloodline."

Blaze clapped Maverick on the back with a grin, which

only caused Maverick's frown to deepen. "You think this cold-hearted bastard could manage to love someone like Wes fucking Calhoun but not you?" Blaze chuckled.

"You've been a Grey Wolf since you were a child," Dean added.

"I've known you since I was born," Maeve echoed.

"And I owe my life to you." A deep voice sounded from somewhere in the back. The group of his pack-mates parted as Wes stepped forward.

"I thought you were on your honeymoon," Colt said.

Wes let out an annoyed huff through his nose. "When we heard you'd been injured, we decided to come back. There are only so many times in my life when I'll have a brother lying in a hospital bed—and you think I wouldn't show up."

"Wait," Maeve breathed. "You're not just Wild Eight? You're Nolan's son?" Her eyes grew wide.

"We'd already established that, darlin'," Austin drawled from where he leaned in the corner.

"Maverick didn't tell me—"

Malcolm hushed her, causing Maeve to glare at him.

Colt looked toward his brother. "Wes, I should have told you, but I—"

Wes shrugged. "Save it. I already knew."

"You did?" Maverick growled.

All his packmates started to talk at once before Wes spoke again. "Course I knew." He gave Colt a know-ing look. "When Maverick told me it was you who'd convinced him to spare me all those years ago, it was downright confirmation."

Maverick nodded. "To be honest, I had my suspicions even back then, and when Belle showed up—"

"Wait," Colt interjected. "You knew who Belle was from the start?"

Every one of his packmates burst out laughing, chuckling as if he had just told a hilarious joke.

"Of course we knew!" several of them cried.

"Unfortunately, brother, you're very vocal when you sleep." Wes grinned.

"And when we hauled you out of the vampires' coven the first time, every other word while you were out of it was 'Belle, Belle, Belle.'" Blaze made a fake gagging noise. "I'll never sit on a porch swing again."

Maeve clutched both hands together and lifted them to her cheek with a dreamy sigh. "So romantic."

Colt was struggling to wrap his head around all this. "If you knew who she was, why let her stay here? Pretend she was part of the pack?"

Maverick shrugged. "Well, it helped that Wes vouched that she was harmless."

"But I mean, why wouldn't we allow her here?" Maeve asked.

"Ain't it obvious?" Austin asked.

Even stone-faced Malcolm was shaking his head. "Even *I* see why."

They were all nodding their heads in agreement. Apparently, the answer was obvious—to everyone but Colt.

"Because you love her, you moron!" The angry comment came from Sierra, who was now standing in the doorway. Her jaw was set, and she looked like she held all the force of a bull prepared to charge inside her—and he was her target. She was clearly pissed. Not only had he never told her he was Wild Eight, but she'd befriended Belle, and Sierra was fiercely protective of her friends.

Sierra stalked toward him. Immediately, Maverick started ushering the rest of them out of the room, leaving only Wes behind. Obviously pack visiting time had shifted into family only.

"What were you thinking?" Sierra snarled.

Colt cast a glance toward Wes, but Wes threw up his hands as if to say *Sorry, not going to help you on this one, bro*.

Sierra was at Colt's bedside, glaring down at him. "You were going to lose her to keep your reputation hidden, and for what? For the sake of a dead man?"

"Sierra…" he breathed.

She raised a hand. "Don't, Colt. Not now."

"Sierra, I should have told you, but I—"

"You think I didn't know?" She placed her hands on her hips, glaring at him. "You think I didn't start to suspect when Wes showed up at the pack? If he cleaned up all his scruff, he might as well be your twin."

Wes ran a hand through his chin-length hair. "Hey now. Colt here is a handsome motherfucker, but don't bash the scruff."

Sierra snarled at him, clearly displeased with being interrupted, before she rounded on Colt again. "I'd always suspected there was some discord between you and Dad, but I chalked it up to the fact that he knew one day you'd take over his position, likely long before he was ready to give it up. The man *lived* to be a soldier. He wouldn't have wanted anyone to take that from him. Not even you."

She pointed to Wes. "But when this troublemaker showed up looking just like you and Maverick spared him, one of our sworn enemies, I knew something was up. Suddenly, all the times Mom and Dad treated me as the favorite made sense, and it didn't seem like funny sibling rivalry anymore. It seemed unfair. Dad always expected more, demanded more of you. I thought it was because I was female, but that wasn't the case. It was because I was his own flesh and blood."

Colt didn't know where to begin. "Sierra, if you knew, why didn't you tell me?"

"Because I thought you didn't know! I couldn't find any records of you before you were five. I assumed they'd been erased, because they took you in as a baby. I had no idea that you knew this whole time."

"I would have told you, but I—"

"Spare me your excuses, brother." She gripped the railing of his bedside. "That's right, I said 'brother,' because even though we weren't born of the same father, you're just as stubborn and bullheaded as Dad was, which is more than enough proof that you're as Grey Wolf as they come, Colt! And now, even though Dad is dead and he should no longer hold an ounce of sway over you, you're going to let him ruin your chance at having something good." She moved to stand inches away from Colt, staring him down. "All because you're a coward," she declared. "If you ask me, you don't deserve the title of high commander."

Colt stiffened.

"Sierra," Wes warned.

She rounded on Wes. "No, he needs to hear this." Turning back toward him, she jammed a finger into his chest, her eyes blazing with anger, frustration, and concern as she did. "You don't deserve to be high commander," she repeated. "And not because you're not a Grey Wolf, but because you're a coward and you've been lying to the pack for years." She was shaking her head as if ashamed of him. "I know you, brother. You may say otherwise, but it's not for the sake of some stupid oath. It was all to save your own pride."

Colt finally raised his voice in protest. "You're right. I am coward, and if you think I don't deserve this position, it's yours to claim by birthright."

Sierra stilled. He knew without a doubt she would want his position. If he were any other person, she wouldn't even hesitate. She'd trained for years with him and their father. She was the fiercest female among them, a far better warrior than most of their men. She'd worked hard enough that Colt had no doubt she could hold her own among the pack's elite warriors. But ancient pack laws denied her the privilege of taking a titled position.

The spark of hope, of ambition in her eyes quickly faded to one of pain. Unshed tears welled. "You think so little of me?"

He hadn't seen Sierra this close to crying since they were children. Their father had told Colt he was a soldier, meant to be Grey Wolf High commander, so he wasn't allowed to cry, and in her quest to be just like the man, Sierra had also taken the lesson to heart.

Colt reached for her. "Sierra."

"No." She held up her hand again to silence him. She didn't allow a single tear to fall. "I know how much your position, your title, your rank define you. They've made you into the man you are, and I love you enough to sacrifice my dreams to make yours a reality. I may want to be a soldier, but I want your happiness more.

When you truly want something, that's what you do; you sacrifice everything, Colt. I just hope you realize exactly what you're choosing to sacrifice."

Sierra stalked toward the door, tearing it open as she made a dramatic exit. She paused only long enough to shoot a glance over her shoulder at Wes. "Welcome to the family, Wes," she said before she slammed the door.

Wes blew out a long breath before he chuckled. "She certainly knows how to make an exit."

Colt raked a hand through his hair and released a long sigh. "You should have seen her in her teenage years."

Wes's grin faded, and he pegged Colt with a hard stare. "She's right, you know. I was and am willing to sacrifice my life for Naomi. But I hesitated, because I was terrified I didn't deserve her."

"And then you realized that you did?"

Wes laughed. "Fuck no. I still don't deserve her, and I'll die a lonely, miserable death if she ever realizes that, but until then, as long as she'll have me, I'll be there." He clapped a hand on Colt's shoulder. "You'll only be defined by being a Calhoun as long as you allow it. I didn't allow having Nolan as a father to stop me from choosing my own path. You should do the same." Wes gave Colt's shoulder a final squeeze before he headed toward the door.

"I liked it better when I only had one sibling to deal with," Colt grumbled.

Wes chuckled darkly. "And I liked it better when you were an arrogant Grey Wolf commander, not the man I owe my life to." Those cold blue eyes softened, and he pegged Colt with a knowing stare. "Don't make the same mistakes I did, brother."

It wasn't until two weeks later when the ranch's mail

came that Colt took Wes's advice to heart. Every day he'd been waiting to hear from Belle about her appointment. Sierra and Maeve had told him she'd left the ranch almost immediately upon returning to Wolf Pack Run, but she hadn't said where she was going. He'd tried to trace her, but as a Rogue, she knew how to cover her tracks. In any case, he knew it was only a matter of time until she returned, and he waited for that moment on pins and needles, so he could apologize, so he could tell her what she meant to him.

Finally, when a letter arrived addressed to him without a return address, he knew without a doubt it was her. He tore the letter open, ripping at the pale-yellow envelope in eager anticipation. He expected it to say when she'd be returning. He was eager to begin planning exactly what he was going to say her, but as he read the letter, his heart sank. It was scrawled in messy handwriting, so nearly illegible, it could have been written only by a doctor.

Dear Colt,

I'll get straight to the point. I've had a miscarriage. It's unfortunately common in the first twelve weeks, and considering the car crash and all that transpired...

I'll recover in a short time. You're off the hook now.

Belle

Colt collapsed into his desk chair as he gripped the letter in his hands. Until now, he hadn't realized how

excited he'd grown over the prospect of having a life
with her, how much he'd hinged his hopes on the fact
that their child would bring them back together. Until
now, he'd never really thought he'd lost her.

What have I done?

As Colt read the letter over again, he lowered his
Stetson from his head before he dropped the crumpled
paper onto the desk and hung his head in his hands.

———

The emotional scars remained, but once Belle recovered
physically, she returned to the rodeo. With her name
cleared, it'd been easy to reclaim her old position. The
rodeo was always in need of more doctors. There was a
plethora of orthopedic-related injuries every night and no
shortage of rodeos in the United States at which to work.

Since she'd left Wolf Pack Run, she'd tried not to
think of Colt, but it was impossible. She missed the
sound of his voice as he teased her, the molten steel of
his eyes, and that wry smile of his as he grinned at her
from beneath the rim of his Stetson hat. Admittedly,
she'd been devastated to lose their baby, but it was so
early in the pregnancy that it hadn't been too physically
traumatic. Dr. Jaffe thought the miscarriage was the
result of the car accident followed by the stress and fear
of being abducted. Though Belle hadn't quite been ready
for the idea of a child, she now had no excuse to maintain
contact with Colt. She told herself the pain would lessen
with time, but if she was honest, she doubted it would.

It was the end of a long day, and she was nearly dead
on her feet. She was standing in one of the arena's exam
rooms when one of her nurses poked her head in.

"Dr. Beaumont," the nurse said.

Belle glanced up from the stack of paperwork she'd been finishing up for the day.

"One of the cowboys says he's having some chest pain. He asked to see you." The woman passed her a manila folder. "Here's his chart."

"All right. One more. Send him in." Belle took the proffered folder. Turning back toward her paperwork, she flipped open the folder as the door opened behind her. The top piece of paper in the manila folder didn't look like a medical sheet at all, but instead, a crumpled letter.

A letter written in her handwriting.

"I've been having some pain in my chest, doc." A smooth, familiar baritone sounded from behind her. Belle gripped the counter in front of her to steady herself.

"You see, ever since I spent one night with this woman, I can't stop thinking about her. It was supposed to be a fling, but it turned into something more. She recognized that before I did, tried to tell me she loved me, but I made a mistake."

Tears welled in Belle's eyes, and she choked down a sob.

"I was too scared to tell her the full truth."

Belle spun to face him. Colt stood before her, his Stetson dipping low on his head as he eased toward her. The low tilt of the cowboy hat highlighted the handsome lines of his face and the chiseled shape of his jaw. And those steely-gray eyes, somehow full of strength yet feral. Wild and free. There was a spark of hope there that she hadn't seen before. As if the weight of his secrets had been lifted off his shoulders.

Belle shook her head. "Didn't you read the letter?

You don't have to say it now. The baby's gone. There's no reason for you to be here."

"I know you're still hurting from the loss, and I want you to know I felt that that pain, too." He continued toward her, approaching slowly and steadily in the way a cowboy might saunter toward a scared and skittish horse. "But I don't need a reason to choose you," he said. "No other reason than that I love you, Belle Beaumont. I've loved you from the first night I spent with you."

She started to protest, but he wasn't having it for a second.

"I was too scared of losing my pack to see it, but I need you to know that I choose you, baby or no baby. I choose you, Belle, and I'll make that same choice again every day for the rest of my life if you can find it in your heart to forgive me." He pulled her in to him. Colt claimed her lips, kissing her with everything he had. It was a kiss that held the full weight of his apology. A kiss that said *I love you, and I can't stand the thought of life without you.*

When he finally released her, she was panting and blushing and warm all over. The things this wolf could do to her with only a simple kiss.

"I'm glad you choose me, but I never wanted you to have to choose in the first place. I didn't want you to resent me for taking your pack away from you, and that hasn't changed. I thought leaving would prevent that from happening."

He gestured to the manila folder with a tilt of his chin. "Read it."

Belle flipped the file open, past her crumpled letter

to a crisp, clean page with the official Grey Wolf letterhead. The top read "Letter of Appointment." Belle quirked a brow as she scanned the letter. "What's this?"

"The Grey Wolves need a physician to head up our new clinic. Maverick seemed to think you'd be a perfect fit for the position."

Belle gaped at him. "But...Maeve said they were only filling this position with Grey Wolves. If that's still the case, then—"

"Then it's a good thing you're a Grey Wolf," he said.

Belle was shaking her head. "You said yourself you can't expect me to keep up the lie with your packmates, Colt. Before I left, I told them the truth, and they—"

"Turn to the next page, Belle." It was a command, not a request.

She shrugged her shoulders, used to his take-charge demeanor by now. In some ways, she'd even come to appreciate it. She flipped past the Letter of Appointment to find an old photo. It was a black-and-white picture of her mother, Caroline, with several other werewolves who all bore a strong family resemblance.

"I...I don't understand."

Colt rubbed her arm in reassuring, gentle strokes. "I saw how you blended in among the Grey Wolves, how much they took to you, and I knew it was more than the fact that you're charming as all get-out. Then when you told me your mother was a pack wolf, I knew I had to do some digging." He released a long sigh. "They were all pissed at me when they found out I was Wild Eight, but I figured they'd have no choice but to keep me around when they found out my soon-to-be-mate was a long-lost blood relative of theirs."

It couldn't be true. It couldn't. But as she stared down at the photo of her mother, she knew it without a doubt.

"I'd guess that's why Silver was so taken with you, too. Persnickety bastard likely sensed all along that *you* were the real Grey Wolf." Colt pointed to a man in the photo who stood next to her mother. "You see that wolf right there?" he asked. "Standing next to Caroline?"

Belle nodded. Her mother would have loved the way her name sounded on Colt's lips. She'd stayed single Belle's whole life, but Belle had always known her mother had been a sucker for gorgeous men, particularly a gorgeous cowboy. "Who is he?"

"You remember that aunt of Maverick's I told you about who ran away?" Colt smiled. "Well…that woman was none other than one Caroline Grey, who changed her name to her grandmother's maiden name, Beaumont, shortly after she left, so that man standing beside her is her brother. None other than Maverick Grey Senior himself."

Belle's breath caught. The photograph was shaking in her hands.

"Belle," Colt said, "you're not just any Grey Wolf. You're one of *the* Grey Wolves. Maverick and Maeve, they're your cousins."

Belle stared down at the photo, her heart overflowing with joy. He'd given her everything she'd ever wanted, not just him and his love but a pack, a family to call her own.

He wrapped his arms around her, but this time she initiated the kiss, and what started as slow and soothing quickly gathered fevered heat. When they both finally came up for air, Belle's tears had dried and she was smiling like a fool.

"You know I've always had a thing for cowboys,"

she said, gesturing to the room. "Some might even say I enjoy seeing them naked." It was far from his level of dirty talk, but it was still enough to cause a growl to tear from his lips.

From the kisses he started to pepper across her neck, he'd caught her line of thinking. Briefly, he flashed her that wry grin of his before he growled against her lips. "Oh, don't worry, sweetheart. I have plenty of that planned, if you'll allow it."

His grin widened. Without warning, he hoisted her up onto the countertop, parting her legs with his knees until the hardened length of him pressed against her center. His words were a delicious purr against her ears. "What do you say to maybe being a bit reckless tonight? Consequences be damned."

Her jaw dropped. "Colt Cavanaugh doing something wild and unplanned? Now that's a first."

The purr he released against the skin of her neck caused her nipples to tighten. "Who said I wasn't planning it?"

Her body responded eagerly. She was already wet and ready for him. "No way, mister. Before we go that route, there are a few rules you need to agree to."

"Rules?" He raised a brow, but she saw the amusement in his eyes at the reference to his old antics.

"Two." She nodded, holding up two fingers. "Rule number one: you're not allowed to have any more ridiculous rules." She ticked off one finger.

"But you are?" He chuckled. "All right, and what's rule number two?"

She grinned. "You have to admit I was never trying to steal your horse."

At that, Colt's smile grew wide, and he gifted her with a wholehearted, full-toothed smile of the kind that could light up a whole room in an instant. And Belle was thankful she was sitting, because she knew if she hadn't been, she would have been weak in the knees.

"Sweetheart, you have yourself a deal." Lifting her with ease, he tossed her onto the examination table, and she squealed.

About the Author

Kait Ballenger hated reading when she was a child because she was horrible at it. Then by chance, she picked up the Harry Potter series, magically fell in love with reading, and never looked back. When she realized shortly after that she could tell her own stories and they could be about falling in love, her fate was sealed.

She earned her BA in English from Stetson University—like the Stetson cowboy hat—followed by an MFA in writing from Spalding University. After stints working as a real vampire—a.k.a. a phlebotomist—a bingo caller, a professional belly dancer, and an adjunct English professor (which she still dabbles in on occasion), Kait finally decided that her eight-year-old self knew best: she was meant to be a romance writer.

When Kait's not preoccupied with writing captivating paranormal romance, page-turning suspense, or love scenes that make even seasoned romance readers blush, she can usually be found spending time with her family, being an accidental crazy cat lady (she has four now—don't ask), or with her nose buried in a good book. She loves to travel—especially abroad—and experience new places. She lives in Florida with her doting librarian husband, her two adorable sons, a lovable, mangy mutt of a dog, and four conniving felines.

And yes, she can still belly dance with the best of them...

COWBOY WOLF TROUBLE

**A new evil will stop at nothing
to tear their world apart**

For centuries, the shifters that roam Big Sky Country have honored a pact to keep the peace. Even bad-boy rancher Wes Calhoun, former leader of a renegade pack, has given up his violent ways and sworn loyalty to the Grey Wolves. But his dark past keeps catching up with him...

Human rancher Naomi Evans cares only about saving the ranch that was her father's legacy. Until a clash with Wes opens up a whole new world—a supernatural world on the verge of war—and Naomi, her ranch, and the sexy cowboy wolf stealing her heart are smack-dab in the middle of it.

"Kait Ballenger is a treasure you don't want to miss."

—Gena Showalter, *New York Times*
and *USA Today* bestseller

For more info about Sourcebooks's
books and authors, visit:
sourcebooks.com

YOU HAD ME AT JAGUAR

First in the new Heart of the Shifter series from
USA Today bestselling author Terry Spear

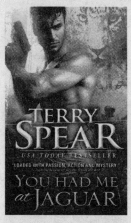

They're not the only ones on the prowl...
but they're the most dangerous...

The United Shifter Force gives jaguar agent Howard
Armstrong an impossible task—to protect fierce she-jaguar
Valerie Chambers, when the last thing she wants is protecting. They're going international to take down a killer, and
he can guard Valerie all day long. But guard his heart? He
doesn't stand a chance.

"Packed with adventure...magnificently entertaining."

—*RT Book Reviews* Top Pick
for *Billionaire in Wolf's Clothing*

For more info about Sourcebooks's
books and authors, visit:

sourcebooks.com

WOLF INSTINCT

New York Times bestselling author Paige Tyler delivers more action-packed paranormal romantic suspense from SWAT: Special Wolf Alpha Team

SWAT werewolf Zane Kendrick will do whatever necessary to take down the man who attacked his pack. His search leads him to Los Angeles, but when he meets Alyssa Carson, the smart, sexy agent who comes to his aid, he's immediately interested in pursuing more than just the next lead. All his wolf instincts tell him that she's *The One*...

"Paige Tyler has a fan in me!"

—Larissa Ione, *New York Times* bestselling author

For more info about Sourcebooks's
books and authors, visit:

sourcebooks.com

SEAL WOLF SURRENDER

The stakes are high in *USA Today* bestseller
Terry Spear's sixth SEAL Wolf romance

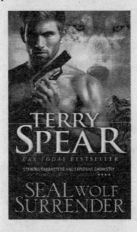

She-wolf Natalie Silverton has inadvertently crossed a
group of dangerous criminals, and she's in dire need of a
bodyguard. Wolf shifter and former Navy SEAL Brock
Greystoke has been tasked with the job. At every turn, their
work—and play—brings them closer to catching the criminals and to each other, but Brock will have to get them out
of this alive if he has any hope of winning Natalie's heart.

*"Great paranormal romance with
depth and dimension."*

—*Night Owl Reviews*
for *A Billionaire Wolf for Christmas*

For more info about Sourcebooks's
books and authors, visit:

sourcebooks.com

THE LEGEND OF ALL WOLVES

For three days out of thirty, when the moon is full and her law is iron, the Great North Pack must be wild...

Don't miss this extraordinary series from Maria Vale

The Last Wolf

Silver Nilsdottir is at the bottom of her Pack's social order, with little chance for a decent mate and a better life. Until the day a stranger stumbles into their territory and Silver decides to risk everything on Tiberius Leveraux...

A Wolf Apart

Thea Villalobos has long since given up trying to be what others expect of her. So she can see that Elijah Sorensson is Alpha of his generation of the Great North Pack, and the wolf inside him will no longer be restrained...

Forever Wolf

With old and new enemies threatening the Great North, Varya knows
that she must keep Eyulf hidden away
from the superstitious wolves who
would doom them both. Until the
day they must fight to the death for
the Pack's survival, side by side and
heart to heart...

---

*"Wonderfully unique and imaginative.
I was enthralled!"*

—Jeaniene Frost, *New York Times* bestselling author

**For more info about Sourcebooks's
books and authors, visit:**

sourcebooks.com

Also by Kait Ballenger

Cowboy Wolf Trouble

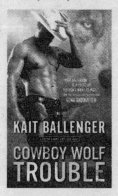